R0301 625416

# PAY DIRT

ERLE STANLEY GARDNER anthologies by the same editors

THE HUMAN ZERO:
*The Science Fiction Stories of
Erle Stanley Gardner*

WHISPERING SANDS
*Stories of Gold Fever and the Western Desert
by Erle Stanley Gardner*

## and Other Whispering Sands Stories of Gold Fever and the Western Desert

BY ERLE STANLEY GARDNER
Edited by Charles G. Waugh
and Martin H. Greenberg

WILLIAM MORROW AND COMPANY, INC.
New York   1983

Compilation, selection and foreword
copyright © 1983 by Martin H. Greenberg and Charles G. Waugh

The stories in this collection were first published
in *Argosy* magazine on the following dates:

Singing Sand November 7, 1931
The Land of Painted Rocks January 28, 1933
The Big Circle September 2, 1933
Pay Dirt April 25, 1931
The Land of Poison Springs April 9, 1932
Stamp of the Desert October 17, 1931
Law of the Ghost Town April 22, 1933
The Law of Drifting Sand August 30, 1932
The Whip Hand January 23, 1932

All rights reserved. No part of this book may be reproduced or utilized in any form or by any means, electronic or mechanical, including photocopying, recording or by any information storage and retrieval system, without permission in writing from the Publisher. Inquiries should be addressed to William Morrow and Company, Inc., 105 Madison Avenue, New York, N.Y. 10016.

Library of Congress Cataloging in Publication Data

Gardner, Erle Stanley, 1889–1970.
  Pay dirt and other Whispering sands stories of gold fever and the western desert.

   Stories first published in Argosy magazine.
   Contents: Singing sand—The land of painted rocks
—The big circle—[etc.]
   1. Western stories.   I. Waugh, Charles.
II. Greenberg, Martin Harry.   III. Title.
PS3513.A6322P3   1983       813'.52       82-20851
ISBN 0-688-01981-1

Printed in the United States of America

First Edition

1  2  3  4  5  6  7  8  9  10

BOOK DESIGN BY NANCY DALE

# FOREWORD

ERLE STANLEY GARDNER (1889–1970) is one of the most popular writers of all time. His books have been translated into thirty-seven foreign languages. The first of his many mystery novels (*The Case of the Velvet Claws,* 1933) has sold four million copies. His paperback sales exceed every other author who has ever lived, and a current estimate of his total sales in all languages and editions would be well over 300 million copies.

Born in Massachusetts, Erle was ten when his family moved to Oregon, and the young boy grew into a hard-working and self-reliant amalgamation of East and West. Though he built a successful law practice, he was an outdoorsman by temperament and became a writer partly so that he could satisfy his taste for a semi-nomadic life-style. Indeed, his profound love for the southwestern deserts is reflected by the fact that he used them as the setting for more than seventy of his earliest works.

Twenty-one of these stories were known as the "Whispering Tales" series. Published in *Argosy* magazine from 1930 to 1934, they take place in what was then the contemporary West. Most involve gold, crime, and romance. All are told in the first person and seventeen feature Bob Zane, a middle-aged prospector who seems to function as a sort of alter ego for Mr. Gardner.

Nine of the stories were collected in the volume called *Whispering Sands*, published by Morrow in 1981, and nine more appear here for the first time since their initial publication fifty years ago.[1]

The first, "Singing Sand," finds Zane guiding a man he distrusts into Yaqui Indian territory to try to rescue a young woman held hostage. Preoccupied with the Yaquis, Zane is less reflective than usual and is, considering the treachery which takes place, lucky to escape alive.

In "The Land of Painted Rocks," the dreams of a seemingly reincarnated Navajo Indian lead Zane and two friends to the Painted Desert, where they are ambushed and pursued by four gangsters intent on murder. But street smarts are no match for hard-won desert wisdom.

Later, in "The Big Circle," Zane is pressed into driving to jail a suspect he believes innocent of murder. To turn the tables on the guilty, Zane plays the fool, risking his reputation.

"Pay Dirt" finds Zane functioning primarily as an observer to Old Pete's attempts to make a man out of a spoiled kid. Initial skepticism ultimately gives way to surprise.

Gangsters chase Zane through "The Land of Poison Springs," where a drink of tempting alkali water means painful death. Yet the desert is hot and some springs are pure.

In "Stamp of the Desert," Zane must solve the mystery of why an accused thief refuses to defend himself. Fortunately, a good woman helps them both.

Perhaps encouraged by this success, Zane becomes the "Law of the Ghost Town" while on a brief sojourn from prospecting. But he resigns after finding justice more appealing.

---

[1] See *Whispering Sands: Stories of Gold Fever and the Western Desert by Erle Stanley Gardner*, Charles G. Waugh and Martin H. Greenberg, eds. (New York: William Morrow and Company, Inc., 1981).

Still mysteries continue to intrigue him. In "The Law of Drifting Sand," he stumbles across one involving Death Valley, gold found in strange places, and murder.

Finally, "The Whip Hand" is a memorable story with a plot seemingly foreshadowing Gardner's later Lam and Cool series. In it claim jumpers, a swindle, and a kidnapping all lead to a richly rewarding climax.

While Zane seldom describes himself physically, he makes frequent observations about life, civilization, and the desert. Indeed, they reveal quite a lot about his (and possibly his creator's) personality, beliefs, and temperament when pieced together as we have done with the thirty-four snippets below.[2]

The city dweller differs from the desert man. ("Singing Sand," 19)[3]

A professor of psychology camped with me for a while. He was out on the desert getting rid of a spot on his left lung. He told me that the subconscious mind was always receptive; that man's environment stamped itself indelibly upon his character, because of the innumerable little things that were soaked up by the subconscious mind, without the consciousness being aware of it.

I didn't get it in just the terms that he expressed it, but I got the idea all right, and I knew that it was the truth. ("Sand Blast," 52–53)

Every place a man lives leaves its stamp upon that man. ("Singing Sand," 19)

Back in the cities a man getting along in the sixties or seventies or maybe eighties without even his next meal in sight and no

---

[2] Bob Zane does not appear in "Stone Frogs" or "Gold Blindness," but we have felt free to use excerpts from both. The first protagonist is an early prototype of Zane, while the second clearly shares Zane's views about civilization.

[3] For collected stories, the page number refers to the appropriate page in Volumes 1 or 2. For "Stone Frogs," the page number refers to the issue of *Argosy* (May 31, 1930) in which the story first appeared. For "Sign of the Sun," the page numbers refer to the issue of *Argosy* (June 27, 1931) in which the story first appeared.

chance of any sort of job, would get panicky, or maybe go to charity. Out on the desert it's a matter of course. No one thinks anything about it.

For one thing old age ain't much of a handicap out on the desert. They get old and dried up, but they always have their health and their strength. They can always get around and fight the desert. And the desert makes 'em fight just enough to make 'em remember they're men. It keeps 'em fit. ("Stone Frogs," 646–647)

We desert men kid ourselves we're looking for gold. It makes the game interesting. What we're really doing is visiting with the desert. It's in our blood: open skies—silence—space—freedom. ("Sign of the Sun," 111)

Why work in the treadmill of civilization? Civilization taxes you almost a hundred percent for the privilege of participating in it.

You have butchers to make your kills, machinery to carry you from place to place, do your work. And yet one really lives in caves. They're made out of concrete instead of cut into the side of a precipice, but they're caves just the same, steam-heated caves. Your liver gets sluggish, and you lose the capacity to enjoy life. ("Gold Blindness," 135)

Out in the desert we get closer to fundamental truths than you do in the cities. ("Priestess of the Sun," 289)

The desert knows the true philosophy of life. Man lives and suffers, and he learns through his suffering. ("Singing Sand," 32)

Mile for mile the desert is the cruelest country in the world, and therefore the kindest. Desert rabbits are the swiftest; desert rattlesnakes are the deadliest; desert coyotes the most cunning. Even the plants have to be coated with a natural varnish, studded with thorns.

Life progresses through overcoming obstacles, and the desert is the greatest natural obstacle. ("Stamp of the Desert," 203)

Things seem sort of out of place to us when they're cruel. That's because we're soft. But it's cruelty that develops character. ("The Law of Drifting Sand," 268)

There's too much mercy in connection with man-made justice. After all, an immutable law that never varies is the one that gets the respect. ("Blood-Red Gold," 202)

The desert doesn't save her weaklings. It's as remorseless as the ocean. A mistake, and the desert strikes. Those who have lived with her are the ones who have learned the ways of the desert. That's her law. Learn her ways or die. ("The Big Circle," 100)

But that's the desert. It's a wonderful mother, and a cruel one. And the cruelty teaches self-reliance, and self-reliance is pretty nearly the object of life, after all. ("Blood-Red Gold," 202)

I've seen men stand on the edge of the Grand Cañon and say that it was a manifestation of the Eternal, a temple of nature and so forth. It's all of that. It's God, showing himself. But those same people turn away with a shudder when they see a cat torturing a mouse. If they only knew it, there's just as much of God manifesting himself in that as there is in the Grand Cañon. ("The Law of Drifting Sand," 268)

It's the law of nature that only the fittest survive. ("The Law of Drifting Sand," 273)

The reason men don't know the law of life is because they're afraid to look Eternity in the face. Out in the desert they have to look at Eternity. It's on all sides of them; they can't turn their eyes away. That's the spell of the desert. ("The Law of Drifting Sand," 268)

The desert is peculiar. It's something that can't be described. You either feel the spell of the desert or you don't. You either hate it or you love it. In either event you'll fear it.

There it lies, miles on miles of it, dry lake beds, twisted mountains of volcanic rock, sloping sage-covered hills, clumps of Joshua trees, thickets of mesquite, bunches of giant cactus. It has the moods of a woman, and the treachery of a big cat.

And always it's vaguely restive. During the daytime the heat makes it do a devil's dance. The horizons shimmer and shake. Mirages chase one another across the dry lake beds. The winds blow like the devil from one direction, and then they turn and blow like the devil from the other direction.

Sand marches on an endless journey, coming from Lord knows where, and going across the desert in a slithering procession of whispering noise that's as dry as the sound made by a sidewinder when he crawls past your blankets. ("Blood-Red Gold," 178)

Now desert whispers are funny things. Maybe you've got to believe in the desert before you believe in desert whispers. At any rate, you've got to know what it's like to spend the long desert night bedded down in the drifting sand before you'll know much about the desert, or the whispers, either. ("Blood-Red Gold," 177–178)

It's at night when the desert's still and calm and the steady stars blaze down like torches that you can hear the whispers best. Then you'll lie in your blankets with your head pillowed right on the surface of the desert, and you'll hear the dry sagebrush swish in the wind. It sounds as though the leaves are whispering. Then you'll hear the sand rattling against the cactus, and it'll sound like a different kind of a whisper, a finer, more stealthy whisper.

And then, usually just before you're getting to sleep, you'll hear that finest whisper of all, the sand whispering to the sand. Of course, if you'd wake up and snap out of it, you'd know that it was just the sound made by windblown sand drifting across the sandy face of the desert.

But you don't wake up like that. You drift off to sleep, lulled by the sound of the sand whispering to the sand. ("Blood-Red Gold," 178–179)

And if you're one of those who love it, you'll get to the point where the whispers mean much. ("Golden Bullets," 290)

You'll finally get so you can almost interpret 'em. Sounds funny, but it isn't. It'll come just as you're dropping off to sleep. You'll hear the sand whisper to the sand, and the sand answer, and you'll be just drowsy enough so you'll nod your head in confirmation. But the next morning you can't tell what it was you were agreeing to. ("Golden Bullets," 291)

# FOREWORD

But a tenderfoot who's frightened of the desert can go crazy if he gets to listening to the slithering comments of the desert. ("Sign of the Sun," 112)

When he becomes afraid of something, he wants to get away from that something. When he starts to run from the desert and finds that it's all around him, he goes clean batty. ("The Law of Drifting Sand," 274)

Nobody knows all that happens, right at the finish, when the desert has her way with a man. It's a grim secret that only the desert herself and the buzzards can tell.

But this much is certain. ("Blood-Red Gold," 169)

When a man finally feels the last agony approaching in the desert, he starts to tear off his clothing and begins to run. Then, at the last, he stoops and starts to dig at the desert with his bare hands, shredding the flesh away from the bone. It is a horrible death—even for a murderer. ("The Land of Painted Rocks," 88)

Go through the desert in a Pullman car and you'll be bored. Travel through it in an automobile and you'll be mildly interested, but disappointed.

"So this is the desert," you'll think. "This is the place about which I've heard so much! Shucks, it's nothing much, just sand and mountains, cacti and sunshine; gasoline stations, not quite so handy."

But get away from the beaten trail in the desert. Get out with your camp equipment loaded on the backs of burros. Or even take a flivver and get off the main roads. See what happens.

The spell of the desert will grip you before you've left the main road five miles behind. ("Golden Bullets," 290)

No more civilization, no more tourist cars, no more roadside hot dog stands, no more fool questions. Just the night—silence—and the desert. ("The Land of Painted Rocks," 60)

By morning you'll either hate and fear it, or you'll love it. I never knew any middle point, not with any one. The desert engenders either fear or fascination, either love or hate. ("Golden Bullets," 290)

There's the sense of being all alone, yet not being alone. A man comes to know himself when he's in the desert. Lots of himself is a lot littler than he ever thought, and a lot of himself is a lot bigger. It's the little part that shrivels away and the big part that grows and becomes company when a man gets out into the desert.

Unless, of course, a man's just naturally a little man all the way through, and then the little part comes leering out through the cracks of the character, sees the naked desert, and gets out of control, like the fabled genie that came out of a bottle. ("The Law of Drifting Sand," 249)

Which is why I love the desert. ("The Land of Painted Rocks," 78)

When you burn off the veneer of convention in the tempering fires of the desert you find what's underneath. ("The Law of Drifting Sand," 286)

Turn a man loose in the furnace heat of the desert for a couple of years and things start happening to him.

If he has courage, the desert will make him. If he hasn't, it'll break him. But there's one thing that's certain, a man won't be a hypocrite with the desert. ("Sign of the Sun," 110)

It'll kill off four-flushers and cowards and make a man find himself. ("Singing Sand," 32)

That's why the desert shapes character better than any other thing on earth. ("Sign of the Sun," 110)

CHARLES G. WAUGH and<br>MARTIN H. GREENBERG

# CONTENTS

Singing Sand 19
The Land of Painted Rocks 53
The Big Circle 93
Pay Dirt 131
The Land of Poison Springs 161
Stamp of the Desert 203
Law of the Ghost Town 227
The Law of Drifting Sand 249
The Whip Hand 287

# PAY DIRT

time. He made a motion with his right hand, then jerked his head toward the man I was watching.

I stiffened up a bit and got back into the shadows.

After a while, the bartender sidled over toward me.

"He's looking for you, Señor Zane," he said.

"What's he want?"

"*Señor*, I do not know, but he wants to see you, and he is impatient."

I get along with those Mexicans pretty well because I can speak their language well enough to savvy their psychology. I knew the bartender for a tough egg, but he professed to be my friend, and now he seemed to be proving it.

"If he is impatient," I said, "let him wait until I come in again."

And I sat back in the shadows of a corner and watched him.

He drank ten whiskies inside of twenty minutes, and he complained about the quality of the stuff. I watched him drink, and waited for him to get a little loose about the mouth, waited for the eyes to get watery.

Nothing happened.

His eyes were as hard as ever, and his mouth was a thin line over a bony jaw.

I tipped the bartender the wink and went out the back door.

Back doors in Mexicali open onto some funny places, and I walked through a cement courtyard that had little doors opening on either side, and then swung to the right, into a sun-swept street, turned the corner and walked in the front door.

"Here," said the bartender, speaking English in a voice loud enough for me to hear, "is Señor Zane."

The tall man with the brittle eyes dropped the elbow that was halfway to the mouth and looked me over. I walked up to the bar.

# SINGING SAND

## 1. Whiskey—Neat

EVERY PLACE A MAN lives leaves its stamp upon that man.

The city dweller differs from the desert man. It ain't always easy to tell just where the difference comes in, but you can tell it. I knew that Harry Karg was from the city the minute I saw him, and I knew he was hard.

It wasn't his body that was hard. It was his mind.

He was in a saloon in Mexicali, and he was drinking whisky. The more he drank the harder his eyes got, the more he watched himself.

Lots of people take a few drinks and relax. Their muscles slacken, their lips get loose, and they laugh when there's nothing to laugh at. But it wasn't that way with Karg. Every time he hoisted his elbow he got more cautious, more wary in his glance, more tight about the lips.

I've seen a few desert men that way, but Karg was the first city man I'd ever seen that was like that.

I watched him, then I looked at the bartender.

The bartender was a Mexican lad that I'd known for some

"Humph," said the tall man.

I ordered a beer.

The tall man set his glass of whisky on the bar, turned to face me, and then walked over.

"Bob Zane?" he asked.

I nodded.

He shot out his hand.

"Karg's my name, Harry Karg."

I took his hand. He hunched his shoulder, tried to squeeze my bones flat, just to show me how hard he was. I knew then he was strong, awfully strong.

I arched my hand, sort of cupping the knuckles, and let him squeeze until he was tired. Let your knuckles stay straight, and pressure may get one of 'em in and another out and hurt like the devil. Arch your hand, and a man can squeeze until his muscles ache.

Karg squeezed.

When he got tired he let go of the hand, swung his left over to the whisky glass, raised it, downed the whisky, slid the wet glass across the top of the mahogany bar and snapped an order at the bartender.

"Fill it up again and fill up Mr. Zane's glass. Then we'll drink."

I drank my beer.

The bartender filled the glass, then he filled Karg's whisky glass, and he shot me a flickering glance out of his smoky eyes.

It was a warning glance.

Some of those bartenders get pretty wise at sizing up character quick.

"Finish this, and have another and we'll talk," said Karg.

"I don't drink over two in succession, and I don't talk," I told him. "I listen."

He tossed off the whisky.

Lord knows how many he'd had, and it was hot. But he

didn't show it. He looked cold sober, beyond just a faint flush of color that darkened his face with a sinister look.

"Come over here to a table," he said. "Bartender, bring me the bottle and a glass. It's rotten stuff, but it kills germs, and I had a drink of water a while ago. The water wasn't boiled."

I sat down at the table with him.

He tilted the bottle until the glass was full, and leaned toward me.

"I'm a hard man," he said.

He wasn't telling me anything. I'd known that as soon as I saw him.

"And I don't like to be monkeyed with," he went on.

I didn't even nod. I was listening.

He waited for a minute, and then flashed his hard, gray eyes into mine.

"That's why it didn't make any hit with me to have the bartender tip you off I was looking for you," he said.

He waited for me to color up, or deny it, or explain.

If he'd kept on waiting until I turned color he'd have been waiting yet. Harry Karg was nothing to me, and if he didn't like my style he could go to hell.

When he saw it was falling flat, he let his eyes shift.

"I knew he tipped you off, and I knew you were studying me," he said.

I kept right on listening. I didn't say a thing.

And his eyes slithered away from my face, over the top of the table, and then stared at the floor for a minute.

Right then I had him classified.

He was from the city, and his hardness was the hardness of the city. If he could get another man on the defensive, he'd ride him to death. But when the other man didn't squirm, Harry Karg felt uncomfortable inside.

"Well," I said slowly. "You wanted to see me. Now you're here, and I'm here."

He laughed uneasily, took a big breath, and got hard again.

It had just been a minute that he'd squirmed around uncomfortably, but that had been enough to show me the weakness that was in him. I remembered it, and let it go at that.

"They tell me you know the desert," he said.

"I'm listening," I told him.

"Like no other man knows it, that you can get by in the desert where another man would starve to death and die of thirst," he said, and his tones were insinuating.

I shrugged my shoulders.

"People will tell you lots of things, if you'll listen," I said.

He reached into an inside pocket and pulled out a map.

It was a page that had been torn from an atlas, and it showed the desert southwest of the United States and a part of Mexico. There was one little spot on it that was sort of greasy, as though somebody had been rubbing it with a moist finger.

He put his finger on the spot.

It was down over the border, in the Yaqui country of Mexico.

"Could you go there?" he asked.

I studied the spot.

"Yes," I said. "Lots of men have gone to that section of the country."

He looked surprised.

"Lots of men?" he asked.

I nodded. "Quite a few, anyway."

"Then I wouldn't need you to guide me to get there?"

"You'd need some one that knew the desert country."

"But I could get there?"

"Yes, I think you could."

"And back?"

I shook my head.

"No," I told him, "I didn't say anything about coming

back. Lots of men have been there, but I only know of one who came back."

"Who," he asked, "was that?"

"Myself," I said.

He spread the map on the sticky surface of the dirty table. Outside, the blare of drowsy music sounded through the sun-swept street. Inside it was darker and the flies buzzed around in circles. He tapped the spot on the map impressively.

"You've been *there*?"

I nodded.

"And back?"

I nodded again.

"What did you find?"

I leaned a little toward him.

"I found a section of the country that the Yaqui Indians want to keep people out of. I found thirst and suffering, and guns that popped off from concealed nests in the rocks, and sent silver bullets humming through the air.

"I found a man, dead. Some one had driven a sharp stake in the ground, leaving about four feet of it sticking up. Then they had sharpened the point and hardened it in fire. After they'd done that, they'd sat the man down on the stake. The sharpened point was sticking out, just back of his neck.

"And I found a rock slab with an iron chain, and the embers of a fire around it, an old fire, and there were bones, and the chain was wrapped around the bones, and the bones were blackened by fire, and bleached by sun. And I found a man who had had the soles of his feet peeled off with a skinning knife, and then been told to walk back over the hot sand.

"It's a country where the Yaqui Indians don't want any one to go. They say it's where they get the gold that they do their trading with."

"Trading?" he asked, and he had to wet his thin lips with the tip of his tongue before the word would come out.

"Yes," I said. "They work up along the ridge of the Sierra Madre Mountains, come down into some of the Arizona towns and buy gunpowder."

"Bullets?" he asked.

"They cast 'em out of silver. They don't need to worry about lead."

He was silent for several seconds.

Finally, he reached in a coat pocket and took out a little bag of buckskin. The buckskin was glazed with dirt and wear, all smooth, dark and shiny. He opened it up.

It was filled with gold.

There wasn't a lot of it, but it was a coarse gold, about the size of wheat grains, and it looked good.

"That gold came from right here," he said, and he tapped the greasy spot on the map with his forefinger. "If you'd go there with me you'd find all you wanted."

His voice was smooth, seductive.

"Did you ever see a placer where the gold was like that?" he asked. "Just to be had for the taking?"

He was trying to arouse my greed.

I let my eyes lock with his.

"Did you ever see a man stuck on a pointed stake?" I asked.

Despite himself there was a little shudder that ran along his spine. I smiled to myself when I saw it. He was hard, but it was the hardness of the city. I didn't think he'd be hard long in the desert.

"I can offer you much money," he said, "a guarantee of success. You can be rich. You can go to the best hotels, eat at the best restaurants, take in the best shows, have the most beautiful women."

I smiled at that. His idea of luxury was the city man's idea.

"Did you ever see a man with the soles of his feet skinned off?" I asked him.

And then he got down to business.

"Listen," he said, and he lowered his voice until it was almost a whisper, "I've got to go there. I'm administrator of an estate. The sole heir is a girl. That girl went there and didn't come back. I've got to find her and bring her out."

I was interested now.

"People who go there seldom come out," I said.

"No," he told me, "she's alive. I've heard from her. She's a prisoner there, and she's inherited a fortune. I've got to find her to keep the fortune from going to another branch of the family that's hostile."

I knew, even then, that there was a chance he was lying, a big chance. But I kept thinking of a white woman, trapped in that country, held a prisoner.

I looked squarely into his gray eyes.

"I'll go," I said, "on one condition."

"That is?"

"That you go along."

He let his eyes turn watery. His lips drooped. His face blanched. He tried to look away from me, and couldn't. I was holding his eyes with my own.

He heaved a deep sigh.

"I'll go," he said.

It wasn't exactly the answer I had expected, and, perhaps, he read that in my eyes.

He laughed, and the laugh was hard.

"Don't think I'm a fool," he said. "I've got an ace up my sleeve you haven't heard about, yet."

He just let his laugh fade into a smile, then the smile was wiped out and his face was hard as rock, hard with a thin-lipped expression of cruelty.

"Yes," he said. "We can go—and we can come back."

And he looked at me.

"There will be four in the party," he said.

"Four?"

"Yourself, myself, and two others."
"The others?"
"A man named Pedro Murietta, and Phil Brennan."
I stared at him. To get a Mexican to go into the Yaqui country was like getting a superstitious Negro to walk through a graveyard at midnight.
"Pedro Murietta?" I asked.
"A Yaqui Indian," he said. "Pure blood."
Then he laughed.
"I told you I had an ace up my sleeve," he said.
I rolled a cigarette.
"When do we start?"
"How soon can we start?"
I flipped away the cigarette
"Right now," I told him and got up from the table.

## II. A Mystery Package

IT WAS THE THIRD DAY that the desert gripped us with its full strength.

The desert is a wonderful place. It's cruel, the cruelest enemy man ever had. And it's the kindest friend. Probably it's kind because it's so cruel. It's the cruelty that makes a man—or breaks him.

Phil Brennan was one of these delicate, retiring individuals. He was always in the background. Pedro Murietta had something wrong with him. I couldn't find out what. He was thin, and he was nervous, and his eyes were like those of a hunted animal.

Harry Karg was hard. He was cruel.

And on the third day the desert blazed into our faces, white hot with reflected sunlight, glaring, dazzling, shimmering, shifting. The horizons did a devil dance in the heat.

The air writhed under the torture of the sun. All about us was a white furnace.

I'd had the two white men keep their skins oiled and covered with a red preparation that kept out some of the sunlight, letting them get accustomed to it by degrees.

But the sun was broiling their skins right through all the protective coverings.

A hot wind blew the stinging sand into little blistering pellets.

"How much longer?" asked Karg.

"Of what?" I inquired.

"Of this awful heat?"

It was the query I'd been waiting for. I faced him.

"You'll have it so long that you'll get accustomed to it," I told him. "Until your body dries out like a mummy; until you get so you know it's there but don't mind it; until you get so you quit sweating, and can go all day on a cup of water."

He cursed.

"Do you know what I heard?" he demanded.

"What did you hear?" I asked.

"That we could have come this far, and fifty miles farther by automobile, and started from there, gaining over five days in time and sparing us all this agony."

"You could," I said.

"Well, you're a hell of a guide," he stormed. "What's the idea in taking us through this hell hole?"

His face was writhing with rage, and his eyes, that had kept so clear all through his whisky drinking, were red now, so red it was hard to see any white in them.

The other two gathered around, made a little ring.

I wanted them to hear my answer, so I waited to make it impressive.

"The object in taking you on this trip was to toughen you up," I said. "If we'd taken the first lap by automobile, you'd have had to drink water on the last lap just like you're drinking it now. You're going to walk through the heat of this desert until you get so you can have one drink in the morning and one drink at night—and no more.

"You're going to walk through this desert until you quit thinking it's a hell hole and think it's one of the most beautiful places a man ever lived in.

"Then you'll be ready to start on the real part of the trip."

And I pushed him to one side and started on.

He was hard, and he was strong, and the heat had frazzled his nerves, and he was accustomed to all sorts of little tricks of domination. It was inevitable that we should clash sooner or later. We clashed then.

He grabbed for me.

I swung my right to his jaw in a blow that was a full-arm swing, timed perfectly. It lifted him off his feet. He flung back his hands and then stretched his length on the sand that was so hot it would have cooled an egg.

The Yaqui said nothing.

Phil Brennan muttered an exclamation of disgust—for me.

I didn't care. I sat down on my heels and rolled a cigarette, waiting for Harry Karg to get back to consciousness.

We have to do things in the desert so that they're done with the least waste of time.

The sand burned into the man's back. The sun tortured his eyelids. He groaned and twisted like an ant on a hot rock. I waited until he had opened his red eyes and realization dawned in them. Then I talked to him.

"You've been hard," I told him, "with men you could dominate. You've avoided those you couldn't. That's been all right in the city. You're in a different place now. You're in the desert. You can't bluff the desert, and you can't four-flush. You're going to tackle a real fight. I'm getting you ready for it.

"Now do you want to go on, or do you want to turn back? Do you want to take that one punch as settling things, or do you want to try a little more of the same?"

He squirmed about like a fresh trout in a hot frying pan. He tried to avoid meeting my eyes. But I held my gaze on him until he had to look at me.

We stared at each other for a full five seconds.

I read hatred and futility in his eyes.

But I knew the desert. I was doing things the only way possible for our own good. His eyes turned away.

"All right," he said. "I guess you know best."

I got up and walked to the burros then, and left him to plod along after he'd got up and scraped the hot sand out of his sweaty hair.

That night I cut down on their water supply. We had plenty, and we were coming to a country where there were springs. But I was giving them a taste of what was to come.

They had about half a pint of water apiece. It was warm water, flat and insipid, and it tasted of tin from the canteen, but they'd have to get used to it.

Pedro Murietta, the Yaqui, took his water.

He didn't seem to care what happened. His devotion to Harry Karg was absolute, and yet it seemed to me to be founded on a hatred. He seemed constantly trying to break away from Karg's dominating influence, yet he couldn't.

Phil Brennan took his water, and he started to protest. Then he averted his eyes.

He wanted to fight, but he hated to oppose his will against that of another man. It wasn't that he was submitting. It was simply that he wasn't fighting. I didn't like it.

Harry Karg started to throw his water in my face.

I guess he'd have done it, too, if it hadn't been for the showdown we'd had earlier in the day.

He finally took the water, gulped it down in two big swallows and held out the empty cup for more.

I turned on my heel and walked away, leaving him with the empty cup. He had to learn his lesson sooner or later. It might as well be sooner.

That night the desert started to talk.

Deserts will do that. They'll be hot and silent, sometimes for days at a time. Then, at night, they'll begin to whisper.

Of course, it's just the sand that comes slithering along on the wings of the night winds that spring up from nowhere with great force, and die down as suddenly and mysteriously as they come up. But it sounds as though the sand is whispering as it slides along, hissing against the rocks, against the stems of the sage, the big barrels of the cacti, and finally, when the wind gets just right, against the sand itself.

But all the desert dwellers know those sand whispers, and, just before they drop off to sleep, they get the idea the desert is whispering to them, trying to tell them some age-old secret.

Some of the old timers will admit it, and claim they can understand the desert. Some of them don't admit feeling that way. But they all have heard the song of the sand.

We lay in our blankets. The stars blazed down, and the sand talked. The spell of the desert gripped us.

I saw a shadow lurch against the stars, and some one came over toward my blankets. I stuck my hand on the butt of my six-gun, and slid back the trigger.

But it was only Phil Brennan.

He paused, then when I sat up, he came over toward me.

"I wasn't sure you were awake," he said.

I didn't say anything. I knew he had something he wanted to talk about.

"The sand seems to be hissing little whispers," he said.

I nodded. He hadn't come over to me to tell me the sand was whispering.

"Of course," he said, "it's nothing but the wind."

I just sat there, listening.

"You said the desert was a beautiful place," he said.
I nodded.

"You meant the sunsets and the colors, the sunrises and the purple shadows?" he asked uneasily.

"No," I said. "That's not real beauty. That's just an illusion. I meant the desert was beautiful because it strips a man's soul stark naked, because it rips off the veneer and blasts right down to the real soul. I meant it was beautiful because it's so cruel. It makes a man fight. It constantly threatens him. It'll kill you if you make a mistake. It'll kill off four-flushers and cowards and make a man find himself.

"Man learns the lesson of life from fighting. Some men are afraid to fight. The desert lures them into itself with its soft colors and its beautiful sunsets and lights and shadows, and then, before they know it, they're fighting, fighting for their lives.

"That's been your trouble. You've been too damned sensitive to fight. Now wait and see what the desert does."

And I dropped back in my light blanket, pillowed my head on the saddle, and let him see I'd talked all I was going to.

I heard him tossing in his blankets. And I heard the desert whispering to him. The sand whispers were soft and furtive that night, sand whispering to sand, mostly, and there was something as full of promise about them as a woman crooning whispers to the man she loves.

Some time after midnight the wind died away, all at once, and the desert became calm and silent, a great big aching void, empty of noise, menacing.

The desert knows the true philosophy of life. Man lives and suffers, and he learns through his suffering.

We plodded on.

The second day found us at the base of a big butte.

I rubbed it in a little.

"Here is where we could have come by machine," I said.

The party was silent. The Yaqui because he was always silent. Phil Brennan, because he was thinking. Harry Karg, because he was afraid to trust himself to speech. He was fighting something now that he couldn't dominate, and it bothered him.

"We'd have reached it in a half a day by auto," I said.

That made Karg's heat-tortured face writhe.

But he kept silent.

I turned, and led the way into the desert that could only be traveled on foot, and my three companions were almost hard enough to stand a chance—if nothing went wrong. They weren't tough enough yet but what a dry water hole would have spelled disaster—but that's part of the game one plays in the desert.

We marched into the shimmering heat until the shadows closed about us. Then we had a little tea, and pushed on until it got too dark to see where we were going.

We made camp. The desert was silent, ominously silent.

The next day was an inferno with mountains that grimaced at us from the distance, rocky, hot mountains that writhed and wriggled all over the horizon.

That was the Yaqui country.

That afternoon I noticed the Yaqui.

After we'd spread our blankets and unsaddled the burros, I went to Harry Karg.

"I don't know what sort of a hold you've got on that Indian," I said, "but watch him."

He laughed at me.

"Leave that Indian to me," he said.

He seemed confident, sure of himself.

I shrugged my shoulders and turned away. I'd told him.

About midnight I woke up. Some one was crawling over the sand, and the sand made little crunching noises under his weight. I got my hand around the butt of my six-gun and rolled over.

The shadow was working its way toward Karg's blankets, and it was filled with menace.

I slid my six-gun around into a good position and thumbed back the hammer.

The shadow raised an arm. The starlight glinted on steel.

I let the hammer down on the shell.

I'd sort of pointed in the general direction of the knife, but I hadn't expected to hit it. It was too close shooting, to blaze away by the feel of the weapon alone. But I guess I didn't miss very far.

The shadow rolled over with a howl.

Karg jumped up out of his blankets, and he screamed as he came awake, which showed how taut his nerves were, and what the country had done to him.

I ran forward, keeping my gun on the squirming shadow.

It was the Indian. I'd missed the knife, but the bullet had ripped off the end of his thumb, right at the first joint.

I kicked the knife into the sand, searched the Indian for a gun, and then made a fire. It was a hard thing to do, but I limited the water for dressing the wound. One cup and no more.

Karg let it boil.

I knew as I watched him that he was a doctor. He took out a little chest of instruments, a folding leather affair of glittering instruments, and sterilized the tips in the water. Then he cleaned out the wound, did something to an artery that was giving little spurts of blood, and bandaged it up.

The Indian said nothing.

Karg took me to one side.

"What do we do with him?"

"Take the guns away, and watch him as best we can. We can't call a cop and have him arrested, and we can't turn him out in the desert, not unless he tries it again."

"Why did he use a knife instead of a gun?"

"Because he wanted all three of us. A gun would have only been good for one."

"How'd you happen to wake up?" he asked next.

I grunted.

"By the time you've lived as long as I have in the desert, you'll wake up when any one crawls around near your bed, or else you'll be asleep permanently."

He nodded.

"All right, then," he said, "you take it."

"Take what?" I asked.

"This," he said, and slid something into my hand. "I'll want it every day, sometimes twice a day. When I do, I'll come to you and get it. Guard it with your life. Don't let any one know you've got it. And don't ever try to look inside of it. It's locked."

I laughed at him; he was mixing in insults and compliments.

"Afraid to keep it yourself?" I asked him.

And there was a look of futility and of fear in his eyes, which showed what the desert was doing to him.

"Yes," he said, "I am afraid to keep it."

So I took it.

The next day the Yaqui was running a fever from the wound, and I took it easy. We didn't dare to stop. We had to keep on toward the next water hole. That's the desert; it's hard.

We came to bones that day. That was when we knew we were in Yaqui country.

The bones were bleached and white, and the skull grinned at us with the eye sockets looming startlingly black against the white brilliance of the sun-whitened bones.

I looked around the bones for signs of clothes. There should have been a few shreds of fiber, but there weren't any.

"Died of thirst," I told Karg. "They always rip their clothes off in the last frenzied run they make. Then they shred the flesh of their fingers into bloody ribbons digging into the sand. Then they die."

Phil Brennan turned sick at the stomach and walked away. Karg's face winced.

The Yaqui glanced at the bones with his smoky, desert-wise eyes, and said nothing.

"And you said the desert was beautiful!" snapped Brennan. I looked him over.

"Yes," I said, "it's beautiful."

## III. A TRAITOR RETURNS

WE STARTED OUR MARCH AGAIN, leaving the white bones out in the clean sunlight, the skull grinning at us. The party was silent. I noticed something gleaming off in the distance, and swung around so the sun glinted from it, then I headed toward the glint.

It turned out to be a burro packsaddle with the cinches cut through, and there were two canteens on the saddle.

I lifted one of them; it was empty. I lifted the other, and grunted my surprise.

It was full.

"Belonged to that dead man, I guess," I told them; "but he died of thirst, and this canteen is full."

It had been there in the sun for a long time, and the top was screwed on tight. The blanket covering was ripped and worn away, and the sun glinted from the metal that was so hot it would have blistered ungloved hands.

I unscrewed the cap and tilted the canteen.

Sand flowed out. It was sand that was so fine and dry that it flowed out just like water.

I laughed.

"What is it?" asked Karg.

"A pleasant little Yaqui trick," I said. "A man comes to a water hole, fills his canteen. The Yaquis follow him and find out what canteen he is using. Then they sneak into camp and pour the water out of the other canteen and fill it with sand.

"That's all they need to do. No rough stuff, nothing violent. The man simply goes out into the desert, not knowing anything's wrong. He travels until he's used up one canteen of water, then he starts on the other canteen—and nothing flows out but sand.

"He's one canteen's distance from his last water hole, usually one canteen's distance from the next. The Yaquis haven't had to follow him out into the desert. They've simply left him and the desert together.

"And the answer is a pile of bones, such as we see every once in a while on the desert."

Brennan stared at me, soul sick, his eyes horror-stricken.

Hard Harry Karg was shivering as with the ague.

"Want to go back?" I asked him.

"Yes," he said, all at once, blurting out the word.

I nodded.

"Thought you would. Well, you can't. You may be in this thing for gold, or for a big fee for closing an estate, or because of some other reason. But there's a white woman held captive at the other end of the trail, and we're going to her. You might as well know it now as later."

I don't know what he would have said just then. I was hoping the shock of it all, and the surprise of my words, would force the truth out of him. The man wasn't a lawyer at all; he was a doctor. And he was a liar.

But the Yaqui had wandered off while I was examining the canteen. I looked up as I finished with my ultimatum to Karg, and saw the Yaqui silhouetted against the blue of the hot sky, on a hill, and he had a pile of green sage in front of him and some dry wood.

It was too far for a revolver shot. I ran for my rifle, and got there too late.

"What is it? What's he doing?" yelled Karg.

He got his answer as I flung the rifle around.

The Indian struck a match to the tinder dry wood. It

crackled into flame. Then he flung himself over the crest of the hill as my bullet zinged through the hot air.

The dry wood sent flames into the oily leaves of the desert plants and a white smoke went up. I smashed bullets into the pile, knocking it into fragments of burning embers, but the damage was done.

The pillar of smoke went swirling up into the air, and ascended high into the blue before little wisps of wind scattered it.

I put fresh shells into the rifle.

Ten minutes later there were answering columns of smoke coming up from the mountains ahead of us.

Karg's face was chalky.

"Yes," he said, "I want to turn back."

Phil Brennan clamped his lips.

"No," he said. "We're going forward."

His face was as white as Karg's, but he was standing straight and his head was back.

The desert was commencing to leave its mark on Phil Brennan.

"Brennan wins. We go forward," I said.

I let them believe that it was because Brennan had made the decision. As a matter of fact, it was too late to go back.

"No, no!" rasped Karg. "I'm paying for this little expedition, and what I say goes. We're going back. Turn back, Zane."

I shrugged my shoulders and pointed back.

"If you want the back trail, there it is, shimmering in the heat. We're pushing forward."

And the thought of being alone in the desert sent Karg huddling close to us.

We marched on.

"The Yaqui?" asked Karg.

"Should be killed, but we can't waste time on him. He's

burrowed into a shelter somewhere, and we'd be all day locating him."

"No," said Karg; "he'll be back, and he'll come asking for friendship." He spoke with calm confidence.

"You don't know the first damned thing about Indian character," I told him.

"Wait and see," he said.

I let it go at that.

But he was right.

It was the next afternoon, late. I could see that some one was running toward us, stumbling, holding his right hand up with the palm out, a gesture of peace.

I got out the gun.

The figure grew in size. It was the Yaqui.

He was haggard. His face was pale underneath its dusky color. His eyes were all red, and his lips were twitching. Little spasms seemed to ripple his skin.

I thought he wanted water, which was strange, because he had undoubtedly seen those answering smoke signals and been able to join his friends.

But it wasn't water he wanted.

And he'd met up with his friends, and deserted them again. For he had a canteen over his shoulder, and a gun at his hip. He'd left us empty handed.

I strode toward him.

But he avoided me. He dodged past and ran straight to Karg, and he was like a dog finding its master.

Karg motioned me to keep back, and then he walked out in the desert for fifty or sixty yards and had quite a little talk with the Yaqui.

The Indian was fawning on him, slavering for something, begging. Karg was hard. That was the way Karg could be his hardest, when some one was coming to him for something.

After a while Karg got up and came toward me.

The Indian remained on the desert, hunched over in a huddled heap.

"Give me the black package," said Karg.

I took it out from under my shirt.

He fitted a key to the lock, snapped it open, walked back toward the Yaqui. They went together down a little depression, walking along slowly.

They just walked through the depression, taking but little more time to it than they would have taken if they'd been walking steadily; but, somehow or other, I had an idea they had stopped for a few seconds.

They came back into sight, and the Indian had stopped talking. Karg motioned to him, and the Indian surrendered the gun. Karg came toward me.

"The Yaquis have got behind us, and they're closing in," he said.

"Don't think you're telling me any news." I said.

"You knew it?"

"Of course. After that smoke signal, there was nothing to it."

"Murietta betrayed us," said Karg. I laughed.

"That ain't news. It's history."

"And was to lead the attack," he said.

I nodded. "He led you here to lead you into a trap," I told him. "He'd been intending to betray you all along. You've got some hold on him, but he hates you."

He made an impatient gesture with his hand, as though he was brushing something aside, something that was unimportant.

"All men that I have a hold on hate me," he said.

"But Pedro's going to lead us through their lines. There's just a chance we can get through. There's a water hole to the south that Pedro knows about. No one else knows of it. If we can win our way through then we won't be surrounded."

"They'll trail us," I told him.

"Of course. But we'll have the advantage of them. We get into a rocky country."

"And Murietta's probably betraying you again."

He shook his head positively

"No," he said, "never again. Murietta knows he has to save me now. He wants to save my life."

I laughed at him, but he was right. I found it out when I got to talking with the Indian. He was frantically, hysterically anxious to see that we won through, and then he wanted us to go back. He wanted to leave.

I knew that if he'd double-crossed his own people and come over to us to get us through, he'd never dare to be caught alive. They reserve their most fiendish tortures for those who turn traitors, those Yaquis.

But I couldn't figure out just what it was that was holding Murietta to Karg.

## IV. INTO AMBUSH

WE STARTED OUT AFTER NIGHT, on a course at right angles, and we pushed through little passes, down little coulees, along dry stream beds, over little rocky ridges. The Indian seemed to know every foot of the way.

Then a dog barked.

Someone muttered something in a hoarse voice and the rocks began to spit little tongues of fire.

The bullets rained around us. Karg wanted to return the shots, but I held his hand. They outnumbered us about ten to one, and the flashes of our guns would have shown them exactly where we were. But, pushing forward in the darkness, keeping under cover, we had them shooting with only a general idea of what they were shooting at.

We lost one of the burros, and, as we were winning clear, I felt something slam into my side with a force that spun me around, jerked me off my feet.

I figured it was the end, but I dropped and didn't say anything. I wanted the others to win through if they could. No use waiting for me.

It was Phil Brennan who came running back.

I tried to send him on, but I couldn't get my breath, couldn't manage to say a word. I made motions with my hands, but he stuck to me, lifted me to my feet.

Then I began to get so I could breathe. I put my hand to my side to see how badly I was hit. I could feel moisture trickling down my side, and my hand came away all sticky. I felt that my side was ripped wide open.

But, when I finally located the place, I found that it wasn't a wound at all. The bullet had ripped into the black leather case that Karg had given me to keep for him, and had slammed it into my side with the force of a mule's kick.

I could talk then, and explained to Brennan, but I couldn't walk, and the Indians were milling around over the country, calling to each other, lighting torches, trying to pick up our trail.

I persuaded Brennan to run on ahead and join the others and tell them I was waiting behind to act as sort of a rear guard, that I was all right, and would join them as soon as I found out just what the Indians would do.

He went on.

After a while I forced my legs into action, and forged ahead as best I could, but I'd lost the others. There was no moon, and the starlight was deceptive. I plugged along in the direction the Indian had said to take, but I couldn't find any trace of the others.

The Indians had the trail by this time, but a trail in rocky country by torchlight isn't easy to follow, and there were mountains off to the left that were great slabs of rock and timber. I figured they'd have to ditch the burros, but they stood some chance of getting through.

I could tell from the noise and the flicker of the red torchlight that I was off to the left of the trail the others had left.

I didn't have any burros, and I was taking time, so I wasn't leaving any trail. On the other hand, I only had a light canteen of water, a little salt, and a small packet of flour.

I got up on a rocky pinnacle, saw the east beginning to turn color, found a place where I could burrow in out of the heat of the sun, and decided to hole up a while.

After this, it would be a case of travel at night.

I was tired, and my side was sore and bruised. I dropped off to sleep.

When I woke up the sun was up.

I was careful to keep from getting so much as the tip of my head against the sky line. I made a survey of the country. It was rocky, a tumbled mass of blistering hot rocks piled in twisted confusion, and stretching from foothills up to high mountains that had timber.

I knew the general run of the country.

There'd be water in those mountains.

But I couldn't see a sign of life, either Indian or white.

I knew the Indians would be perched up on the rocky crests, waiting and watching. And I hoped Murietta would be true enough to keep the others from moving around in daylight. To move was to invite sure death.

I made sure my hiding place was pretty safe, and crawled back in the shade of the overhanging rock. The sun crept up, and the heat began to turn my little hiding place into an oven.

I thought of the leather packet that had saved my life.

I took it out from underneath my shirt. The bullet was of the type I knew it would be, almost pure silver. It had ripped into the leather and smashed some bottles, and it was the liquid from those bottles that I had felt trickling down my side.

I looked at the bottles, and then I knew the truth—knew the reason the Yaqui had been such a slave to Harry Karg. Karg had made him a dope fiend, and the leather case contained lots of little vials of dope, ready mixed for hypodermic use. And then, in case that wasn't enough, there were some bottles of morphia, heroin, cocaine, all in little powders and tablets.

Most of the mixed stuff had broken under the impact of the bullet and had soaked through the case, but the upper end of the case that had the tablets in it was uninjured.

There was a letter wadded in there, a letter written in a feminine hand.

I saw Brennan's name scrawled on a margin.

Some people may be hesitant about reading letters that are written to other people. I'm not—not when the other person has got me out in the Yaqui country with an Indian that he's made a dope fiend out of, and it's beginning to look as though he lied to get me there.

I spread out the letter.

The bullet had torn off one corner, but the writing was intact. It started out: "Harry," not "Dear Harry" or "Friend Harry" or any of that mushy stuff, just "Harry."

The message was the kind that showed just how the woman felt. She didn't mince words.

Harry:

I know now that you tricked father into coming here. You knew he would. You didn't count on his taking me with him.

I know now that you tricked me, through father, into promising that I would marry you. You knew I loved Phil Brennan, and I think he loves me. But he's too retiring to fight.

I give you the credit of really loving me, and think that my money doesn't enter into it. But, as you said, so frequently, "a Kettler never goes back on a promise." And you got my promise, both to you and to father.

Father came here after specimens, and the Indians killed him. I'm inclosing a bit of map torn from his atlas which shows where I am. I won't tell you how I'm managing to keep from being killed, whether or not I'm a prisoner.

I've promised I'd marry you, but you've got to come for your bride. If you want me badly enough to come and get me, and bring Phil Brennan with you to see fair play, I'll remember the promise I made father. If you don't come within three months after this message is delivered I'll consider you don't want your bride badly enough to come for her.

I'm sending this by a Yaqui I can trust. You remember telling me a hundred times that you liked me well enough to come to the ends of the earth for me. Well, this isn't exactly the end of the earth, but it will be a good test of whether or not I'm to be released from my promise.

SALLY KETTLER

I read the note and knew a lot more than I had before.

Evidently Harry Karg had used some sort of pressure to get a promise from the woman, but he had to come to her to get her to keep that promise. He was now at almost the exact spot on the map the woman had marked, the spot from which the mark she had made had been obliterated by the oil of many fingers smearing over the colored surface of the paper as they pressed down on it. I wondered how many guides Karg had tried to engage before he had hit on me, had thought of making a dope fiend out of the Indian messenger.

I wondered what the Indian would do when he realized Karg had no more dope for him. Apparently he had been a slave to Karg until he got within striking distance of an Indian doctor. Then he had gone to the Indian medicine man, told the story, been treated.

But the herbs of the Yaquis had been of no avail against the gnawing of the drug hunger. And the Yaqui had realized, too late, that he had only one chance for satisfying that terrible craving—to find the man he had betrayed.

But now . . .

It was just the faintest suggestion of sound, the bare hint of a pebble rattling down a rock, but I grasped my weapon and rolled swiftly to the little rim of rock.

I determined I was going to make them buy my life at a dear price.

But it wasn't an Indian.

Down below me, toiling along, carrying a rifle and a heavy canteen, was Phil Brennan, working his way with what he thought was great caution.

I couldn't imagine how the Indians could have passed him up. He hadn't even figured out the advantage of areas of low visibility sufficiently to keep in the patches of shade. He was trying to walk quietly, but the keen senses of the Yaquis would hear sounds that I couldn't, and I had heard him from seventy yards up the slope.

I was afraid to signal to him, afraid he would give a shout or betray himself still further through a scramble up the slope. I slid the rifle forward and concentrated on his back trail, ready to pick off any one who followed.

But no one seemed to be following, which was a mystery to me.

Then I caught a flicker of motion and the sights of my rifle snapped into line. I had the hot stock pressed to my cheek, and was ready to squeeze the trigger, when the person stepped out from between two bowlders, and I got a brief glimpse.

It was a woman, slender, graceful as a deer, clad in a garment made out of tanned skins, and the flesh which was disclosed over the top of the skins, and down below the hem of the short skirt, was as sun-tanned and bronzed as old ivory.

She was following him, and she was moving with the lithe grace of a wild animal.

Phil Brennan sat down on a hot rock. He mopped his forehead, gazed apprehensively about him. But he didn't see the girl. For that matter, I couldn't see her any longer. There had been just that one brief, flashing glimpse. She was as intangible as a deer slipping up a brush-covered slope.

Brennan unscrewed the cap of the canteen, raised it.

I frowned, considered flinging him a low word of caution. This was no time to be wasting water.

But I held my speech. After all, there were more important things than water.

I saw Brennan fling back his head, throw the canteen from him. His fingers clawed at his mouth. He looked as though the water from the canteen had been some deadly acid that burned its way into his flesh.

For a second I couldn't understand, and my eye flashed to the canteen.

Then I understood.

A white stream was slipping silently from the mouth of the canteen, a stream, not of water, but of sand.

## v. "Isn't It Beautiful?"

I THOUGHT PANIC was going to grip the man when he realized that he was in the midst of a hostile desert without water, that there were enemies surrounding him.

He got to his feet, swung around, took a running step or two, and came to a dead stop as he heard my voice raised in a low command.

It took him a little while to locate me, and, in that interval, I knew he was getting himself under control.

"Here I am, up here. That's it. Now work up here towards me, and take it slow. Keep to the shadows. Don't get impatient and try to come too fast. Take it easy."

He came up to me, then, listening for my commands.

I kept him well under cover, as well as I could. The sunlight was beating pitilessly down on the rocky slope of the hill, but that made the darkness of the shadows the more intense, and I hoped there was a chance, perhaps one in ten, that he could make it without betraying himself to watching eyes.

I couldn't understand why those eyes hadn't seen him before this, didn't understand it until the sound of a rifle shot, thin and thready in the hot air, came to my ears. Then there was another shot and another, a rattle of swift fire and then silence.

Then I knew, knew even before I heard words of confirmation from Brennan. He and Karg had separated. Karg had been thinking over the Yaqui trick of putting sand in a canteen and getting a man trapped into going into the desert country. It had been just the sort of scheme he liked. He had tried it on Brennan.

They had separated, Brennan tricked into taking the canteen of sand, and Karg had forged ahead with the water. But his cleverness had been his undoing; the Yaquis had spotted him. They had signaled their discovery, concentrated on Karg, and then—torture.

I greeted Brennan. He was mouthing curses against Karg and his trickery.

I interrupted them.

"We stand a chance," I told him. "The mountains. The Yaquis have been spread out, doing scout work, searching for us. But when they found Karg they all swung in together for an attack. That leaves us unguarded, and if we can get to the mountains there's a chance."

He was interested, looking up at the white-hot slopes of the rocky mountains, then back at the tumbled mass of foothills.

"How about Karg?" he asked.

I shrugged my shoulders.

He sighed, got to his feet. "Let's go," he said.

I said nothing about the form of the girl I had seen on his back trail, nor did I say anything about the letter in the bullet-ripped leather packet.

We gained the mountains, kept to the hot rocks, leaving but little trail. From time to time, I paused to search the back trail, but I could see no one. And yet I had the feeling that we were being followed. I wondered if it was the girl, or something more sinister.

The afternoon shadows lengthened. I proposed a rest. We'd have to travel long into the night.

"In which direction?" asked Brennan.

"Back of course."

He shook his head.

"No; I haven't got what I came here for, yet."

I said nothing.

We waited. I watched the back trail. We could hear the distant barking of a dog, an hour or so after sunset.

"How about Karg?" asked Brennan.

"That's the second time you've asked about him," I said.

"It's the hundredth time I've thought about him."

"Don't worry about not being revenged. The Indians will take care of that."

He shuddered.

"That's exactly it. Think of the stake in the ground ... Ugh!"

I looked at the stars, steady, bright, giving lots of light.

"There's perhaps a village out where that dog is barking," I told him.

"They'd take him there?"

"Yes."

He got to his feet uncertainly.

"Okay. Let's go back. I've got to save him. I hate the sight of him. After I rescue him I'll beat him to a pulp. But I can't run away and leave him."

I warned him.

"You don't stand any chance. They will hear us. They will simply capture us, too."

"Us?" he said. "You're going?"

"Of course, if you go."

He wet his lips.

"I'm going," he said, and took a stride forward.

I've lived in the desert for a long time. I think I know something about woodcraft and the way men stalk in the open. I'd have sworn no one could have crawled up within listening distance without my hearing. But I'd have been wrong.

A slender shape rose from the rocks like a wraith.

Brennan recoiled.

"Phil!" she said.

"Sally!" was torn from his throat, and the word, as he said it, was an exclamation, a prayer, a benediction, and a great longing.

I dropped back, down behind the rocks.

I heard her voice.

"It's too late," she was saying. "He dug his own pitfall. The Yaqui murdered him when he found there was no more of the drug. It was the sound of that shot that brought the others."

They came to me later on.

The woman had established herself with the natives. They considered her as something of a priestess. The desert had done something to her, brought out something of the lithe grace which is inherent in youth and beauty. She had become as a wild thing, perfect in strength, poise, figure.

The Indians considered her a goddess and the priestess of the godhead. She came and she went as she saw fit. And she was promised to a man she didn't love; wanted the love of a man who loved her, but who would not speak.

So she had brought them into the crucible of the desert.

"If Harry had come," she told me privately, "openly and fairly, the Indians would have given him safe passage. But he came by trickery and deception. He tried to enslave to the dope habit the guide I sent, so there could be no question of treachery, and, by that treachery of his own, he brought about his own destruction."

"If he was to have come in safety," I asked, "why did you make him come at all? What was to be gained?"

She looked at the stars.

"Perhaps it was just to postpone things," she said softly; "perhaps it was a woman's intuition. But I have come to know the desert places. I thought that if I could get those two men together out into the desert . . ."

And I thought of what the desert had done, of how the man who had thought he was hard had had the surface hardness cut away by the hissing sand and the melting heat, until the craven soul beneath that surface had stood forth for all to see.

And I thought of how the tempering fire of the desert heat had fused the character of the other, melted away the surface weakness, and brought to light the inner strength of character.

And I continued to think, long after the two had left me, long after the desert had begun to talk, a wind hissing the sand against the rocks of the mountainside.

They were off to one side, sitting close, talking in low tones, and the desert whispers were sending an undercurrent of whispering sand against the crooning tones of their voices.

I was lulled into a doze.

I awakened with Phil Brennan's hand on my shoulder.

"Isn't it beautiful?" he asked softly.

I looked at the grayish white of the desert sand, at the inverted bowl of golden stars, blazing steadily.

"Isn't what beautiful?" I asked.

"The desert, of course!" he said.

# THE LAND OF PAINTED ROCKS

## 1. Dreams

I RUBBED MY EYES the first time I saw him, because he didn't have any business being where he was. Not that some strange people didn't come out of Bessie Crayton's place. We get used to that in the desert. Bess ran a lunch counter restaurant, looked the world in the eyes, and served it meals. She didn't talk. She was a good listener, though.

Lots of people couldn't figure Bessie at all; but I could. She had a heart as big as the desert, steady eyes the color of moonlit sand, and an abiding faith in human nature. Girls from the dance hall would walk across the stretch of sandy street to have dinner at Bessie's place, and Bessie would treat 'em like sisters. She'd listen to their troubles, give 'em a word of encouragement, and throw in an extra cup of coffee.

Gamblers from the joint a couple of hundred yards down toward the mill would come strolling in for a late cup of coffee, and tell Bess about their hopes and secret ambitions. As for the mining men, they just worshipped her.

She was straight as a string, steady-eyed and calm, with a natural talent for mothering people, even if she was only twenty-five. "We're all just people," she used to say, "livin' here together, and not quite sure what it's all about. Just because some of 'em make their livin' in funny ways, don't be so sure they ain't just as good as you are."

Which was all right; but when I saw this man walking out of Bessie's place I rubbed my eyes, looked again, and rubbed 'em some more. For this man was a Navajo, and his clothes were of buckskin, with silver coins for buttons. You could see where he's had hard luck and had pulled the dimes off, here and there, to use for cash.

I waited until he'd gone down the sandy street, and then I sauntered over to Bess's place. I needed a little Mocha anyhow, and I was curious.

She handed me the coffee, looked at me with steady eyes, and smiled. "Curious, Bob?" she asked.

She'd called the turn. I grinned at her and nodded.

"I saw him go out," I said. "He's 'way off the reservation. He should have been out in the Painted Desert, not over here in the Mojave."

She let the smile light die out of her eyes. "Did I ever tell you about Hoste-Ne-Bega?" she asked.

"Don't be funny," I told her. "You never told anybody about anything. You're the champion listener."

The smile light was back in her eyes. "I'm going to tell you something, Bob Zane, because you've got to be in on it. I want somebody I can trust; a man who can point a six-gun if he has to."

"What's the matter with Ed Kaplin?" I asked her.

She nodded her head slowly. "Yes. I think Ed Kaplin, too. I need you both."

I stirred my coffee, and waited.

"Hoste-Ne-Bega was a Navajo who had troubles," she said, "and he told me about them.—He wasn't the same Indian that you saw coming out of here a little while ago, but he sent that man to me as a messenger."

I nodded, wise as a tree full of owls. A girl who could make gamblers confide in her could make an Indian open up without any trouble at all.

"He got to dreaming dreams," she continued, and her own eyes were dreamy.

She drew up a stool back of the counter, and started to talk. Outside was the desert, the sun beating against the walls of the little shack as though it was trying to dissolve it in sunlight. Flies droned around the screens outside. The heat was like a blanket that had folded itself around everything in a suffocating pall.

"His name was Hoste-Ne-Bega, and he had been banished from the tribe," said Bess in a dreamy voice. "He didn't have anything to eat. They'd put him out of the Navajo country, and he came to me, tired, hungry, almost ready to fall. He didn't have any money. The silver coins that they use for buttons were gone from his clothes. He'd held the buckskin together with bits of wire and old nails. He was too proud to beg, and he was Indian, and wouldn't work for his food. He preferred to starve if he had to—which was what he was doing.

"When I heard about him he was camped outside the mining camp, sitting down with his face to the west, waiting for the end. I went out to him with some hot soup, but he was too proud to eat. I had to talk to him. I made him understand that I wanted him to eat.

"After a while he took the soup. It was cold by that time,

but it had nourishment that gave him new strength. The next morning I took him more food, and finally he came into the place here and let me feed him.

"He'd been here for three days before he began to talk, then he told me of his dreams. Always he'd dream of an old life before the coming of the white man. The Indians were plentiful then, and strong, but the tribe had sickness, and then came the warriors of the other tribes, and there was a big battle, and the Indians were almost all killed.

"An eagle flew overhead, and a feather came drifting down from its wing.

"The medicine men decided it was an omen that the tribe should move to a new ground. They were to begin all over, entirely anew.

"The tribe was not like the Hopis. They lived chiefly by hunting. But they had some crops, and they took enough seed to plant. The other things they left behind. There were big earthenware water pots and cooking pots and a great store of treasure. He told me particularly of the treasure. It was made from a deposit of yellow metal which had been discovered many years before by one of the braves. They made their ornaments from it, and at first the gold had made them prosperous. Then it had proven to be a curse. It had attracted other tribes, who had come in search of the source of the treasure, had come to do battle over the ornaments of yellow metal.

"So the high priests of the tribe decided that all of the misfortunes of the Indians came from this yellow metal. They closed up the place where the mine had been, a place that had been so cunningly hidden that no one had ever found it, and they took just the bare necessities of life, their bows and their arrows, their stock and their little store of seed, and they migrated to a new dwelling place."

She stopped and looked at me with her level gray eyes. She was so convincing that the Indian's dreams almost sounded logical.

I lit a cigarette and finished the cup of coffee. "This was all a dream?" I said. "The dream of an old Indian who had suffered the pangs of hunger, and whose mind had probably become affected?"

She nodded her head.

I was impatient. I'd have liked it better if she'd argued that maybe it wasn't a dream after all, or that it might have been founded on fact.

"That was a dream of something that must have happened, not when he was a little boy, but something that happened long before he was born." I went on. "I know something of the Navajos. They had trouble with other tribes. But what this man tells about must have been years and years before he was born. There was a great invasion . . ."

She nodded. "Yes," she said, "he admits that. You see, he remembers his childhood perfectly. It was always spent in the one place. What I'm telling you about was a dream. He's had that dream again and again, ever since he can remember. And in it he lives over the old days of his tribe."

"Probably something that his father told him when he was a very little boy. His memory played tricks on him when he got old and hungry, and he got to remembering those stories vaguely, and thought they were dreams. He's absorbed the legends of the tribe."

"Probably," she agreed.

"It couldn't be anything else," I told her, impatient at her docile acquiescence.

"Certainly," she said. "It couldn't have been anything else—but I grubstaked him."

"You *what?*—Grubstaked him for what, in heaven's name?"

"To go to this land of his dreams. It was to the south and east. He said he'd know the place when he came to it. It wasn't far—only a three or four weeks' march."

I stared at her. "You grubstaked a man to go and find a

dream?" I demanded. "What chance did you think you stood?"

"I didn't think I stood any. It was purely for his sake. He was old, and those dreams had been haunting him. Since he got older and had been banished from the tribe, those dreams had become more vivid. I got him a couple of burros and gave him some of the surplus provisions from the restaurant. He started out with those, and was happy."

"How long ago?" I asked her.

"Two years."

"Ever heard from him?—No, you wouldn't. Two years—grubstake a dream ... No, you wouldn't hear."

She reached under the counter, took out something and slid it across to me. "Yes," she said. "I got that from the other Indian who was just in here. It was sent to me with a message to come to Cameron and wait."

I picked the object up. It was virgin gold, a bracelet that had been hammered and carved with the cunning of the Indian craftsman. It was studded with turquoises, and there were a couple of stones in it that looked like rubies. I had never seen anything quite like it. It was old, I could swear to that.

"Cameron?" I said, fingering the heavy bracelet. "That's in Arizona, over in the Painted Desert."

She nodded.

"He could have made this himself, of course," was my comment. "Does he want any more money?"

She shook her head impatiently. "He simply sent this with the message that I should come to Cameron, and that I should bring my young man with me."

I thought of Ed Kaplin, a quiet, softspoken man of the desert. He was young, about her own age, maybe a year or two older. He'd lived in the desert and knew its moods. He and Bessie were interested in each other—the sort of an interest that's quiet and deep-founded.

"Well?" I said.

"And somehow or other, I wanted you to go along, too, Bob Zane," she said, softly.

"Why, Bess?"

"Because you know the desert."

"What's that got to do with it?"

"I don't know. I feel funny about it all. It's weird and uncanny. I grubstaked this man because I thought he was hitting the last trail. I never expected to see him again. I didn't think he'd last out the grub I gave him. It was just because he was an old Indian who had been banished from the tribe . . . But it's got me guessing."

She busied herself with the dishes.

I sat and thought. The flies droned about the sun-swept shack, attracted by the odor of the food. The glare of the light on the sandy street was so intense that it made the eyes ache.—And, in the background was the desert, a great expanse of sweeping sand and cacti, of Joshua palm and greasewood, sage and rock.

"I'll go," I told her abruptly.

She looked up then. "We start at midnight," she said. "I've already hired some one to run the place for a week or two."

I nodded. Then I got up and walked out. I'd have work to do—getting my flivver ready with provisions, sleeping bags, shoulder packs, and canteens would take some time. Then I'd have to get some sleep.

## II. Strangers in the Night

At midnight I swung the car around to the lunch shack. Kaplin was there, waiting with Bess.

"You're tired," I told them. "Try and get some sleep while I drive."

They crawled into the car. The engine roared, and the desert miles began to unreel. The stars marched in silent procession; the headlights showed the same monotonous ribbon of winding, sandy road. The flivver rattled and swayed. Bess sat dozing on the front seat, at my side. Ed Kaplin was over on the roped-in pile of dunnage.

Toward dawn we struck the main road running to Needles. The sun came up over the desert, illuminating the barren mountains, plunging the gray sand almost at once into torturing heat that started the horizon to dancing. We stopped by the side of the road, got out some of the camp stuff and had grub.

We crossed the Colorado below Needles, crossed some level country, and then started climbing. Bess took a trick at the wheel, then I relieved her in the afternoon. We got into Flagstaff—up where it was cold, in the high, dry air, with the pines giving tang to the atmosphere and the jagged silhouettes blotting out star segments.

Then we swung off the main highway and headed for the Painted Desert. I heaved a sigh of relief. No more civilization, no more tourist cars, no more roadside hot dog stands, no more fool questions. Just the night—silence—and the desert.

We camped for the night out where the big pines gave way to the stunted cedars, out where the desert began to reach out with an arid hand and claim its own. The wind began to make the sand whisper against the stunted trees. I fell asleep listening to those sand whispers, indescribably soft and seductive, the crooning lullaby of the desert—to the men who sleep on her bosom.

Daylight found us astir. Shortly after the sun was up, we dropped down to the Painted Desert and to Cameron. It was just a little trading post with a few Indians about, and a man who had hard, twinkling eyes—eyes that saw a lot. He looked us over. The Indians looked us over. We camped and waited. Hoste-Ne-Bega was to have met us, or if not, to have left a message.

## THE LAND OF PAINTED ROCKS

We didn't ask any questions, and no one asked questions of us. We were in the real desert now, where a man may do as he pleases.

Toward afternoon we moved camp. All around us were the vivid reds and blues of the Painted Desert, rock walls with brilliant colored strata, stretching above the sea of sand like petrified rainbows, held there by some secret process of nature.

We didn't talk much. The desert doesn't make for lengthy conversation. We camped and waited.

At night the sand whispered again. This time we heard the most subtle sand whisperings of all, the sound of sand slithering along on sand, or hissing against some jutting promontory of sand-carved rock.

In the morning we rolled up the things, lashed them into place, and went back to Cameron. We sat around. The sun crawled up in the hot blue of the cloudless sky. About the time the shadows shortened into almost nothing, Ed Kaplin came over toward me.

He had a piece of paper and a strange story. He'd taken a little walk, and a Navajo had appeared from behind a rock, standing very erect and dignified, as though he'd sent some mental messenger for Kaplin, and had just been waiting for him.

Ed had pieced together the story from what the Indian had said, and from signs.

The man was a friend of Hoste-Ne-Bega. He knew we were coming. But Hoste-Ne-Bega had expected to meet us in person. In the event something happened so that he couldn't, he had commissioned this Indian to give us a map. The Indian had seen us yesterday. He'd waited, however, expecting Hoste-Ne-Bega to show up. Then, when nothing happened, he'd delivered his message, and then gone.

We studied over the map, checked it with that knowledge we had of the Painted Desert. We figured that some of the way we could go in the car. The rest would be with shoulder packs.

We started out, following the map. The car had to be abandoned after the first ten miles. We stripped the very bare essentials out of the pack stuff, and made shoulder packs. Then we started out on the long hike.

Every section of the desert has an individuality of its own. Sometimes you'll find one section that's something like another section, but the resemblance is more or less superficial. A man who really knows the desert can be put down in any section of it, walk for a few miles, and come pretty close to telling where he is.

The Painted Desert runs to color, of course, but, more than that, it runs to weird rock formations. Little outcroppings of rock thrust out from the main formations, standing up to a height of from ten to a hundred feet, have had the sand whipped against them for thousands of years, until the sand has carved them into freakish designs.

These rocks are formed of strata of different hardness. Some of them the sand wears away in a few hundred years, some last three or four times that long; and the rock finally takes on a peculiar appearance, as though big pancakes of different sizes had been plunked down, one on the other, all of different color. Then the profiles show up in strange shapes against the blue black of the desert sky.

At nightfall, we had a few swigs of water, stretched out our blankets and slept.

The next day was a tiresome repetition of the first. The water was low in our canteens, despite the fact that we were trained to disregard the "mouth-thirst" of the tenderfoot. A little water at morning, a few sips at night, and we could travel all day.

It wasn't until late afternoon of the next day that we came to the end of the mapped road. It was a little spring of clear water that trickled out of a rock fissure. We filled the canteens.

There was no one to meet us, no sign of any one. But we knew something of the Indians. We looked around.

Fifteen feet from the water, we found a little forked stick, apparently dropped carelessly on the ground. It pointed northeast. We followed the direction of the stick.

Toward dark we found another stick, just a little forked branch of desert plant, dry and brittle. It pointed northeast. We kept on until it got pretty dark. Then we made camp on a little rise of ground.

There was a little crescent of moon, in the west, a moon that was a couple of days old. We watched it slide down below the horizon. Then I noticed a pin-prick of red light, off to the east and north. I looked at it and it disappeared. I didn't say anything about it, but I kept watching.

A coyote *yap-yapped-yippety-yapped* a few preliminaries, and then burst into a full-throated screaming of hysterical discord that sounded like a dozen brazen throats getting into play at once.

I kept watching the place where I'd seen the red pin-prick of light. Then I saw it again. This time it was brighter. I lined it up with one of the low stars, and then told my companions about it.

"Somebody's got a little campfire over there," I said.

They both saw it when I pointed.

"We can come back later on and get the packs," I said. "It may be our man, and it may not."

I could hear them getting to their feet. They didn't say anything at all. That's the nice part about desert-bred companionship. People aren't always babbling half-formed ideas, valueless reminiscences and meaningless words. There's a dignity about the desert that impresses itself upon the people who live in it and love it. After a while it does things to their natures. Notice any one who's spent a lot of time in the desert. He'll have sun-bleached eyes, a voice that has something of the stinging of drifting sand in it, and he won't talk much. The desert leaves its imprint upon all of them.

We trudged along toward that speck of red light. The starlight reflected from the sand showed something of the surface of the desert, enough to enable us to keep from floundering over ridges, slamming into sagebrush, or dropping into ravines.

Walking in a dim light that's almost no light at all is a strain, however. The eyes keep trying to focus, as though they could stare more light into the surroundings.

The campfire got brighter as we got nearer. At that, it was quite a distance. It wasn't an Indian fire. I could tell that when we were a quarter of a mile away.

We reached the illumination after a while and we could see four black shadows between us and the firelight.

I called, "Halloo!"

The four black silhouettes scrambled into motion that was as abrupt as though I'd dropped a bombshell into their midst. I could see hands tugging weapons from holsters.

"They aren't desert men," I said.

I heard Ed Kaplin grunt assent.

Then, abruptly, the figures scattered into the darkness on either side of the fire.

"But they've got a desert man with them," I went on.

And again I heard Kaplin's grunt of assent. It was a cinch that a desert man, surprised when he was near his campfire, would never have remained outlined against the light of the fire—not if he'd been suspicious enough to go for a gun when he heard the hail. The fact that those men tugged out their guns, and then remained against the light of the fire showed that they were city bred; just as the fact that they moved with a swift unison which showed that some word of command had been spoken, indicated that some desert-wise man in the shadows had given an order.

That would mean five men in all.

I wondered if the one who had given the order might be Hoste-Ne-Bega.

"We're friends," I called.

"Well," said a voice from the blackness, "come on in by the fire, and let's have a look at you."

I didn't like the sound of that voice.

"They've heard my voice," I whispered to Kaplin. "But they don't know that you're here. I'll go on in with Bess. You stick around and wait until you're sure that everything's all right before you come in. If anything happens, you'll have the drop on 'em from out here."

He hissed a whisper that showed he understood, and Bess and I walked into the circle of firelight.

After a while the men began to ooze in out of the darkness. They were a sorry looking lot. From the minute I saw them, I didn't like them. They were of the city all right, but they'd been in the desert a while—long enough to allow their skins to become brown and to get over the first angry red which comes to the city born when they tackle the desert.

There were four of them, right enough. But there was another man who stuck out in the darkness. He must have been there, because it had certainly been a desert dweller who had sent them tumbling out of the firelight, and these four men were city men—definitely. I could tell it from their hands, from the way they stood around the fire, from the guns they used—automatics that gave lots of shots fast, but weren't the guns a desert man would have used as holster weapons.

Not that we pack guns around in the open, when we're around our fellow man. The old prospector may have a gun in a slick holster, worn black and smooth by years of use—when he's out on the desert. If he's going on a trip, when he thinks he may run into a claim jumper, he'll have it with him pretty steadily. But for the most part the desert man will have his gun in his war bag, when he's around his fellow mortals. A desert man would never make the mistake of going for his iron, and then remaining outlined against a campfire.

I had my own gun at my hip because I'd rather expected some sort of trouble, following the hunch Bess had. And she had stuck a gun down the front of her blouse. But neither of us were making any false motions toward the guns. When we pulled 'em there'd be action, and we wouldn't stick around a campfire, either.

The men sat down on the sand, and they sat awkwardly. Bess dropped to a sitting position, light as a feather. I sat on my heels, the way of the desert man who's making himself comfortable for a short visit.

"Looking for an Indian who's supposed to be in these parts," I said.

"Yeah?" asked one of the men swiftly. "What's his name?"

Bess told him the name. I wouldn't have done it, not just then—not until the other man showed up, at any rate.

"Hoste-Ne-Bega," she said.

The men exchanged glances.

"He's got one of those little timber-and-mud houses up here a half mile or so. It's hard to find at night, but you won't have any trouble at all in the morning."

"We can find it," I said, confidently.

"Better wait until morning. Then we can show you right where it is. He used to come over and visit with us at night some, but we haven't seen him for a couple of days."

I lit a cigarette.

A voice, hard, dry, and brittle with menace sounded from the darkness. "Well, friend, suppose we both walk in—together."

It was the fifth man, the one who had been wise to the desert. He'd evidently circled around until he'd got behind Ed Kaplin, and had got the drop on him.

I heard Ed's voice, closer than it should have been. "Sure," he said. "I was sort of lookin' for you."

The words made the men around the fire go for their guns again. Bess and I, however, sat motionless. Kaplin was a nice chap and he knew something of the desert, but there are some things a man learns only after he'd had a flock of years in the open spaces.

For instance, when he saw but four men in there he should have gone 'way back, so that it would have been impossible for a prowler to circle him. Then he should have lain down back of a bush and listened. The way it was, he'd probably crowded on in to hear what the men near the fire were saying. Then again, he was in love with Bess, and he wanted to be where he wouldn't miss if he had to do any shooting.

Anyhow, he'd been discovered. We could hear the sound of the feet crunching the loose sand of the Painted Desert, and then they came in near the campfire together, two shadows looming up out of the night.

I sized up the man who brought him in, and I didn't like that man any more than I liked the city chaps. He was part Mexican, I guess, for his skin was bronze, and his eyes were a smoky, restless black. He had a gun at his hip; and something about the way the right hand flicked around the top of the holster made me feel that he might be able to use that gun to advantage if he ever started for it. He'd probably snake it into action without wasting any time.

I merely grunted a greeting and sat motionless, puffing out smoke.

"He's looking for Hoste-Ne-Bega," said one of the men. "Think they could find him at night, Pete?"

And the desert man grunted an affirmative. "Sure," he said, "this man here, squatting down by the fire, is Bob Zane. He could find anything in the desert."

I looked at him sharply, but I couldn't remember where I'd seen him before. The name didn't mean much to the city men, evidently. They looked me over with a placid curiosity. Now that this Pete had come in by the fire, he seemed to be the dominant spirit.

"Maybe, if you'd sort of give me the direction, we'd find the place," I said.

He grinned, and his teeth were white against the bronze of his leathery skin. The light from the campfire glinted from the matched rows. I didn't like him any better when he grinned.

"It's over there to the east and north," he said. "You'll find a little draw running in that direction. He's made his *hogan* just over the little ridge, where the draw heads. He's been here for some time, I guess."

I watched the smoke from my cigarette. "Here when you came here, then?" I asked.

"Yes."

"Been here long?" I wanted to know, realizing that I was violating the etiquette of the desert in asking so many questions, but feeling vaguely uneasy, knowing that there was going to be trouble anyway.

"So-so," he said.

I watched the night wind take a little eddy of smoke from my cigarette. Glancing over at the light of the campfire, I turned so that I could see something of their outfit. It was an outfit that had been packed in by manpower—light and compact.

"One of the boys said it had been a couple of days since they'd seen the Indian," I said.

"Did he?" asked Pete.

"Yes," I said.

"I see," he remarked.

That finished the conversation. I finished the cigarette, and then straightened.

"We'll be moseying along, I guess," I said.
"Good luck. See you later—maybe," observed Pete.
"So-long," I told him.

I motioned to Ed and Bess to go ahead; I stayed a little behind. After they'd got off into the desert a short distance, I moved over to one side. The men we'd left behind were spreading out, too. They were moving in unison, as though there'd been another order. They shifted around on the other side of the blaze, so that the fire was between them and us. It made them almost invisible. I hurried up to catch Bess and Ed.

## III. Six-guns Versus Rifles

"Think we'll find the hogan here?" asked Ed as I caught up with them.

"Can't tell," I answered. "We'll push right on toward it, and if there's a little ridge there, we'll wait on the other side of it. If we see anything silhouetted against the stars we'll ask it to get its hands up."

I could tell from his grunt of assent that he didn't like the outfit any better than I did. Bess wasn't saying anything, which was one of the things I liked about Bess. She took things as they came. I knew that her eyes would be steady, her hand ready, and that if she had to get her gun, her aim would be true.

We found the draw and worked up along it. There was a little ridge, all right, and we dropped over that and waited. I thought I could hear motion, but I couldn't see anything. Down the slope was a blotch of blackness that was probably the *hogan* we wanted.

I pushed on down toward it, saw that it really was the *hogan*, and called for the others. Then I walked around to the east. There wasn't any entrance to the place. I looked it over as well as I could in the starlight, then I leaned forward and felt the side of it with the tips of my fingers. There'd been an entrance there, all right, and it had been moved.

I walked around the structure. There was a low entrance to the west, then the little tunnel that ran into the cone-shaped structure. I whistled, a little whistle of surprise.

"Something fishy here, all right," I said, pausing to listen.

A rock rattled somewhere on the slope.

"Quick, Bess!" I said, pulling her back. "Get out of there. Don't go in that place!"

"Why not?" she asked.

"The entrance," I told her. "That's one thing about the Navajo. He'd never go into a *hogan* that had an entrance to the west. They build them with the entrance to the east. You can even feel where this entrance has been on the east side, then was changed to the west. That's a warning to us that there's something wrong."

I led her out, away from the *hogan*. Ed Kaplin was right with us, pushing through the sand with swift strides. We covered distance as fast as we could, going toward the west.

I heard another rock, and I thought I caught a glimpse of a shadow, moving across the blurred reflection of desert light. Then there was the spurt of flame from a rifle, the roar of an explosion, and I could hear the *thunk* of the bullet.

Other rifles joined in the chorus. I could pick them out from the location of the flashes. They had the *hogan* surrounded on three sides, and were pouring lead into it. One man was standing with his back to us, rattling a fusillade down the entrance to that *hogan*.

I grunted permission to Ed, and cut loose with my six-gun. It was shooting in the dark, and the work had to be done by the feel of the weapon rather than the alignment of the sights. But a man who knows his gun can sometimes do quite a bit of execution, shooting just by a sense of touch.

They'd figured that we were trapped inside that *hogan*, and when they found out that we weren't it was something of a shock to 'em. Their bullets had been tearing through the mud-and-timber structure, and if we'd been inside, it'd have been just too bad. However, we weren't there. The first hail of lead that came from our guns, toppled over the man who had been shooting through the entrance to the *hogan*.

But that first volley was all the advantage we had. After that, they whirled and concentrated their fire on us. They had rifles—we had six-guns.

I saw that things were getting too hot for us to stick it out, and so I told Ed and Bess to separate and start working back. I dropped down to the ground and reloaded my six-shooter to guard the rear.

When our fire stopped, the others began to draw together. That was a poor move. They were huddling together like sheep, and from that I figured the one we'd knocked down was the man who had been the brains of the thing, the one who had circled out into the darkness and picked up Ed Kaplin.

But I didn't do any more shooting. Most of my surplus cartridges were in my shoulder pack, and I'd left that pretty far back. Having shown their hands, I didn't know but what they might be foolish enough to try and make a rush. If they'd done that, I'd have needed every shell in the gun to protect the two who were retreating.

They didn't rush. Evidently they figured we might be trying to circle around them.

They got nervous, and after a while they went away.

I got up and walked to the west, whistling like a whippoorwill to attract Ed's attention. He'd heard me give that call on previous occasions; and after a while he answered me. I worked over and joined Bess and him.

About that time a rifle cracked from over by the *hogan*—just a single shot. I listened. There weren't any more shots, and there was not anything to indicate the cause of that one shot.

"They got the Indian," I said. "Somehow or other they got wise to what he had, and they followed him in here. But the Indian was wise. He knew they intended to kill him. He couldn't leave us any other message, warning us of danger, except to change the entrance on his *hogan.*

"The man who knew the desert better than any of the others knew it pretty well, but he didn't know this section of it. That is, he didn't know the Indians. Otherwise he'd have known that that switched entrance was a danger signal. No Navajo ever lived in a *hogan* with the entrance to the west.

"So Hoste-Ne-Bega left us a warning—that was all he could do."

"The Indian must have discovered the cache of treasure, and maybe the mine itself," said Ed.

"Sure. That's why they followed him in here. But they didn't find the mine; otherwise they'd have lifted the treasure and gone. And they probably didn't know we were coming, or they'd have ambushed us somewhere along the trail in."

Bess sighed. "Anyway you've a mind to look at it now, we're in an awful pickle!"

I nodded silent agreement to that. We'd expected that there might be a little trouble of some sort, and we'd packed six-guns and a few shells. But we certainly hadn't expected that we'd run into a band of desperate criminals who were armed with rifles as well as revolvers, and who would shoot to kill, without warning.

"The first thing to do is to go get our sleeping bags and provisions," I said. "Then we'll try and locate what the Indian found."

"But they'll be waiting for us to find it, and then they'll open up on us with rifles," said Bess.

"Sure," I told her; "that's part of the fortunes of war. We've just got to take that as it comes."

She sighed. That sigh sounded tremulous in the darkness. I knew how she felt. Personally, I'd rather take a chance on being killed than on backing up. It was different with her. She was young and she had a lot to live for.

We trudged on through the darkness.

Of a sudden an idea hit me. It was an explanation for that lone rifle shot that I'd heard.

"Wait a minute," I told them. "I'm going to go on a little look-see trip before I make any sudden moves. I've just had an idea.—The night's young yet. You folks wait here."

So I got them located in the shelter of a little greasebush, and started feeling my way back toward the *hogan*. There was a possibility that those bandits had been hard, and that their very greed had trapped them.

I worked pretty cautiously, getting in toward the *hogan*. But the men seemed to have gone. I figured they'd worked back toward their campfire.

After I got within fifteen or twenty yards of the *hogan* I could see a figure sprawled out on the sand. I went up to it cautiously. It was the man who had been firing through the entranceway, into the *hogan*.

He was dead. We had wounded him with a bullet.

As near as I could tell in the dim light which came from the stars, we'd fired a shot through his leg that had brought him down. The others had done the rest. They'd fired a rifle shell through his heart, at point blank. He had his hands up, as though he'd been trying to ward off a blow or stop a bullet or something. The quiet clay was more eloquent than words of the futility of the gesture.

I saw the situation now. This man had stumbled on to the Indian's secret. He'd known that Hoste-Ne-Bega had found a treasure. He'd known the general direction in which the Indian was going, and he'd enlisted his band of city cutthroats to help him. They'd followed the Indian, and had probably killed him. Then when we happened along, they decided to wipe us out. But we'd managed to get free, and they'd found themselves with a fight on their hands. The leader had been wounded, and they'd decided that there was no use bothering with a wounded man; so they'd killed him off, which made one man less to share in the treasure.—But in killing him, they'd lost their only man who knew the desert.

I ran my hands over the figure. They'd stripped him of everything of value. Rifle, revolver and even his jackknife were gone.

I moved on past him and took a chance on going inside the *hogan*. It was as bare as only an Indian's *hogan* can be. There was a little parched corn in a buckskin sack, and that was all.

I struck matches, once I was inside, knowing I was taking a chance, but realizing I was in a tough spot. Then I mentally kicked myself for being a fool. The entrance pointing toward the west was more than a signal of danger; it gave a direction. To make sure that we would get the direction, Hoste-Ne-Bega had left another of the little forked sticks on the sandy floor of the place. It was just a dead branch of desert shrub, and it was pointing to the west, the same direction as the entrance to the *hogan* pointed.

I went back and found the others, telling them of what I'd found. Then I led the way in a long half circle back to the place where we'd dropped our blankets. I got out some of the concentrated provisions, and we had a bite to eat, washing it down with water from the canteens.

Then Ed and I took turns standing watch, and Bess crawled into her blankets and slept.

With the first faint suggestion of dawn in the east, we were up. I didn't dare to chance a fire, no matter how much we screened it. We munched on some more cold rations, and then rolled up the blankets and cached them as best we could.

Filling our canteens back at the spring, by the time the sun was up, we were ready for a day of fighting.

It didn't take us long to see what we were up against.

Bess pushed her head over a ridge to take a look at the

country. There was the sound of something *plumping* into the sand, and a shower of little sand particles flung up in a stinging spray.

The noise of a rifle was swallowed up in the hot silence of the desert. Bess ducked back behind the ridge. The shot had been fairly close.

"How far, Bess?" I asked her.

She rubbed some of the sand out of her eyes. "Couple of hundred yards, I guess."

I got out my gun and wormed my way to the top of the ridge. I figured the other two were working somewhere close, and that they'd probably charge. I cocked my gun and slid over the ridge.

They weren't charging, however. They were still two hundred yards away, waving signals to another pair that were away over on another ridge.

They saw me, and both rifles cracked. The bullets were too close for comfort. It was close shooting, all right. These men knew how to handle their weapons. What was more, they'd worked out a pretty slick strategy. They weren't going to charge. They were going to separate, keep out of range as far as they could, and gun us out as though we'd been coyotes.

"We've got to move," I told Bess and Ed, sliding back down the slope of the sand ridge. "And we've got to keep pretty much out of sight while we're moving!"

I knew then how a wild animal feels.

## IV. INDIAN TRAIL

THERE WAS A DRAW which ran along for fifty or seventy-five yards, inclining upward steadily. Then there was a little saddle, running down into some broken country. We kept pretty well doubled up so that our heads wouldn't show, and ran up the draw.

We were at the top of it when one of the men from the second couple swung around so he could see us. He opened up.

Whoever was first over had the best chance, so I sent Bess over the top on the run. Guns roared and little geysers of sand whipped up. Ed Kaplin made a running dive. The bullets were coming closer now. One of them actually whipped dust from his coat, but he wasn't scratched.

I was between two fires. The man who had swung around, so he could see me, was working the pump on his gun at a distance of three hundred and fifty yards. There was a cross fire over the saddle, and the men who had seen Bess and Ed go knew I'd have to go over, too.

I ran a few steps back down the draw, then charged the side hill and went over the ridge fifteen or twenty yards down from the low saddle where the others had gone over. That saved my life. They'd concentrated their fire on the saddle. The necessity for shifting their aim threw them off on the first shots. I was going like a plummet on the second shot.

I dropped into the other little cañon and joined the others. We ran for the lower level, crossed a wash, and scrambled along a curving cañon that ran up on the other side. We managed to cross the next ridge before they could get to a spot where they could even see us. It was hot work. Perspiration was streaming from us, and we were breathless.

Bess looked at me, and her eyes were glittering with rage. "They're hunting us down like dogs!" she flared.

I knew that my own feelings weren't any too calm and tranquil. "When night comes," I said grimly, "it'll be our turn. Our guns will give us an advantage at ranges that are short enough. We'll keep in touch with them, and close in when it gets dark."

Ed Kaplin nodded. Bess clamped her lips in a thin line.

"Our problem," I told them, "is going to be to keep going until it does get dark. They're tracking us, and they're going to keep us on the move, constantly. If they can guess where we're heading and get us cut off they'll have us between two fires. Those are high-power rifles. They'll be effective at enormous ranges."

We swung in a great circle, getting up on the high places from time to time to see what the others were doing. They were pushing on at speed. Two of them were following our tracks. The other two had swung far out, one on either side, and were pushing forward at top speed, trying to get us where we'd be outflanked.

We kept trotting wherever we could, and it was pretty evident that we couldn't stand the pace for any great length of time. On the other hand, the pursuers were also showing signs of slowing.

I contemplated a scheme of getting over to the side and ambushing one of the men who was trying to flank us. But that would have split us up, and with a woman along it was better to keep together.

Obviously, our game was to make the men walk twice as far as we did, if we could. And so I swung our party over to the east; put them to it to use their last remaining strength. Then I swung them back to the south, in a little cañon, told them to sit down and rest. I crawled up to look things over.

The man who was trying to gain the east flank went past me, within a hundred yards of the place where I was concealed. He was gasping, almost staggering, but he kept on going. The man on the west flank was keeping pace with him. But they were out of contact with each other because the country was more broken here.

I slid down the ridge, moved back along our tracks. The two who were tracking us were behind. They came into sight, running shoulder to shoulder down a slope, toiling slowly upward again.

I rested the barrel of my gun on a rock, got a good aim down the sights, allowed for elevation, and pulled the trigger. The shot was just a couple of inches high. It caught the crown of one of the hats, whipped it off. I pulled the trigger again.

The bullet went between the two. The third shot I put to one side. But the fusillade sent them running for cover, trying to locate me. I remained motionless.

I could see the men who had tried to flank us, now some two or three hundred yards on ahead, turn at the sound of the firing, and give every ounce of strength they had to a last desperate run.

I slid down the side of my ridge, ran back to the others, and called on them for another sprint. We sneaked around, got to the cañon up which the men who had tried to flank us had come, and started on his back tracks.

The country was rough here. We slowed somewhat. A rocky ledge gave us a chance to lose our tracks. I didn't figure these men, being city men, were much on tracking. We crossed over a couple of ridges.

Once I caught a glimpse of the men. They were closing in, cautiously, concentrating on the ridge where I had been when I fired the shots; and they were going cautiously, too. I'd opened their eyes a bit to what a long-barrelled revolver can do at a distance.

We were to the west of the *hogan* now, and our tracks were pretty well covered. But is wasn't yet noon, and there was a long hot day ahead of us.

The desert was merciless. The sun glared with eye-aching brilliance down upon the varicolored sand. There wasn't a breath of wind. The hot air came radiating up off the rocks as though it had been blasted from an oven.

But we three knew the desert. She was cruel, and yet her cruelty was kindness. The price of a mistake is pain. Therefore, one learns not to make mistakes.

Which is why I love the desert. It is a place where character is tempered in a furnace heat. It is the cruelest mother a man ever had, and therefore the kindest.

Bess was following me. Ed Kaplin brought up the rear. Our

guns were ready in our hands, and the hot metal would have raised a blister had we held our hands on the barrels.

Of a sudden I stopped. There was a twig on the ground, a broken branch of sage, with a fork at one end. It was like the others. To the uninitiated it was merely a twig, a desert-dried bit of branch.

I stopped and looked at it, and then I bent closer. There was something on it, a little blotch of red that had turned to a brown rust.

"Hoste-Ne-Bega came this way, and he was wounded," I said.

We stared at each other. We had been going on the theory that the Indian had been killed. But if he had been merely wounded we had another responsibility. We must find him, hoping that our help would not be too late.

I lined up the direction in which the twig pointed. We walked in that direction, scrutinizing every inch of the ground. Yet there seemed to be no more twigs.

We climbed up the slope of a huge mesa or butte with sharp sandy sides, when another bit of brush caught my eye. It was just a clump of sage, but the topmost branches were bent. They were not broken off entirely, but bent over at right angles, in a direction almost at right angles to the direction in which the twig had been pointed.

Then I saw what I should have seen before. At the top of the mesa was a rimrock, and there was a little hole in that rimrock. Had it not been for the eye-aching brilliance of the sand, the glittering refractions of hot air from the rimrock itself, I would have seen it. It was barely more than two feet in diameter, and it was nestled in against the folds of rock in such a way that a person might have walked past it without seeing it.

I motioned to the rock. "This way," I told them.

They didn't see the little opening until they were almost

upon it. I dropped to my stomach, started to crawl into the hole, on my guard against snakes.

The hole was just a little opening into a chamber which had evidently been hollowed out of the rock by hand. A foot or two beyond the entrance, the chamber opened up. I straightened up inside, and found that I could stand erect, but I could see little, as yet, after the glare of the outer world.

"Okay," I said to the others.

They pushed their way in, momentarily blotting out the light as they filled the passageway. Then, when Kaplin was in and the girl was also standing at my side, the daylight filtered through once more, and I could see the vague outlines of the chamber, my eyes gradually becoming accustomed to the half darkness.

I saw a human form, stretched out at one side of the rock. I went toward it, extended my hand. When I felt the firm, quiet body, I knew what had happened. Hoste-Ne-Bega had been wounded, and had dragged himself to the secret cave where he had died—Indian fashion—alone, proud.

I turned to Bess. "It's too late," I said.

She dropped to her knees beside the figure. I struck a match. Apparently he had died only a few minutes after he had gained his sanctuary.

She straightened again as the match burned down to my fingers and I dropped it on the floor of the cavern.

That floor was thick with the dust of ages. The cavern had a dry, dusty smell. The fine sediment rose as a dust to our nostrils as we moved about, stirring it up. It was far finer than flour—a dust that was like a mist.

"He never *dreamt* of this place," I said. "It was old when he was born."

"How did he find it then?" asked Bess.

I shrugged my shoulders.

We looked about us. There were little niches cut into the wall, and in these niches were bags of what had evidently been buckskin. Now they were but shreds of dusty ruin. But back of these dusty curtains gleamed yellow metal. There were niches filled with gold nuggets, other niches that were filled with cunningly wrought gold jewelry, turquoise-studded works of Indian art and craftsmanship that far surpassed any examples of workmanship by the modern Indian.

I picked up several objects and examined them.

Then my ears heard the sound of a rock falling. Bess gave a little gasp.

"We've forgotten about those men!" she said.

I grinned. Forgotten nothing! We were in exactly the right sort of place. Let them find us here and try to get in. Let them try to stand off and pepper us with their rifles! The opening faced upon a ridge of rock not more than twenty yards away. We were on the inside, safe from attack save in one direction. Let them come!

But they had lost our trail, and they were worried and cautious, mindful of my previous accurate shooting which had almost proven fatal.

I could hear their voices as they called to one another. Then they stumbled on, keeping below the rimrock. The opening into the rock chamber was out of their sight.

I made an examination of the dead Indian.

He had been shot twice, once in the shoulder and once through the side. The shots had come from rifles, and probably he had been shot down, without a chance to defend himself or to flee.

The glint of tears was on Bess's cheeks as the light from the cave opening showed the side of her face.

"He was old," I said. "He couldn't have lived long in any event."

She nodded, choked.

"I know. It's the cowardice of it! Think of it! Ambushing a lone Indian, murdering him this way!"

I shared her indignation, but I wasn't showing it. There

was work to be done, and there was some thinking to do. These men had killed Hoste-Ne-Bega; but they would never have killed him unless they had been satisfied he had led the way to the cache which they sought. Nor had he been shot very far from the cave. The nature of his wounds was such that he couldn't have gone far.

It was fair to suppose then that these men were pretty hot on the scent. Within a few hundred yards, they knew where the cache was located. They must have been satisfied they had learned from Hoste-Ne-Bega all that they could learn.

Emerging from the rock cave, the Indian had found himself ringed around by the enemy. It had probably been night, or dusk. He had marked the way to the cave, hoping that ours were eyes that were wise in Indian lore to follow. Then he had been trapped.

There was a shooting. Perhaps the Indian had shot in his own defense, but probably his bullets were unavailing. And just before the end he had crawled into the cave.

The men had become convinced that the Indian had either escaped, or else hidden himself so cunningly he could not be found. They had devoted their attention to locating the treasure. So far they had failed, but that failure would not be for long. Inch by inch, they would comb the desert.

I thought somewhat of letting them know where the treasure was, so forcing them to come and fight it out. I was hungry, and the prospect of getting food didn't seem very favorable. Then an idea gripped me. I'd been overlooking the best ally we had.

## V. The Desert Speaks

The sounds which indicated the passing of our hunters died in the distance.

"We're safe here," said Bess.

"Safe," I said, "except that we're going to run out of food

and water. If those men get wise, they'll go back to the spring and hold it against us. We'll have to have water. We've got one chance. You remember, we brought along a little dynamite. It's in our blankets. Also there's a little food there. Now, I suggest that we go to the place where we left our blankets, and get that dynamite. Then we'll blow up the spring, which will put us all on an equal footing."

"But they'll still have the rifles," said Bess.

"They can't drink rifles," I reminded her.

"But we'll be suffering, too," said Ed. "Our canteens are just little ones."

"Sure," I told him, "but we know the desert, and the desert is kind to those who know her."

Bess took a deep breath. "Come on," she said. "It's going to be a nightmare. Let's get it over with, and let's get to that spring before they think of holding it."

We wormed our way out of the treasure cave, sliding down the rocky ledge, keeping up where the chunks of rimrock had broken off, so that we wouldn't leave too plain a trail. Then we headed for the spring.

We hadn't been going very long when we saw that the others had also got the idea of concentrating at the spring. We could see them, although they hadn't seen us. They were pretty well to the north of us, and we were between them and the spring. They were coming right along, hitting the ridges and keeping an eye out for us, heading toward the water.

Which meant that we had to run again. We got down behind the ridge and broke into a jog trot. We were pretty well up to the place where we'd left our blankets when they saw us, and by that time the distance was too great for accurate shooting. Bullets whizzed around us, striking the sand, humming overhead, but they weren't very close.

I got out the dynamite and some of the concentrated food. We didn't have time to salvage anything else, and we couldn't be burdened with weight. We had to leave the packs and run for the spring.

We got there, filled the canteens, put in the dynamite.

The country around the spring was too open to enable us to hold the place. It would have been easy for them, with their rifles, to have held it against us, but it would have been suicide for us to try it.

I lit the fuse, and we started away on the run. When they saw the trickle of smoke going up from the fuse, they got the idea. They started to run toward the spring, and they quit shooting at us. But they saw they couldn't make it. Then they tried to shoot out the fuse. They couldn't shoot well enough for that, at the distance.

The blast went off. There was a lifting column of smoke, dust and crushed rock. The hot air of the desert expanded with the roar of the explosion, then settled back like a blanket.

I couldn't see whether or not the shot had killed the spring, but I could see the four black figures. They'd reached the spot now, and the way they ran around and waved their hands told me all I needed to know.

Time was precious. I got out some of the concentrated rations. We sat down and ate, washing the food down with water. Our canteens were small. Unfortunately we'd left the big ones back in the car. The enemy had larger canteens, but in all probability they had little more water left than we had in our three small canteens.

Then the shooting started again. We retreated, and the four men followed us. But we could play that game as long as they could. They could hold us to the rocky country until it got dark. After that, they couldn't hold us at all.

The sun beat down with merciless fury. Little mirages appeared here and there. The rimrock showed up in the mirages in weird, shimmering shapes.

The enemy kept pressing us. They were desperate now. If they'd only had more sense they'd have realized that killing us wouldn't have helped matters any. They were fighting something far more menacing than any human enemy, but they didn't realize that until the shadows began to lengthen. Then they huddled together in a conference.

I gathered that they were thirsty; I could see them passing around a large canteen. From the way they tilted it, I gathered that it was about half full. Then they struck out to the south.

"Well," I said, "they've come down to earth now. They know what they're up against. Here's where *we* start."

So we filed out of the rocky country and started to follow them. At first they fired a few long distance shots back at us. But they'd lost their enthusiasm. The bullets went wild, and they didn't bother to correct their aim and try again.

They were murderers, these men, yet I couldn't help feeling sorry for them. Nor was I any too certain that I shouldn't start to feel sorry for ourselves. We knew the desert, but it was going to be a battle. We'd had a day and a night of exhausting toil and fighting. We'd been running over the sand in the hot sunlight. We'd been living on insufficient water and rations.

All around us shimmered the Painted Desert, beautiful as a tiger, and as cruel. We were in her grip now. She seemed to be leering at us, reminding us of the price of a mistake, the doom of failure.

There was a brief period of dusk, and then night blotted out everything except the outlines shown by the moon that was now riding higher in the heavens. We lost sight of the men with rifles.

We were walking slowly now, our legs swinging in the stride of the desert dweller, a stride that pushes through the sand without wasting too much energy. Sand is funny stuff.

You can fight it, but it requires more than twice as much energy as is required by those who know how to take it easy. You can't fight the desert; you've got to humor it.

The moon went down, and it was slow work feeling our way along, avoiding pitfalls and sagebrush. After an hour or two of it my nerves were on edge.

"Far enough," I said. "We're not gaining anything now. We've got to rest and save ourselves for to-morrow."

Bess staggered as she came up to me, gave a little gasp, and sank on the sand.

Ed Kaplin was breathing hard. I could sense his taut nerves, his clenched fists, his quivering legs.

We dropped down to the sand. It was cool now, but not cold. We had a sip of water each, pillowed our heads on the sand, and dropped off to instant sleep.

I woke up an hour or so before the first streaks of light. The wind was blowing and out in the dark the desert was rustling to life. There were whispers, hissing sand whispers. It seemed as though the desert was trying to tell us something. Yet there was a menace about those rustling noises, too. It was a sound such as a rattlesnake makes when he starts to twist his body into a striking coil, when the dry scales slither along against the dry scales of writhing coils.

Nothing ever remains the same in the desert. The restless sand, the beating sun, all take their toll. Man does not remain the same in the desert. Bit by bit, the desert changes and hardens him.

Then I quit thinking about the desert and deliberately willed myself to sleep.

The desert was hushed when I again awoke. The first faint streaks of light in the east showed outlines of the mountains which were thrust up from the floor of the desert.

The other two were sleeping on the sand, mere lumps of dark shadow against the half-lighted gray of the desert. They heard the sound of my stirring. Wordlessly they rolled over, sat up, got to their feet, flexed their tortured muscles.

"All aboard," said Bess, and laughed. It wasn't a care-free laugh. It was a grim laugh, the laugh of one who goes out to face death—unafraid.

We had some water. There was a little powdered soup left, and one of the canteens had a bottom that slid over the canteen and could be used as a little cooking pot. I started a tiny fire of twigs of sage. We poured a little of the precious water into the pan, then added the powdered soup. We did not heat the liquid too much, because heating makes for evaporation; we merely warmed the soup enough so that it felt warm to our stomachs as we swallowed it.

Then we started.

We had been freshened by the few hours' rest—and we had an automobile which would save us the last ten miles. The others didn't have any machine cached. When we got to Cameron we could brand them as outlaws, and they would have to flee the desert. Yet every step of flight would take them into hostile country.

They had probably pressed on during the night, and continuous progress in the desert exacts a fearful toll.

We walked steadily. The east flared to crimson, then gold, then the sun leapt up over the rim of the desert and the weird colors became vividly apparent. The heat began to sway the outlines of objects.

Crossing a sandy stretch, Ed Kaplin paused to stare and to point. There were tracks crossing that bit of sand, and the tracks were single, those of a lone man.

"It may be one of the four," he husked.

I nodded. We had nothing to fear from him now. We were three to one, and the country was open enough so that he couldn't ambush us. We pushed on, following his tracks.

The tracks showed that the man was running at times,

staggering at others. Twice I found where he had sat down, only to get up and start to run. That was a bad sign. Panic can strip a man of strength and vitality quicker than any known agency. Panic accounts for many deaths, even in the forest, where man has firewood and water, and usually a supply of game. In the desert panic is fatal.

Presently I saw something gleam on the sand. We walked to it. It was a rifle. There were some cartridges in the magazine. I stooped and felt of the barrel. It was so hot that the hand couldn't be held against the metal.

"Been here over an hour, anyhow," I said.

I looked ahead. There were some brass shells, fully loaded, glittering where they had been flung into the desert.

"We won't need it now, and we can't carry any surplus weight," I said.

We left the rifle, loaded, lying there in the sun, and pressed forward. The painted rocks rose on either side now, and seemed to dance some weird devil-dance against the blue of the sky. I could see where the man we followed was running again. He veered now to the east, then, after a while, his tracks crossed ours again, this time going west.

Farther on something white appeared on the surface of the sand. It was a shirt. I knew the meaning of that. When a man finally feels the last agony approaching in the desert, he starts to tear off his clothing and begins to run. Then, at the last, he stoops and starts to dig at the desert with his bare hands, shredding the flesh away from the bone. It is a horrible death—even for a murderer.

We pushed straight ahead. We did not try to follow the tracks that had wobbled across our path. Nor did we see them again.

The shadows lengthened. Our feet were tortured by the hot sands. There were blisters which had formed and broken, and every step was an agony. My mouth was dry and my stomach was clamoring for food.

Bess and Ed Kaplin trudged along, single file, saying nothing, chins up, eyes steady.

The sun set. The moon, riding constantly higher, gave more light. We dared not rest now. Our tortured feet would have stiffened. Yet we dared not hurry. Every step was made with a stride that would consume the least energy, yet keep us moving.

The canteens had long been empty, and we had thrown them away. Our mouths were dry. But worst of all was the constant quivering of the tortured muscles, the demand of our tortured, fatigued bodies for nourishment.

I saw a weird butte against the moonlit sky, and recognized it. Our car would be at the foot of that butte. It seemed to be a haven of refuge, that battered flivver. Yet we walked and walked, and the butte might have been a mirage. It retreated step for step, apparently.

Then the moon slid down and darkness blotted out even the outline of the butte. Still we dared not rest. We trudged on, stumbling and falling once in a while, when our fatigued muscles refused to coordinate in time to enable us to avoid pitfalls or rough places.

It seemed endless hours that we had been upon a treadmill of sand. Then something loomed directly ahead of us. It was the butte again, this time high against the stars. As we walked, it blotted out more and more stars. Then a shape showed slightly to one side. It was the battered flivver, covered with dust, but ready, waiting.

We fell upon it. I opened a door and rummaged in among the provisions. There were two cans of tomatoes, priceless in the desert. I found them, but I couldn't wait to use a can opener or knife. I tugged out my six-gun and shot holes in both cans. We took turns passing them around, letting the cool liquid trickle down our parched throats. Then I cut the cans open and we ate the tomatoes.

We sat down on the sand, and almost at once my muscles

began to stiffen into pain. I could hardly move when I crawled up, half an hour later, to drag provisions from the car and make a little fire.

We had coffee, canned beans, even some half-stale camp bread that had been left in the car, beneath the blankets. Then we slept, on the bare sand. I got up some time after midnight and dragged out some blankets. Every step was torture. I flung blankets over the others, wrapped myself up and dropped off to sleep again.

Wind came up before dawn, and the desert began to talk. I lay, half dozing, listening to the song of the drifting sand.

At last day dawned, and I lay there as the first rays of the sun brought out the varied colors of the rimrocks on the big butte. I looked about me. Everywhere was the riot of color which marks the Painted Desert. It well deserved its name. The rocks were painted, and they were cruel.

I let my bloodshot eyes stare out over the desert to the north, straining them to see if there should be moving specks—if any of the four men had survived that terrible ordeal. Nothing moved.

The desert is kind to its own, cruel to strangers. The painted rocks were placid in their calm indifference to what had happened out there in the waste spaces.

Bess stirred in her blankets, caught her breath as her aching muscles started to function. Sitting up, she stared out into the desert. Then Kaplin flung aside the blanket, groaned, grinned, got to his feet. He also stared out into the desert.

But still there was no sign of life. "It's a judgment of the desert," I said. "They have been tried and executed."

Now that we had won to safety, those painted rocks above us seemed softer in their coloring, somehow seemed to tower over us protectingly, almost maternal.

The desert is cruel, but it protects those who love it.

Those four men out there had violated the laws of God and Man. They had been flung upon the mercy of the desert, and the voice of the painted rocks had spoken. At night the sand would scurry hither and thither, bearing the message of that which had happened in the hot silence of the Painted Desert, telling each bit of sage, each outcropping of wind-carved rock.

# THE BIG CIRCLE

## 1. OUT OF THE DESERT

THE MAN WAS A PROFESSIONAL GAMBLER, which meant that it was difficult to read his thoughts. One who had ever been familiar with gamblers could never have mistaken him for anything else.

His eyes were alert but calm and steady. His face was utterly passive, and there was that hard, smooth polish about him which is more than a veneer. It's a poise that seems to defy the entire universe to do anything which can jar it. It comes from having endured losses which wipe out everything at one swift swoop of ill fortune.

Never a professional gambler but who has won and lost fortunes. To-day they are millionaires and to-morrow paupers. Winnings are balanced by losses, losses by winnings. And the gamblers have to learn to be plunged from prosperity to poverty, and to carry on with the same suave urbanity which puts the loss of yesterday into the limbo of the past and lays the foundation for the winnings of to-morrow.

Out in the desert we get to classify men pretty quickly. We have to. Nature gets in the raw out in the desert. The veneer of civilization strips off, and the primitive emotions come to the front.

Perhaps that's why the gamblers are so noticeable. They're about the only class of men who can go out into the desert and keep that polish which serves to hide the inner soul from the glance of the curious.

Nevada is a strange State, and a little understood State.

It's a State of big places, and it's a breeder of men. Nevada has always been impatient of the shams and hypocrisies of civilization. Nevada has never tried to reform its citizens by laws. Gambling remains a legal vocation in the State of Nevada.

I looked at Nell Hastings, and then at the gambler. I wanted to see if Nell knew who he was. If she did, she gave no sign.

"What'll it be, Bob?" she asked me.

"Get me something good," I told her. "I'll leave it to you."

The gambler flashed me a swift glance, then his eyes went back to his plate.

Nell Hastings ran the little restaurant there, and did a rushing business with it, too. There wasn't a table in the place, just a long counter that ran the length of the building, with a stove at one end, a cash register at the other. Both were kept busy.

The mining camp had sprung into a boom with the rush of interest in the gold bearing properties that lay round about. Talk about a shortage of gold! Nevada's lousy with it. Let conditions get to a point where labor and raw materials are down in price, and it pays to work mines that have long lain dormant. The gold's there, tons of it. It costs too much money to get it out the way conditions are ordinarily.

Now we were having a gold boom that was like the old days. The camp was running full blast. The pound of the stamps in the mills furnished an undertone of rhythmic noise which jarred the placid silence of the desert. The big mines were working full shifts, and prospectors outfitted to disappear in the desert, their places being taken by silent men who came shuffling in from the great spaces, a string of thin burros plodding behind them.

Nell brought me some roast beef.

"You can always count on that," she said.

"And you," I told her.

She grinned and got me some coffee.

"Business good, Nell?"

"And how! I'm so tired my feet ache."

"That's good. About the business, I mean—not the feet."

She started to say something, and then held her breath as the door banged open. A man was weaving about on the threshold of the place.

He was covered with desert dust. His eyes were gray, seemed to be dust covered themselves. But the places which should have been white were all flecked with red. There was a growth of stubble all over his face and neck, a white, bristly stubble that was inches long and made his face look like two red-rimmed bloodshot eyes peering out of a white mop.

Back of the tangle of white bristle that masked his mouth I could get a glimpse of something that was swollen blackish purple. I knew it for the tip of his tongue. He'd been without water, and, if the bony frame was any indication, he'd been without food.

I took that one first, swift look at him, and knew the symptoms. I had sprung to his side by the time he started to fall. He tried to speak, and couldn't. Then his eyes closed and he lay still in my arms, a little wisp of a man who was so frail it seemed a good breath of desert wind would blow him away.

And yet he'd been out in the desert, fighting it for days, perhaps weeks, and he'd won back to civilization.

"Quick, Nell," I said, "some sort of fruit juice first. A little hot soup later. Some orange juice if you have it, and a can of tomatoes. We'll drain off the juice."

She didn't say a word, but just went back of the counter, all swift motions, all flying hands and deft fingers. That was Nell. You could count on her to back you up in any sort of an emergency.

The gambler came over and stared curiously. Just from the way he looked I could tell that he was new to the desert.

"Been out of water and food," I explained to the gambler. "Even if he'd had food, he couldn't have eaten it without the water. You can see where he came from."

And I nodded my head toward the country that was visible from the open door of the restaurant shack.

It was desert, a mountain desert that showed naked, stark and cruel. There wasn't anything that even resembled a tree, not even the desert palms that grow in some of the more fertile stretches of desert. There was just the great expanse of glittering, eye-aching space, tumbled into cruel crags, twisting cañons, and sharp cliffs. There was sage and greasewood, little stunted plants that dotted the desert.

Here and there the steep slopes were scarred by mines, many of which were deserted. There were tumbledown shacks that had lain in crumbling decay ever since the gay nineties. And the nineties *had* been gay in this camp. Make no mistake about that!

Another man came through the door. Pedro Gonzales, sort of Man-Friday to Pete Blaine, the manager of the big mine that kept the town going.

He stared at the spectacle of the man who was stretched out, the gambler and myself bending over him.

I opened the man's shirt at the neck, took a glass of water and a spoon, and trickled slow drops of water on the swollen, cracked lips, the big, blackish tongue.

Something fell out of the shirt, a something that thudded as it fell. A thong came loose, and the floor was cascaded with bits of yellow metal.

Men who live with gold a lot get so they can tell much from it.

Those chunks of gold were placer, and they'd come from a field that was rich, the sort of a strike that makes the desert quiver with excitement, and makes towns spring up like mushrooms. There were coarse grains and nuggets that were hardly rounded down.

It looked like gold that started at the surface of the sand and went down clear through to hardpan.

I made a dive for the dirt-glazed buckskin sack and put the gold back in it, fastened the thong around the neck of the sack, and stuffed it down the front of the shirt again.

Then I knew why it had fallen out so easily. There were other sacks in there, and there was a leather belt with pockets down next to the skin.

I tried to get the shirt back in place.

But, when I looked up, I saw the eyes of Pedro Gonzales, and the eyes of the gambler. Neither pair of eyes had missed anything.

"Where did he come from this *hombre?*" asked Pedro.

"Lord knows," I said. "He staggered in out of the desert somewhere. And, look you, he was suffering, but he didn't stop any passer-by and ask for help. He used the last bit of remaining strength he had to walk into a public restaurant. Then the smell of the food and the knowledge he had won out snapped the nerve tension, and he keeled over."

Pedro nodded. His eyes were squinted and glittering.

The gambler said: "Is there anything I can do to help?"

"I don't think so," I said. "He's going to pull around all

right after a while. He ain't so far gone. I've seen 'em worse. He's had a hard fight and it's jarred him, but he's a desert rat, and he's got the constitution of an ox."

Nell came with the tomato juice. We dropped little doses of it in the lips we'd pried apart, and saw the throat make convulsive gulps, having difficulty swallowing the liquid because the throat and tongue were so swollen.

"The last thing this man wanted," I said, "was a crowd around him. He didn't want any one to see the things that we've seen. How about it, boys? Shall we get him some place out of the way and agree to forget what we've seen?"

Pedro Gonzales was of the desert, and his answer was prompt.

"That," he said, "is agreed. We can take him to my room."

The gambler hesitated a moment, then he said:

"Of course, it's not my business, and I'm not in the habit of speaking of those things which are not my business."

Nell looked at me.

"Taking him anywhere, the way he is now, will attract too much attention. I've got my tent out here in back. Put him there. There's a cot."

We carried him around behind the counter, out through the little screen door in the back to the tent where Nell lived. It was a little affair with a board floor and sides, canvas above that and over the top. She'd fixed it up with those little touches of feminine skill which made the place seem comfortable and homelike, for all it was nothing but a tent house thrown up in a rough mining camp where there was nothing in the way of conveniences.

The man was dirty. He was covered with the grime of the desert, and no one knew the first thing about his past or who he was. But Nell unhesitatingly had us put him down on her bed, and said to me:

"Close up the restaurant, will you, Bob? This man needs some one to be with him. I'm going to stick here."

That's the way of the desert.

The gambler spoke to me as we were going back to the restaurant. "You live here?"

"No. I live in the desert. I come and I go. I don't live any one particular place. Just so it's the desert."

"You know the people here?"

"Some of them."

"Know any one named Blaine?"

"Pete Blaine?" I asked.

"That's the one."

"Sure," I said. "He's the big chief up at the mine here. He has charge of the whole thing for the Desert Rand Syndicate. Pedro here can tell you anything you want to know about him. Pedro works for him, sort of assistant, you know. He's usually with Blaine on the job."

The gambler whirled to stare at Pedro Gonzales.

"Oh," he said, "I see."

"What was it you wanted to know?" asked Pedro.

"I thought I knew this man, Blaine, back in Las Vegas, New Mexico. Was he ever there, do you know?"

"I've heard him speak of it."

"Fine!" said the gambler. "He's the man I want. I'm quite certain I knew him there. I'm going to hunt him up."

"I'll tell him you're looking for him," said Pedro.

"Don't," the gambler said. "I want to see about getting a job from him, and I'd rather tackle him right out of a clear sky."

I flashed an amused glance at the gambler's hands.

They were soft as silk, and the fingers were as smoothly efficient as the fingers of a trained surgeon. I knew that those hands and the dexterity of those fingers were a good part of the gambler's stock in trade.

"He only has jobs in the mine," I said. "I think the office staff comes here from the outside. It's all hired in New York, and then sent on here. They don't do much office work, anyway, just time-keeping, and the checking of a few records. Most of the book-keeping is done in the East, you know."

The gambler didn't say anything. His silence indicated that whether he wanted to work in a mine or not was none of my business. I grinned and let it go at that. He was new to the desert.

We filed out to the street and separated.

## II. Murder

A DESERT CAMP IS A PECULIAR PLACE, no matter how you take it.

This camp had lots of things in common with the camps of the early days. There are dozens of those places in Nevada right to-day, running full blast.

There were electric lights, and part of the place had running water. Some of the old-time houses were still in service, and there were some new ones put up out of boards and canvas. It was wide open.

Over all were the stars, the great, silent, unwinking stars that stared steadily down as they do in the desert. The camp was a blaze of light in the darkness of the desert night, a single bright spot that flared out into prominence and could be seen for miles.

All around it was the dark silence of the desert, black and mysterious, grim and cruel, the desert that has waited for always, and will always wait.

It seemed to mock at the puny efforts of these men whom the desert had trapped, surrounded in this little inclosure of light and noise. Here was light, water and food. Outside in the desert was darkness, thirst and death. The desert waited, patient, cruel, remorseless.

And it's that which makes the desert the kindest mother a man ever had. The desert doesn't save her weaklings. She's as remorseless as the ocean. A mistake, and the desert strikes. Those who have lived with her are the ones who have learned the ways of the desert. That's her law. Learn her ways or die. But once you learn to get along with the desert, you realize that cruelty is, after all, the highest form of kindness.

Say what you want to about the desert. Say what you want to about ruthless cruelty which strikes with deadly aim and baffling speed. But you'll have to admit one thing. Take desert trained men, men who have lived with the desert and know her ways, and you'll find men who have thrown aside the cloak of mediocrity and have developed character.

That, too, is the law of the desert.

I strolled about the camp, looking at the types.

There were men from the Rand mine, typical laborers of the mining type, heavy muscled, good natured adventurers of the open places, broad-minded, tolerant, slow to anger, but, when once aroused, fiends incarnate.

There were girls, imported girls who had come in from the outside, trekking across miles of desert to taxi-dance with the miners, giving those rough men of the open a feminine companionship without which man sooner or later goes mad.

There were gamblers, men who sat at tables, green eyeshades on their foreheads, their faces pale with the pallor of skin that is exposed much to the artificial light of the night and but little to the sunlight of day. These men sat calmly expressionless, their hands flashing in swift motion as they dealt cards, pushing chips out to the center of the table without an instant's hesitation, or else throwing down their cards when a bet was made.

They never paused to consider in that lather of anxiety which marks the indecision of the amateur. They either had good enough cards to take a chance with or else they didn't. If they took a chance they received the verdict of the showdown with faces that didn't change a muscle. If they won, they raked in the chips. If they lost, they remained utterly motionless. They won without triumph, and lost without despair.

I was staring at a game of draw poker when a hand touched my arm.

It was Pete Blaine.

"I understand there was a man looking for me," he said.

I remembered that the gambler had said he preferred to speak to Pete Blaine himself, and had asked us not to mention his inquiry. But Pedro Gonzales didn't have any will of his own so far as Blaine was concerned.

"Seems to me I heard some one mention you."

"Can you describe him, Bob?"

"Not very well. He was tall and dark, looked like a professional gamber."

"Did he have a little scar over his right eye?"

I thought for a moment.

"Yes," I said. "I believe he did. You know him, then?"

"No," said Blaine. "I don't know him, but Pedro told me about him and about the scar. I wondered if he had been mistaken."

"He's around town, somewhere," I told him. "You'll run on to him probably."

He shook his head.

"No. That's why I was asking the questions. There's a big deal pending, and I've got some information from the mine that they have to have at once. I'm leaving within ten minutes. I'm going to drive over the Jawbone Cañon road and try and make the railroad by daylight. I don't know how long I'll be gone, and if this man were really a friend of mine I'd like to have seen him before I leave."

"I'll tell him, if I see him," I said.

"I wouldn't bother," he told me. "I'm satisfied it's just another one of those drifters who want to make a pretense of former friendship in order to get some easy work."

I nodded. I knew that the camp had its share of that type, men who were willing to work if the work wasn't too hard, and the pay was plenty. The desert isn't kind to men of that type. They drift, for the most part, around the cities.

Along about nine thirty, which is late for the desert, I decided that I'd stroll around and see how Nell was making it, and whether there was anything I could do to help her with her guest who had stumbled in out of the desert. I figured he'd have recovered enough to go to the ramshackle hotel and get a room by this time. Or he might have been one of those fellows who were hardy enough to pull out and make a camp in the open. For the most part the hotel housed the people from the outside. Your true desert dweller hates a roof over his head when he doesn't need protection from rain—which is seldom in the desert.

Nell was closing up the place.

"How's the patient?" I asked.

"Coming along," she said. "I kept his head sopped in wet towels, and by the time the tomato juice had started his saliva trickling he was yelling for water. I didn't give him too much, just a little bit at a time. He'd been in the desert before, and he knew enough to help me. I guess he's gone by this time. I had to come back here for the supper trade, and he said he'd be all right.

"I sort of thought he'd come in and see me before he left, but he didn't. Guess he's over at the hotel by this time."

"I'll go take a look with you," I told her.

She had an electric flash light. Together we walked out to the tent. I raised the flap. She flashed the torch into the interior of the tent.

Things have a way of being grim in the desert. The veneer gets stripped off of everything. That holds true for murders. I've seen a murder or two in my time, and always the murders that take place in the desert are killings that haven't any sugar coating.

This one wasn't any exception.

The man lay on his back on the cot. There was a cut in his throat, a thing of red horror that made a gap between his chin and his chest.

One glance and I knew that Nell would never be able to use the bedding again.

The white illumination of the flash light, boring into that dark interior of the tent house, caught the form on the bed, the head that was tilted back at such a grotesque angle, and made a shadow of horror on the canvas side of the house.

I caught Nell as she screamed and her hand became limp.

The flash light rolled to the floor, slipping from her numbed fingers. She clung to me in the darkness like a child clinging to its father. Then she shuddered, took a deep breath, and said:

"I'm sorry. I dropped the flash light. Do you want to go in and make an investigation, Bob?"

"Yes," I told her, and picked up the flash light.

"I'll stay out here," she said.

"I'm sorry," I told her, "but I'd like to have a witness. The gold, you know."

"I'd forgotten about that," she said.

We went in. I opened the man's shirt.

The gold was gone.

"That's all I wanted to know." I said. "Now we'll get in touch with Stan Walker. He can take charge."

Stan Walker was the resident deputy sheriff. He was an excitable sort of cuss, and I knew he'd resent it if he wasn't told of the crime at once. Perhaps as a desert man who's been accustomed to the reading of trail I might have discovered something if I'd looked around, but Walker would have resented that.

Nell was trembling as she put her hand on my arm, but she didn't say anything, and she walked along with firm steps.

The desert was big and silent and dark over on the left. The lights of the town made the sky bright over on the right.

A phonograph made music from a scratchy record. A girl laughed in the darkness; a low, seductive, throaty laugh.

"Walker was in a poker game about half an hour ago," I told Nell. "I'll see if I can round him up."

But I didn't need to take the trouble. We were coming to the lighted section of the town when I saw a figure come out of the dance hall. It looked like Stan Walker, and I whistled. He turned and I saw it was the man I was looking for.

He looked us over with that look of halfway hostility that he always had for me. Now that he was a deputy, Walker took himself seriously, and I wasn't inclined to take him so seriously, remembering back to the time when he'd got drunk in Mojave and tried to steal a locomotive.

"What is it?" he asked.

Before his appointment he'd always worn a sensible Stetson with a color that matched the desert dust. Now he'd broken out in one of those dressy, wide-brimmed black hats that are worn by sheriffs out in the West.

"Stan," I said, "there's been a man murdered."

He stared at me, then seemed to swell up with importance. "Who was he?"

"I don't know, a prospector who stumbled into Nell's restaurant."

"Who murdered him?"

"I don't know."

"How did you happen to discover the crime?"

I told him, in a few words, telling about the man's arrival, the gold, the gambler.

Stan Walker was a weatherbeaten cuss who'd seen fifty-five or fifty-six years go by in the course of his checkered lifetime. He had a bony face, a long, catfish mouth and eyes that he tried to make look penetrating now that he was a deputy.

"The motive," he said, "was robbery."

"Apparently," I told him.

"Four people are under suspicion," he said. "That is, there

are four people who must explain their whereabouts. The murderer is certain to be one of the four."

"Yes?" I asked him.

"Yes," he said.

"Well," I told him, "If you're going to figure it that way, I can see where you can suspect the gambler, and Pedro Gonzales, and myself, but I don't figure the fourth."

He fastened his steely eyes on Nell Hastings.

"There's Nell here," he said. "She had equal knowledge, and probably a better opportunity."

I could feel my face getting red, and my knuckles were pushing against the skin on the back of my hands. I kept myself in check, though.

"If you want some advice from a bystander," I told him, "you'd better get the sheriff here just as fast as you can. You start handling this thing by yourself and you're going to get hurt."

He stared threateningly.

"Who's going to hurt me?" he asked.

"You are," I told him.

He clamped that catfish mouth of his into a grim line, and said:

"I want you to understand, Bob Zane, that this is murder, and the law doesn't take cognizance of individuals. I don't give a damn whether a man is friend or foe. I suspect him until he can prove his innocence."

"All right," I said. "As an efficient officer, would you rather visit the scene of the crime, or would you prefer to stand here and debate about your devotion to duty?"

He couldn't answer that with words.

"Where is it?" he asked.

"Nell's tent."

"Come on," he said. "I want you both to remain with me until I release you."

I was mad, but Nell laughed, and the sound of that laughter made Stan Walker's back bristle up like an angry cat's. He stalked with the imposing dignity of a man who takes himself very, very seriously.

We trailed along.

## III. Who Is Guilty?

STAN WALKER EMERGED from the tent with a look of professional gravity.

"It's murder," he said.

"What the hell did you think it was?" I snapped, my nerves rubbed raw by his unjust suspicion of Nell Hastings.

"That'll do," he said. "This is a serious matter. The motive was robbery. Now we're going to round up Pedro Gonzales and this gambler. When we've done that we'll have an investigation."

There wasn't any use arguing with him. He represented the law, and law should be respected, even when it picks funny agents.

"I'd suggest the gambler first," I said.

"You get his name?" he asked.

"No. But we won't have any great trouble finding him. He's registered at the hotel, and they won't mistake him for any one else. I say he's a gambler. Of course I don't know, but I'm betting he is. His hands, his eyes, the way he holds his face..."

Stan Walker interrupted.

"It has been my experience in detective work that it's pretty hard to place a man simply from his appearance. You should have got his name and found out definitely what he was doing here."

"Yes," I said, with mock meekness, "I was under a disadvantage when I was talking with him."

"How was that?" asked Walker.

"I forgot that there was a murder intended, and didn't

know you'd want all those facts. Otherwise I'd have had them."

He clamped his mouth the more firmly. There wasn't any use trying to reason with that *hombre*, or trying to be sarcastic either. He pursued the even tenor of his ways and figured he was the biggest man in town. Watching him that night, I was reminded of the description of him a mining engineer had given after he'd talked with the deputy.

"Ten inches taller than God," he'd said.

And the description fit.

We went to the hotel. Walker routed out Bill Fincher, who ran the joint, and asked him if he'd rented a room to a man of about forty-five years of age with black eyes, dark hair, a scar over his right eye.

Fincher scowled thoughtfully.

"Fellow who looked like a gambler, Bill," I said.

Fincher grunted and remarked:

"Oh, that guy! His name's Madison, and he comes from El Paso."

Walker said:

"Shut up, Zane, I'm asking the questions."

I didn't say anything.

Fincher went on:

"He's a funny cuss. He sneaked out a couple of hours ago, and we haven't seen him since. He acted as though he didn't want anybody to ask any questions, and—"

"What's his room?" asked Walker.

"Come on," said Bill.

He took us down the corridor, paused in front of a door. He knocked. It was a typical mining camp hotel, a long barnlike structure with a single corridor and rooms on either side. It was made of boards thrown up on frames and strips of batten covering the spaces between the boards. In summer it was hot. In winter it was cold. And it was the best the town afforded.

There was no answer.

Bill tried the door. It was locked.

He took a pass key and we went in.

The gambler had unpacked his suitcase and had the contents scattered over the bed. There was the usual assortment of things that a man uses when he's living out of a suitcase. There was a heavy cowhide telescope bag in the corner. It was strapped. Stan Walker unpacked it.

Halfway down in it he found three buckskin bags. They were glazed with dirt and empty. He opened them carefully. With a magnifying glass we could see the bits of gold that adhered to the seams.

Walker was excited now. He explored around and found a money belt that had also contained gold, and which was now empty. And then he gave an exclamation as his hand pulled something else from the tangle of stuff that he'd thrown out of the telescope bag.

Nell Hastings gave an exclamation of horror.

It was a sheath knife, and the red horror of it told only too well what it had been used for.

Walker straightened.

A key sounded in the door. The door opened. The gambler stood there on the threshold. He stared at us with an impassive countenance. Whatever his emotions were, we couldn't read them. Walker dropped the knife and his hand streaked for his gun. He was quick with a gun.

But the gambler was just as quick, if not quicker.

I flung myself against him and grabbed the wrist.

"The law," I said.

I held the gun where he couldn't use it. Stan Walker came forward, the gun boring into the gambler's middle.

"Drop that gun," he said, "or I'll blow your stomach out."

The gun thudded to the floor. The gambler's face remained impassive. I released my hold on his wrist.

"I arrest you, in the name of the law," said Stan Walker,

"for the murder of an unidentified man, and maybe there'll be a charge of grand larceny, too. I ain't sure how they handle that. But I'm warning you that anything you say will be used against you."

"You're crazy!" said the gambler.

"Maybe," said Walker. "Put handcuffs on him, Bob, and keep out of the line of fire when you do it."

He handed me handcuffs.

"Put out your wrists," I told the gambler.

He held them out. His face was the color of chalk, but there wasn't any expression on it. I felt him wince as the handcuffs went around his wrists and clicked home. I was willing to bet it wasn't the first pair of handcuffs that had been on his wrists, but I wasn't saying anything. It was Walker's show. He could run it to suit himself.

"Where was you about an hour ago?" asked Walker.

The gambler smiled. His face was white as desert chalk, but his eyes were steady.

"I'm answering no questions," he said.

Walker shrugged.

"I'm goin' to take him down to the county seat," he told me. "There'll be a lynching sure if he's left here."

"Better look up Pedro Gonzales," I told him. "You want to check up on all four of us, you know."

He acted just a little embarrassed.

"No hard feelings," he said. "But I had to be impartial. Now that we got the evidence on this *hombre,* I can treat you unofficial like. But I couldn't play favorites."

Bill Fincher spoke up and said:

"Pedro Gonzales left with Pete Blaine to take the trip through Jawbone Cañon. They left before dark."

Walker turned to Nell.

"Was this murder done after dark, Nell?"

"Yes. I was talking with the old man after eight o'clock."

Walker nodded.

"That lets Pedro out," he said. "We got the guilty man, all right; and I'm going to get him down to the county seat. Bob Zane, I'm going to draft you to take us there. There's only one way we can make it in time to get back here with the sheriff and take charge of the case, and that's to drive through Jawbone Cañon. I want somebody that knows the desert to do the driving. You're hereby appointed a special deputy to see that I get to the jail with this prisoner."

I shrugged my shoulders. Not that I wanted the job, but I figured it'd be a lot better to get down and get the sheriff on the job than to let Walker mess around with it; and he was right when he said that there was some danger of lynch law.

"When do we start?" I asked.

"Now," he said. "We'll go in my car."

The Jawbone Cañon road is a short-cut, all right. It saves over forty-one miles of desert road. It's only a matter of sixty-four miles to the county seat over the Jawbone Cañon road. But it's tough going.

There used to be some mines in Jawbone Cañon that kept the road up. The mines were abandoned, and the road got in bad repair. But it was a road, and a good driver could get over it with a light car. None of those shiny finished boulevard cars could make it, but a rough and ready desert rattle-trap could.

Down below Jawbone Cañon where the road struck the flat desert was a place of shifting sand and hard pulling, but it was pretty much on the level. Jawbone Cañon was rough and twisting. At that a man could make time over the road if he was in enough of a hurry. But cars mostly went the long way around. It was easier.

Stan Walker appointed Bill Fincher as a deputy to take charge of the body and see that it wasn't disturbed until we could get back with the sheriff. He got his car filled up with oil and gas, and we started.

I'm more at home with burros than with a car, but I guess I

know every foot of the desert as well as the next man. I know it well enough to respect it without being afraid of it, to love it without taking chances with it.

We jolted along the plateau road until we topped the big barren ridge of colored mountains and started winding down Jawbone Cañon.

We'd got pretty well down into the middle of the cañon, where the road twisted and turned and was all rutted and rough, covered with bowlders of varying sizes, and with occasional stretches of sand. The high walls of the cañon stretched up until they blotted out the steady stars with rims of black that were like ink.

I swung the wheel getting the car around a curve, and saw a man waving his arms frantically. I slammed on the brakes. The car skidded around some and stopped. The man came into the glare of the headlights. His coat was off, his arms semaphoring wildly.

I saw it was Pete Blaine.

And the gambler saw him, too. There were the three of us in the car, the gambler, who sat up in front with me, his wrists handcuffed, and Stan Walker who sat in back with his gun out. I was driving, up at the wheel.

I could see the gambler stiffen when Blaine walked into the headlights.

"That the man you knew?" I asked him.

The gambler said nothing.

Blaine walked up until he could see into the car.

"Hello, Zane," he said. "And there's Stan Walker. Hello, Walker. Gee, I'm glad to see you two. We had a bust-down, smashed into a rock and collapsed the front wheel. I've got to get down to the railroad. Can you give us a lift?"

Walker said importantly:

"We're on official business, Blaine. But I guess we can give you a ride."

Blaine snorted:

"You can't leave us here. There ain't a car a week over this road. I thought we were stranded for keeps. Gee, but I was glad to hear the sound of the motor in your car!"

He was dressed after the fashion of mining engineers, with corduroys and lace boots. He was going down for a consultation with the representatives of the mine, and he wanted to look important and well dressed. A real desert rat would have turned up his nose at the rig he wore, though.

And then his eyes lit on the gambler.

He stiffened, backed away, and said: "You!"

The gambler stared at him and said nothing.

Blaine said: "Is this man a prisoner, officer?"

Stan Walker liked the word "officer." He swelled out his chest.

"He's under arrest for murder," he said. "You know him?"

"Know him!" said Blaine. "I'll say I know him! I knew him when he was convicted of robbery in Las Vegas, New Mexico, and sentenced to seven years in the penitentiary!"

Walker said gloatingly: "A jailbird, eh?"

And the gambler said nothing. He sat very straight, very tense, and very silent.

"Well," I told them, "this ain't getting us any place. If we're going to the county seat we'd better get started."

Blaine got to the running board.

"The car's down there a hundred yards or so. Pedro's with it. He got hurt a little bit, a sprained ankle or something. I heard the sound of your car and came up here to make sure you didn't smash into us when you came around the curve."

I drove slowly until we rounded the sharp curve on a steep grade. There was Blaine's car with the left front wheel caved in. The car was sitting down on the axle in front, and looked pretty much out of the running.

Pedro Gonzales came hobbling out.

He was glad to see us, and insisted on shaking hands all around like we'd been long lost brothers. He heard of the murder and was surprised. He said there wasn't over five hundred dollars' worth of gold in the sack. He evidently didn't know about the other sacks I'd felt in the man's shirt. I told him about them.

"How'd the accident happen?" I asked.

"I don't know. I was asleep. Blaine was driving. All of a sudden, bang, down we went."

"What time?" I asked.

"Must have been over two hours ago," he said.

I went over to look at the car. It was hopeless without a new wheel and a lot of minor parts. Things on one side were smashed pretty much. I could see that there were suitcases in the car, and that Blaine had taken off his coat and folded it over the hood of the car. I put one hand on the coat and leaned over to take a look at the wheel. My bare arm slid along the top of the radiator, and I jerked it back as the metal burnt my flesh.

"You must not have any water in here," I told him. "Your radiator's pretty hot."

Pedro answered: "Yes. We were speeding."

It was a poor road to speed on. I turned to Walker.

"Well," I told him, "you're the boss. What are you going to do?"

"You can take me to the railroad," said Blaine.

Walker shook his head. "We're turning the other way. We won't hit the railroad until we get to the county seat. We can take you there."

Blaine was impatient.

"Look here," he said, "this is important. It's a matter of business that—"

"This," said Walker, drawing himself up and swelling out his chest, "is murder. It's my duty and it comes first."

Pedro said: "He means it, chief. He's just that kind of a guy. Better let me ride in to the county seat with them and bring back a repair car. We'll get this fixed up. You can stay here. If some one else comes along that's headed for the railroad you can go with them. If you can't get a lift I'll be back with the repair car."

Blaine thought it over.

"Go ahead," he snapped. "You'll hear more from this, Walker."

"I'm sorry," said Walker, "but duty is duty."

I had a sudden inspiration. I slid my hand around the hood of the car and dragged Blaine's coat down to the place between the hood and the front fender. Then I turned and leaned my back against the fender, my right hand dropping down to the coat. I fumbled around in the pocket until I found the leather wallet which Blaine always carried in the coat pocket. I slipped it out and put it in my hip pocket as I walked away from the car.

Blaine was walking up and down and sputtering, but there wasn't any use, as far as Walker was concerned. Walker was as immovable as the Rock of Gibraltar.

"Let's go," he said.

Pedro got in the car with us. I sent it on its way, leaving Blaine there.

Pedro was nursing his foot. Walker was keeping both eyes on the prisoner. Neither of them knew too much about this section of the desert. There was a place at the bottom of the grade where an old road turned off. If I could get their attention distracted when I came to the forks of the road, I had an idea I might put a plan of my own into operation.

## IV. LOST

WE HIT THE PLACE where the old road turned off. I jumped as though the gambler had made a sudden move, and Walker jabbed his gun into the gambler's shoulder blades.

"None of that!" he said.

I swung the wheel and we were fighting our way along over the old road. If you know roads in the desert, you know y it takes so long to get places. This road was never repaired. It was cut up with channels cut by water from the cloudbursts. There were stretches of sand, long gullies of stone, steep hills.

Walker said after a while: "I had no idea the road was this bad. We'd have saved time by taking the long way around and forgetting the Jawbone Cañon road."

"I believe we would, at that," I said. "This is awful!"

I kept on fighting the road. It had turned now and was winding up a long draw where the sand was so heavy I had to keep down in the gears. Walker was getting nervous.

Pedro Gonzales said: "There's something wrong here. I was over the road once before, and it wasn't this bad."

"Maybe the thing'll get better when we top this grade," I said.

I kept the car running.

An hour passed, another hour. The passengers were getting fidgety. We dropped down a steep slope, crossed a place that was all sand, and started another climb. The road had been cut into a grade, and there were lots of bowlders that had rolled down. Four or five times I had to get out and roll rocks away. Then we went down into the flat desert, broken only by rolling stretches. This was harder going than anything we'd struck. There was sand, lots of sand.

Walker pulled out his watch.

"You've got us on the wrong road, Zane," he snapped.

"I don't think so," I told him.

I was watching for landmarks. At last I saw them. I knew right where I was.

There was a dry wash with bowlders, and the road dropped right off into it, a drop of two feet at least.

I put it in low and stepped on it.

"Look out!" yelled Walker.

I grabbed for the emergency brake, but I stepped on the throttle. The front of the car took the drop. There was a terrific jar. Then a stone went through the transmission. A front wheel gave way, and there we were. Water was hissing and boiling, streaming out of the radiator.

"You clumsy fool!" yelled Walker.

I turned around.

"Anybody hurt?" I asked.

Nobody was much the worse for the shock. Pedro's ankle was pretty bad. It was bothering him. Walker was sore. The gambler had cut his wrist with the side of one of the handcuffs as the car had made the plunge. Aside from that, they were all right.

"I told you, Walker, I was more at home with a burro than an automobile."

He got out and surveyed the mess.

"All due to clumsy incompetence!" he stormed. "For years I've had you pointed out, Bob Zane, as the man who knew the desert, the old timer who knew every single inch of the desert as far as there was any desert. And here you go and get us on the wrong road, and then put your foot on the gasoline instead of the brake pedal!"

"I'm sorry," I told him.

Pedro and Walker took turns in cussing me.

The gambler said nothing.

"Well," I told them, "we'll have to wait for daylight now, and try to see where we are."

Walker stormed around and threatened to file charges against me for interfering with an officer in the discharge of his duty, and a lot more stuff.

Pedro was having trouble with his ankle. He cursed in a low, sullen undertone. The gambler was very suave, very much of a gentleman. He asked Walker to take off the handcuffs. Walker finally unlocked one and locked the other around the robe rail.

It wasn't a comfortable night, what was left of it.

Morning showed us just what I knew it would show us, the

most desolate, God-forsaken stretch of barren country that one could imagine.

There were rolling hills that seemed to stretch in an unbroken sea of glittering desolation. We were down in a sort of cañon.

The car was hopeless. The water had even drained out of the radiator and made a moist place in the thirsty sand.

The sun sent its rays beating down fiercely.

There was no shade.

The men took stock of the situation. Walker was going to remain with his prisoner, come what might. Pedro's ankle prevented him from walking.

"You've got to go and get help," said Walker, "and don't bungle it like you did in getting us out here."

"Okay," I said, "providing you remember to stay with the car. That's where trouble starts on the desert. The car gets wrecked, one man goes for help. The others get impatient and start out to search for him. When help comes the men are scattered all over the desert. By the time they find 'em it's too late. You can sit still in the shade of the car and conserve your strength better than you can by bucking the heat of the desert."

"Get started," Walker snarled. "You'd think you was putting on a talk for tenderfeet. Get started."

I headed east.

Walker yelled at me: "Don't tackle *that* road. It leads back to Jawbone Cañon eventually, and there's no traffic over that. Head to the north. You should strike the main highway by midnight!"

I kept on walking due east.

Walker came running up alongside of me. I could hear the crunch of his feet in the sand and the rattle of his voice in angry expostulation; but I didn't pay any attention to it. I just kept plugging along.

After a while I said:

"How about your prisoner? I thought your duty was to look after him."

Walker whirled, looked back at the car, cursed me some more, and then jog trotted back. I didn't look at him. I just kept on going due east.

After an hour I'd lost sight of the car and the road. There was nothing around me but desert, a vast furnace of heat. The hot sand burned through the soles of my shoes. The sun beat down mercilessly.

The white-hot glare of the light on the sand made the eye muscles ache until the whole brain throbbed with a dreadful weariness from which there was no relief.

I swung down a wash between two hills, heading toward the south.

I walked until afternoon, making a big circle, taking great care not to leave prints within a long distance of the car. It was three o'clock when I topped a little hill 'way over on the west of the car and looked at it.

The car cast a splotch of shadow, and that splotch of shadow showed jet black on the glittering sand. The men were sprawled in that area of shadow, motionless, lifeless in appearance.

I was tired. I lay down and slept.

Toward sunset I looked at them again.

They were stirring around a little. I knew I was practically invisible with the sun in the heavens back of me, but I had only the very top of my head sticking up, and I was cautious.

When the sun started to slide behind the mountains in the west I ducked down into my cañon and picked out a place to spend the night. I gathered a lot of scrub sage and piled it in a sheltered place against a ledge. By the time it was dark I took a last look.

The men had a fire going. It would be cold there in the desert at night, and they'd gone out and picked up some sage and piled it around. They'd conserve their fuel.

I went back to my bed of sage and went to sleep.

When morning came I kept in the bed. I was a little chilled, but the sun started stoking up the surface heat of the desert, and the horizons started to shimmy.

I kept under cover all morning. Not until the sun started down in the west did I dare to risk looking out at them.

They weren't keeping so quiet now. They were standing out, staring over the desert, straining their eyes for some sign of help.

They figured I'd have hit the Jawbone Cañon road by night and should have been showing up with help.

I knew how they felt, listening for the sound of a motor, every time a breath of wind made a noise as it rustled past the sage their hopeful ears would interpret it as sound made by a motor.

It was dry work, and it was hungry work. I hadn't eaten, and I hadn't had anything to drink. I'm an old desert man, and a man who's lived a long time in the desert doesn't sweat as much as a man who hasn't dried out any. Even at that, I felt the heat and had to carry a pebble in my mouth to keep any saliva on my tongue.

I watched the men.

They got impatient. Once or twice Walker would move out a ways and climb to a little hill where he'd look all around. I could see Pedro when he moved. The foot was bothering him.

The desert was silent, vast, unchanging, patient.

The men moved about; little, aimless motions that relieved the tension of the mind, and yet built up more nervousness. I watched them until almost sundown. Then I went back and lay down.

There was a restlessness, a feeling of fear. Well as I knew the desert, well as I knew my own plans, I had that peculiar feeling. It comes from experiencing the pangs of hunger and the suffering of thirst when one's out in the desert.

No matter where the place in the desert, there's that sinister silence that comes thundering to the consciousness, the vast, aching space that's a breeder of panic in those who don't know the desert and love it.

For just a half second I felt the urge of that blind panic, the fear of the very bigness of the desert, the contagion of the void which seemed to creep into my soul and suck the very life out of me.

Then I took a deep breath and the feeling left me.

The desert had stamped its mark upon me, and branded me for its own. Gone was that feeling of panic. In its place was one of calm peace. The desert had ceased to terrify me with its waiting patience, and had inspired me, instead, with its tranquillity.

I slept.

I awoke at night and heard the desert talking.

It's a strange experience, lying out in the desert and listening to the sand slither along on the wings of those mysterious night winds which spring up from nowhere, blow violently, then die down again.

The sand scurries along on the wings of the wind, and rustles against the sage and the cacti. Then, as the wind freshens, sand rustles along on the surface of the sand itself. The whole desert seethes into life, and every grain rubs against the other grains, giving forth a faint suggestion of inaudible sound which, multiplied a thousandfold, comes to the ears as an intangible whisper.

You try to pin it down to some definite sound, and it's just a peculiar undertone of faint noise underlying the desert wind. Relax and immediately it becomes a whisper, slitheringly insistent, hissing and mysterious.

I've known men to go almost crazy when they were alone out in the desert and the sand started to whisper.

I crawled up on the ridge and looked over at the men around the machine. They were keeping the fire going, and they were huddled around the flame. They wanted companionship more than warmth. That's the way with men who are plunged out into the middle of the desert.

They find themselves alone with their own souls. They strive to keep from facing themselves, clutching at every vestige of human companionship, yet always being swept into the silence.

These men were clutching at each other as a drowning man clutches at straws. And the attempt to avoid the inevitable was as futile. They were facing their own souls, stripped stark naked of the artificial standards of a civilization that's coated with gilt.

Back amongst their kind they'd have standards of success in life that would be measured by gold, by power, by an ability to wrest from their fellow men.

Out here in the desert, standing face to face with themselves, with the grim specter of death jeering at their elbows, there was only one standard of life. The great whispering desert, and the steady silent stars, knew what that standard was. Remorselessly, inexorably, the desert was holding her mirror to these three men.

I nodded my satisfaction, and stumbled my way down to my bed of sage. I lay and listened to the desert talk to me.

Morning. The golden rays of the sun touched the tops of the mountains. The purple shadows shrank into little pools which hugged the face of the desert, then disappeared. The heat beat down like a smothering blanket. The skyline of the mountains wavered, tilted, wavered, and broke into a devil dance of its own, a thing of heat distortion and mirage.

I risked peering over the ridge.

The last semblance of self-control had vanished. The men were moving about. That is, Pedro and one other man were moving. I could tell Pedro by the limp. The other man might have been either the deputy or the gambler. I couldn't tell at the distance.

They made frequent journeys to the tops of the knolls, and they broke into running steps at times, running steps which their panic-sticken minds finally controlled, beat into a walk. But, ever and anon, the control of the mind would slip. The sight of death, jeering at their elbows, would send them into a run again.

I waited until it was noon, until the tongue in my mouth felt like a great ball of dry blotting paper that was sucking the soul stuff from my blood. Then I topped the ridge and came stumblingly down the slope.

I'd gone two hundred yards before they saw me.

Then they paused in their restless motions to stare at me, little sticks of black standing grotesquely against the white glare of the desert.

Then they ran toward me.

I had a pinch of tobacco in either hand. I put a bit in my eyes. The eyes streamed water, then flamed into red anger. I stumbled on and stared with those red eyes at the two men who came weaving their heavy-footed way across the hot sands.

Walker tried to speak, and could not.

Pedro Gonzales limped after him. He stared at me with incredulous eyes.

"You didn't find it?"

I pretended to be delirious.

"Help," I said thickly. "Three men in an automobile in the desert. I came east. They're west!"

I pointed a wavering finger at the horizon which shimmered in hot mockery.

"Go to them. Give me water. Water! *Water!*"

Pedro Gonzales cursed.

"Walked in a big circle like a damned tenderfoot! This is the end!"

Walker mumbled. "Too late for us to try now. We're dying!"

They stumbled their way back to the car. I staggered after them.

The gambler looked up. His face was calm as the desert, utterly expressionless. He smiled a greeting.

"Hello," he said. "You got back?"

"It's the end, you fool," said Pedro Gonzales. "He walked in a circle . . ."

"Sure, I know," observed the gambler. "We have to face it some time."

They stared at him with their reddened, feverish eyes.

I flopped over on the sand and kept mumbling for water.

The sun beat down on the dazzling sand which shifted and swayed in the heat waves. The eyes ached with the white glare. The heat seemed to have started the blood boiling.

"It's the end," said Pedro Gonzales, mouthing the words in toneless, foolish repetition.

I sat up on the sand and stared at him with my bloodshot eyes.

"Why don't you die clean?" I asked him.

## v. The Confession

WALKER SAID: "Don't mind him. It's the delirium. They get the strength of ten men, run up and down and tear their clothes off and talk crazy things. He doesn't know what he's talking about."

I got to my feet and let my eyes get big and staring.

"Don't tell me I don't know what I'm talking about!" I said. "I was crazy when I came here, but I know now what I'm doing. I found Pete Blaine out there on the desert. He had tried to walk for water, and he was dying when I came on him.

"He'd gone on ahead in the dark, and fallen over the edge

of the cañon and broken his leg. He knew he was dying. I was there with him when he died.

"He couldn't die with murder on his soul. He told me all about it. Pete and Pedro killed that old prospector. Not for the gold, but because they wanted this gambler out of the way.

"They were going to frame an alibi. They left town and pretended they were going on down the Jawbone Cañon road. But they didn't. They sneaked back and killed the old prospector and took the gold, to make it look like robbery.

"Then they went down the Jawbone Cañon road, but they were only about twenty minutes ahead of us. They smashed the car on purpose, so that they'd have an alibi. They said the car had been broken down for about two hours. It wasn't anything of the sort. The car had only been broken down about twenty minutes. That's why the radiator burned my arm when I touched it."

I stopped and stared around at the men with my reddened eyes.

The gambler sat quiet, almost detached, his face absolutely expressionless. Pedro Gonzales's face had twisted into a spasm of expression. His eyes were staring.

Walker looked at me with his jaw sagging open. It was pathetic to see this man, face to face with death, realizing that he might have made the mistake that had caused all this.

"Blaine confessed," I went on. "He told me all about it, and he scribbled a confession in his notebook and gave me the notebook and wallet, so that I could turn in his confession and make what restitution he could."

Pedro Gonzales husked: "That's a damned lie!"

I shook my head and pulled the wallet from my pocket.

Every one of them knew that leather wallet. It was Blaine's, and one that he was proud of, one that had the edges laced together with a leather thong, and had his monogram embossed on the leather front. I took out the notebook that was inside of it, and thumbed through the pages.

Pedro Gonzales pushed forward.

"It's a lie!" he said again.

I looked at Gonzales and then let my face settle into a cunning leer.

"Oh, no, it ain't a lie," I said. "I've got the confession right here, but you aren't going to get your hands on it. You'd destroy it!"

And I pushed the notebook back in the wallet, put the wallet in my pocket.

Stan Walker said: "Bob Zane, that's evidence. I command you to deliver it into the custody of the law!"

I laughed at him mockingly.

"There isn't any law," I said. "As far as you're concerned, the law is finished. As far as I'm concerned, the law is finished. As far as Pedro Gonzales is concerned, the law is finished. The law can't do anything to any of us. We're going to a higher court! We're dying!"

Pedro Gonzales stared at us with his bloodshot eyes.

"Blaine wasn't the one that did it," I said. "Gonzales was the one who did the real killing. Blaine only helped."

Gonzales said nothing.

Walker turned to him and said: "Gonzales, is that right?"

Gonzales still kept quiet.

I said: "Of course it's right, you fool! Don't you see? How could the motor of that car have been so hot that I burned my arm on it if it had been standing there in Jawbone Cañon for two hours? They smashed the car just to make an alibi."

Nobody said anything for a while. There was silence. Then I got up and said: "You can do what you want to, but I'm not going to die with a murderer."

I got to my feet and started to walk away, but I only went about twenty yards, and then staggered, stumbled, and fell down on my face.

I heard some one running toward me, and knew that it was Pedro Gonzales, from the way he limped when he ran. I could hear the sound of his feet crunching in the sand, one foot coming down harder than the other.

He flung himself on me and started clawing and scratching at my pocket, trying to get hold of the wallet that I had there.

Stan Walker was running after him, yelling for him to stop.

Gonzales got his hands on the wallet, but couldn't drag it from my pocket because I flung my arm across my body so that I held the wallet close to my body.

Walker shouted something inarticulate and flung himself at Gonzales, knocking Gonzales back into the desert.

I sat up and stared at them. My eyes were red-rimmed and bloodshot, and my voice was husky.

"There's no use fighting about it," I said. "It wouldn't make any difference. There's no escape. We're going to die. We can't reach water, and no help will come to us here. All that I ask is, don't let me die with that murderer!

"Blaine died, but he died with a clean soul. He confessed."

The strain was too much for Gonzales. He got to his hands and knees there in the desert and stared at us with his red-rimmed eyes glittering malevolently, his lips working and twisting. He was like some wild animal there, with the fierce sun beating down on his face, showing the ravages of thirst and hunger, the oily scum which had collected on his skin, the growth of stubble which was pushing out from his chin.

"He didn't die clean, damn him!" he snarled. "I didn't kill him; Blaine killed him! I only helped Blaine with his getaway. The dirty double crosser! He came to me and told me that this gambler had something on him, and that he had to kill him. I don't know what it was, but the man had been following Pete for years. So Pete killed the prospector, and took the gold. He wanted to make it look as though the gambler had done the killing. Then he figured that the boys would string up the gambler. All I did was help Pete plant the gold in the gambler's room and plan the alibi so that Pete would have a chance to alibi himself if anybody made any accusation."

Walker said: "Gonzales, I arrest you in the name of the law."

Gonzales jibbered at him with a face that was like the face of some great ape.

"You damn fool!" he said. "You can't arrest anybody. We're dying. All of us are dying. It's the end! There's no escape! Blaine's dead. The gambler's going to die. You're going to die. Bob Zane's going to die. I'm going to die. All here together, we're going to die!"

The gambler said calmly:

"Well, at least let's be men about it."

I rolled over and got to my hands and knees. I sat up and stared at one of the mountains, and then pointed to the outline of a saddleback.

"I know that mountain!" I yelled. "There's a prospector got a camp on the other side. The road's only a little ways from his place, the main road that has travel on it."

"Delirium," said Walker, trying to calm me.

"Anyhow," said the gambler, "we can see if he's right. Personally, I'm tired of this place. I'd like a change of scenery for my death. I don't want to die by the side of this automobile. It lacks distinction."

I staggered away toward the mountain.

"Come on," said the gambler.

Pedro tried to keep up, but his ankle was bad. He was limping and staggering.

I led the procession.

It was hard going in the hot sun, toiling up the little slope. We topped it. There, not half a mile away, was a little shack with a road running in to it, and a flivver standing in the sun, covered over with burlap. There was a trailer with a big water tank on it.

The men broke into a run.

The prospector came out when he heard us shuffling through the sand. He gave us water and made us some soup. We went out and got Pedro Gonzales.

The water brought us around all right. The fever left our blood.

Walker came over to me. His manner was more changed. It was deferential and somehow apologetic.

"Zane," he said, "I had better take that confession as evidence."

"You don't need it now," I told him, "not after having heard Gonzales' confession."

"I know it," he said, "but nevertheless it's evidence and I should have it."

I grinned at him and said: "Well, you won't get it."

He stiffened.

"Why not?"

"Because," I told him, "there isn't any confession."

He stared at me with his eyes getting bigger all the time.

"I knew you were making a mistake right from the start," I told him, "and when I touched the radiator on that car down there in the cañon and it was red-hot, I knew that the car hadn't been standing there for any particular length of time.

"Then I looked it over a little bit and saw that they must have driven into that rock on purpose in order to smash the wheel. I put two and two together, and figured that they wanted an alibi. So I slipped Blaine's wallet out of his coat pocket, figuring that I might be able to fake a story about a confession if I ever had the opportunity."

But I didn't tell him that I had deliberately driven the car off the road in order to make the opportunity. He might not have appreciated that.

"Then Blaine really wasn't dead?" he asked.

"No," I said. "I didn't see Blaine. I just wandered around on the desert, and didn't see anybody."

Walker didn't like it, but there wasn't very much he could do about it.

By midnight we could travel, and the prospector put us all in his flivver and headed for the main road to the county seat. It wasn't over five miles from his shack, that main road, and we were at the county seat by daylight.

The sheriff heard the story.

Then he organized a posse and rounded up Blaine.

There was only once when the sheriff threatened to give me away. That was when Walker was telling about how I got lost in the desert and walked in a big circle.

The sheriff was seized with a fit of coughing.

He'd known me for ten years, been in the desert with me. Many's the night we'd lain and listened to the tale of the whispering sand as it slithered along on the wings of the wind.

# PAY DIRT

## 1. A Dying Man's Wisdom

I COULD TELL THAT HE WAS GOING TO DIE, almost from the first minute I saw him. I've lived too long in the desert to be fooled on those things.

He was running, if you could call it that. And that was a bad sign. Then again he had most of his clothes torn off. And he was soft and he had been fat. Those things weigh against a man when the desert has her way with him.

It was along in the afternoon, and the sun was sending out long shadows. The man showed as a speck at first, wobbling in a crazy zigzag. His shadow was jet black, as is the way with desert shadows in the summer.

Old Pete knows the desert even better than I do.

"Get that second burro unpacked," he told me. "There's some canned tomatoes in that pack, and we'll need the canvas, and all the water. Take one of the blankets and soak it in water."

We weren't over five miles from Owl Wells, so we had water and to spare. I started throwing off the pack ropes. Pete went out to meet the running man.

I caught a glimpse of Pete trying to flag the man down.

He waved his arms, shouted, yelled. It wasn't any use. The guy was plumb loco. Pete finally had to catch him. Then the guy let out a whoop and started to struggle, as though Pete had been a cannibal. Then he went limp and Pete eased him down to the desert.

"Make it snappy!" he yelled at me.

I started the burro over that way, sopping water on the blankets as I came.

The fellow was an awful sight.

His skin was like a boiled lobster. His lips were cracked until they were taut, drawn back from the teeth. The tongue was black and swollen. Most of the clothes were gone. Pete took off the few rags that remained. We lay him on the wet blanket, put a little tomato juice in his mouth, sprinkled him with water, made a shade with the big bed canvas.

"Any chance?" I asked, knowing that there wasn't, but just to be sociable.

Pete shook his head.

The man had been too fat. Thirst and heat had sizzled the lard off of him.

And when that happens there's some sort of an acid poison that gets into the system. It does with every one who gets out in the desert when it's hot. But a fat man gets it worse. That's why we always use tomatoes instead of water. It helps to cut that acid.

We worked until sunset with this party. Along about dusk he opened his eyes and was conscious.

We'd been feeding him tomatoes and keeping his skin sopped with water.

As soon as he came to, we gave him some more water. He gulped it down as though he had been a piece of dried blotting paper.

"More," he said.

Pete shook his head.

"Not yet. Try to sleep."

The man rolled his head from side to side.

"The judge," he said.

Pete frowned.

"What about the judge?"

The man tried to talk, but his tongue got in his way and he was awfully weak.

"The automobile—broken axle—tow car—judge—"

He closed his eyes.

Pete looked at me and frowned.

"Say, d'you s'pose there's another one of 'em out in the desert? They must have come in from the auto road. Tried a short cut, maybe."

He cocked his eye over toward the east. A full moon was tipping its rim over the hills.

"Say, Bob," he said, "d'you s'pose you could track this pilgrim by moonlight?"

"Maybe."

"If you can't, you can stay with him and I'll go."

I reached for my hat.

"I can track him if you could," I said, which wasn't exactly true. There's no man can hold his own with Pete Harder in the desert. But then, I wasn't going to let Pete get too puffed up.

I waited to see if he was going to make any come-back.

"The quicker you start the sooner you'll find out," he said. "This guy's got about one chance in a hundred. I'll know by morning. If he can move I'll make Owl Wells. What I'm afraid of is that there may be a woman—"

I didn't hear the rest. I was moving away in the desert.

You can track easier when the moon is angling up or down. It makes shadows back of the little ridges of disturbed sand. When it's straight overhead, it flattens things out too much.

I wanted to cover all the ground I could, so I pushed right along. After five miles I got a hunch my man had been walking in a circle. I cut across at right angles, and picked up his tracks again within half a mile. I backtracked those for a mile, then did the same thing, and made another short cut.

This time the steps were more evenly spaced and were in a straight line. Looked as though he'd been more certain of himself then, and a lot stronger. I pushed right along. The course he was traveling would have been a short cut over the Red Mountains to the automobile road, and I knew a short cut that would take off a whole lot of miles from that. I acted on a hunch and took that short cut.

As soon as I came down out of the mountain pass on the old Indian trail I could see the machine. The moon was pretty much overhead now, but the shadows were black as ink, what there was of them. The road was an old short cut some of the oldtimers used. There wouldn't be a machine over it in a month.

They'd taken out the rear axle all right. The car was right there and was going to be for some little time. I poked around in it. There were suitcases, a couple of bags of golf sticks, some overcoats, and a lot of junk. The baggage was expensive.

There wasn't any sign of a canteen. Either they didn't have any or they'd taken 'em with them. I was inclined to think they hadn't had any.

There was a little pile of charred embers by the side of the running board, an empty thermos bottle, and some grease-stained papers. I looked around and found some chicken bones and bread crusts.

Looked as though one of the men had gone for help, the other had stayed with the car—for awhile. He'd eaten the lunch. The embers weren't so awfully old. I looked at the radiator and found it was full of water, looked around the car and found the tracks of two men all milled up. Then one set of tracks headed out over the desert. Those were the tracks of the man we'd found. I poked around and found the other man's tracks. He'd started back down the road.

He'd started running almost at once. Maybe he'd got thirsty waiting, maybe he'd just got the lost-panic. People get that way when they're left alone in the universe with themselves. They want to start running. It's just a panic, fear feeding on fear.

I swung back down the road. Within two miles I found a coat and vest. There were papers in the pocket, a watch in the vest. It had run down. There was a big Masonic emblem on the chain, gold set with diamonds.

I kept on. The man had simply run himself to death. Maybe it had been the heat, maybe it had been his heart. I found him blotching the road in the moonlight less than five miles from the car.

His tongue wasn't swollen, his clothes were on and he hadn't shredded the flesh from his fingers, digging in the coarse sand with his hands at the last, so I knew he hadn't died from thirst.

That seemed to account for everybody. Just two men.

I buried him where I found him in a shallow grave that would keep the buzzards off, even if it didn't stop coyotes. I figured on coming back and finishing the job later.

I put the papers from his coat in my pocket.

He'd been a judge of a superior court some place, and his name was Charles McNaught. I had some canned tomatoes and cooked up a little bacon and warmed over some beans. I was tired. I'd been on the move all day and most of the night. The moon was getting pretty well in the west.

I figured on making Owl Wells because it was nearest and if Pete had been able to move the other man he'd be there.

If he couldn't move him by morning it'd mean there'd be two graves instead of just one.

The burro would have liked a long lay-off, but I gave him only two hours. Then we hit for the wells.

It was ten o'clock in the morning when we got there. Pete was there—alone.

"Cash in?" I asked.

He nodded. "Find the judge?"

"Yeah. If he'd waited at the car he'd have been O.K. If he'd thought of the radiator he'd have had enough water to have lasted him a week. But he ate a fried chicken lunch and then started to run. His pump stopped."

Pete ran his fingers through the white stubble along his chin. There was a funny look in his eye.

"Listen to me, and listen careful," he said. "My man got conscious along toward morning. He could talk. I knew he was going and he knew it, too. His name is Harrisson Bocker. He's a millionaire. He's got a son named Edward that's in college some place or other. I've got the address written down.

"The guy could talk rationally about some things. Other things he was goofy on. Seemed he'd made some sort of what he called a 'spendthrift trust' for his boy. The judge was the trustee. Old Bocker figured the judge was maybe croaked. That'd invalidate the trust and mean the boy would take the money all in one gob. Bocker said he'd blow it in. He always was an easy mark, sort of a rich man's kid.

"Well, the long and short of it was, he made me his trustee if old McNaught had cashed in, changed his will accordingly. I'm sole trustee. What I say goes. The kid don't get any money until he's forty unless I say he can have it. I can let him have all I want. If he gets married without my consent he loses everything. What do you think of that?"

I looked old Pete over.

"I think the guy was batty and you let him go ahead knowing he was crazy as a loon. He never even saw you before. What do you know about trusts?"

Pete chuckled.

"That's what you think. Nobody can prove nothin', and I've always wanted to have the handling of one of these rich men's sons. Let us go get the coroner. I want this here official."

## II. A Desert Man's Ward

I WAS A WITNESS AT THE INQUEST, and then I lost track of Pete for a few months. I heard generally what was happening. The kid didn't take kindly to Pete as a trustee. He got a lawyer and they fought for a while, but the codicil to the will was in his dad's own handwriting all right, and Pete gave some pretty strong testimony. The kid couldn't even get money to pay a lawyer unless Pete let him have it, after the first court sustained the trust. So the kid gave in and accepted Pete.

In summer vacation Pete stopped the kid's allowance and brought him up to Kernville.

Kernville's up in the mountains on the rim of the Mojave Desert. It's where the big mountains and the edge of the big desert meet, and it has something of both the desert and the mountains in its climate.

Looked at in one way, it's civilization, but it's pretty close to the jumping-off place. The desert sends streamers licking at the foot of the mountains like dry tongues. The cañons are filled with sand, prickly pear, Joshua trees, the weird desert cacti. The mountains are high, dry walls of crumbling rock with snow glistening on the ridges. Then, on the other side of the mountains, are roaring streams, pine timber, shaded slopes.

The Mojave Desert stretches to the east, runs into Death Valley, then sweeps along through the Pahrump Valley down through Nevada and Arizona, way on into New Mexico. It's all the domain of the desert, although the desert changes in every locality.

Men grow hard in Kernville. Big Bill Bruze lived in Kernville and he was hard. Nell Thurmond waited tables for

Martha Stout, and Big Bill was sweet on Martha's help. And you couldn't blame him. Nell was pretty.

I was there when young Bocker arrived.

He gave his name as E. Reed Bocker. Pete asked him why he did that and the kid said Edward was common. He was like that.

Pete glared at him. "Your name's Ed Bocker up here," he said, "common or not." And E. Reed Bocker became Ed Bocker.

Pete put him to work in the mine.

Big Bill Bruze was foreman at the mine.

Ed Bocker was one of those handsome men. He had a profile like a movie picture actor, and his eyes were big and soulful. He was well muscled, not strong, just beautifully molded. His waist was slim, his shoulders broad and he drawled his a's when he talked.

I guess it was the first time that Pete had seen the kid at close range. He sure was enough to make a man go take a drink of rotgut.

He was so soft his skin would blister if he made three passes with a shovel. His hair had to be combed just so, and he had to have his suits pressed every couple of days. He brought along a bag of golf sticks "for exercise."

That was when Pete stopped his allowance and put him to work.

Within three days Ed Bocker was the most hated man in Kernville. He was everything he shouldn't be: a patronizing, educated, snobbish, weak-willed nincompoop, and three years at college hadn't helped him any.

Martha Stout was the only one who saw anything good in the kid.

Martha had trained animals in a circus before she got so fat she couldn't wear tights.

"It ain't the kid," she said. "It's his training."

And she sold Nell Thurmond on the idea, because Nell started returning the kid's smiles.

That started the fight.

The kid thought he was working in the mine. He actually wasn't earning his salt. Pete was paying the superintendent for the privilege of having the kid draw wages. And the kid was snobbing it around, telling everybody how everything should be done.

Then he and Nell fell for each other. She liked his soulful eyes, and she and Bill Bruze had a spat over something anyhow.

The two went to the picture show, Ed and the girl. Big Bill was waiting outside.

Ed had confided to me that he'd taken boxing lessons in school, and had stood well at the head of his class. He seemed to think he could handle Dempsey with one hand.

But Big Bill called him.

The kid turned up his upper lip.

"I don't brawl," he said, and stuck out his arm for Nell to take.

Nell looked at him.

"Aren't you going to stick up for your rights?" she asked.

Big Bill Bruze stepped forward and slapped the kid across the mouth. He flushed, but kept his eyes straight ahead.

"I don't brawl," he repeated.

Nell's eyes blazed.

"Well, you're going to brawl if you go with me, big boy!" she said, and pushed him into Big Bill. At the same time Big Bill stuck out his left. It smeared the kid up a bit.

The kid adopted the correct boxing attitude.

"Very well," he said.

Big Bill swung a right. The kid made the correct college block. But Bill's fist ripped the blocking arm to one side and crashed the kid on the jaw.

Ed Bocker's features bore that look of dazed incredulity that a mathematician would have if he saw the multiplication table go haywire.

He made a ladylike left lead.

It was technically correct. It landed squarely on the point of Bill's jaw. But it might have been a mosquito buzzing for all the good it did. Bill walked right into it, planted himself and swung a right to the stomach.

The kid was out the minute that right crashed.

But Bill Bruze was a bully and a killer. He was six feet of whipcorded strength, and he was jealous. What was more, he hadn't got the kid's looks, and he was sore at the kid because of that profile.

Bill measured the distance.

His right smashed the beautiful nose to powder. His left took out a couple of front teeth. His right put a permanent scar over the left eye. Then the kid hit the cement like a sack of meal. The bystanders prevented Bill kicking in his face, after he'd swung his foot for the second time.

Ed Bocker was four weeks healing, and then he looked like something the cat had dragged in.

He went to Bakersfield and a doctor told him a plastic surgeon could fix him up. Pete wouldn't let him have the money.

"You're gettin' over one handicap now," he said. "That damned beauty of yours. If you could only forget your education and the way you dawdle along on your a's when you talk, you might make a man."

The kid cried, he was so mad. Pete said things about a bawl baby and walked away.

Women are funny. Both Martha Stout and Nell Thurmond stuck up for the kid. Nell gave Big Bill Bruze the gate. She kept all her smiles for Ed Bocker. But the beating seemed to have turned Bocker plumb yellow. Bruze threatened to beat him up again if he even looked at Nell, and Bocker kept away.

The way I figured it, any man who would let fear of a beating keep him away from a girl he liked wasn't worth shooting.

Pete was worried about it. The summer was about over, and it looked like his whole plan was a fizzle. The kid was just a false alarm.

Pete asked me what I thought, and I told him.

"He ain't worth bothering with," I said. "Give him all his money and hope he drinks himself to death. Better yet, buy him the booze yourself. Or else pick a dark night and bump him with a club. Far as society's concerned he's a total loss."

Pete clawed at his white stubble.

"That's about the way I figure," he admitted, "but Martha Stout knows a lot about animals an' about men. She says he's got pay dirt. That it's his trainin' that's to blame. He's just one of those kids that was born with a gold spoon in his mouth. He tells me his dad wouldn't let him associate much with the kids at college, because they were common. It's his trainin'."

I shrugged my shoulders.

"You an' me ain't got no education to live down," Pete went on. "We don't know nothin' about the handicap this kid's got."

I walked away. Pete's adopted kids were nothing to me.

### III. YELLOW

PETE WENT OUT IN THE DESERT on a prospecting trip. He left the kid there without any money. The kid had hardened his muscles a bit by working in the mine. But he was yellow all the way through. His spirit was just as soft as it had been the day he landed.

He avoided Nell Thurmond because Bruze told him to. Nell wouldn't notice Bill Bruze. And the kid's face had healed up into a crooked mask that was a distortion of his former beauty.

I was worried about the whole thing. Seemed like Pete should have left this kid to live the only sort of a life he knew.

Then Pete came staggering into town with some gold that was enough to make a stampede. It was coarse gold, like wheat grains, and Pete was loaded with it. His coat had gold in all the pockets.

But Pete was in a bad way. He sent for old Doc Smith.

Doc Smith is sort of a father confessor to the town. He's young in years, but old in knowledge. He came to the country that borders the desert because he thought he could do some good there. He writes philosophy, acts as judge, and patches up the sick.

Doc Smith treated Pete, and then he sent for me.

"Pete's cashing in," he said. "He's located a bonanza, but his heart gave out on him. He wants you to take his kid and go back there."

"His kid?"

"The adopted kid, Ed Bocker."

"That kid couldn't live in the desert."

Doc Smith shrugged his shoulders. He gave me a pencil scrawl. "Here's a map Pete made before he became unconscious. He gave it to Martha Stout, who's acting as nurse. She gave it to me. Pete was unconscious when I got there. He won't ever regain consciousness. You've got to start right now, before some one tries to trail you."

I looked at the map and whistled.

It was a bum map, but I could tell where the main range was. It was down in the worst section of desert I'd ever been in. Pete had scrawled on the bottom. "It's up one of these cañons marked with a circle. My heart went bad on me, and I walked for days without remembering where I was."

That was all. It was a heck of a map.

"I want to see Pete," I told Doc Smith.

"Walk on tiptoes," he said.

I followed him into the room. Martha Stout was there, fat and efficient. Pete was stretched in bed, his face like wax, his eyes rolled up, his lips blue. He was motionless. I touched his flesh. It was like ice.

"He'll die inside of two days at the latest. If he wakes up and finds you haven't started the shock will kill him right then," said Doc Smith.

"I'm startin'," I told him.

I groped around until I found Pete's limp, cold hand, shook it, and promised him. I thought the eyebrows might have moved a little. Then I groped for the door. My eyes were all swimmy. Pete had been a pal of mine for years.

I got the kid rounded up.

That beating had done things to his soul, more than it had to his face. He was like a frightened quail, and he'd cringe every time he saw a man look at him real hard. That tickled the boys. There were lots to look at him real hard.

The things we needed I threw into a car. We'd outfit at Needles. We made Needles by daylight the next morning. The kid was helpless when it came to doing anything. He couldn't even drive the car.

We got our burros together and started out into the desert.

That's real desert, down south of Needles. There are stretches of it that don't see a human being once in five years. And there are stretches where the sand hills get up and walk around.

Down toward Yuma they couldn't build an automobile road across those hills for years, until some slick engineer figured out a way to hold the road. For years they had a long road of planks fastened together so the road could be lifted and shifted. When the sand hills would march over the road they'd pull the road up and around. It would have broken a snake's back to follow it. And it broke the motorists' hearts.

They've solved the road problem, but the sand hills still walk around.

That's the section of the desert where the whispers hang out. Every night the desert seeps with whispers. Of course they aren't really whispers, just the sand slithering against the sand on the wings of the wind. But it makes lots of whispering noises, and, just when you're dropping off to sleep, it sounds like whole words and sentences.

That's the true desert. People who have lived in it for a long time get the same way the desert is, hard and gray, and with a whispering note in their speech.

Ed Bocker and I headed into that desert with three pack burros and two saddle burros.

Misfortune dogged us from the start.

One of the saddle burros was gone the second night. The third night the other saddle burro followed suit. I'd hobbled him, but he gnawed through the hobbles.

It was funny. I'd never had anything quite like that before. I wouldn't have believed a burro could have gnawed those hobbles, but I found 'em in the desert in his tracks.

Seemed like the first burro had followed him up and enticed him away. I found the tracks.

After that Ed and I had to walk.

His feet blistered and his face peeled. He sobbed and wanted to go back. I threatened him with a beating if he even looked back over his shoulder, and he stumbled on.

It was Pete's dying request, and I was going to see it through, but it sure was a trial. That kid was a thorn in the flesh, and I don't mean maybe.

We had to limit our water. Virtually none for washing, just enough for drinking to keep us going. It was awfully hard at first, particularly on Ed. After a while we toughened to it. I naturally got used to it first.

The work in the mine had toughened him up some, but his trouble was lack of grit. The desert toughened him more, walking every day through soft and shifting sand, scrambling over hard ridges of rock outcropping, working along valleys of rough float.

I kept wondering how those saddle burros had got loose. Then one night I heard a rifle shot. I rolled out of my blankets and got away from the light of the camp fire, jerked my Winchester from its scabbard and waited.

There was nothing more.

In the morning one of our pack burros was dead, shot through the heart. I worked for an hour before I picked up the tracks of the man who had fired that shot. He had been two hundred yards from the burro, with only moonlight to see with. It had been real shooting.

I tried to follow the tracks, but the man was too wise to leave a trail. He hit a rocky ledge and followed it.

I went back to the kid. I was worried now.

The desert is nothing to fool with. We were way out of the beaten track, in a wilderness of sand that was almost unexplored. Maps weren't much good because the sand would get up and walk around overnight. Big mountain ranges were the only things that stayed fixed in that country.

The kid was whimpering. He was frightened. It was too strong for him.

I figured we could carry the lighter packs on the two remaining burros. But how about getting back? And who was following us?

It looked as though some one had been wise to that map and was using us to lead him to the place where the gold was.

Finally we reached the shoulder of the ridge of mountains that Pete had marked with a circle. And I ran on man tracks in the soft sand, tracks that were fresh.

He was a man and he was a big man, and he had two

burros with him. I figured he'd be the one who had shot our other burro, and I got the rifle ready as I swung in along his trail.

There was enough of a moon to follow it after the sun set. By midnight I came on his camp. I didn't let the kid know. The camp was just over the ridge. With the first gray of dawn I kicked the kid out.

"Buckle on your six-gun," I told him, "and come along."

"Game?" he asked.

"Game," I said.

He followed me over the ridge. We caught our man just as he was making his breakfast fire.

I thought there was something familiar in his motions the way he reached for his gun when he heard us coming.

"Little late, ain't you?" I asked him, looking down the sights of the Winchester.

He looked up so I could see his face, all twisted with hatred.

It was Big Bill Bruze.

"Gone into the hold-up business?" he asked.

I kept the rifle ready.

"You're not dealing with any college kids now," I told him. "You've called for chips in a man's game and you want to be prepared to play your hand."

He squirmed a bit, looked at the kid.

"Got a chaperon to fight his battles now, eh?"

"Maybe. What are you doing here?"

"Prospectin'. It's government land."

I jerked my head toward my camp.

"They weren't government burros you shot and ran off," I told him.

I could see his face twist with surprise and thought at the time he was doing some good acting. And that made me mad, madder than if he'd denied it with a wink or a grin.

"Never mind opening your trap," I said. "You might bite

off a soft-nosed bullet. Just open your ears and do some listening. You've followed us down here, thinking we'd lead the way to a mine you could steal. Well, we're not playing *Santa Claus* with any mines, but I've got lots of ammunition. If we have any more trouble there's likely to be some careless shooting and you might get hurt. I've forgotten more about this desert than you ever knew."

And I stopped to let the words soak in.

He was a great big bulk of a man, hairy-chested, big-jawed, broad-shouldered. His shirt was open at the neck and the big muscles of his neck and chest stood out in cords of strength.

"Put down your gun and come ahead," he invited.

I laughed at him.

"My gun's my advantage," I told him. "It's my ace in the hole, and I ain't aiming to lay it down. There's nothing about your face that looks good to me, and the only way I can even bear to look at it is over the sights of a gun."

"Huh!" he retorted. "Speakin' of faces, what's that you've got with you? His face looks like it had been through a sausage grinder. What happened to it?"

"A coward kicked it," I said.

He flushed at that.

"If there's any more trouble I'm going to take your guns away," I promised him, and then I motioned to the kid and we went back over the ridge to our camp.

I kept an eye out for ambushes.

## IV. A VISITOR

THAT AFTERNOON there was a droning noise from the sky. I looked up and made out a plane swinging in wide circles. It's a funny sensation, being out in the desert and seeing a plane snarling through the blue sky like some great bird. That plane had left Needles maybe less than three hours. We'd been toilsome days in coming.

The plane spotted us. The circles got more and more narrow. I looked up at it. Something dark was coming out of the middle of the thing. That something dark hung poised for a minute, and then separated from the plane. I turned sick.

A man was being thrown overboard. Even as I looked, he broke loose and came down, a hurtling black speck, arms and legs spread out, spinning, turning, twisting.

I looked, my mouth warm with a rush of saliva, my stomach weak with horror. Then there was a puff of white. Almost at once a great mushroom of glittering white came out against the blue-black of the sky. It was a parachute.

The plane sailed off.

The black speck dangled and swung against the big mushroom of white. Slowly it drifted to the earth. I could see it was coming down almost on top of us.

It slid down back of a ridge some two hundred yards away. We walked over there, the kid's face white and drawn, my own rifle ready.

I could see it was a girl, untangling herself from the harness of the parachute. She came toward us.

"Nell Thurmond!" I yelled.

She smiled. Her face was a bit pale, and her knees were a little wobbly. It takes nerve for a girl to make her first parachute jump.

"I came to warn you," she said.

Ed Bocker's face was getting red and white by turns.

The girl didn't seem to even notice him.

"Martha Stout went crooked," she said. "She made a copy of the map, and she sold it to Bill Bruze. Bill's here, and he's got three other men who are camped up separate cañons so you can't surprise them all at once. They're planning to let you find the mine and then see that you don't leave the desert. Martha had to copy the map from memory, and they figure that yours is the best map. They think you'll be more likely to find it than they will."

I knew my eyes were bulging. I couldn't figure Martha Stout as a crook, no matter how I went about it.

"Pete?" I asked.

"He died the day after you left. He never regained consciousness."

I looked her over.

"You came to warn us. How about getting back out?"

She shrugged her shoulders.

"I'll take my fortune with yours . . . Hello, Ed."

He twisted his broken nose as he grinned.

"Hello, Nell."

I looked at the burros. We never would get out now. We had one more mouth to feed, one more person to divide drinking water with.

"Bet you were frightened when you climbed overboard from that plane," I said.

She didn't even hear me. She was looking at Ed Bocker.

I sighed and got the burros together. We were getting to where we could make a permanent camp, though we had little to make it with. Pete's map had showed the location of a spring of water up at the head of one of the cañons, and I figured that cañon was the second over. If there were hostile people in the country the first thing was to get to drinking water.

We marched over the ridges. About dusk we came to the cañon that had the spring.

Two people were camped there. What was more they had monuments on the ground and a location notice.

"Howdy, folks," I said when we came up.

They weren't cordial about it.

"You can't camp here," one of them said. "This here is a located mineral claim."

I tried to keep smiling. "I can get water here, anyway."

He shook his head. "Nope. We can't afford to take no chances on having the claim jumped."

I started getting the canteens off the burros.

"Well," I told him, "we're not jumping any claims, but we're almost out of water, and we're filling up. What's more, we're goin' to come back from time to time and fill up some more."

He came toward me.

"I gotta stop you."

"You and who else?"

"My partner."

He was just a little uncertain, but his right hand was getting pretty close to the holstered gun that swung at his belt.

Living in the desert doesn't give you much weight, but it gives you a lot of strength per pound and it makes a man plenty active. I got within reaching distance before the right hand could connect with the butt of the gun. My left cracked him on the jaw, staggered him back. Out of the corner of my eye I saw the other man reaching for a gun. Then I saw Ed Bocker get into action. After that my hands were full.

I finally got my man where I could take his gun away from him, and looked around to see what luck Ed was having. He wasn't having much. His footwork was all the college professor on boxing could have asked for, but it wasn't getting by in the soft sand with a clump of sagebrush to tangle his feet every once in a while. His broken nose had stopped another punch and it hadn't done the general effect any good.

But he was swapping punches, and his blows had a little steam to them.

I rolled myself a cigarette.

"Now then, son," I told him, "are you going to knock that gent out, or are you going to be a sissy all your life?"

He turned to look at me when I spoke, and the reception committee that had taken him on, slammed home a terrific wallop to the chin.

Ed was punch-groggy, but there was something that gleamed out from the back of his eyes I hadn't seen before.

He was forgetting some of his complexes and getting down to raw human nature.

He went in, and, for a second or two, he showed speed and strength. His boxing helped him time his punches, and something that had been dormant in him made him put snap in them.

The left measured the distance, the right crossed over, and a sprawling figure staggered backward, poised for a second and then went down with a thud that jarred the earth.

Ed Bocker stood over him, staring with a species of dazed incredulity.

"I knocked him out! I knocked him out! I knocked him out!" he kept repeating.

I didn't pay any attention to him in particular. I left that for the girl. I was busy going through the camp and confiscating firearms. I got two six-guns and a rifle, and I took all the shells I could find.

The one that Bocker had knocked out stayed out. My man was sitting up, nursing a black eye and a bloody nose and gazing at me moodily. My lips were split, and one of my front teeth was wobbly. The sand was all dug up with man tracks. We were a great-looking outfit.

"Any guy that tries to corner water in the desert is a so-and-so," I said. "And, what's more, you guys ain't to be trusted with firearms. You might get hurt."

He didn't say anything.

I filled the canteens, loaded on the captured arsenal, and led the way over the ridge, down a cañon, over another ridge and camped at the head of a little draw where the ridges would break the wind.

We were getting into the region of drifting sands.

No one said very much that night. Twice I caught Ed Bocker looking at his skinned knuckles with a sort of wide-eyed incredulity.

"I knocked him out," he said once.

"Sure you did," I told him. "That's what your fists are for. You box for points in college, but when you get out in the world you fight for knock-outs. It ain't a sociable pastime."

Nell Thurmond didn't say anything. Her eyes were starry.

I made a little camp fire because I wanted some tea, and we had to cook some rice.

But I kept every one but myself away from the circle of firelight, and when they made up their beds I had them bed down far from the fire.

Some one was watching us, it seemed to me. It was an uncomfortable feeling.

I'd just got the rice ready and the tea water boiling when the rifle started to talk.

"*Bang!*" it went.

I heard the crack of the bullet rushing through the air toward me, and I heard the "*thunk*" as it struck.

I grabbed a rifle and rolled over to one side. I caught the flash of a second shot and answered with a snap shot that must have given the hombre something to think about.

There were no more shots.

I remembered that second bullet had a tin-panny sound when it struck, but I couldn't be bothered just then. I was streaking up the ridge, keeping just below the skyline, watching the skyline of the second ridge over. If I saw anything move against the stars I was going to throw lead. This had quit being a joke.

But I didn't see a thing. Somehow or other, I got the idea I was up against some one who knew as much about the desert as I did, maybe a lot more—only I wouldn't have missed those first two shots.

I went back to camp. They'd had sense enough to kick the fire out, but I could see the glow of an isolated ember here and there.

"Get those embers covered," I said, and began kicking sand over all I could find.

"He hit the canteens," said Nell.

"What?"

"Yes. A hole through each one."

I whistled. "Any water left?"

"Yes," said Ed Bocker. "I knew I couldn't do any good with a gun, so I beat it out to some of the mesquite and whittled plugs. They help, but the water seeps out around them, no matter how tightly I push them in."

I didn't say anything. The water would leak out. With bullet holes in those two big canteens we could never make the long march back out of the desert. It would mean one of us would have to try it, and leave the other two. And I didn't like the idea of leaving the girl with only Ed Bocker to protect her. That stretch of desert was getting mean.

I salvaged as much of the rice as I could, and we had weak tea, not too hot, and rice. We ate in the dark.

I rolled the two into their blankets, pretended to crawl into mine. But I crawled out on the other side and started playing Indian.

The shots had come from a rifle. The two citizens at the spring might have had a rifle cached, but there was Big Bill Bruze to be reckoned with. Maybe he'd done the rifle shooting.

I crawled up along the sandy ridge, sniffing for wood smoke. Finally I located a camp. It was Big Bill, all right. I started to wake him up and have a show-down, then I figured on a better lesson. I still-hunted into his camp, picked out the biggest of his canteens, carried it out into the desert and buried it where I'd find it again. Then I went back to my blankets.

That night the desert began to whisper. The sand hissed over the sand on the wings of the desert night wind, and the whole darkness literally crawled with whispers. I could tell the others were awake, listening.

The desert is a fearsome thing out at night in the land of

the marching sand hills when the wind brings the sand to life and the desert begins to whisper. Listening to those whispers will do things to a man's soul. They bite deep. I didn't sleep much.

## v. Show-down

Morning, and I organized things. We needed access to that spring and I intended to have it.

"I'm going over to the spring," I told Ed Bocker. "You stay here with the girl. Use your head. If anything happens to me you've got to get her out of here."

He didn't argue, just nodded. The desert was doing things to him. I could see that. But I had other things to think about. I went over to the spring. The two looked at me, surly-like.

I kept my eye on them and went through the camp, looking for a rifle. I couldn't find anything that even looked like a rifle. I told the two a few choice sentiments and went back to camp.

There I made the two a little talk.

"We came into this country to find a mine. We're going to find it," I said. "What's more, we're going to have trouble. A little trouble all the time. A devil of a lot of trouble if we locate the pay dirt. Let's go."

We started out. I had the map and did more exploring than the rest. I left Bocker to do most of the guard duty. The girl did the cooking. I covered cañon after cañon: and always I had the feeling of being watched.

Day after day, the program was about the same. It was hard work, looking for gold and watching back trail. It did things to my disposition. It also did things to Bocker. He got thinner, more whipcorded. His eyes were steadier, and his lips took on a firmer line.

Then one day I stumbled onto it. It was up a winding cañon, and I could see there had been some old camp made at the mouth. A little ways on up I found a can with a piece of paper in it. The paper had some of Pete's writing in lead pencil:

IT'S UP AT THE END OF THIS CAÑON

That was a funny message, but I figured it was because Pete's heart had started to go bad on him when he was coming out and he'd left this paper to guide him when he came back.

I stood staring at the piece of paper when a rifle cracked. The report sounded thin and stringy on the hot desert air, but the bullet came cracking through the heat and whipped up the sand within two feet of me. I ducked for cover and got my own rifle into play.

I spotted him up on a ridge, just over the crest, four hundred yards away. He'd been following me, looking at me through binoculars. When he saw me pick up the can with the paper in it, he figured it was a location notice and had gone into action.

I decided to try a trick I'd seen once south of Tucson.

I started walking straight toward the ridge, firing often enough to keep him under cover, making him take little snap shots that went wild at the distance. Fifty yards, and I came to a protecting ridge that ran up and headed the ridge he was on.

I didn't come over the top of that ridge the way he figured I would, but I started running for all that was in me, working up toward where the ridge joined the main formation.

I got up there, eased over the top, waited until I got my breath enough to hold the gun steady, and then began to slip down, on the same side of the ridge where my friend was.

Two hundred yards, and I got where I could see him. He was stretched out just back of the crest, his rifle at his shoulder, waiting for me to show myself against the skyline as I came across.

I could see he was getting a little nervous, from the way he was stretching his head.

But it never dawned on him to look up his own ridge.

I got my rifle at ready and cat-footed down to him.

When I was within twenty yards he heard me. He flung around and started to throw up the rifle. There wasn't any time to waste in chatter. I slammed a bullet in the general direction of his gun arm and worked the repeating lever as I jerked in a fresh shell. That one was due to rip his heart to ribbons if he didn't take the hint of the first one.

But the first shell hit the rifle on the lock and slammed it out of his numbed and nerveless fingers.

"Had another gun hid, I see," I told him.

He was the same hombre I'd had the fight with at the spring. He'd evidently had one rifle buried in the sand, and they'd kept it cached.

I made him take his shoes off and pass them over. Then I took my rifle and started back down the ridge. He wouldn't do much mischief in the hot sands of the desert in his stocking feet.

"You take my advice and head for camp," I told him as I left. "Your feet won't stand over a mile of this, and you'll need all the mud you can puddle out of that spring."

Sure it was cruel, but he had it coming.

Then I heard firing from the direction of my camp. The shots sounded thin and weak, but plenty rapid. I started down the ridge just as fast as I dared to take it in the sun.

I topped a ridge and looked down on camp from four hundred yards. A black speck was perched on a ridge, making talk with a rifle. Another black speck was wading out to meet him, shooting as he walked, shooting calmly, unhurriedly.

Another black speck was behind the blanket rolls, peppering away with a six-gun. It wouldn't do any good at the distance except keep the guy with the gun occupied.

I knew Nell Thurmond was fully aware of that fact. She

was just joining in. I elevated my sights for four hundred yards.

And then I held my fire. The black speck on the ridge had tossed away his rifle and was running down the slope. It was Big Bill Bruze. I could tell from his awkward, sidelong gallop.

Ed Bocker held his gun for a moment, at his shoulder. Then he tossed it away and started running up the slope, toward Big Bill.

I uncocked my rifle and shortened the distance as fast as my legs would cover the ground, and I could see some one else running toward the two enemies, a long-legged cuss who had sprung up from nowhere out of the desert. He must have been buried in the sand. I hadn't seen him.

Big Bill Bruze and Ed Bocker met on a little level space. The sand was soft. There was no chance for college footwork. It was primitive man against primitive man.

I got there just as it finished. I'd seen some of the action while I was running, not as much as I'd liked, and I had to keep an eye on the long-legged stranger with the rifle who was quartering down the other slope.

Big Bill went down for the count as I came up.

I got a look at his face. His nose was ground to powder. His eyes looked like pieces of hamburger steak. His lips were ribbons.

Ed Bocker had some marks, but, on the whole, he seemed fairly beautiful compared with the other guy. I flung my rifle in the general direction of the long-legged customer.

"Now then, you get your gun stretched out in the sand and your hands up, and—"

My jaw sagged. The long-legged cuss was old Pete himself. He started to laugh. And the girl was laughing. Ed Bocker was as speechless as I was.

Pete did the talking. "I never had but one school, the old desert. I knew there was pay dirt in this kid, but he'd had things too soft. Civilization wasn't bringing it out. So I framed it with old Doc Smith to give me some sort of a powder and paint my lips blue. Then I planted some gold and pretended to have a mine out in the worst section of the desert goin'.

"I didn't intend nothin' else, not me. But Martha Stout embellished the idea. She said Ed would never get no self-respect until he'd mastered Big Bill over the girl. So she let Big Bill Bruze bribe her for a rough copy of the map and started him out here. Then they shipped the girl in by plane.

"Big Bill got a couple of his buddies to locate on the spring, figuring they'd keep you from water and make you surrender the map for water. He just didn't figure you right.

"I wanted Old Mother Desert to take this lad in hand and bring out the pay dirt in him. I was the one that followed you and run off the burros and punctured the canteens. I been watchin' all the time. And I been waitin' for Big Bill to find out the girl was here and come after her.

"The old desert took things in hand and ripped off some of the softness from my boy and done brought out the pay dirt."

I let the information soak in.

"One of those guys might have killed me," I said.

Pete snorted.

"If'n you can't take care of yourself in the desert you'd oughta cash in your chips."

"And there wasn't any gold at all?"

He shook his head. "Only what I bought from a placer mine and stuffed into my pockets."

I could feel myself getting madder and madder.

"And all this time I thought I was carrying out your dying wishes I was just playing schoolma'am for a kid that couldn't absorb nothing from college?"

Pete's eyes got sort of gray, like the desert sand. His voice had that whisper to it that comes to those who have lived long where they can hear the sand whispering to the sand, a dry huskiness.

"The desert did the teachin'," he said. "She's the cruelest and the kindest mother a man ever had. Now I can give this kid his money an' let him get married and know that the money won't ruin him. We've brought out the pay dirt, you an' me. You're mad now, but you'll be glad for what you've done 'fore you get back out."

I turned my back and walked away.

That night though, when the sand commenced to whisper, I could see things in a little different light.

I lay and listened to the sand. Then the wind died down, and I could hear Ed Bocker and Nell Thurmond talking in low tones over the embers of the fire.

And I could hear something soft and hissing that I thought was sand whispering; but the wind had lulled. I propped myself up on an elbow to hear what it was.

It wasn't sand. It was old Pete, the damned old galoot, chuckling to himself, and his throat had got so dry from years in the desert that it sounded like a sand whisper.

Then I knew how much I liked the old cuss, and I got over being mad and commenced to chuckle, too.

Nature had played a funny stunt when she'd delivered Harrisson Bocker and Judge McNaught into the desert. If the old judge had been trustee for Ed Bocker he'd have trained him up to be a pampered son of luxury, never worth a damn.

But the desert had taken a hand. Seemed sort of like she'd known what she was doing when she slipped Pete in as guardian and trustee of young E. Reed Bocker.

And then the wind, which had lulled, sprang up again, and the sand began to stir and rustle, and it sounded just like Pete's chuckle. I got to wondering if the desert was chuckling, too, and was still wondering when I dropped off to sleep.

# THE LAND OF POISON SPRINGS

## 1. A Strange Expedition

IF THE GIRL HAD COME CLEAN WITH ME, right from the start, it wouldn't have happened.

But my first contact was with the man.

He was all dressed up for the desert, the way a Los Angeles tailor thinks a man should be dressed to go hunting. His boots laced all the way up, and his breeches were tailored to a tight fit, pegged out and pressed. The shirt was one of those sport affairs, and the coat was pinched in at the back.

But out on the desert we don't notice clothes so much, even when they are so gosh-awful as these. We look at the man.

"You're Bob Zane," he said, walking up to me in the back of the grocery store where I was outfitting. "I'm George Fargo, and I want to see you on a matter of business."

He didn't offer to shake hands, and his words were close clipped, like the words of a business executive who's accustomed to make men grovel before him or else lose their jobs. I didn't like the tone, and I didn't like the eyes.

Out in the desert we don't grovel. We're too close to blue skies, the quiet of the stars, and the edict of nature that says the fit ones are going to survive, while the weak ones get pushed under, grovel or not.

"Yes," I said, "I'm Bob Zane, and I don't take out fishing parties."

He frowned.

"I didn't say anything about a fishing party. This is different. If you're interested in twenty dollars a day I can talk."

Twenty dollars a day is big money anywhere. Out in the desert it's bigger.

He saw my eyes light, and he turned away, so I'd have to follow him to the other end of the store.

I hesitated, weighed the twenty a day against what I'd have to put up with, and turned back to my groceries.

He paused, looked back over his shoulder, saw I wasn't following, and had to swallow his pride and come back to me. I knew then that we were going to hate each other.

"Go on and talk," I said.

He straightened, very rigid, very much under control, and very mad down underneath it all.

"My business can't be discussed right here," he observed.

"I'll drop around and see you then, after a while," I told him, getting the groceries put in the *kyaks* so that they balanced about even. "*My* business is right here, and if I get these things outa balance it's going to mean a sore back for my burro."

He lowered his voice.

"I am interested in a mine," he said.

"Yeah?" I observed, getting some flour wedged nicely into a corner.

"And I must start right away. There are three men and a woman in the party."

I straightened, dusted the flour off my hands.

"Okay," I said. "A woman's different. Where do you want to talk?"

He walked back to the other side of the store. I followed him. He was so mad his eyes were pale, but he managed to keep control of his voice.

"They tell me you know the desert as no other living man," he said, grudgingly.

I said nothing.

"I must have the best guide that money can buy. Can you get a pack train outfit together, get provisions and blankets and leave by afternoon?"

"It'll take a lot of money to get an outfit like that on such short notice. We'll have to pick up local stuff, and they'll stick us."

"I have the money," he snapped.

"I can get the stuff," I said, and my tone was just as crisp as his.

"We want to go to Burro Springs," he said.

"That all?" I asked.

"That's all," he said.

"No reason for all the secrecy then. Hundreds of people go to Burro Springs. You come in a car?"

"Yes."

"Better store it and get something to eat then. Meet me here at three o'clock, and we start. Give me some money now."

"How much?"

"Three hundred dollars."

I thought the sum would scare him out and then I'd be free to go back to my own business. But he took out a roll, peeled off the three outside bills as though he'd been tossing scraps of meat to a stray dog, and walked away.

I hated his insides, but I couldn't turn down twenty dollars a day. I started getting the outfit together.

This much I'll say for him, he was on time.

They showed up at three o'clock, on the dot. I had the whole thing packed and ready to go. Some of the saddles were pretty ancient, but they'd make the trip, and they were the best the desert town afforded.

I saw the girl then, and the other two men.

No one introduced us. They just asked which burros they were to ride, and climbed aboard. I lengthened the stirrups on one of the men's saddles and shortened those on the girl's saddle, and then we started.

She was slender, gray eyed, and silent. There was a poise about her that I liked. The other two men were puzzles to me. They walked with a swagger, and they wore city clothes and looked as though they'd like to fight the world.

Oh, well, the desert would take that out of them.

I led the way. The afternoon start gave us the sun at our backs, made it possible to get 'em broken in to the saddle without killing 'em, and caught the desert when the glare wasn't so bad.

We angled down the steep slope of colored mountains, watched the shadows fill the cañons with purple, and came to the camping place I'd picked.

"Where's the water?" asked Fargo.

"In the canteens."

"Isn't there any spring?"

"Not here. To-morrow night."

"I want to wash."

"Go ahead. There are four canteens, one apiece. Use that water any way you want. It'll last you until to-morrow night."

He turned on his heel and walked away.

I got a campfire going and put on some tea water. Then I looked around to see who was doing what. Evidently I was the only customer. No one seemed to think they should do anything, except the girl. She came over to help with the cooking.

"I'm Vera Camm," she said. "I know your name. You're Bob Zane. I want to help."

I saw her right hand thrust out, and took it in my grizzled desert paw. I liked her smile and her voice. We cooked them up a good meal. The girl straightened up the dishes. The men did nothing.

The campfire died down, and the desert mountains got a tang in the air that penetrated.

Fargo shivered, looked at me.

"The fire's dying down," he said.

I nodded.

"We need some more wood," he said, after a while.

I waved my hand toward the side of the mountain.

"There's lots of sage. It makes a good fire."

He sat still, and I sat still. The cold crept in. It's a dry, insidious cold, but the air's so light that it gets into your blood. The fire was just coals, and the stars came out and blazed steadily as the light of the fire shrank.

I kicked off my shoes and rolled up in my blankets.

After a few minutes Fargo turned to one of the two men. "Harry," he said, "go get some wood."

The man got up and looked steadily at Fargo for a minute. "Yeah," he said, "we'll all go."

The other man got up. They both looked at Fargo. He squirmed. I could hear his breath suck in as he started to say something. Then he got to his feet. He was reluctant about it, but he went.

They came back with wood and threw it on the coals. It made quite a fire. They sat up and talked for quite a while. I went to sleep, woke up once or twice, found 'em still huddled there, the girl had gone off to her blankets. I noticed that she spread 'em so I was between her and the men.

About two o'clock in the morning I woke up.

Everything was quiet. The stars were steady, and the coals had gone down until there was just a reddish glow under the ashes.

The wind was coming down the slope.

Pretty soon the desert would start to whisper. That's the way the desert does, nights. The wind springs up without warning, dies down the same way. The sand slithers along on the wind and rattles against the sage until it seems to whisper. Then, when the wind freshens, the sand slithering along the sandy surface of the desert makes the most elusive whisper of them all, the pure sand whisper.

A lot of old timers claim they can hear words when the desert starts to talk and they're drifting off to sleep. It's just a trick the ears play on a man's brain when he's dozing off, of course, but it's something you'll hear from almost anybody that's spent much of his life in the desert.

I listened as the wind freshened and the sand started its hissing whispers. All around me I could hear the people stirring in their blankets, shifting about. I could have cut sage for them and made a pretty comfortable mattress under each blanket roll, but I didn't do it. I had a hunch they might be out some time, and it'd be better to let 'em get hardened up. The desert's cruel, all right, and it's kindly. It's the cruelty that makes it kind. It licks people into shape.

Mercy and kindness are funny things. Sometimes you can be more kind to people by being cruel to 'em. Lots of times you see people that have been pampered and humored all their lives until it's done funny things to their characters. The desert ain't that kind. It don't pamper anybody. It's like the ocean. One mistake, and that's all.

The desert breeds men.

I drifted off to sleep. When I woke up the east was getting greenish with a streak of red on the opposite range of mountains that shut off the first of the sunrise colors.

I kicked out of my blankets and started after the burros.

I figured they'd either get up and start the fire and the coffee, or they wouldn't. If they did, they'd get a good breakfast. If they didn't, they'd take what they got. *I* could travel a long ways without much grub; I figured the others were accustomed to city stuff.

One of the burros was a drifter. I cussed. That meant the others were following along, hobbles and all. A burro that's a good drifter can do a lot, even with hobbles.

I was some little time getting 'em located. Then they were down a mean cañon. Only a burro could have gone down the way they went; a horse would never have done it, not with hobbles.

The sun was slanting along the high slopes as I started back with the burros. I topped the ridge and heard a crisp revolver shot. Then I heard another and another.

I hadn't strapped on my gat, but left it in my bed roll, which is the proper place for a gent's gun, the way things are nowadays in the desert.

But those revolver shots sounded like business.

I slid off the burro I was forking, and crawled up to the ragged summit of the ridge, picked a place for my head where it wouldn't be too prominent, and looked down.

They were the two men who were with Fargo. At first I didn't get it. They were making funny motions, jumping about and shooting. I thought maybe it was a rattlesnake when I saw the bullets kick up the dust.

Then I saw what they were doing. They were practicing. They had shoulder holsters, and they were putting the guns back in them between shots. Then they'd crouch, whip their hands to the guns, rip 'em out, and fire at a bowlder that was on the ground.

They didn't seem to be hitting the bowlder. But they were coming close to it.

I went back to the burros and strung 'em along the little

trail that they'd made coming down. By the time I got into sight the firing had stopped.

The girl had the fire going and coffee ready. She was wrestling with the cooking, but campfire cooking is different from stove cooking.

I came in and helped her get the hang of it.

"You need a helper," I said, looking at where the three men sprawled on the ground.

No one said anything.

I went to the burros and started to get on the saddles and packs. It took some little time. The girl had breakfast ready when I was about half finished. It consisted of pancakes that were burnt on the edges and raw in the center. The bacon had burnt, and the coffee was too strong.

The men grumbled about the food, looked at me.

I grinned at the girl.

"You're doing fine, Miss Camm," I told her.

Her eyes were red from the smoke, and her hair had straggled down around her forehead. She didn't look happy, but she was game.

"Well," said Fargo, "Zane won't have to pack the burros at noon, so he can cook us a regular desert banquet."

I waited until his eyes met mine.

"We don't stop until to-night," I told him.

He flushed.

"I'm running this show," he said.

"Go ahead and run it any time you want to," I said. "Two of these burros are mine. The rest are yours."

He didn't say anything. One of the men snickered.

We got started, and the sun began to do its stuff.

I rode close to the girl. "Got some cold cream handy?"

"Yes."

"Put it on thick, and leave it on. Put lipstick on your lips. Don't wash your face in water. Use cream."

Then I rode away.

The sport shirts of the men left their necks exposed, places where their collars usually covered. And the desert sun, reflecting from sand, is pitiless.

After a while they covered up their necks with handkerchiefs. But the damage was done by that time. They looked like boiled lobsters. They fidgeted about in the saddles, got off and walked part of the time.

It was a day that wasn't pleasant for them, any of them. They almost had to be pulled from the saddles and their legs straightened when we made camp.

I pushed the girl away from the fire and did the cooking. I gave them some good grub. It was wholesome, but it wasn't any banquet. The men grumbled. They were hungry and tired.

"The thing for you to do," I said, "is to start dividing up the work. You'd better make arrangements right now, one to get the wood, one to do the dishes, one to help the girl with the cooking."

Fargo glared.

"I'm not accustomed to manual labor," he said.

I nodded.

"You're going to change. Either you'll get accustomed to manual labor, or your stomach'll get accustomed to going without grub."

The girl stared at me, startled.

Fargo struggled to his feet, towered over me.

"When I say anything," he snarled, "it goes. See?"

I motioned toward the fire with my hand.

"See if you can tell the fire to burn without wood," I suggested.

He stood there for a while, then shifted his position. I didn't even let on I knew he was there. The fire went down and it got cold. The girl was ready for her blankets. She rolled in. I kicked off my shoes and coat, crawled in my blankets.

"I'm cold," said Fargo. "The blanket rolls you got were too light, Zane."

"You'll get used to 'em," I said, and yawned. "Build the fire up if you get too cold."

And I dropped off to sleep.

When I woke up the fire was crackling. One of the men had gone for wood, perhaps all three of them. They were huddled together, talking in low voices.

The next night we made Burro Springs.

The girl took out a pencil and paper. She wrote a document, read it over, frowned, scratched out a word here and there, and handed it to Fargo.

"This," she said, "gives you your protection."

Fargo folded it, stuck it in his pocket without reading it, grinned at the others, nodded to the girl.

"Thanks," he said.

They got wood for the campfire without any argument. The camp was commencing to function smoothly. I drifted off to sleep. The three men talked over the campfire.

The next morning I had the usual chase after the burros. It was a long chase. I figured on turning the drifter loose and getting along with one less pack burro. He sure was a nuisance. I came on in with the string and I was sore.

The sunlight caught something white at just the right angle, and glittered. I saw that it was a piece of paper. There were others near it. The papers were rustling in the first of a morning breeze. I knew it'd spring up hard for half an hour or so, and then go down.

I got to wondering about the papers. Perhaps some one was ahead of us. I swung the burros so I went over past them. It was still a quarter of a mile from camp.

The paper looked familiar. I saw there was pencil writing on it, and that it was a woman's writing. I picked up a piece of the paper, then got interested and went out after the others. When I had them all, I fitted them together.

It made interesting reading. It was the paper the girl had given Fargo for his "protection."

I, Vera Camm, hereby certify that I grubstaked a man known as Panamint Kelley, a prospector. That Kelley located a valuable mining claim and died before he could record it. He mailed me a map and directions for getting there, giving the letter to a prospector he met when he started to get sick. George Fargo has financed my trip to the mine, and is to receive a one-tenth interest in the mine. He is to pay all expenses, and furnish guards to hold the claim. (Signed)

VERA CAMM.

I read it over two or three times, and the more I read the funnier it all seemed. That paper evidenced the understanding between the four of them. Evidently the two men were bodyguards or mining claim guards, as you'd want to call them. They thought they were on the trail of a rich mine. The girl evidently had the directions.

She'd given Fargo this writing. Under its terms, Fargo was to have a tenth interest. Without it, he only had the girl's word. I'd heard of people whose words were as good as their bonds, but I'd never before heard of a case where words were better.

But Fargo had taken this paper out in the desert, torn it up, deliberately and derisively, and thrown the pieces away. Why?

In one way it wasn't my business. In another way it was. I put the pieces of paper in my pocket, and went into camp.

## II. BETRAYED

"THIS IS WHERE YOU WANTED TO GO," I said, "Burro Springs."

They looked at the girl.

She had her answer ready.

"Go twenty miles up the valley between the two ranges. Then look for a peculiar notched peak in The Last Chance Mountains. The notch is like this."

And she gave us a sketch.

I knew the peak, but I didn't say so.

"Twenty miles?" I said.

"Twenty miles," she said.

"It's a tough country up there, up near the head of Death Valley, and the desert is none too friendly anywhere along in there.

"We go through a pass?" I asked, knowing we'd have to to get to where the peak showed just that profile against the sky.

She looked confused.

"Oh, I'd forgotten about that. Yes, we go through a pass after we've gone three miles. We turn to the left."

I nodded.

"Better look at your sailing directions again and make sure," said Fargo, and he grinned, a big, friendly grin. It was the first time I'd seen him twist his lips in anything like a friendly grin. But, even then, his eyes were hard.

She shook her head, decisively.

"It is not necessary," she said.

Fargo hesitated for a minute. His lips were cracked, and his neck and face looked sun tortured, his temper was worn thin and his eyes were flecked with red veins, but he controlled himself, and kept friendly.

"It's lots of fun, ain't it?" he said.

One of the men laughed.

"It's going to be more fun," he said.

I went over to my blanket roll and got out my gun and the cartridge belt, strapped it on.

The two guards looked at me.

"Zane must be expecting to hunt a rabbit," said Fargo.

I shook my head.

"You sometimes run into a coyote along in here," I told them.

"You kill 'em?" asked Fargo.

"Not always," I answered, "but I like to have my gun where I can reach it—when I'm dealing with coyotes."

I thought that little warning would be all they needed.

We got started. That afternoon, late, we were where the peaks cut the sky.

"Now what?" asked Fargo.

"We turn up this cañon," she said, and her voice was tremulous with excitement.

"You sure?" asked Fargo.

"Yes. The map's as plain as can be from here on."

I led the way up the cañon, and I decided I'd have the old six-gun ready to yank out. I didn't like the attitude of the men.

"How far?" asked Fargo.

I didn't get the immediate significance of what followed. The girl reached for the front of her blouse, and one of the men who had been to my right sort of hitched in his saddle.

"We're all partners now," said the girl, "and there's no further need for secrecy."

I sensed something of surreptitious motion, and whirled.

I was staring into the business end of an automatic, and the grinning teeth of the man who went by the name of Harry Osgood.

"If you'd unbuckle that gun belt, I could hoist the whole works over here onto my saddle," he said.

I looked in his eyes, and knew he meant business.

The girl screamed.

Fargo had simply thrown his arms around her, and held her hands pinioned. There was a scrap of paper in one of them, something that was slick and dirty, the sort of paper a prospector would have used for a penciled map.

The other gunman was standing, well away from his burro, his automatic in his hand. The afternoon rays of the sun were sending long purple shadows along the cañons. There wasn't a soul within sight save the members of our party. It was a wild, unfrequented stretch of desert.

Fargo tore the paper from the girl's grasp.

I know death when I see it in a man's eyes. Killing men is something like the dope habit. Some killers get so it's an obsession with 'em. They like to pull the trigger and see an adversary crumple. It's just like dope to the complexes that they build up.

This man Osgood had the eyes of a killer. He was getting ready to pull the trigger.

I'd expected there might be trouble if we got to the mine and found that it was rich, but I hardly thought they'd try murder over something that was just a dubious pencil cross on a rough sketch map. It just shows what happens when a man gets too trusting in the desert.

Osgood eased the gun over to his saddle.

"Now, you rat, take this, and . . ."

Fargo interrupted.

"Wait. We'll see if we can find it first. Remember, this man knows the desert."

Osgood stood snarling at me, his eyes glittering with the gleam of a killer.

"Not yet, not yet, Harry," called the other gunman.

He went by the name of Rankin, and I thought he was more likely to be a leader than Osgood. He had more power. What I hadn't counted on was Osgood's killing complex.

Osgood hesitated. Rankin came up. They slipped a rope around my shoulders. One of them heaved. I went off the burro, and one foot caught in the stirrup. I got dragged and stepped on before I could kick free. The three men got a great kick out of it. They laughed long and loud.

They had the girl tied by the time I was free of the stirrup and on my feet again. They knotted my elbows so my hands were behind me, and stuck a gun in my back. Fargo was studying the sketch map he'd taken from the girl.

"Okay?" asked Rankin.

"Okay," said Fargo.

"Let's go."

They went up the cañon. Fargo read the trail from the map.

They turned up a branch cañon, climbed to a mesa. I could see where some one had camped in there, making a dry camp. It had been some little time ago.

They still consulted the map, but I could see the little foot-trail that went to a rock outcropping that had been opened up.

They found the rock. The wild whoop that went up from Fargo's lips was all I needed to tell me that our death warrant had been signed. That was why they'd jumped us before they had actually located the mine. It was one of those fabulously rich mines that have jewelry rock right on the surface.

I cursed the impulse that had sent me out to guide these crooks. I had some mighty valuable mining properties in a corporation. I didn't really need the money, only I had a desert man's horror of borrowing money and pledging stock as collateral. I was keeping that stock free and clear, and earning my living until the stock paid dividends, and now it looked as though the life insurance companies were due to pay up on the policy I'd taken out a couple of years ago.

But the men were so excited over the gold they forgot us. The girl was near me.

"What will they do?" she asked, but her tone and the dark terror of her eyes showed that she knew, without having to ask me. The men were gangsters from the city, gunmen who had perfected their skill in the art of killing. There had never been a badman in the desert who was as ruthless as these killers.

I tried a grin.

"Maybe get drunk," I told her.

They were drunk, too, drunk with greed and gloating with avarice. They broke off chunks of rock, jumped around, flung up their hats.

Finally they thought of us and the burros. It was getting dark, almost dark enough to have warranted us in making a break. But they came to their senses in time.

They put me down with my back to a rock, and the girl beside me. Then they started to unpack the burros. Osgood was having a talk with Fargo. Fargo was shaking his head determinedly.

"There's going to be a rush here, and digging all around the place. We've got to make certain we've got a place where there won't be trouble. Wait a while."

I hoped the girl didn't know what they were talking about. They were figuring on killing us. But Fargo was thinking ahead. He wanted to have it so our bodies wouldn't be found. I knew his type. He was one of the kind that likes to gloat. He'd come and gloat over us, tell us he was going to make us dig our own graves, and all that.

The girl was dry-eyed. I thought maybe she'd burst into tears, but she just stuck her chin up and took it.

They piled all the blankets, all the grub, all the saddles into one big pile, and they didn't know anything about hobbling the burros. They just turned 'em loose. I could tell them something about those burros, what with that drifter along. But I wasn't doing any talking just then.

They got a fire going. It got dark.

Fargo came over to us, sneered gloatingly at me.

"Sucker," he said.

I didn't say anything.

"Thought you was going to be the big man and make me respect you, didn't you? You wasn't going to be a servant, not you. You were just the guide. We could divide the work up.

Bah! I'll tell you what you're going to do. You're going 'way up the cañon where there's a nice quiet place and work half the night digging a big hole. I won't tell you what's going in that hole—not right now I won't. I'll save it for a surprise."

And then he kicked me in the ribs.

The girl screamed.

Fargo laughed, walked over toward the campfire. The girl was breathing hard, as though she'd been running. I heard a dry sob come from her lips and the shoulders heaved quaveringly. But she didn't turn on the weeps.

## III. On the Cañon's Wall

I SAW THEY WERE TALKING AGAIN, having another of their low-voiced conferences. The rock I was against had a jagged edge, and I started to saw, making my arms go up and down against it.

It was a forlorn hope. That rope would take a great deal of sawing, but then, it gave me something to do. I was furious with myself for being trapped so easy.

But I got a break. The rope caught on a projection. I pushed my weight down on my arms to pull the rope free, and I felt the knot slip. These men were tenderfeet in spite of their viciousness, and they'd tied a knot that had some slip in it.

It doesn't take much slip to give a man's arms quite a bit of play. The rope slacked. I worked my arms. The rope dropped.

I had a knife in my pocket.

Before the girl knew what was happening, I had it out and her ropes cut.

There was a little wash behind us. We were against a rock that was right on the rim.

"Over backwards, light running, keep down the cañon, the shadows are deeper there. One ... two ... three."

We went into a back somersault and down the wash just as though we'd rehearsed the act.

There was commotion above us, but I didn't have any time to see what was going on. The men ran toward the bank and started to shoot. But they'd been staring into the flames of the fire, and it gets dark quick in the desert.

I didn't want to keep right with the girl because two make twice as big a mark as one. So I let her go first, and I stumbled along behind. There were rocks in the bed of that wash and where it opened into the main cañon there was a steep drop of about ten feet. The girl slid down it. A bullet clipped the rock by the side of my head as I followed suit.

I caught up with her fifty yards or so down the main cañon. She was panting, about all in from the shock, the run, the excitement. I could hear the others coming pell mell down the cañon after us, and I knew they could outrun her.

But they were tenderfeet, and they wouldn't go too strong on reading trail. Also it was dark. So I guided her up a rock outcropping.

"Now you've got to keep your nerve, and don't make any noise," I told her. "They'll come closer. But just be a sport and keep your head."

We went up.

It was slow work, climbing. And running down the cañon was a lot faster. The pursuers came clattering down the rocky bed of the stream when we weren't over fifty feet above them.

I flattened the girl down so there'd be no silhouette showing against the sky.

They went past on the dead run. One of them was shooting into the darkness, and I could see the stabbing flashes of the automatic.

The girl stopped breathing. It was a strain on her. I thought she was going to faint. But the men went past. I chuckled, just to help her keep her spirits up, and then quit chuckling. The men had come to a sudden stop, not over twenty yards below us.

"They couldn't have gone down there," said Fargo's voice.

"Listen," said Rankin. "See if we can hear 'em."

They listened.

If they were wise they'd know that we must have gone up, and it wouldn't take much of a search to find us. By myself, I could have laughed at them. But there was the girl.

Then I got a break.

The shooting had alarmed the burros. There was a clatter down the cañon. To ears that knew the desert, it was only too apparent what that noise was, burros stampeding down the cañon, half a mile away. But these men had forgotten about the burros and their ears weren't trained to the desert.

"Way to thunder and gone down there!" snarled Fargo. "How could they have covered all that distance?"

"A short cut, maybe," said Rankin.

"Let's follow and kill 'em. They gotta stop. They ain't armed."

That would be Osgood, the killer.

Fargo gave the vote.

"No. They've got no food, no water. The desert will get them. Even if they do get to civilization, no one will believe their story if we deny it. And we'll locate this claim, rush in to get her recorded, then make a fake sale to a corporation and skip out. The corporation will run it. We've got possession, and remember it's possession that counts. The girl never did locate the claim. She had the sketch map. We got here first and located."

"We'll follow 'em in the morning, anyhow," said Osgood. "The girl can't go far. We got lots of water. They ain't got any. The canteens are all in camp."

Sitting up there on the side of the outcropping in the still desert night, hearing every word they said, it seemed strange that we weren't discovered. But these men were city men, green to the desert, and the burros were still making a racket. The shooting and the bullets that had cut around them were enough to start a stampede, even without a drifter along.

We didn't have anything, food, water, blankets or guns. I thought some of trying to jump down and beat them back to camp, trusting to find my gun there in the pile of stuff, and fighting them off.

But they'd hear me before I had gone ten feet, and there was the girl ... I waited. They turned back up the cañon, walking below us, once more, and they were talking.

"It'll be moonlight after midnight. We can get started then. They can't have gone far. The girl was all in anyway, and she had a blister on her heel. She mentioned it this morning, remember?"

Fargo growled an answer.

"I'm going to put bullets right between that guy Zane's ears," said Osgood. "If you guys had let me pull the trigger this afternoon we'd be out of all this mess now, and everything would have been all nice and regular."

"You've got to hide the bodies," said Fargo.

"Hell, I never did see such a fuss made over a stiff. I've bumped 'em by the score, and left 'em where they got bumped, for the most part. Once, in a hick town, I did pack the corpse on the running board, so I could dump him on the lawn of the courthouse, where the officers could have him handy ..."

"This is the desert," said Fargo.

"Aw, you give me a pain in the belly," snarled Osgood.

There was a sudden cessation of steps. Fargo may not have known it, but he was close to death at that time. Then I heard Rankin say something in a low voice, and they went back to the camp, clattering up the wash. After a while I could see their silhouettes moving against the fire. I waited until I was certain they were all three together there.

If they'd been wise, they'd have kept one man out for a listening post. But they were hungry, and they all crowded around the campfire.

I figured it'd be a good time to put some spirit into the girl. We had a hard trek ahead of us.

"Well," I said, "we got out of that lucky. Now we can make a forced march, get to the automobile road and find a car, get to civilization and swear out warrants for that bunch of crooks."

She sighed, that same tremulous, dry sobbing sigh.

"But can we do it?"

"Oh, I think so," I said.

"We haven't had anything to eat or drink. I remembered what you said about a dry camp, and I haven't eaten all day or taken a drink. I was getting toughened up. They'll have lots of food and water. And even if we get into court we can't fight them. They'll swear we tried to take the mine away from them. After all, possession counts, and we never did make any location."

There were all those difficulties ahead of us, all right, but they were bridges we could cross when we came to them. What worried me was whether we could make the auto road, and whether there'd be a machine along it in time to do us any good. I had a hunch these men might start getting some sense, and patrol the routes toward the highway. There were some passes . . .

And then finally the girl started to sob.

I have a hard time when a woman sobs. I don't hear it often enough. She cried for maybe a full minute, and then clung to my shoulder and quit it.

"I'm trusting to you," she said. "I wish I'd confided in you right at the start."

That would have been a wonderful idea, if she'd had it sooner, but it wasn't of much use now. There was no time to waste figuring what would have been a good move to make if we'd made it.

"Let's go," I told her.

I helped her ease her way down the outcropping so she wouldn't make any noise, and we started to walk. It was slow going, trying to be silent, and I knew that the faintest noise would bring them down on us. And they'd know then what we'd done to throw them off the trail the first time. It wouldn't be so easy the second time.

We got pretty well out of the cañon, and I turned the girl so she was angling along a slope. I knew a short cut to a road on the other side of the mountains. We'd have to climb, but I thought there'd be water in one of the springs that was near enough to the route to make it worth while stopping to find out. But it'd be tough.

I could see her limping, and knew the blister wouldn't get any better. Her boots were more of the department store kind that make a nice window display, but rub raw places on the feet when you get them out in the mountains.

Then she pitched, flung up her arms and went down.

I was afraid of the answer, even before I realized what it was. She tried to get up, lurched forward, and lay still. I felt for the ankle. She winced.

"I'm afraid," she said, "that it's broken."

She might have been commenting on the weather, for all the expression of pain that was in her voice. But I knew how she felt.

It was the end.

I sat there. The ankle wasn't broken, but it was a bad sprain, and I could feel it swelling. I managed to unlace the boot before we had to cut the leather. We sat in a huddle. It wasn't a nice fix.

Then the wind sprang up and the desert began to talk. I could hear the sand whispering softly down the slope, rustling against the sparse sagebrush, hissing against the rock outcroppings.

"What a nasty, cruel place the desert is!" she spat.

"It's the nicest mother a man ever had," I told her.

"It's cruel," she said.

"And cruelty is really the best form of parental kindness. It makes one self-reliant."

She sighed and pitched over so that her whole weight was resting against my shoulder.

"Well," she said, "there's a chance, and just a chance. You leave me and start traveling for help. You can leave a fire and some wood for me to keep it going. They'll find me, of course, but they won't dare to kill me, not with the story you can tell. They've either got to kill you, get rid of you, or else leave me alone."

I broke it to her gently.

"That's exactly what they would do—leave you alone. They'd just pretend they hadn't seen you, would walk off and leave you here, alone in the desert, without food or water, and with a sprained ankle. Then, when people found you . . . they'd be blameless. The cause of your death would be all too apparent."

I didn't tell her just how they could tell. There was no use rubbing it in. People who die of thirst in the desert die a death that isn't pleasant. And the last thing they do is to start digging with their hands. The cruel gravel of the desert rips the flesh from the bones . . .

We sat there in silence. The desert talked.

"Somehow, it seems like the desert's talking to us," she said.

"That's what lots of people think when they've lived in the desert for a while," I told her.

"But it seems to be saying something."

I knew that it was only her imagination.

The desert whispers do that to people. Their ears get so fed up with the vast, aching silence of the place that they are anxious to interpret sounds as words. The mind is lonely, and the parts of the brain that hear speech get hungry. Just the same way the sound of the wind in trees will always sound like water to a thirsty man.

We sat for a spell in silence again. There was nothing else to do. It was the end.

I couldn't carry her and reach any water. I doubted if I could get help and return to her.

The stars wheeled by majestically overhead.

And then the desert spell caught me, the desert seemed to be trying to talk. I shook off the feeling, knowing it was just the desert hypnosis. But the feeling came back.

I listened to the desert for a while, and then I started talking to the girl in a low voice, telling her what I'd been thinking.

"I've been laying down on the job," I told her gently. "We should never have figured on running away. I should have fought the thing out. That's what the desert's trying to tell us."

"Don't be foolish. You're one man, and you're unarmed. They're three, and they're armed, and they've got all the advantage."

I shook my head. The thought was taking a firmer root in my mind now. "Wrong," I said. "I'm not just one man. I've got the desert on my side. These people don't know the desert. I'm going to tackle them, and the desert's going to help me. You can think I'm foolish and that the desert's cruel, but I'm telling you that what I say is right. The desert's going to help."

She turned to stare at me. I got to my feet.

"You'll have to be brave, and wait here. Keep out of sight, and wait for me. I'll come back. It'll be a long time, perhaps to-morrow night. You won't dare to make even a fire. Hunger and thirst will be terrific, but the desert will win for us. When you begin to feel thirsty and the sun beats down on you, just be brave and know that it's the desert helping."

She was quiet for a little while, and the sand, slithering along on the sand, seemed to make whispers of encouragement.

"I think I understand," she said. "I am not afraid."

I patted her shoulder.

"Be brave," I told her. Her hand came groping up mine, patted the side of my face.

"Good luck," she said, and I surely needed it.

And I slipped down the slope into the darkness.

## IV. Desert Tricks

I didn't want her to know exactly what I was planning on doing, so I waited until I'd covered a hundred yards or so before I started to put my plan into execution.

There was a juniper tree, twisted and stunted, but a regular tree of the desert places. It had been forced to weather cruel heat and dry days, to stand up against twisting winds and hissing sand. The desert had been cruel to it, and it had received the reward of the desert. It had become tempered and strong.

I cut a limb and flexed it into the shape I wanted. It was green, but it had plenty of spring. The Indians make bows out of the juniper tree. It's a tempered wood, one you can trust.

I took my bootlaces and split out a thong from them that was strong enough for my purpose. Then I started to climb. I wanted pine, and pine grows up near the summits. I knew where there were a few trees.

It was a hard climb, and I took it as easy as I dared. It was going to be a big battle, and I needed to conserve all my strength.

The desert seemed to have whispered long enough to attract attention to itself as an ally, and then to have quieted down. It was silent now, the wind had ceased, the sand was still.

The faintest breath of air was stirring, but not enough to make the sand start to talk.

I collected some of the sort of pine I wanted, pitchy knots that were bone dry and would burn like tinder, and stay burning. Then I went back down the mountain and made the juniper branch into a bow, strung it taut with the leather thong, and tied the pitch knots on to the ends of some makeshift arrows I whittled from the straightest of the dead pine. It wasn't so much of an outfit, but would serve.

I started a still hunt up to the camp. The three men were in one of their huddles around the campfire. The possibility of being attacked by a lone, unarmed man was one of the things that hadn't entered their minds. They were having lots to talk about and lots to think about, and the most of the camp equipment was where they had left it.

I've stumbled onto a bonanza myself once or twice, and I know the feeling. A man doesn't sleep right away, no matter how tired he's been.

I inched my way up into the overhang of a rock outcropping. The eastern sky was commencing to pale with the coming of the moon.

I could hear wind rushing down the slopes of the mountains. It would reach the cañon in a minute and the desert would start talking again.

I struck a match and lit one of the pine knots.

Then I drew back the flaming arrow and shot the bow.

It wasn't far, and the first arrow went straight to the mark, lit right on the pile of stuff they'd taken from the burro. I knew there were some caps and some giant powder in that pile, somewhere.

I fitted another arrow.

The flickering light of the blazing pine knot caught their

eyes, huddled around the campfire as they were, and one of them turned. Just as he yelled, I launched the second arrow. I tried to keep cool. Perhaps it was the excitement, perhaps it was the crude arrow and the green bow. But the arrow was short and to one side.

They saw my position then.

I was lighting the third knot as the bullets started to spatter. They were doing some fair shooting, too. I could feel the vicious spat of the missiles striking on the face of the rock. But I had pretty fair protection, and they were shooting without being able to line up the sights.

The third arrow sailed out, straight and true. It lit within three feet of the first, lodged right on a roll of blankets, right under a box.

I wondered if that box was the one that had the giant powder?

Still the fools didn't realize their danger. They continued to rake the side of the mountain with gunfire. I had a fourth knot ready to light, and was even groping for the match when I saw what was happening.

The fire had gotten under some sort of grease—bacon, perhaps—perhaps some oil for cooking. Anyway, it flared up in a big sheet of snarling flame that writhed and twisted about a border of greasy black smoke that vortexed in swirling confusion. And the solid bank of wind, rushing down the mountainside, caught the flames and sent them billowing out in a flat sheet.

One of the men yelled something about the grub and the water. Then another remembered the powder. If he hadn't called the warning, it would have been all over within ten seconds. But the warning gave them time to fling themselves down the cañon, get the shelter of the dirt walls.

Then it happened. The red flame suddenly expanded into a great, white hot ball of fire, a mushroom of blasting destruction. Objects, looming as black as the silhouette of a dead tree against a lightning flare, were tossed up on the fringes of this burst of flame. The ground seemed to part.

Then there was a terrific roar. The mountainside shook. A blast of air was shot upward by the force of the explosion, a hot wave of sound-filled air that puffed up the mountainside. Then everything was black, and the distant ranges started reverberating back the roaring echoes of that explosion.

I started on a run down the mountainside, and the moon lifted up over the top of the range at the very instant my plodding feet started churning the earth.

They saw me when I had covered fifty yards, and they opened fire. It was what I'd been hoping for. I ducked behind a rock, angled into a side cañon, went down instead of up, and showed myself along the moonlight that gilded the slope of the next ridge. That drew me some more shots.

I kept going.

They were following, strung out behind me, casting grotesque shadows in the moonlight. I went over into the shadows and headed straight down. They rather expected me to keep on angling. I had to show myself in a patch of moonlight, wait for a moment, to let them see me and draw their fire. Then they came boiling down after me.

I crossed into the shadow and doubled back.

They came on past me, running, stopping, peering.

I heard Fargo's panting words. He was the thinker of the crowd.

"We're wiped out ... food ... water ... all gone ... Follow him ... he knows a spring ... don't shoot any more."

I chuckled to myself. They'd got the idea sooner than I expected they would.

I waited until they'd gone past, then I went on down the shadowed slope, taking it easy. I was conserving my strength now. They were still running, combing the side of the mountains in breathless panic.

No one needed to return to the camp to see what had happened. That explosion had wiped out the little mesa, just as though a volcano had opened up under it. There wasn't any camp equipment left. They knew it and I knew it. We were starting on an equal basis, except that they were one meal ahead of me, and several drinks of water. But I knew the desert and they didn't. The desert is kind to those who have grown to know her, and cruel to those who haven't slept out under her stars long enough to learn her rigid ways.

I let them comb the mountainside as long as I dared before I came out on a ridge well down toward the flat of the desert. They saw me, and there was a shout as they conveyed the information. Then they started down after me.

I kept in plain sight after that. I was out of range of their revolvers, anyway, but I was safe. I was their only hope of getting out. They didn't know where they were, nor which way to head for water. The burros had gone, and their equipment had puffed out in smoke.

I hit the level surface. The shadow I cast was shorter now, but black as ink against the desert sand. I looked up at the slopes, and wondered if the girl was watching. She was going to have a long wait ahead of her. It would sear its way into her soul with suffering. But it would give her more calm power than she'd ever had before in her life. That's the way of the desert, but she hadn't learned it yet.

The men strung out behind me. Once or twice they tried to close the distance, but I kept ahead of them. They found I could foot it as fast as they could, faster if necessary.

I knew how they were, panting from their run, worried, anxious, perspiring; and perspiration makes for thirst. I had kept going just fast enough to keep my muscles limbered up, but I wasn't sweating. We who have lived long in the desert learn not to sweat much. It's one of the first lessons the desert teaches.

And I headed right up the rim of the desert, skirting the

mountains, headed for the land of poison springs. I kept a pace that would press them to the limit, keep them sweating.

My stomach told me it needed food, and my throat was parched. But I've lived a long time in the desert, and I've been hungry and thirsty before. And there's this much to be said for traveling on an empty stomach—it's better than to try and make time right after a full meal. The processes of digestion make for an acid condition that doesn't help thirst.

We traveled, and we must have presented a strange sight to the night prowling coyotes that looked us over from the shadows cast by sage clumps. One man, pushing on ahead fast. Behind him, strung out over the glittering surface of the desert, three straggling shapes, that were put to it to keep the pace.

There wasn't any running now, trying to catch up and overpower me. It was a straight question of pushing themselves to the limit to keep me in sight.

We reeled off the miles as well as we could with the loose footing. It was hard work, tiring work, soul wearying work.

Daylight rimmed the jagged crests of The Last Chance Mountains, and I took a bearing on the ranges. We were getting toward the country I wanted to hit, and it was a bad country, a tumbled mass of barren slopes, arsenic springs, water that would rot out a man's insides.

The country was stained with colored rock outcroppings, strata of vivid soil, and strange conglomerates. The men behind me were all in, and I was keeping the pace myself only by an effort. I looked behind and one of them frantically waved a white handkerchief.

I thought of the girl on the hill, and pushed on. I would have no truce with the trio of crooks. It was whole hog or nothing as far as I was concerned.

The colors to the east went through a swift range of vivid beauty, but my eyes were on the desert, watching every step, figuring distances and my strength.

The land of poison springs was ahead.

The sun came up over the range and the rays threw instant heat. It was going to be a day when the heat would shrivel a man's soul inside of his skin. I knew the men behind me were sweating now, tired, almost at the point of dropping. One of them was limping badly.

I knew what would affect them worse than travel now.

I picked a bit of shade to the west of a clump of mesquite and stopped. They pressed on eagerly. I got going. After a few hundred yards, I tried it again. This time they had the idea. They stopped. They were glad of the rest. After a minute or two, one of them came toward me. I started moving. I would have no conversation with them, would not let them get within talking distance.

From time to time I watched them.

One of the men had been carrying my gun and belt thrown over his shoulder. I'd noticed that when the first streaks of dawn gave me light. Now he didn't seem to have it. He'd thrown it away as so much dead weight.

The desert was as sizzling hot as the business side of a frying pan now, and the men were desperate. Fear gripped them. They didn't know the location of the nearest roads, probably hadn't even kept their directions well enough to know the route we'd taken.

I had ceased to be their enemy. I was the only guide they could get to lead them to water.

I pushed out in a great swinging circle.

They were too panicky and too green to even note what was taking place. They followed blindly.

I hit their tracks after a while, and pushed back along them. Green as they were, they knew what was taking place then, and the fear that surged up in their breasts sent them running toward me, waving their hands and yelling.

I broke into a jog trot.

We ran in the baking sunlight, ran for two hundred yards,

which is a good run in the desert, even when a man is fresh—and we had been pressing ourselves all night.

I came to it then, that which meant a great saving of my strength, the gun and belt which one of the men had been wearing as additional protection, the old six-gun which had pounded at my hip through all sorts of misfortune and triumph.

They had thrown it away as excess weight, and they hadn't bothered, even, to take out the shells and throw them away. It hadn't occurred to them that I would double back.

That was one trump which the desert had put into my hand. Slowly but surely I was winning. The very desert herself was taking part, and the men realized in a surge of black panic just what they were up against, just why I'd doubled back.

## V. Desert Torture

I TOOK ANOTHER CIRCLE, and headed back for the country of the poison springs.

They followed, plodding, desperately tired, their muscles aching.

I picked a place where I could watch the back trail and flung myself on my side to rest. They dropped without argument. The rest seemed almost as welcome to them as water would have seemed.

I chuckled.

That rest would finish things.

It was hard on my muscles, and years in the desert have dried my muscles to fine strings of sinew on which there is no fat, and in which there is little surplus moisture.

But these men were from the city. Booze gangsters, gunfighters, soft livers. Bah!

Half an hour of rest and their tortured muscles would cramp under the gruelling fatigue. I gave them that half hour. Then I got to my feet and started out at top speed.

## THE LAND OF POISON SPRINGS

All three of them limped now.

The time had dried the exudations from the broken blisters on their feet, had set the tortured muscles into stiffness, had made their joints as rusted hinges.

I had all the trumps now.

And the country of the poison springs was just ahead.

There's arsenic in the desert, lots of it, and, every once in a while, the water spurts out in the arsenic country. The result may be deadly springs from which an emanation of death surges upward in such gaseous clouds that birds flying over the water will drop dead. Or the water may be discolored and coat the rocks in the bed of the purling stream with a black slime that spells "death" even to the uninitiated. Or the water may be pure and clear to the eye, slightly wrong as to taste, but deadly as to the effect.

The country toward which I was heading had all of the three sorts of springs. And, interspersed, here and there, was some good water.

I led them first to a spring that didn't need the sign that was over it to warn them. It was a spring the water of which oozed a deadly gas. The bed of the rivulet which trickled down for a hundred yards, before the greedy sand swallowed it was jet black, and slimy.

The government surveyors had placed a warning sign over it:

WARNING. POISON. DO NOT DRINK.

I walked to this spring, apparently surprised to find the sign, then I walked away. They caught the glint of water, and came up on the run, eagerly flinging their arms toward the sky, shouting hoarsely in their eager gratification at the purling stream.

Then their nostrils caught the odor. Their eyes read the sign. They paused, crushed, disappointed. They were almost insane with the black despair which surged up in their souls.

For these were city men. And each man can face the form of death he has accustomed himself to face. But show him death in a suddenly sinister and strange form, and panic grips him. That is why the thought of a horrible death in the midst of this confused mass of jumbled hills and barren mountains caused them such fear.

I swung in a circle. They stayed by the poisoned spring, arguing. One of them even bent to taste the water and the fumes slumped him over. The others dragged him back.

I waited until they came after me once more, stumbling, staggering, every ounce of spirit gone from their craven souls. They were almost insane with the strain of it all.

I swung once more in a circle and walked back to the poison spring. They couldn't get the idea, and they stood on a hill to watch me. Then they got the thought that maybe I was going to drink the water, after all. If it was safe for me it would be safe for them. I knew the desert. They didn't.

But I waited until a little rise hid them, and took the sign from the edge of the spring, the sign which marked it as poison. And then I started out of the little cañon where the spring was located, going on a half run.

They did what I thought they would do, what their fatigued muscles demanded that they should do, cut over the ridge to save themselves the extra yardage of climb. They didn't go near the spring itself.

I had all the trumps. It only was necessary to play them.

I climbed the divide. There was a sweet water spring just over the summit of the first ridge. It was a cold, clear spring, bordered with moist sand, and a fringe of vegetation.

I ran to it, dropped on my hands and knees where the moist sand would hold the imprint of my tracks, and drank. And I was careful not to drink more than a swallow or two. It was agony to tear my face away, but I know the deadly cramps that come from drinking too much water when one has tasted the hot torture of the desert's thirst.

Then I moved over to the other side of the little stream, and planted the sign that I'd taken from the other spring. I put it in some of the green stuff so it wouldn't show to casual observation.

Then I went on.

From the shelter of a rock outcropping, I watched them come over the crest in a stumbling run, watched them as they saw my tracks going toward the stream, and the fringe of cool greenery that broke the eye torture of the glaring sands.

They saw where I had knelt down and placed my face to the water, and they plunged their own red faces down into the cool depths, gulped, strangled, sputtered and gulped again. There was no one to tell them to take it easy. They simply let their appetites dictate their actions. It was the way they were accustomed to live.

I waited, watched.

It wouldn't be long until the cramps would claim them. They had made hogs of themselves, and Nature would have her way.

They finally finished their mad orgy of first draughts, and looked casually around them, searching for me. I had led them to water now, and I had ceased to be something they needed. They would shoot on sight.

They would have gone after more of the water, when they had finished their inspection, had not the eyes of Fargo chanced to light on the sign.

He stared at it with unbelieving eyes.

Then he shouted, an inarticulate shout that conveyed meaning more by the note of panic in his voice than by the words. He pointed his finger.

The others saw the sign.

Then, as their minds concentrated on their stomachs, seeking the first sign of alarming symptoms, the preliminary spasms of cramp became noticeable.

Fargo pressed his hands to his stomach. The color drained

from his sunbaked face. His eyes were wide with fear. Osgood stared incredulously, then slowly twisted his torso, rolled over and tried to retch the water from his system.

As well have tried to coax moisture from a blotter.

His parched tissues had swelled under the moisture which had entered his stomach, and it was that very absorption which was causing the sudden pains which now gripped them all.

I chose that moment to stand erect against the sky.

They didn't see me.

I came down the slope, my gun holstered at my side, my hands swinging free. The first they knew of my presence was when I spoke.

"Good Heavens!" I said. "You didn't drink it?"

They stared at me.

Fargo snapped out words in between moans.

"You drank it!"

"Not a drop. I only bent and cooled my face in it. It's not like the other. It doesn't send off a gas, and you can touch your skin to it. But it's sure death to drink it. There's a good spring over the hill. I drank there. I only cooled my face here."

They stared with utter incredulity.

"I'm dying!" said Osgood. He said it in the tone of voice which one would reserve for some great cataclysm. Like so many killers who have accustomed themselves to killing under such circumstances that the other man stands no chance, these gangster gunmen had always been certain of victory before they would enter battle. That was why they were so arrogant. Now, brought face to face with impending death, they thought that the whole scheme of things had gone awry, that God had stepped down from heaven, and that the world was ending.

I grinned at them.

"Well," I said, "we've all got to die sometime. I hate to

think of what's on your souls. Personally, I'd hate to take such a load into eternity with me. When my time comes, I hope that . . ."

Osgood, the killer, was Osgood the whiner. He interrupted me with a plea for mercy, as though I could have spared his life or washed his craven soul free from sin.

I shrugged my shoulders, turned my back as though to walk away. I thought that would bring home a more vivid realization of their predicament—to have me walk calmly away and leave them to their torture.

I was almost too late in remembering those with whom I had to deal. They were sneaks and cowards. They were the type of men who shot from ambush. They were accustomed to line their sights on a man's back.

I whirled.

Osgood, his face drawn into a spasm of hatred, his sneaking soul grasping at the opportunity for a mean revenge, had his gun halfway from the holster. Those gangsters were undoubtedly fast with a gun.

Out in the desert men learn to use a gun as a tool of the trade. Many the time a rattler has to be shot with a snapping motion of the wrist before the foot descends. Many a time a man has to take a snap shot at a running rabbit when his belt buckle is pushing against his ribs.

I snapped out my gun.

Osgood doubtless thought he was unbeatable on the draw. City dwellers get some strange ideas, and then, again, man is ever prone to judge his worth, not from any fixed standard of merit, but purely from the comparison he can make with competition.

There was staring incredulity on Osgood's face as my gun was the first to spit fire, and the automatic's explosion came a fraction of a second after my slug had torn into his forearm, spun him half around.

The automatic dropped from his hand. He stared at me,

then at the bleeding arm. His left hand clutched at the wound, the fingers gripped around the arm.

Carl Rankin, his own gun out, stared at me, met my eyes, and dropped the gun.

"The trouble with you city gangsters," I told them, "is that you're too accustomed to shooting in the back."

Fargo came toward me, staggering a tentative step or two.

"Save me! Save me! You know the desert. You know what to do. There must be something! I can't die like this. I can't! I can't! I can't!"

They were a sorry spectacle. The three who had been swaggering about, talking of making us dig our own graves, gloating over the mine and the good fortune which had come to them. Now they were staggering about, whining and whimpering.

The sun and the blue vault of clean sky looked down upon them, and must have laughed at the manner in which the self-assurance of these mortals had evaporated.

I came over, picked up the guns, tossed them into the water.

"I'm afraid there's nothing that can be done. You'll have cramps for about half an hour. They gradually increase in violence. After that the pain isn't quite so severe. That's when the nerves are getting paralyzed. As the pains quit you can prepare to make your peace with whatever sort of God gangsters like you worship."

I seemed so utterly indifferent about it that my very indifference made them wail the louder with self-sympathy. Fargo ripped cloth from his shirt and tied up Osgood's arm. Between spasms of cramps they condoled with each other, glowered at me.

I smoked a cigarette.

"I'll wait until you die," I told them. "Not that there's anything I can do, but it'll be company for you."

Rankin sneered a reply. "Don't let us delay you!"

I smiled paternally at him. "It won't be long." I looked at Fargo. "Of course there's one thing that might make a difference," I said casually.

"How do you mean, a difference?" he asked.

I regarded the smoking tip of my cigarette.

"If you didn't drink too much of the water, there's an antidote that the Indians use. If you felt like signing a confession of what you've done, and admitting that the claim is the girl's, I might be able to help you."

They stared at me with incredulous eyes and fear-grayed faces. They had been staring certain death in the face, and now I gave them a hope of life.

Without a word Fargo got out a fountain pen and a notebook. He scrawled the confession, stopping his writing twice to double with cramps. They were caused in part by the water, in part by the suggestion of the poison sign.

Osgood and Rankin clamored to get in on it. They yammered to sign their names, babbled pleas for mercy. I remained cold and aloof until they had finished the confession; all three signed it. I glanced it over, saw that it was sufficient, made them ink their fingers and impress their inked fingertips over the sheet, giving it an absolute authenticity.

Then I gave them the "remedy." It was the first thing that came to my mind.

"Eat the leaves of the plants that are growing by the fringe of the stream. Then lie down flat and scoop up the surface sand that's warmed by the sun and pour it on your stomachs and abdomens, putting it right next to the skin. When it loses its warmth, get more hot sand."

"Will that cure us?" asked Fargo.

"That," I promised him, "will cure you."

I started up the slope.

Fifty yards away I paused and looked back.

A bullet zinged past my head. Rankin had retrieved his gun from the stream, shaken the water out of its mechanism, and fired. Fargo also had his gun. Honor among thieves? Maybe—but not in that crowd. I snapped up my gun. They scurried for cover like rabbits. They had seen something of my accuracy with my weapon, and didn't want to see more.

I dropped over the ridge. They didn't follow. They were "saving their lives." The warmth of the sand would help, and the suggestion of chewing the leaves would also help.

It would undo the harm that the planted sign had done. I hit for the north.

It was noon before I struck a branch road. There was a speck of dust off to the left—a car, coming my way. I built a fire, put on some greenery, took my coat and made the smoke column into signalling puffs.

A man who was green to the desert would have ignored the Indian telegraph. But, as the dust speck grew larger and disclosed the little black dot of an automobile scurrying along at the head of it, I could see that the driver was a desert man. He swung from the road and started grinding his car over the surface of the desert. I ran down the slope to meet him.

He was a desert prospector, one of the type who prospects in an automobile and knows his stuff. The car was battered as to body. The paint that remained was checked and scaling under the effects of scouring sand and desert sun, but the motor ran like a watch.

The car was light enough to go over the surface of sand, and had great oversize tires, only partially inflated, giving it lots of traction.

He looked me over. "Huh!" he said, and reached for the canteen.

"You could dig me out some cold grub," I told him. "And I've got an interest in a claim all staked out for you. You drive and I'll eat and talk. Head down the Eureka Valley. You'll be rich by dusk."

He looked me over, opened the door of the car.

"Get in," he said. "There's part of a cold haunch of venison in the center of the blanket roll in back, where it'll keep cool."

I dug into the blankets. The car ground into motion, snarling its way over the desert. After fifteen minutes, my eyes caught sight of three specks outlined against the sky on the top of a long ridge. The three specks were running, signaling, waving their hands.

The prospector was at the wheel, his faculties concentrated on driving. He didn't see them. I didn't tell him. Maybe they got out—back to their city warrens. Maybe not. I don't think it would matter much to the world.

We covered the ground I'd walked over at fast time. It was a good car, and one that was accustomed to desert work. We picked up the girl in the late afternoon. She had suffered some from thirst, and she was weak from hunger. But she gulped the warm water from the canteen, gnawed at some venison, and grinned at me.

"Did you hear the desert talk early this morning?" she asked.

"I was busy," I told her. "Did the sand whisper?"

She nodded solemnly.

"I think . . . I think it *does* say words, sometimes," she said.

The old prospector, a four days' growth of gray stubble on his chin, nodded his head in agreement.

"You're dog-gone tootin' it does," he said.

But we didn't ask her what the desert had said. Out in the vast spaces of sand and sun each person has the right to think his own thoughts in his own manner.

The desert is a cruel mother, but she's kind to those who know her. And that lonely vigil had left its mark upon Vera Camm. There was a poise, a calm patience, a steadiness of purpose about her. . . The mark that the desert leaves upon those whom it mothers.

# STAMP OF THE DESERT

MILE FOR MILE the desert is the cruelest country in the world, and therefore the kindest. Desert rabbits are the swiftest; desert rattlesnakes are the deadliest; desert coyotes the most cunning. Even the plants have to be coated with a natural varnish, studded with thorns.

Life progresses through overcoming obstacles, and the desert is the greatest natural obstacle. Men who have lived long in the desert are clear of mind, keen of eye, swift of hand—otherwise they don't live long in the desert.

Which is why we knew Fred Conway wasn't of the desert.

He looked the part all right when he got off the stage. He was rigged out in clothes that were covered with desert dust. His boots were light, but sand proof and a good protection against the strike of a sidewinder. His shirt was of just the right color, sun faded, serviceable. His skin was bronzed by sunlight.

But there was too much moisture in the man.

His eyes weren't bright. His fat was too much like suet. He was too well nourished, and he moved with that careless, casual assurance which comes to man when he lives in protection.

Your true desert dweller is dried out to hard fiber muscles. He walks with an easy grace, but it's unconscious, and he's always poised, always gives the impression of being ready to strike from any position.

But lots of men came to Deuces. The mine brought in some of them. The free gold that was known to be in the sun-distorted hills brought more. And there was a type that came in because Deuces was a mining camp.

I'd seen them come, and I'd seen them go.

I looked at Fred Conway, catalogued him, and looked at the other passengers on the stage. A woman, dressed in city style, her features beautiful, her skin fresh, and in her eyes just the glint of a bit of panic. A college bred mining engineer, attired in corduroys and leather high boots that screamed of newness. He was too sure of himself, and the sun had been unkind to his skin as he traveled the long desert miles in the stage. Then there was a tough old desert rat, back from civilization, and there was Sam Wint, manager of the big mine on the hill.

Sam Wint was a power around Deuces. He hired and he fired. He expanded or he shut down. Maybe he got his general orders from the big bugs in the East, but he was the one who put those orders into effect. The town looked on Sam Wint as a despot.

With Sam was his foreman, Ned Monger.

Ned wouldn't have made much noise if he'd had only his own two feet to stand on. But Ned Monger was close to Sam Wint, and Sam Wint was power, as far as the desert mining town recognized power.

I heard a little gasp from behind me, and I shifted around

so I could get a glance out of the corner of my eye.

It was Catherine Lane who had done the gasping.

Catherine was sole owner and manager of the Treat 'Em Right Restaurant. She was a desert kid. I'd known her daddy before he and Bill Pierce had had the big fight over the mining claim. Lane had died subsequently from the bullet holes Pierce had put in him. But he'd kept possession of the claim so his daughter would have something to give her a start in the world. Pierce had gone out into the desert, nursed his own wounds and faded from sight.

Catherine had buried her dad and started working the claim with a hammer, drill and giant, a big gun strapped around her slim waist, and a thirty-thirty propped against the windlass hoist.

The claim was a frost. The vein faulted out within a week. Catherine started the Treat 'Em Right Restaurant. She asked no odds of any man. She looked eternity straight in the eyes and did her stuff. She was a desert girl.

"Know him, Catherine?" I asked her.

She resented the question until she saw who it was that had asked it. Then she nodded, a curt nod.

"I did, once," she said, and walked into the restaurant.

I watched him.

He was a well-built chap, and he moved with the general air of a man who was going places and planning on doing things. But he had a little too much assurance, was a little too casual in his motions.

He got a pack outfit from Porcupine Withers and I saw him start out into the desert the next day. He hadn't been near the Treat 'Em Right Restaurant.

It was hot when he got away. The skyline was dancing in the heat and a mirage distorted the base of the purple mountain range off to the east. I was heading out into the desert myself, but I let my outfit wait for a couple of hours. A man can travel farther and easier if he starts after the sun's slid halfway down the west than if he starts when it's overhead.

Toward dusk I crosssed his trail twice. When it came dark I could see his camp fire up on the shoulder of Red Rock Butte. Probably he could look over and see mine. We were about three miles apart.

I got the start of him the next morning. I had the burros in and was swinging out on the trail when I caught the first glow of his camp fire. The east was commencing to color up. The stars were down to pin points. It was cold, with the dry numbing chill of dawn in the desert high places.

I made time.

By sun-up I was around the shoulder of the ridge. By the time it got hot, I was at Mesquite Wells. I gave the burros a rest and fought flies in the shade of the mesquite.

About two o'clock I heard the burros getting restless, and I went out for a look-see. Instead of four burros I had seven, and three of 'em were from Porcupine Wither's outfit, the ones that he'd sold this chap.

I cussed every tenderfoot a blue streak.

He'd left the burros unhobbled. They'd heard my outfit starting out, and they'd crossed over and followed, taking their time. They were nice and chummy with my stock, and I had to back-track a day's travel to return 'em to the pilgrim.

If he'd been a desert man he'd have known where to look for 'em, and I'd have tied 'em up. But, on the other hand, if he'd been a desert man, they wouldn't have got away in the first place.

I cached my stuff so I wouldn't have to pack it twice, threw a saddle on the best of the burros and headed on back to where I'd camped. I got there about sundown. Then I cut across to where the other camp fire had been. The man wasn't there.

I was sore by that time. His stuff was on the floor of the desert, and I could see where he'd started out on foot to chase the burros.

I trailed him until it got dark, too dark to see the tracks. The more I trailed, the madder I got.

Here was this pilgrim within half a day's walk of a fairly good-sized mining town, letting his burros get away from him, and starting out in the desert looking for 'em, without even having sense enough to track them. He was just looking.

That's the way many a man has been swallowed into the maw of the desert.

I tied up the burro near a little feed, stretched out on the sand. It was going to be cold later on, and I decided to get a little sleep and then gather some sagebrush for a fire. I'd have to use it pretty sparingly unless I wanted to keep moving camp.

I guess I slept for an hour. Then I woke up and saw the glitter of a fire way over to the south. I got the burro into protesting action and rode through the night. I came up on the camp fire about midnight. The pilgrim was by it, shivering and frightened.

"Water!" he yelled at me when I came up. "Have you got water?"

I swung off of the saddle and unslung the canteen. He couldn't have been very bad. A desert man wouldn't have even begun to get thirsty. What he was suffering with was a mouth thirst and panic. He swigged the water. I took the canteen away from him when he had it tilted up at right angles. I hadn't had a drink since I'd left Mesquite Wells.

Then I sat down on the desert and told him lots of things. I cussed him out good and proper, and I finished up by pointing to a shoulder of Bald Mountain.

"Right over the line of that mountain," I said, "you can see the lights of Deuces. That's the place for you. It's a desert town. There's enough of the desert about it to be interesting, and enough of the town about it to be safe for tenderfeet, providing their feet ain't too tender. You're going back there to-morrow."

He squirmed around and finally blurted out that he didn't want to go to the town. Then he told me why he was in the desert. It was the damndest reason I'd ever heard.

Most of the time it's the lure of gold that brings them into the desert. But this man was prospecting, and yet wasn't particularly interested in gold. No, what he wanted was to get self-reliant.

It had me cheated.

I quit being quite so sore when I found out that he had sense enough to realize that the desert was the best school in the world, and I tried to find out what particular brand of loco had made him want to get toughtened up in the desert.

He wouldn't give any explanation.

After a while I went to sleep. When I woke up the sand was talking.

Sand talk in the desert is a funny thing. The wind blows the sand against the sage and cacti, and it gives little whispering noises. Then as the desert wind freshens, it gets the sand slithering along on the surface and you get the weirdest whisper of all, sand talking to sand.

And don't think the sand whispers are imagination. Any of the old-timers can tell you how they've started out of a sound sleep thinking some one was whispering to them, only to find one of those sudden, mysterious desert winds had sprung up and the sand had started talking.

I looked over to where Fred Conway was huddled over what was left of the fire. He'd been working hard to keep it going.

"I'll tend the fire for a while," I said. "You get some rest."

He shook his head.

"Why?" I asked. "You'll need your strength to-morrow."

He shook his head again, more emphatically.

"I'm listening to the sand," he said.

I nodded. He had the makings of a desert man.

"Go to Sam Wint over at the mine and tell him Bob Zane said to put you to work," I told him. "You stay with the mining job for a while, and then you can go out in the desert and get self-reliant without having to take a guardian along." Then I went to sleep.

Three months I stayed in the desert. Once I got some supplies at a little jerkwater store. The rest of the time I lived on the country and what grub I'd burro-backed along with me. When I got back to Deuces I had a few samples of ore and not much else.

I found Fred Conway a little harder. He was walking with a spring in his stride. His eyes were clear and hard. But he wasn't a desert man, not yet.

He was eating at the Treat 'Em Right Restaurant. He was being better than tolerated. But there was a tension between him and Catherine Lane, a peculiar sort of tension that told of lots of things.

But I didn't ask any questions, and I didn't notice anything, not to let on.

The mine foreman was eating at the Treat 'Em Right, too. Ned Monger was a regular customer. He'd been making quite a campaign for Catherine.

I hoped she wouldn't pay any attention to him, but that was just a hope. She seemed to like him pretty well.

Ned Monger looked over at Fred Conway a couple of times and frowned. I didn't like that frown.

I shook hands with Conway, spoke to Monger, got a smile out of Catherine, and a piece of my favorite pie that the kid bakes special whenever she hears that I'm in from the desert.

Monger walked out. Conway shifted from one foot to the other as though he wanted to say something, and then he drifted out to the street. I gave Catherine a chance to talk.

She didn't take it. I wanted to ask a question or two, but figured I hadn't better. Catherine was a desert girl.

So we sat in the silence which is born of the desert, and is more intimate than conversation.

"Like the pie, Bob?" she asked after a long while.

I set down the coffee cup.

"Fine, Kittens," I told her.

She leaned forward. She might have said something else, but there was the roar of a heavy caliber revolver. It sounded from about fifty yards away, down the street.

Catherine jumped as though the bullet had struck her, and started for the door.

"No, no, no, no, no!" she screamed.

I grabbed her as she went through and got my body in front of hers as she crowded to the street.

Men were running. A figure was standing in front of the Okay Pool Room, emptying a heavy caliber Colt.

Somebody else was streaking it down the street. He was the target. I could see the spurts of dust. He was going some place in particular, and there was lead cutting the atmosphere around him.

The man that was doing the shooting was Ned Monger. The chap who was going places in a hurry was Fred Conway.

"Stop him!" yelled the girl.

I looked at her to see which one she meant she wanted stopped. It was Ned Monger. Her face was as white as a mountain of drift sand in the moonlight.

I lugged the forty-five from the holster and stepped out to the center of the street. I didn't know much about the merits of the thing, but if Catherine Lane said she wanted somebody stopped, I was the guy to stop him.

But the foreman's gun was empty. He was yelling something, something about hi-grading and he started to run. I got in his way. He grabbed me. His face was purple.

"Don't be a damned fool! He's the head of the hi-graders.

I've got the dope on him, accused him. He's trying to get away."

Catherine was quivering like a bit of dry sage in a desert wind, and she didn't say anything about letting Ned Monger go, so I kept a hold on him, and he stayed right there.

People poured out of various places. Everybody tried to talk at once. Monger was cussing me. It was language a lady shouldn't have heard. But Catherine was a desert girl and Ned was excited.

By that time he had an audience, and he told them his story. There'd been hi-grading up at the mine where he and Conway both worked. The hi-grading wasn't any secret. They'd been working through jewelry rock for several months, and lots of it had been disappearing. But they couldn't find out where it had gone.

It's hard to keep miners from hi-grading when a mine's working in jewelry rock. But it's not so easy to dispose of it after it's hi-graded. A miner can pick out a particularly rich bit of ore and pry out the chunk that's got the most value, with the gold all wire on the side that's been pried loose. He simply sticks that high grade ore in a nice place of concealment and, later on, lifts it out to the surface. Maybe it's worth twenty-five dollars, maybe a little more. Take half a hundred men and start a few of them hi-grading and it runs into money.

Monger was dancing around.

"I caught old Charley, the breed, with some high grade. He was taking it some place. I'd put him to work at the mine knowing he was a hi-grader. The idea was, I wanted to find out who was getting it from him. Well, he went to Conway's room. I collared old Charley and made him confess. Conway had been buying it.

"Then I started for the deputy sheriff, and Conway tried to make a get-away. I figured he'd been tipped off. Like a fool, I let Charley get away.

"So I yelled for Conway to stop, and he took to his heels. Then I tried to stop him with my gun, and this old desert rat"—he looked at me with hatred—"butted in."

There was a murmur from the crowd. Hi-grading in a mining camp is something like rustling in a cattle camp. They started to mill about, then they started to move.

I know when a man's played his hand. I didn't try to stop 'em. I tried to lead 'em.

"That's Monger's story," I said. "Now let's go hear Conway's." And I kept in the lead.

There wasn't much of a chance for Conway to get away. We found him in his room. He'd barricaded the door and was going to shoot it out. The man in the pool room downstairs said he'd heard stuff thudding out to the ground after Conway went into the room.

We got Conway out, after a while, without any shooting. It was a mean situation. The mob was ugly. Somebody got a flash light and started searching the desert, out back of Conway's window. We found what had been thudding to the ground. High grade, lots of it. There was seven hundred dollars in jewelry rock.

"You threw it out!" yelled old Pete, the man that runs the pool room.

Conway didn't deny it. He didn't say anything. He sat tight-lipped.

They were for getting rough right then, the mob. I'll say this for Monger, he didn't want a lynching, and he tried to get 'em to hold Conway where he'd have a trial. But mobs are funny things. They finally decided to get old Charley and hear his story.

Getting Charley was a different story. He was a breed, old and shifty. He never used much water. About half a pint a day for his insides, and not a damned drop for his outside. But he knew the desert, and when he was in trouble he went for the desert like a seal for water.

There was a desert all around Deuces. It would have trapped an ordinary man, held him to the town. To Charley it was just like a refuge. There were a few of us that knew the desert pretty well. We set out to trail Charley.

We might as well have spared ourselves the trouble. It was slow work, trailing by the light of electric flash lights. And old Charley headed for the shifting sand country. I couldn't figure at first what was taking him there. There wasn't any water and there wasn't enough cover to hide a jack-rabbit. But about midnight I knew.

The stars were awfully clear that night. That's sometimes a sign of wind. It was that night. Charley had smelled the wind. He got us into the shifting sand country just about the time the wind came like an evil spirit.

You could hear it whistling down the cañons of the barren mountains for fifteen minutes before it arrived. It's a weird sound, wind coming down out of the mountains in the silence of a desert night.

The sound was a low roar at first, so low-pitched and indefinite that it wasn't sound at all, but just an undertone of menace that made the hair bristle with little cold chills of fear that rippled up the spine. It's the reaction of the man animal, unconscious, bred in the bone through thousands of years.

Then the rumble became specific sound. It grew into a roar. A curtain of white sand blotted out the stars, came sweeping down on us. You couldn't hold your face against the wind. The sand would cut the skin right through. It was a case of drifting down wind and looking for shelter.

The wind blew for an hour. When it quit, it stopped as suddenly as it had started. Charley was gone as completely as though he'd been swallowed up. There wasn't a track or anything that looked like a track.

Back to town we went, and we started sweating Conway. He didn't sweat. He kept his lips tight together. Once he said that he never explained, that his friends shouldn't need an explanation. His enemies wouldn't believe one. It's old stuff with fellows who get in a position where they can't explain. But, somehow or other, I believed it.

The crowd got to milling again. Monger was the one to remind them that, without old Charley, there was no chance of a conviction in court. And Charley was in the desert. He'd crawl in a hole and stay there until the thing blew over.

Some one suggested the tar and feathers.

I drifted across to the restaurant. "I can stop this," I told Catherine, "if Fred Conway will just say enough to give me something to go on. It'll take a little shooting, maybe, but I don't think so. Anyhow, I can stop them, but I can't play it blind. I've got to know what it's all about."

She shook her head. I was surprised. But her lips were pressed together so tight they were white. She was worse than Conway.

"Do nothing," she said.

I did nothing. The mob put on the tar and the feathers, and they got a rail. Day was breaking when they put Conway out on the border of the desert, gave him a ragged outfit of clothes, a big canteen of water and some shoes. He looked like a bedraggled chicken.

I hunted up Catherine.

"I'll trail him after the excitement gets over," I told her, "and help him get the tar off. That won't be hard to do with the sun that'll be shining. Then I'll see what can be done."

She was mad.

"He could have stopped it if he wanted to!"

I smiled at her, trying to let her see my attitude was paternal.

"No, Catherine," I said. "A man doesn't get tarred and feathered just because he wants to. And he's floated out to the desert. He can't come back now."

That's the code of the desert. Sometimes they give the coat

of tar and feathers, sometimes they don't. But it's the same in any event. When the committee gives a man a canteen, that's his ticket out of the desert, and if he's wise to desert customs he starts traveling right then.

Catherine lowered her voice and shifted her position. She was talking now almost in a whisper, a whisper that was like the desert whisper.

"Have you noticed how friendly old Charley has been with Louie Bann?"

I nodded and tried to prod her along.

"Louie's a simple sort of a cuss," I said. "He's got a prospect way out on the other side of the Panamints, and he got in a fight with the storekeeper at Skidoo, and he packs all the way over here to buy his supplies. He comes in here once a month and loads up, and he's got quite a string of burros. Takes him about half his time lugging in provisions."

She let her eyes bore into mine.

"He trades at the company store," she said.

I nodded again.

"He buys provisions in bunches," she went on.

I nodded again, keeping my nods just about the same, sort of a nod of invitation.

She was silent for a while. Her eyes narrowed.

"I got a look at his purchase card the other day," she said. "He doesn't buy so much stuff. His bill the last time in was only twelve dollars and a half."

That was funny. I told her so.

"What's the angle?" I asked.

"There isn't any," she said, and laughed.

I kept after her. Finally she blurted out a story.

"Fred Conway didn't hi-grade," she said. "He don't have to hi-grade. He's got money. I met him down in Mojave. He's the rich son of a rich dad. He thought he was falling for me, Fred did. So did his dad.

"I went to his dad like a little lady. I told him that Fred

was just green, impressionable. He'd been used to society women that couldn't do a thing except drive a golf ball or know the patter of auction bridge. I said he was attracted to me because of the novelty of meeting a woman who made her own way in the world.

"The father is impossible. He's one of those cold jellyfish who thinks all his thoughts with a dollar sign around them. He thought I was trying to make a grand stand to get his son's affections and win over the father. He asked me to go away and keep from letting the boy know where I was. He wanted to pay me. I wouldn't touch his money. I left.

"Then the boy found me. I think he hired detectives. He came to me and wanted to marry me. I told him the truth. I wouldn't marry a man who had been brought up in the atmosphere he had. I was afraid some of it might stick to him. I didn't want him to get like his dad, only I didn't say it that way.

"So he swore he was going to give up everything and come into the desert until he became the same sort of a man that I'd picked as a possible future husband.

"His dad raised a scene when he found it out. He did the usual stuff, disinherited the boy, and called me an adventuress. I came to Deuces and opened the restaurant. I thought that time I'd left a trail no detective could follow. But I guess he managed it some way."

I began to see a lot now. I'd known that after Catherine's mine had faulted out and after she'd gone to Mojave there'd been a spell when I didn't know where she was at all. And I sort of figured lately that she'd been taking a little shine to Ned Monger and that there was, maybe, a jealousy between the two men.

I didn't say anything about that. I shook hands with the girl, wished her luck, told her to quit worrying about Louie Bann's grocery bill, said things would come out all right in the wash, and went over to the pool hall.

Over there I started a hell of an argument, until I'd dragged most of the men in as spectators or talkers, and then I slipped out the back way, got some stuff on my burros and started out over the desert, figuring I wouldn't be noticed.

It wasn't hard to pick up the trail of Fred Conway. There were still feathers clinging to the sagebrush.

I was doing something that's against the code of the desert. When a man is handed a canteen he's done. No one is supposed to go out and give him succor. He's a pariah, floated out of the community. But I had faith in Fred.

And I couldn't understand Catherine. She'd always seemed to be a pretty sensible kid to me. Why any one should pass up Fred Conway to moon around over Ned Monger was more than I knew. But I knew that there are some subjects that are sacred as far as the heart of a girl is concerned. Trouble with us oldsters is that we want to go busting in where we've no business.

Conway's trail got fresher. He'd stopped to work off a ball of tar and feathers. Then he'd started on again. He was traveling fast, going out toward where he'd had his camp the night he lost the burros.

I got to where the camp had been. There was the black circle that marked the camp fire. And I could see where Conway had dug something up out of the sand. Then he'd headed off again at right angles. He was making mighty fast time. Guess the work in the mine had hardened him up. I started trailing him.

I stopped stock-still when the thought struck me. What a fool I'd been!

Louie Bann was a peculiar cuss, all right. Come to think of it, it was funny he'd come all the way into Deuces to buy provisions for a mine that was way over in the Panamint country. And, come to think of it, I didn't know just exactly where that mine was.

But it was the girl that I was thinking about. She'd started to say something about Louie Bann, and then when I scoffed at her idea of getting concerned over Louie's grocery bill, she'd dried up.

I was betting a hunk of pure quill against a chunk of porphyry that the girl was starting out to make some sort of an investigation of Louie Bann. And Louie Bann was the sort of a man that it wasn't exactly safe to monkey with. Let him get the idea that Catherine was trailing him, and he'd get rough. And if Catherine's surmises were correct, he'd shoot her down in cold blood.

I turned right around and headed for the Panamints. Fred Conway had been able to find that place where he'd made his old camp, and that made it seem as though he'd commenced to get onto the hang of the desert. If he had, he'd get out all right. If he hadn't, he could just shift for himself. I was going to see Catherine through.

I dropped down the slope of the Funeral Range and hit Death Valley. It was night by that time. But the stars showed some clumps of sage and rocks clearly enough to keep me from getting tangled up with 'em.

Daylight found us well up in the Panamint district. We were slowed down a bit, but still moving. I topped the ridge in a pass that I'd prospected through ten years ago, and sat down and got out the binoculars. Way up to the north I could see moving specks that danced around in the heat.

The glasses gave me magnification, but they also magnified the heat waves, and I could only guess at what those specks were; but they looked like burros, a whole string of burros. I decided to head toward them. They were working toward the south.

I had a job of it. I was dog-weary, and it was so hot the tops of the rocks would have blistered a man's hand. I topped a side ridge and saw the train of burros coming my way, not over half a mile off. And I saw something else.

I saw that there was somebody trailing that string of

burros. That somebody was moving slow, but determined, and seemed to be keeping back, trying to keep the train in sight, but not catching up with it.

Under those circumstances it was up to me to join the procession until somebody made a move. I wasn't going to butt in on something that was no concern of mine. On the other hand, if Catherine took cards in the game I was going to see that she had top hand when it came to the show-down.

The train went past me on the slope, not over three hundred yards down the hill. I let 'em pass. They were Louie's burros, all right, and he was riding with the string, with two other men. One of those men was Charley.

I was doing some tall thinking. I looked back through the binoculars at the woman, for that's who it was. I could see her plainly now, Catherine Lane. She looked tired, judging from the way she drooped over the saddle and swayed a little bit.

She should have been tired; she had ridden fast and hard.

I was wondering what I was going to do about getting a show-down before I got too sleepy, when I saw one of the riders below me swing back and around. Then they put the burro string in a little box cañon. One of the men stayed behind. The other went up and joined the man who was doubling back.

I slid my rifle out of the saddle holster, took a look at my six-gun, staked my burro, and started slipping down the ridge.

But somebody was beating me to it. He came up from a side cañon, toiling in the heat like an ant, crawling on all fours, running when he could, scrambling, slipping, stumbling.

One of the men opened fire on Catherine. It was just a desert warning, a shot that was intended to plump up a little dust.

But the chap coming up the slope didn't know what that

shot was for. He stopped and flung up a rifle. His first shot clipped a burro out from under old Charley as neat as you please. It was a good miss. He'd shot for the man.

That started hostilities. The two men figured they'd run into some sort of an ambush. They hadn't seen the figure toiling up the slope. The two got to cover and started shooting to kill. Catherine was off her burro and behind a rock. The man was still coming up the slope. It was sheer suicide. I turned the glasses on him.

My first hunch had been right. It was Fred Conway. I wanted to yell at him to get under cover, but I knew he couldn't hear me. There was one thing I could do, though.

I got a fine sight on old Charley's shoulder as he settled his rifle down to a deliberate aim. I knew that he was the most dangerous of the pair. Charley was a shot. When he pulled trigger something was due to drop.

I squeezed the trigger first. It caught his shoulder, and his gun dropped. He didn't know who had hit him. He rather fancied it was the girl. She was very much in the fight now, coming fast, slipping from rock to rock, firing whenever she got a chance.

There was only one man who was left in the battle, and he was between two of 'em. He didn't seem to have much heart in it. He fired a few times, started to hold up his hands, then fired another magazine full, mostly at random.

His cover was getting unhealthy. The girl from one side, Conway from another. He threw down his rifle and put up his hands.

I settled back on my haunches and grinned. Nobody knew I was in the picture.

Then my eye caught a flicker of motion off toward the burros. I swung the glasses down and caught the glint of sunlight on blued steel.

It was Louie Bann, and he was playing his hand just like a man of his type would. He didn't want to miss. He was going to get to a position where his fire would count, and count hard.

What he intended to do was to let Catherine and Fred Conway get together, and then smash home the lead from ambush. They hadn't figured on him. He'd been left with the burros, but the shooting had brought him up.

So far no one had suspected that I had the drop on the whole bunch, being up the slope, and having a good rest for the rifle. I slid it over a bowlder and waited.

Catherine and Conway met. They were keeping the drop on the man that had surrendered. Old Charley was tying up his shoulder. Once or twice he looked back up the slope. I think he'd commenced to suspect the truth.

Then Louie got into action. He stepped out from behind a clump of sage, dropped to one knee, and flung up his rifle.

Conway sensed the danger. He whirled, took in the situation, and fired from the hip. It was a snap shot, a hip shot at a hundred yards, and there was not one chance in a thousand that a tenderfoot would connect.

But, at the crack of his rifle, Louie Bann had gone over as though he'd been knocked with a sledge hammer. And that was because I'd pulled the trigger myself, from sixty yards.

By the time I got the glasses on him I saw that I'd caught his right arm, just below the shoulder. Evidently the bullet had shattered the bone and then crashed the stock of the rifle he had been holding. The rifle stock was a mass of splinters.

Fred and the girl had a busy fifteen minutes. They tied up the man that had surrendered, helped old Charley with his bandage, and did what they could for Louie's right arm. Louie was cussing. I could hear him up the slope, his words thin and rasping in the hot desert air.

Old Charley was saying nothing. He wouldn't; he was too much Indian.

After a while the pair went down into the box cañon where the pack train had been cached when the hostilities commenced. I figured that was the signal for my exit. I got my burro out into the open and slid down the side ridge on an angle, then crept into the shadow of a big clump of juniper.

Out in the desert, shadow is a pretty good place of concealment, particularly if you're up a mile or so above sea level. The air is so dry and rare that the sunlight is dazzling in its white hot brilliance, while the shadows seem black as ink and sharply defined.

I went to sleep for an hour. When I woke up they'd gone, pack train, captives and all. I coaxed my burro into motion and started back toward Death Valley. I rolled in and had a good sleep that night.

The next day I pushed forward and made good time. I was way over on the slope of the Funerals when I saw a camp fire. It was along toward eight or nine o'clock and I was about ready to make a camp. I pushed over to it.

There was a string of burros, and the silhouettes of two figures that were sitting against the ruddy glow of the flames, figures that were sitting so close together they seemed just a single blob of black shadow.

When I spoke they jumped apart as though some one had exploded some dynamite in the camp fire. The man reached for his gun.

"Not so hasty, Fred," I said.

He stepped back.

"Oh," he muttered, "you!"

"Yes," I said.

The girl laughed, nervously.

"I want to tell you the news," she said. "It's all right. Louie Bann didn't have a mine at all. He just had a string of burros. He'd come into Deuces, claiming he was after provisions, and he'd shop around and only really buy enough to load up one or two burros. Then he'd meet the head of the hi-grading outfit and load up the rest of the string with high grade ore.

"He'd start his string over the Panamints, and then work

down into Randsburg and sell the ore as having come from his mine up north in the Panamints. Then he'd start back again for another trip to Deuces."

I expressed proper surprise.

"And Fred," she went on, "had it figured out, but he didn't dare to say anything when they tarred and feathered him because he knew Louie would get tipped off and ditch the stuff from the pack train.

"That's why Ned Monger framed the hi-grading on him and got old Charley to skip out. Monger knew Fred was getting pretty close to the real solution. So he decided to beat him to it. He planted a lot of high grade stuff in Fred's room, then started a shooting. Fred got to his room, found the planted ore, and didn't know what to do.

"But when he'd lost his burros in the desert, he'd buried his stuff, including a rifle and some shells. And, what do you think? He got in a gun fight with Louie Bann and cleaned him up. He made a shot from the hip at over a hundred yards that was a Lulu!"

I nodded again.

Fred was sitting back, his chest out.

"Yeah," he said, and his tone had the casual drawl of a desert man, "we had a little argument with 'em when we caught up with 'em. The real credit goes to Catherine. She doped the whole thing out and trailed Louie."

I expressed proper surprise.

"How about the prisoners?" I asked.

"The sheriff's got 'em, and the ore, and they've got Ned Monger. We're going back and see the finish. After that I'm going back to work in the mine. Then we're going to build a house right there in Deuces."

I shook hands.

"Congratulations," I said.

We sat around the fire after that. He was quiet now, self-contained, sure of himself. The desert had set its mark on him. He'd graduated from the finest finishing school man ever knows, a school that doesn't give a fellow a parrot-like smattering of book knowledge, but a school that builds character.

After a while I went off a ways, rolled into my blankets and went to sleep.

The desert was crawling in the wind when I woke up, and the sand was whispering its ceaseless song of age-old mystery. Lying awake, I listened to it. I thought it was saying words. Then I became sure of it.

"—he doesn't know, but I know. I was so proud when you didn't say a word—"

I rolled over in my blankets. It was Catherine. She'd crawled out of her bed roll, and was whispering to me, knowing that I'd waked up.

"I back-tracked you," she said. "I thought it was funny you hadn't found Fred, and when I looked at the bullet holes I saw the direction was wrong. Old Charley kept looking up the slope, besides. So after a while, when Fred was busy with the ore, I crept up. You were lying asleep under a juniper. I saw the empty shells where you'd fired twice.

"But Fred thinks he did it, and that thought has done wonders to make him self-reliant. I'm so proud of you!"

And she kissed me. I squeezed her hand there in the midst of the whispering sand.

"He's a different man," I said to her. "He's a real man now."

She nodded. I could see her eyes above me, illuminated by an orange peel moon and the stars. Those eyes were the same as the stars above them.

"The desert's set its mark on him," she agreed.

Then she patted my hand and crawled back to her own blankets. The wind freshened and the whispering sand seeped through the sage, hissing its sibilants of sound as it went. And more delicate than all was the subtle whisper that began to permeate the night, the sound of sand slithering along sand, the pure sand whisper.

I lay and listened to it, and, finally, I dropped off to sleep, lulled by the lullaby of the whispering sand.

Catherine was right. The desert had set its mark on Fred Conway ... and they'd be happy, a desert woman and her desert man, their characters tempered in the cruel fires which, after all, are the kindest.

# LAW OF THE GHOST TOWN

I TOLD HIM that I didn't want the job of deputy, and he talked me into it.

"You're fearless, handy with a gun, know the desert, and know the men," he said.

When a man hands out that much of a line with a deputy badge, there ain't much to say except to take the badge. I took the badge. Bob Zane, deputy sheriff of Bodie!

Of course Bodie ain't much any more. There are a few of the old mines working, and mostly they're held by the old timers who have confidence in the future of the place only because they remember its past. Back in the early days, Bodie was a live town. Plenty live! They still talk about the Bad Man from Bodie. But now it squats up on the crest of a ridge, in a high depression, right up among the clouds, with the desert mountains all around it. The old buildings, built, for the most part, out of flattened tin cans, still stand.

Every once in a while there's some sort of a dispute, where men get personal; and I guess Bob Clark, the sheriff, sort of figured that he could save himself some trips over there to Bodie if he had a deputy residing on the ground.—Not that I was permanent. But I'd be there for a matter of six months yet.

This man Sellers drifted in, and I don't know just why it was I didn't like him. He certainly put himself out enough to be agreeable to me. I couldn't place him, yet I couldn't like him. He wore boots and breeches, which is usually the sign of a mining engineer or a tenderfoot in the desert. And he was interested in the Pinto Mountain district.

"I'd certainly appreciate it, Mr. Zane," he said, in that purring voice of his, "if you could introduce me to some one who is familiar with that Pinto district."

I started to ask him why; but asking questions is one thing the desert man ain't very good at, so I just nodded.

"There ain't nobody in town right now that knows that district," I told him. "But you stick around, and Tom and Harry will be driftin' in. They pick around those Pinto Mountains all the time."

He let his lips slide back far enough to show me a whole assortment of gold teeth. I started to tell him that if there was as much gold in the hills as there was in his mouth, the prospectors would sure get rich. But I didn't.

"Who," he wanted to know, "are Tom and Harry?"

"Prospectors—old timers. Harry's got a busted heart, and he's out forgetting it."

I don't know why I told him that. It was Harry's business, not mine—and certainly not this guy Sellers'. But there was a funny thing about the man's eyes—the way they rested on you, and all. They made you start telling things.

"Oh," he said, "he's a young man, then! I thought you said they were old timers."

"I did, and they are," I said, sort of nettled because I'd told him so much. Then, as he fastened those eyes on me again, I heard myself telling him more.

"It was back when the old Butterfly Dance Hall was running wide open," I told him. "There was a dance hall girl named Kate. Maybe she had another name; nobody ever heard it. She was just Kate. She was just the same as all dance hall girls, in lots of ways; and in lots of ways she wasn't.

"She got so she was like a big sister to the men. She encouraged 'em when their claims were petered out, or when the assay didn't show up so good; and she'd go out and nurse 'em when they were sick.

"Harry fell in love with her, and she fell in love with him. There was a gambler that wanted her, too. They all had it out one night, over in the Butterfly.—That's been forty years ago. Kate offered to go with Harry. She was quitting the dance hall racket. She loved Harry, all right, and Harry loved her. But Harry had some of the old New England notions in his head. He wouldn't marry her because she had been a dance hall girl—no matter how much he loved her.

"The gambler grabbed her in his arms that night. Harry walked out of the dance hall. She stayed there in the gambler's arms; but her eyes, over the gambler's shoulder, were watching Harry. He looked back at the door and saw her. Her eyes were all filled with tears. He tells about it—to his close friends.—He's been in the desert ever since, trying to forget."

Sellers flashed his gold teeth at me again. "A very pretty tale, Mr. Zane. And what happened to the girl from the dance hall? Was she happy with the gambler?"

"She didn't go with the gambler," I said, "not long enough to get married. Before the preacher came, the girl had gone—out into the desert perhaps. Harry realized his mistake then, and he tried to find her. He couldn't. Years later he struck it pretty rich, and he spent most of the money on detectives, trying to trace the woman. He never found her."

Sellers nodded. He seemed pretty satisfied with himself and superior—that smug sort of a superiority that a city man gets when he's talking with some one from the country.

"A dance hall girl wouldn't amount to much," he said.

"Don't ever lose sight of the fact that human beings are human beings," I told him. "And don't ever kid yourself that dance hall girls aren't human!"

There was a little edge on my tone. Kate had been in Bodie long before my time, but I'd heard stories of how she nursed the men—particularly the time there was an epidemic of smallpox in Bodie. Men who have lived their lives out in the open don't forget that sort of thing.

And then Tom and Harry showed up, right while I was talking with Sellers. I just had time to give him a word of caution.

"In talking with Tom," I told him, "don't ever let on that you know anything about Harry's history; and of course the same thing goes for Harry. And don't ever make any slurring remarks about dance hall girls when you're talking with either of them."

He surveyed the two figures coming down the dusty road, a string of burros behind them.

"You mean those two bums?" he asked. The word had slipped out without thought on his part. I doubt if he even knew he'd said it.

"Yes," I said, "the two gentlemen coming along here with the string of burros."

"Give me an introduction, will you?"

"You don't need one in this part of the world," I told him, "but you can sort of stick around when I start talking to 'em. When Harry gets lit up, he gets to thinking it's still the old days, and he goes and digs up his six-gun and cuts her loose. As the representative of law and order in these parts, I've got to have a talk with him."

And I moved forward.

They recognized me when I was forty or fifty yards away, and Harry let out a whoop. Tom was the quiet one, almost taciturn, even with those he knew best. Harry was more of a mixer.

I grinned, walked up and shook hands all around. They looked at Sellers, and he showed them his mouthful of gold teeth. I explained Sellers. "A newcomer," I told them. "Interested in the Pinto Mountain country. I told him you could tell him anything he wanted to know about that territory."

Sellers showed them the teeth again.

Harry whipped off his old Stetson, slapped it against his leg. A cloud of white dust flew up.

"See that dust, stranger?" he asked.

Sellers nodded.

"Well," said Harry, "that there's dust from the Pinto Mountains; and so help me, stranger, there's a hell of a lot left where that came from!"

He laughed, a dry, desert cackle.

Sellers waited just a tenth of a second too long, and then he joined in the laugh with a well-groomed haw-haw.

I took Harry off to one side.

"Harry, how long you been on the wagon?"

"Five years," he said. "When I get too much of the stuff, I get to thinkin' Bodie is back in the boom days an' I strap on my six-gun an'—"

"I know," I told him. "Going to get drunk this time?"

He shook his head. "Why?" he wanted to know.

"Because," I told him, "I'm the law in these parts now."

He looked me over, and I could see the little wrinkles around his desert-bleached eyes begin to deepen.

"Well," he said, grinning, "they're sure as hell careless

who they get for dep'ties around here!" And he reached out and gripped my hand.

I knew then I wouldn't ever have any trouble with Harry. I looked over at Tom. He and Sellers had gone into a huddle, and Tom was showing him some specimens of rock that they'd brought from the Pinto Mountain country. Sellers was shaking his head gloomily.

I said a few words to Tom, and then went on. Sellers stayed behind.

Late that night, I heard the sound of a gunshot. Then there was a whoop and a couple of more shots. I rolled out of my blankets and reached for my gun. Three more shots rang out quick, and I heard the bullet from one of them as it tore into the tin of a building across the street.

I began to poke around the streets. Bodie is a ghost town. There are a few people who live there, but for the most part they're the holdovers of a past generation. The buildings are all ghosts—ghosts with strange memories. Walking through the silent streets at midnight, I felt like a man prowling around in a cemetery.

I saw a man running. He saw me and slowed to a walk. I crossed over to him. It was Sellers.

"You're up late," I told him.

The starlight showed me his face well enough so that I could tell he was making teeth at me again.

"You folks may consider twelve-thirty late. In the city, I don't usually go to bed before one or two."

I looked down at his hand. "Hear any shots?" I asked.

"No," he said. "Were there shots?"

"Six," I said. "What you got in your hand?"

"A rock," he said.

"Rock?"

"Yes. I—er—I picked it up. I was a little afraid to be walking home through the dark streets unarmed, so I picked up a rock."

He tossed it away into the darkness. It hit with a *plump* in the dust of the road. There weren't any more shots.

"I'll walk up to where you're going," I said. "Then you won't have to pick up any more rocks."

There was whisky on his breath.

We walked up to the place where he was staying. He said good night, and didn't seem very cordial about it. I wasn't any more cordial than he was. After he had gone in I went back to where he'd tossed the rock.

I groped around for a while in the dust of the road, and then I found it. It was heavy. I took it home.

In the morning I looked at it. It was just rock, as far as I was concerned, only it was awfully heavy. I put it away and looked around town.

A little later I saw Tom. He looked kind of sheepish.

"I heard some shots last night," I told him.

He was anxious. "Nobody was hurt?" he asked.

"Not that I heard of," I told him. "Don't you know?"

"No, how should I know?"

"That's right," I told him, and then I waited a few seconds so that it would seem just significant enough.

"Where's Harry?" I asked.

He stared at me. "Don't you know?"

"No. Why?"

"Nothing, only I—er—I kinda thought that maybe you'd taken him and put him to bed somewhere. You know—sort of locked him up for something."

"What would I lock him up for, Tom?"

"I don't know."

"Neither do I."

He looked at me for a few seconds.

"When you see him," I said, "tell him that I want to talk with him."

He fidgeted around a bit. "I guess I got a new partner," he blurted.

"New partner?"

"Yes. In a way. It ain't a partner—not a general partner—just a partner in a prospect. It's a funny sort of prospect, too. Sellers was telling me how much he knew about certain formations in the Pinto Mountains. We had some funny rock I'd picked up there. We came on a ledge of it. It looked ordinary, but it was awfully heavy. We filed on it, just to be doing something.

"I showed Sellers the rock and asked him if he knew what it was. He said it didn't amount to much. He wouldn't give five cents for a carload of it. But last night Harry sold his interest in that claim.—Leastwise, Sellers said he did. —Sellers said he was called in as a witness. Harry was selling out to some chap Sellers said was named J. Stanley Petersen. He says he was called on to sign the instrument as a witness."

"J. Stanley Petersen!" I said. "Who's he?"

"I don't know. I thought you would know."

"I never heard of him."

"Uh-huh," said Tom.

He kept shuffling around in the dusty road. He had nothing else to say. Nevertheless he stuck around. I knew there was something on his mind. For the space of a cigarette or two, we sat and looked at the cloud shadows on the hills. Then Tom said what had been on his mind.

"Somebody got into my saddle bags last night."

"Steal something?" I asked.

"Ore samples," he said.

I thought for a while. "Take a walk with me," I told him, and led him up to the place where I had my blankets. I picked up the rock that Sellers had been carrying, tossed it over to him.

"Ever see that before?"

His eyes bulged. "Gee," he said. "That's a piece of that Pinto rock."

"Stolen from your saddle bags?" I asked, getting ready to

get some action that would pull the lips of Sellers down over his gold teeth for a while.

He shook his head. "No. That's the piece that came from Harry's pocket. He was carrying that piece around with him. Just sort of trying to find out what it was. I had some bigger specimens. Those were the ones that were stolen."

"You don't know where Harry is?"

"No."

"Didn't I once hear you boys say something to the effect that you had some sort of an agreement by which Harry had only forty-nine percent of a claim?"

"Oh, we had some sort of an agreement that Harry'd have forty-nine per cent. I was to have control. That was because Harry was impulsive at times."

"Okay," I told him. "I'd remember that. When this J. Stanley Petersen shows up, I'd be sort of hard-boiled. I don't think I'd do anything that he wanted me to do. I'd be inclined to keep the mine undeveloped, if he wanted to develop it. And if he wanted to bring in capital, I'd prefer to sit tight with it, see?"

His face lit up. "You'd be a witness that Harry only had a forty-nine per cent interest in our partnership?"

"I'd be a witness," I told him. "I remember you boys talking about that other claim. Maybe a lot of it was kidding, but I remember what was said. I can even repeat the words, though I can't repeat the tone of voice."

"That's white of you, Bob Zane," he said, and shook my hand.

"When you see Harry, tell him I want to have a talk with him," I told him as I walked away.

I took the rock sample back and put it in my blanket roll, and then I sort of skirmished around. I didn't find any one who had ever heard of J. Stanley Petersen, nor did I see anything of Harry.

That night it looked as though Harry had folded up and

gone somewhere. Nobody'd seen him all day. It was funny.

I unrolled my blankets late and crawled in. Something seemed to be hitting my mind in connection with those blankets. I couldn't go to sleep right away, thinking about it. Then I remembered. It was that bit of rock. I'd put it in the blanket roll.

I got up and looked around for it. It was gone.

J. Stanley Petersen showed up. He was a flat-chested guy with guinea-pig teeth, and eyes that blinked out from behind thick smoked glasses. It was hard to see into his eyes, back of those glasses.

He had the bill of sale, all signed by Harry and witnessed by Sellers. Sellers claimed he didn't know the man at all, that he'd just seen him talking with Harry, and that Harry had asked him to sign his name as a witness to the transfer of a claim.

Sellers said he asked Harry if he knew just what he was doing, and that Harry had taken him off to one side and whispered that the rock didn't have anything in it. It was just heavy, and Petersen was a tenderfoot with a chunk of money to invest. He'd gone crazy over the rock merely because it was heavy, and he had been willing to pay some real money for Harry's interest.

That was the same story that Petersen gave. It was a question of the word of two men against that of nobody. Harry's signature was genuine, all right. Tom admitted that. And that was all that counted—that signature.

They found out about the fifty-one per cent owned by Tom. The instrument that Petersen had drawn up merely called for a sale of all of Harry's interest in the mine.

Petersen had ideas about operation. Tom was convinced that those ideas weren't any good. After a while, Petersen got the idea. Tom was going to play a game of opposites with him. Anything Petersen wanted Tom didn't. Anything Petersen mentioned that he didn't want, Tom was for. That made a deadlock.

By that time, almost everybody in the whole camp was interested in the thing, from a standpoint of seeing what was going to happen next. Opinions were divided about the rock. Most of the boys had seen the samples. Some of them thought that Petersen and Sellers were a pair of slick ones who were looking for something, and that they'd stumbled on to what they were looking for, in the rock that Tom and Harry had brought in. But those people had to admit that Petersen seemed to be a fool and that the rock didn't seem to have any possibilities.

There was also the gang that figured Petersen and Sellers were plain fool tenderfeet who had gone ahead and bit off something that they didn't know anything about chewing. Every one suspected that Petersen and Sellers knew each other, and had known each other when the deal was made—in spite of the fact that they claimed they'd been strangers.

Over all there brooded the blue-black sky of the desert, the desert silence, and the little whispering winds that sent the sand scurrying along on the wings of the wind, making mysterious whispers against the sagebrush as it hissed its way across the desert.

Tom did the logical thing, of course. He started back into the Pinto Mountain country to get some samples of the ore. He was going to have them taken to a first class assayer and find out exactly where he stood.

He outfitted his burros, and started down through the cañons, and over toward the barren, heat-distorted ridges. Just before he went, Petersen came to him with an offer. He'd give a thousand dollars cash for the outstanding fifty-one per cent.

Tom came to me to get my advice. I didn't have any. It

was a gamble. All I was interested in was the mystery of this missing rock—and the whereabouts of Harry.

So Tom turned down the offer and plodded on out into the desert. The town of Bodie settled back into its patient waiting.

The old ghost camp had waited for years. Time, there, seemed to be different from what it was in the bigger places. The whole camp seemed to have been sucked into the patient silence of the desert. Clocks didn't seem to measure time there any more; time was something that couldn't be measured. The future was all mixed up in the present, and the past dominated both. You can't describe it. It's the rhythm of eternity which sways everything in the desert.

Tom didn't come back, but Harry showed up. He came into the camp one day, clear-eyed and thin-lipped.

People questioned him about the sale of the mine. He looked at the instrument of sale, and nodded his head. That was all. When he was questioned as to where he'd been or what he'd done, his lips just got the tighter. He seemed to have taken over Tom's nature. He wasn't the loquacious one any more; he was taciturn and broody. He kept looking into the purple distances, looking over toward the Pintos.

Then he came to me. He sat on his heels in the shade for a while, rolling a cigarette, getting it to burn, seeping smoke out through the corners of his tight lips. I knew he had something to say, so I waited patiently.

After a while he fished into his pocket. "Bob," he said, "I'm going to give you something that no one else has got."

"What's that?" I asked.

"Knowledge of the exact place where Tom went," he said. And he pushed a map into my hand, a map that was all tied up with various landmarks. I saw he'd taken a lot of time making that map.

"You sold your interest in the mine," I said.

He nodded, "I sold what interest I had," he admitted.

"Then these others must know just where the mine is."

Crow's feet sprang up all around the edges of his eyes. "That instrument of sale was hurriedly drawn," he said. "I was dead drunk when I signed it. But I left right afterwards. I'm bound by what's in that instrument, that's all."

"Well?" I asked.

"That claim ain't been recorded," he said. "Tom was the owner of the controlling interest, and he didn't want to record it."

"Do you mean to tell me that Petersen doesn't know where the mine is—the mine in which he owns a forty-nine per cent interest?"

He looked at me and grinned. "I ain't telling you anything," he said, "except the route that Tom took and the place he was to go to. I want you to go look Tom up."

"Look Tom up?"

"That's what I said."

"Why?"

"Because he's been gone too long."

I thought that over. "Tom's a desert-wise individual," I told Harry. "He doesn't need to have some one ride herd over him every time he gets off the beaten track."

Harry was obstinate. "I wish," he said, "that you'd look him up. Certain people have been looking around, getting data on Tom's full name and who his heirs would be if anything happened to him."

I whistled. "Are you sure?"

"Of course I'm sure. There ain't all the cards on the table in this deal. For certain reasons, I've got to stay here. I can't leave. I'm telling you that I wish you'd take this route that Tom took—and see what you find. I've got a string of burros all ready to start."

He didn't say any more after that. He'd made his point, and that was all there was to it. He sat on his heels and smoked.

I smoked a cigarette in silence, thinking it over. Then I got up.

"Where are the burros?" I wanted to know.

"I've got 'em down a cañon where no one will see 'em. You can start any time you're ready."

"I'm ready," I said, getting up.

He led the way. The string was all packed. I swung into the saddle and moved down the cañon. By nightfall I was in the real desert, down off the real high places, and into the high barrens. I was still over a mile above sea level, but I was steadily working downward.

The next day was a torture of heat. But I was used to the desert. The horizons danced a devil-dance. Here and there, black buzzards were dots against the deep blue of the sky. I kept plugging along.

That night the desert started to talk. Unless you've heard it, you'll never realize how the desert talks. The sand slithers along on the wings of the sudden night winds that spring up, and the whole face of the desert becomes alive with sand whispers. Rolled out in your blankets, under the stars, clasped to the bosom of the desert, you can almost hear the desert breathe and talk.

I drifted off to sleep with the desert whispering; and perhaps it was the sound of the sand, perhaps just my imagination, but I dreamt of the old romance between Harry and the dance hall girl. I seemed to be living through the moment when she had given Harry his choice and Harry had turned his back on romance and love.

The desert had known the emptiness of his heart. The desert must have known of the dry bitterness of his hatred of the man who had taken the girl he loved. Too late, he had found out what that love meant to him, how much of his life it was.

Then I slept more soundly, awaking to find the desert graying to dawn. I got the string in, packed, and was away while it was still cool.

Before the sun was up an hour, I found him. There was a pile of bones; there were the remnants of a pack—empty canteens—all the signs of a desert tragedy. It looked as though he'd lashed himself to his burro when he found himself giving out, so that the animal could lead him to water. But neither animal nor man had made it.

It was pretty late to read trail, but I did the best I could. Those canteens interested me. I couldn't see how a man like Tom ever would have allowed himself to run out of water in the desert—not unless there'd been some very unforeseen accident. I looked the canteens over.

I shook out dry sand particles. Those sand particles were on the inside of the canteen. That's a trick that's been worked, off and on, by men who are human fiends and who have wanted to murder without the danger of being caught, or risking a face-to-face conflict. Fill a man's reserve canteens with dry sand. The weight is there, and he thinks he's packing a reserve supply of water. When he goes to fill up his smaller canteens, he finds he's out of water in the middle of the desert.

I squatted down by the bones and thought things over. Then I started back for Bodie. And I made it a lot quicker than I'd made it on the road out. I was pushing the burros for all they were worth. I was in a hurry. I thought I was beginning to get the answer.

Finally I swung down the pass from the divide and into the plateau, the cup-like depression which marks the location of the ghost city.

On the street I found one of the old prospectors. I tried to make my tone casual, and asked for Harry. He chuckled.

"Gettin' ready for a shootin'," he said.

I stiffened. "Yeah?"

"Uh-huh. You know how he used to be with liquor. Well, he's gone the same way again. That taste he had that night loosed the fire in his blood, I guess. He's taken up with some new chap that's here, and they've hoisted a few, just in moderation. But to-night they started out goin' after their hooch serious.—And, say! Guess who's in town? Lita Cooper!"

"Who?" I asked, my mind on Harry. "Who is Lita Cooper?"

"She's Tom's daughter. Nobody ever thought much of his last name, but it was really Cooper. And his daughter's out here for a visit. Seems like somebody got up a contest of some kind and put up a prize of a trip to the old mining camp of Bodie. She knew her dad was out here, and she entered the contest—and won.—We never heard of the contest out here, but Lita won it, and she's here. This guy with the gold teeth is showing her around the town—the old buildings and all that stuff."

I digested that information. The contest had probably seemed innocent enough to Lita. She had inherited the old man's mine, though it couldn't be worth much. She controlled a fifty-one per cent interest.

She'd come to town; Harry was drunk; and Sellers was piloting her over the town. It didn't look like a good combination to me, and it didn't look like just an accident, either. It had all happened with too much regularity, too much purpose.

I didn't have enough on Sellers to arrest him. I couldn't prove anything. I could only think. But I was thinking a lot, and I could get to the girl before she signed any papers. That'd help.

I started looking for this daughter of Tom's. Half-way down the street I got the news. She'd signed some papers. It had all been conducted as if it was a joke. They'd persuaded her to sit in one of the old office buildings and sign away all of her rights to any mine she might own. It had been a grand lark. No one knew exactly what was in the paper she had signed. She hadn't even read it herself. Sellers had flashed his gold teeth, and it had been handled like a lark all the way through.

I started on the run. Some one said they were down in the old Butterfly Dance Hall. That's a part of the city that's truly deserted, and almost nobody ever goes there except an occasional straggler from the outside who wants to see what the town once looked like that produced the most notorious badmen of the West. I had the district to myself.

Then I heard laughter and the shuffle of feet in the old dance hall.

I pushed my face up against a window. She was trim and well formed, and she was laughing. She was dancing with Sellers, just a few steps of a dance without music. Presently they paused and made bows to an imaginary audience. Their faces were smiling, the girl's with the joy of life and of youth, Sellers with that smirk that an older man has when he's trying to act young, and when he's just put something across.

And while I was watching, I saw another face against a window on the other side. It was Harry's distorted face, and he was crazy drunk. I could tell it. He stared with reddened, glazed eyes, then he lurched around to the front door and walked in.

"There you are!" he bellowed.

Sellers looked at him, and his face lost the glitter of gold teeth. Though it was moonlight, I could see the thing indistinctly. When I'd first seen Harry, the moon had been shining strong on his face. When he walked inside I could see pretty well, but not well enough.

Things happened so quickly then that I didn't have a chance to get caught up with events until they'd moved on to become a part of other events.

Harry weaved across the floor. "I've been looking for you, Caspar Moray, for years. You've got her with you, too! They said you'd treated her bad. Maybe it's so.—Hand her over. She's mine!"

It flashed on me then. Harry, drunk as a lord, had been put away some place with the idea that he must be kept out of the way. He had broken loose, come to the dance hall, and was reënacting the scenes of the old tragedy that had ruined his life. The man in the center of the floor was the gambler, so far as Harry was concerned, and the woman was Dance-Hall Kate.

I wondered if she had looked like this, that Dance-Hall Kate, back in the dim long ago when the town of Bodie had been a roaring camp. If she had, she'd been a mighty attractive woman—slender and willowy with energy and life force, her every motion a thing of grace.

Then, suddenly, Sellers seemed to get the idea. "Harry," he said, "you are crazy. I'm your friend. This isn't the old Bodie. This is the ghost city!"

Harry weaved on his feet, laughed scornfully, waved a hand around at the cobwebby walls. "Yeah! And all these people, this dance orchestra. These gambling tables—they're just things that ain't, huh?"

Sellers tried to explain. Then he saw Harry's crouching attitude, his hands holding the rigid fingers wide-spread, crooked, like claws, the right hand hovering over the butt of the big, holstered forty-five that swung at his right hip.

Sellers made his fatal mistake. He went into a panic, and his hand streaked for his hip pocket.

There in the vivid desert moonlight I had a chance to see things as they had been in the old days. I saw Harry's hand streak into motion so swift that you could hardly see it. The gun was a single-action. I couldn't see the mechanics of the draw, nor the way the gun was cocked. But I could see Seller's snub-nosed automatic, the deadly weapon which modern science has perfected for the killer, come out and spit into action. There was no question but what that small, light, well-balanced automatic handicapped Harry at the outset.

Yet Harry's skill and speed actually made up for that handicap! The single-action roared, and the automatic spat. Of course, I couldn't be quite certain, but it seemed to me that the shots from the single-action crashed out even faster than the shots from the automatic.

This much was certain: they were more accurate.

Ever see a man get shot? The bullets sound with a peculiar *thunk!* as they plunk into him. The dust whips up from his clothes in a fine powder, a twisting bit of dim white that spirals upward.

There were three of those little white spirals in the air about Sellers before he went down. Then he went hard.

The woman screamed and ran from the building. Harry laughed, a demoniac laugh of triumph, lurched forward and fell into a drunken stupor. He was unhurt.

I caught the girl. "Listen, Lita, I was your father's friend," I said.

She struggled against me. "Let me go, let me go! It's awful. It's murder!"

I held her by main force, and calmed her until I didn't need to use force.

"Promise me you'll do this much," I said. "Go to your room and say nothing. This man Sellers murdered your father."

She gasped. "Father—!"

I gave it to her, straight from the shoulder. If she was Tom Cooper's daughter, she'd have the old stuff in her, I knew. She'd be able to take it on the chin. I handed it to her straight.

She did take it on the chin, though she became very white, very silent. She promised she'd do as I said.

I walked into the dance hall. Sellers was dead. Three shots had hit him. My hat brim would have covered all three.

Harry was just drunk—crazy, blind, stupid drunk.

I went through Seller's pockets. I found the paper signed by the girl. I took it and put it in my pocket. The rest of the things I left as they were.

Getting Harry onto my shoulder was a job. I hoisted him and walked slowly through the shadows. I didn't put him down on the ground until I was three hundred yards from the place. Then I took his old gun and belt. There was the ruins of an old mine there. The shaft had partially caved, but there was an opening, a black hole in the ground. The timber had rotted, and no one would think of going down there now. I tossed Harry's gun and belt down there.

After a while I went back to Lita. I told her the whole story. She was Tom Cooper's daughter, all right; she just clamped her lips together and listened.

After that, we went out and walked up and down the street, casually, so that no one would think she'd last been with Sellers.

They didn't find Sellers until the next noon. How he'd died was a mystery. But the gun was in his hand, and he'd been shooting at some one.

They notified me. I notified the sheriff. He came over by fast machine.

Harry came awake eventually, and I handed him the news. "Sellers is dead," I said. "Somebody shot him."

He stared at me with sagging jaw.

"Gosh!" he said. "That changes things! Thank heaven I got two alibis. The first is, I was too drunk to move. The second is that I couldn't find my gun.

"You know, sometimes when I get on a spree I start shootin' up the town. This time I couldn't find any gun when I woke up."

I nodded, and told him of finding Tom and of Lita's being in town. His bloodshot eyes narrowed.

"A frame-up," he said. "They knew she was coming, and

they got me drunk so I'd be out of the way. She didn't sign anything, did she?"

I shook my head. "She signed some foolish papers, but it was just a prank. There wasn't anything on the paper except a Mother Goose rhyme."

He took a deep breath. "Well," he said, "now I can tell you—"

I interrupted. "That you got drunk before and sold your mine interest. You knew something was fishy about it, and so you went into Tom's saddle bags while he was asleep, got the rest of the ore samples, dusted out, went across the desert to an assayer some place, had 'em assayed, found out the mine was rich in some rare form of ore that the ordinary prospector doesn't know about, came back here to tip off Tom—and found he'd gone."

He stared at me. "How'd you know?"

"I just guessed," I said. "You've said nothing about it, and I wouldn't. You can tell Lita. She's a daughter of Tom."

He straightened. "I'll go to her," he said. "That ore was tellurium. It didn't look like gold, but it's really rich with it."

I went over and met the sheriff. We went over the ground of the shooting pretty carefully.

He looked at me. "Funny. They tell me they heard the shots. But Harry was drunk, and he always shoots up the town when he gets drunk. Only, it's the old part of town, where the life used to be, and where nobody lives any more. So they let him shoot. They figured the shots were from Harry's gun."

"Yeah," I said. "He was too drunk to move, though, and he ain't seen his gun for a long time. It's missing."

The sheriff stroked his chin. "I hate to have a plain case of murder go unsolved," he said.

I thought of the bones out there on the desert. "Oh, I don't know," I told him. "This ain't like a city. The desert has its own way of settling things. Probably Sellers fired the first shot at whoever did it. He had his gun in his hand, and he'd shot three times."

Bob Clark sighed. "For a deputy," he said, looking me over, "you somehow take a funny view of the shooting. If you'd been on the job, you'd have investigated those shots."

I unpinned the star and handed it over.

J. Stanley Petersen faded out of town. They never saw him again. After a while, the owners of the fifty-one per cent interest in the mine froze out the outstanding minority interest. Harry's got that interest now. He doesn't get drunk any more.

The town of Bodie still lays sprawled in the sunlight, with the desert winds whispering across the sand just as it always has. The desert has ways of her own of doing things.

Some people might think that it was all a part of some scheme of things, the way Harry's heart was broken in the old dance hall, the way they tried to get rid of him when Lita came to town by getting him drunk, and the crazy notion that made him go back to the old dance hall and start shooting.—I don't know. I just know what happened.

# THE LAW OF DRIFTING SAND

## 1. A Sample of Ore

OUT TO THE WEST stretched the desert, silent, inscrutable, cruel. The town hung to the edge of the desert. It was a gold town; the place lived, breathed, ate and thought gold.

Men came to this town, stayed for a space, then were drawn out into the grim silence of the desert, just as iron filings are drawn to a magnet. Some came back. Some didn't. Occasionally the desert would give up a part of its hoard to some favored one. Occasionally the buzzards would circle over a staggering figure that ran aimlessly, its swollen tongue turning black, its glassy eyes staring at the white expanse of glittering torture.

Such is the way of the desert.

There were hard-bitten men in that little desert town.

They were the men who had learned much of the laws of the desert. They had been tempered in a furnace heat, and they had survived. There were also the bloated, soft parasites who fed upon those who work, and tenderfeet who were being tempered by the desert fires.

The man who came in on the stage from Las Vegas was new to the desert. That much could be seen in his sun-tortured visage. His skin was crimson, the bloodshot rims of the eyes had gazed too long upon white wastes. He had not stood the trip well.

There was a scar on his forehead, a jagged, irregular scar, and the blistering sun had made that scar stand out as a white star against the red of his forehead. Except for that scar he would have been considered handsome, judged by the standards of the ballroom. He had an erect figure, a certain self assurance, a jaunty set to his head which even the long stage trip hadn't conquered— and the trip by auto-stage from Las Vegas was cruel beyond belief to those who had never been adopted by the desert.

He came in to the Pay Dirt Café as I was eating. He hitched himself aboard one of the high stools, planted an elbow on the imitation mahogany counter, and grinned familiarly at Bessie O'Day.

He was good looking and young, not over twenty-five at the most. His manner was that of one who is accustomed to having women fall all over themselves being nice to him. His voice was deep, richly resonant, the sort of a voice that stirs the romantic thoughts in a woman's breast. There was just a little undertone of harsh selfishness in that voice, but that note was almost drowned out by the rich resonance.

"Roast beef, and a smile," he said.

He got them both. The smile was only a lip smile, but he didn't notice that.

"Know a man named Bloom?" he asked the girl as he picked up knife and fork.

"Harry Bloom? He's dead," said Bessie. "He was murdered. Somebody ambushed him and killed him with one shot from a rifle."

The man with the scarred forehead shoved in another mouthful. "Yeah," he said indifferently. "How'd it happen?"

Bessie's eyes were troubled.

"Nobody knows. Harry Bloom had been out on a prospecting trip. He was coming back. From the way his packs were arranged, and the stuff that had been thrown away, the old timers figured he'd made a strike and was bringing in the gold. They don't know. Somebody shot him, not ten miles from town. They found his body, lying just as it had been pitched down from the saddle. There was one bullet hole in the side of the head."

The man nodded. "What happened to his stuff?" he asked.

"You mean the burros, the saddles and the canteens?"

"Yeah. I guess so, whatever it was he had."

"The coroner took charge of it."

The young man speared the last of the roast beef, scooped the mashed potatoes on it with a swipe of his knife, opened his mouth and shoved in the whole thing.

"Wasn't there something else?" he asked. "Wasn't there an ore sample?"

She shook her head. "Not that I know of."

I joined the conversation.

"There was just one rock, and it wasn't ore," I said. "I saw them when they brought the body in. Harry Bloom had one jagged chunk of rock in his poke, and that was all."

The youth looked at me. "What happened to that?" he asked, scraping his plate with his knife, sliding the knife along the edge of the fork and swooping down on the fork with eager mouth.

"A Mex got it," I said. "Jose Diaz, the gambler. He thought there might be some charm in the thing, the only rock brought in by a murdered man."

The man with the scarred forehead pushed back his stool, sized me up.

"Yeah?" he said.

Bessie O'Day asked him a question.

"You interested in Harry Bloom?—Know him, or related to him or something?"

"Nope. Just read about the case in the newspapers," he said. "There was a paragraph. It mentioned the name of this place, and said it was one of the typical desert, wide-open mining towns. I thought I'd come on and see what a wide-open mining town looked like. I'm a curious cuss, myself."

And he flipped a half dollar on the counter and strode to the door.

Bessie looked at me.

I shrugged my shoulders.

"He's good looking—if it wasn't for that scar," she said.

"He looks like a matinée idol," I told her. "We'll wait and see what the desert does to him. So far as I'm concerned, it's character on a man's face that makes him handsome."

## II. A Good Investment

I saw him again that evening. He was over in the Miner's Retreat, talking with Jose Diaz. He was talking earnestly, as though he was trying to sell something, and Jose Diaz seemed reluctant.

The Miner's Retreat was one of those places. There was a bar and a stack of bottles behind the bar. There were some round tables in the back, covered with green cloth, and with hanging lights dangling from the ceiling over the tables. Men sat at those tables and played poker, hour after hour, night after night. There were men with pale complexions, nervous hands and big eyes. They always won. There were just two ways of making a living in the camp. Either make it from the desert, or make it from those who made their livings in the desert.

Jose Diaz finally went out. The man with the scarred forehead sat at the table, waiting. Poker games were going on all around him.

Diaz came back, his pocket bulging. He passed something over under the table.

The man with the scarred forehead made little shoulder motions as he turned the object over and over in his hands. He talked. I could see that his lips were speaking in numbers. The eyes of the gambler glittered with greed, but he shook his head.

After a while the man with the scarred forehead passed the mysterious object back under the table. Jose Diaz took it, crammed it in his pocket, got up, flashed his teeth in a grin, and went to a poker game.

The man with the scarred forehead got up, started for the door. Seeing me, he came over.

"I talked with you in the restaurant," he said.

"I remember," I replied.

He thrust out his hand. "Trask is my name. Fred Trask."

"Zane, Bob Zane," I said, and shook hands.

His hand was firm and strong. The fingers wrapped around my hand, gave a firm pressure. He was looking me straight in the eyes, but his voice was not so richly resonant as it had been in the restaurant. It had an undertone of harsh, grasping greed.

"I want you to do something for me," he said.

"What?" I asked.

"That Mex has got that bit of rock which came from the body of the murdered prospector. He won't sell it for anything reasonable. I can't get him to name a price, even. He's turned down twenty dollars. I don't want to arouse his suspicions, but I want that rock. I'll pay a hundred dollars for it, if I have to go that high. He knows I'm a greenhorn, and he's trying to hold me up. I want you to buy the rock for me."

He pushed over a roll of bills.

"There's the hundred. Get the rock, and you can keep the hundred. If you get it for any less, it's your profit."

"You offered him twenty?" I asked.

"That's all. Five at first, then ten, and then twenty."

"Where'll I meet you when I get the rock?" I wanted to know.

"Over at the hotel," he said. "And make it as snappy as you can."

"It's going to take a little while," I warned him. "I've got to wait until Jose has a run of poor luck at cards, and then I'll sit in the game and tear into him for all I can. I'll tell him he's having bad luck because the murdered man's ghost is haunting the rock."

His voice was impatient. "I don't care how you get it.—I want it."

I didn't like him and I didn't like his tone. But when a man comes to camp and offers to pay a hundred dollars for a chunk of rock that was the only thing which was found in the poke of a murdered prospector, I aim to get a look at that rock if it's at all possible. And buying this particular rock seemed about the only way I could get a look at it.

I'd seen it before, when they brought Harry Bloom's body in. The whole camp had seen it. But we hadn't thought anything of it. It was just a chunk of plain rock, and it wasn't even mineralized. It really wasn't rock, but conglomerate, hard, and jagged.

I strolled over to the table to watch Jose's luck at the cards. Jose grinned at me, scraped back his chair, flashed his teeth at me with a smile.

"He is a poor liar, that boy," he said.

I raised my eyebrows.

"Yes," he said. "And I saw him talking with you. He has asked you to buy the rock for him. No?"

I wasn't going to lie to Jose. "What if he did?" I asked.

He rippled a laugh. "He offered me twenty, fifty, seventy-five dollars," he boasted. "Am I a fool to sell a plain rock for that money? If the rock is worth that much it is worth more."

I was mad. Jose had his faults, but he wouldn't lie, not to me.

"So he offered you seventy-five dollars, eh?"

"*Si, señor*, he did that! And I told him that I would not sell for less than a hundred and twenty-five dollars."

I put my cards on the table.

"He told me he hadn't offered you more than twenty," I said. "He gave me a hundred to buy it with. I was to keep any difference."

Jose chuckled. He was in fine humor.

"Do you know why he did that?" he asked me.

"He said he thought you were trying to hold him up," I replied. "He said he thought I could buy it cheaper than he could."

Jose nodded. "He did it because I told him I would not sell the rock at all unless some one who was very expert upon the value of stones told me it was not worth money for the ore that was in it. He asked me if I thought you knew stones, and I told him that your judgment was good anywhere in the desert. That is why he went to you, *amigo*.

"But this matter has become very peculiar," he continued. "We will not trust to any one's offhand judgment. We will go to an assayer.—The only difficulty is that the man refused to pay anything for the rock if it was broken. Can you imagine that?—He is crazy, and he is a liar. He has tried to deceive you; therefore we shall put all of our cards down together. Come, and we will see Señor Garland, the assayer."

I nodded.

We hunted up Phil Garland, who is big, fat, good natured and honest.

"We've got to know what's in a rock, without smashing it up," I said.

Garland looked at us suspiciously, then led the way over to

his little office, in a shack with a galvanized iron roof, where he did most of his work at night. The place was too hot, daytimes.

We went in. Jose Diaz produced the rock. Garland took it in his hands.

"It's the rock they found in Harry Bloom's saddle bag, ain't it?" he asked.

I nodded. He sat down and looked at it.

"Funny," he said. "You know, I thought there might be something of value in this thing, and I looked it over pretty carefully for metal at the time it was found. I'll look it over again, though."

He sat down at his bench, put the rock on scales to weigh it. Then he took a glass jar, filled the jar with water, weighed the jar and the water, then dropped in the rock. A lot of water overflowed. Garland weighed the water that was left and the rock. He scratched his head.

He took the wet rock, studied it, dried it, looked at it with a magnifying glass, and shook his head.

"The darn thing is just a chunk of conglomerate," he said. "There's miles and miles of it around here. From the texture of this, though, I'd make a guess that it came from around Hole-in-the-Rock Springs. But there isn't any mineral in it, and there wouldn't be anything worth while even if there had been any mineral in it. It's nothing but a sort of natural cement, holding together a smear of round stones.—You can see the cement-like nature of the binding material, and these round pebbles are gripped here by a natural cement. They were picked up by the binding material a few million years ago; and the fact that one of the little rocks might be pure gold wouldn't mean anything at all, so far as mining operations are concerned."

Jose grinned at me.

"One hundred and twenty-five dollars, Señor Zane, and that is my limit. I am a gambler. The rock is worth nothing to me; but I know it is worth a hundred to the man with the scar on his forehead, and I think you are curious enough to invest twenty-five dollars of your own money."

I knew Jose. He was bluffing his way through, figuring, just as he said, that I would put in twenty-five dollars of my own money. But he was a good gambler. If I refused, he'd sit tight and hold that rock until he died.

"You are a good judge of human nature, Jose," I said, and handed him a hundred and twenty-five dollars.

"I have to be," he said, "in my profession."

He handed me the rock, pocketed the money, and went back to the gambling games.

I walked directly over to the hotel. They called it a hotel; it was really a ramshackle structure put up over a stone store, and divided into little cubicles. There was a pitcher and a bowl in each room, a table, a chair and an iron bed. Sheets were unknown.

Fred Trask was registered. He sat on the straight backed chair in his room, waiting. He'd picked up an iron mortar and a pestle from some miner, and he had it on the floor at his feet all ready for me.

His eyes lit up when he saw me bring in the rock.

"You got it?" he said.

"I got it," I told him. "But I found you'd offered more than twenty dollars for it."

"Who told you that?" he asked, reaching for the rock.

"Jose Diaz did," I said.

"He's a liar," said Trask, speaking easily, as though the words were of no particular import. He picked up the iron pestle and started mashing up the rock. It was pretty hard, and I noticed he struck light blows.

"Here," I said, reaching for the pestle. "You can't get anywhere that way. There's nothing in the binder, anyhow. If there's anything worth while, it'll be in some of the small rocks that . . ."

He pushed me away, snarling.

"Who's doing this?" he rasped, and his lips drew back from his teeth, his eyes glittered, and the deep timbre had entirely gone from his voice. The words were just barked out.

As he spoke, the pestle came down hard on the conglomerate and a piece broke off. That piece was a chunk that had a round pebble about the size of a very small potato in the center.

Something else rolled out, too: a chunk of pure gold. I've seen gold too much not to know it when I glimpse it. This was gold, all right; and it had a peculiar, rippled appearance. The nugget was as big around as a half dollar, and a little thicker. It was bent a trifle, and the top surface was all waves and ripples. The gold was all shiny and new looking on top. A strange looking nugget.

Fred Trask swooped for that bit of gold and scooped it into his hand. His eyes stared at me and were hostile.

"I knew that rock was mineralized," he said. "Now get out of here!"

I got out of there. I'd invested twenty-five dollars, and it was a worth while investment.

I waited around the hotel. Fred Trask came out in about fifteen minutes. His feet were pounding the ground like those of a man who's going places in a hurry. He went over to the Miner's Rest and got hold of the bartender. They chatted for a while, and then the barkeep called over Dick Rose.

Rose was a man who hung around on the edges and snapped up anything that offered a long profit with no investment. He wasn't scrupulous in his business dealings, and he'd had a couple of enemies who had been mysteriously shot from ambush. No one could prove anything on Dick Rose, and they didn't try particularly hard; but we local men all knew him and gave him a more or less wide berth. Not that we were afraid of him. It was just the way we felt toward rattlesnakes. We didn't like 'em.

Rose and Fred Trask had a drink. Then they went off into a corner and talked. Trask did most of the talking. He was voluble and convincing, but full of words. Dick Rose stared at him with eyes that were slitted and glistening. Eyes that glittered like diamonds through the blue haze of cigarette smoke.

After half an hour or so of talk, they had a couple more drinks. But Dick Rose kept his eyes half closed, and they still had that diamond hard glitter in them when the two men at length left the saloon.

### III. Auto Versus Burro

The next morning they were gone. They'd pulled out in the early dawn. Dick Rose had gone to the hotel with a string of burros and he'd had Sam Pitch along. Sam was an old buzzard who'd have shot his own grandmother in the back for fifty cents cash and a drink of whisky.

I thought over the fact that they'd pulled out. Then I went to the hotel, on a hunch, and looked around under the window of the room that Trask has occupied.

I found what I wanted, a bunch of rounded rocks and some jagged binder. It was the last of the pounded up conglomerate. I also found the piece that had clung to the big rock, the one that was the size of a small potato and had masked the chunk of gold. I examined that piece. Looking at it from the back side and in the daylight, it seemed different. The side that had been on the outside of the chunk of conglomerate looked natural; but there was a peculiar, colorless something on the back of the rounded rock.

I pocketed it and hunted up Garland. He was asleep, after a night of work, and some drink. I shook him awake.

"Take a look at this," I told him.

His eyes focused on the rock. "Banquo's ghost!" he said.

"Go on," I told him. "It may keep turning up, but there ain't no banquet."

"That's right," he said, and reached for his boots.

In his little office he looked the thing over more carefully.

"Well," he said, at length, "it's been doctored—salted and all that sort of stuff. But what the hell a man would want to salt conglomerate for is more than I know. Every once in a while you come on a piece where the sun or moisture has rotted the cement out of a round rock, so that that rock can be pulled out. That's what happened to this rock. Then somebody evidently hollowed out the chunk, working through the hole left by the removal of this little rock. The gold was then inserted, and this rock cemented back into place. That's what this stuff is that you see on the back of the round rock—cement."

"Thanks," I said. "Go back to sleep."

I handed him ten dollars, which gave me a thirty-five dollar investment in something that wasn't even a salted mine.

Of course, the purchase of the rock had made news in the little town, sprawled in the sun on the edge of the desert. Everything that pertained to gold had the highest news value. If this rock had been anything but conglomerate, there would have been some action. But when the boys figured it out, they figured that it was just another case of a tenderfoot going goofy.

I yawned and shrugged my shoulders. I didn't tell anybody about the gold, nor about the cemented rock. And I knew that Garland wouldn't talk.

I didn't want to leave too soon after Trask; so I waited until night, and then slipped out into the desert, taking advantage of a half moon.

The desert was cold and still, like the surface of some vast tombstone that stretched out cold in the moonlight. The utter silence, the lack of life, the big expanse of space gripped me. I always feel like that when I'm starting out into the desert. There's the sense of being all alone, yet not being alone.

# THE LAW OF DRIFTING SAND

A man comes to know himself when he's in the desert. Lots of himself is a lot littler than he ever thought, and a lot of himself is a lot bigger. It's the little part that shrivels away and the big part that grows and becomes company when a man gets out into the desert.

Unless, of course, a man's just naturally a little man all the way through, and then the little part comes leering out through the cracks of the character, sees the naked desert, and gets out of control, like the fabled genie that came out of a bottle.

I made camp when the moon went down, and got a few hours of sleep before the first crack of cold dawn. Then I got up the burros, lashed on the packs and started. I was headed in the general direction of the Hole-in-the-Rock Spring, and for the surface of the desert which lay down below the level of the sea. I was traveling fast, too, and I had a pair of powerful binoculars on the horn of my saddle.

The sun grew hot and the desert seethed in the dazzling glare of day. The last of the Funeral Range topped the sky before me. I swung through a pass and looked down on Death Valley.

I don't care how often a man sees Death Valley. When he looks down on it from the top of either the Funerals or the Panamints, something happens inside of him. It's as though his insides looped the loop and left him without any breath.

There weren't any tracks in the pass. I got the binoculars and looked down on the floor of the valley. Nothing moved. It lived up to its name, a valley of death. For many years now it had been luring men to destruction.

I swung the glasses in a survey of the passes, boring into the black shadows that seemed inky after the glittering flood of sand-reflected light.

Nothing moved.

Putting the glasses away, I went down into the valley. That

night I slept beneath the blazing stars. When they had receded to pin points with the coming of dawn, I was once more on my way. I was headed toward the north.

The heat robbed the air of oxygen. The hot air, rushing upwards, was as devoid of life giving qualities as the air which rushes up the flue of a furnace. I took it pretty slowly, which is the real way to make haste in the desert.

There was a queer, droning sound. At first I thought it was the sound of the blood pounding through the arteries in my ears. I stopped and listened. The sound came and went, droning into a crescendo of pulsating noise, then dying away. I looked upward, but I couldn't see any plane.

I paid no further heed to it, and plugged on. The burros wagged their ears, cast short shadows, inky black. I could feel the hot sand burning up through the soles of my shoes.

Then the sound came to me louder and louder. I knew it then for what it was, a motor toiling through the sand. The engine sounded pretty bad. There wasn't any road within a matter of miles. I wondered what sort of fool would push a car through the floor of the valley in the heat.

I rounded a spur of drifting sand. The car was ahead, a black dot against the shimmering outlines of the sand hills. It was coming toward me, and not making very much headway.

Four times, while I pushed on toward it, the motor stopped. Whenever it did that a black figure would run out to the front of the car. I knew what was happening; a man was pouring fresh water into the boiling radiator.

At last the motor gave a series of backfires. Something harsh and metallic made clanging noises, far louder than the roaring pulsations of the hot motor. It was a bearing. There was a moment or two of that noise, and then a terrific bang.

A dense cloud of white steam and smoke puffed out from the hood of the car like a mushroom, and then there was silence.

The car was still some distance away. I dipped down into a

wind ravine between two sand hills, and found firm footing. I followed the windings of that ravine.

After a while I figured I must be pretty close to the car. I angled up the slope of sand and found that it was less than two hundred yards away.

There were two figures out in front of that car, staring at it after the manner of stranded motorists the world over. It seemed as if they thought they could get the thing started just by staring at it, if they stared long enough and hard enough.

The sad truth dawned on them as I got within earshot.

"We've got to walk," said one of the figures. And I could tell from the voice that this one was a young woman, although she was dressed in boots and breeches.

The man's voice sounded frightened. "Walk *back*," he said.

"We can't be far now," the woman told him.

"But we're out of water, in the desert . . ."

Then the sound of slithering sand as my burro train pushed its way along the white hot sand hill carried to their ears. They turned and stared at me with big eyes.

They'd evidently been a day or two in the desert, and the sun had done things to their skins. The woman was of that brunette type that simply browns, and her face was as brown as a berry, her eyes big black pools. She had adapted herself naturally to the desert, but as far as her complexion was concerned, she'd soon come to look like an Indian.

The man wasn't of that type. He'd peel and blister. His face was swollen, red and painful. His eyes were watering. The lips were beginning to crack. Neither one of them was over twenty-five.

"Did you use all the water you had in filling the radiator?" I asked them.

The woman answered me, "Yes," she said. "The car took every drop. Then we ran out of water, and that's when it burned out the bearings."

I nodded.

"We've got to get out of the desert," said the man.

I'd heard people talk like that before. His words were coming rapidly, and his eye shifted a little bit as he talked. He was afraid, and the fear was getting bigger as he tried to fight it down.

"It's a long way to water," I said.

"Why, we passed a watering station not over two hours ago!" the girl said.

"Two hours in an automobile, and two hours walking are two different things, ma'am."

She thought that over, turned to look at the fellow who was with her. "Let me talk with you a minute, Ted."

He joined her. They walked forty or fifty yards away and started whispering. They pulled out a paper, started pointing, then rubbering around at the mountains that rimmed the valley. There were the Panamints on one side, and the Funerals on the other, and both ranges were dancing about in the heat, the horizons twisting and writhing grotesquely.

The woman reached the decision. I could see her lips snap out the words. Then the man nodded, and the woman came striding over toward me.

"Do you know this section of the desert?" she asked.

"I've been through it a few times."

"Do you know of a twisting cañon that makes a right-angled bend just beyond the shifting sand hills?"

I puckered my forehead. "I don't remember anything like that offhand."

She bit her lip. "How far are the drifting sand hills from here?"

"You're getting into 'em now, ma'am. They're off here to your right. I made a swing so as to avoid 'em."

She batted those big eyes of hers swiftly, then peered into my eyes steadily, searchingly. After a second or two she nodded her head.

"I'm Lois Beachley," she said. "The man with me is Ted

Wayne. We want to find that cañon over beyond the drifting sand. Some one sold me a site for a homestead somewhere over in there."

I kept my eyes on hers. "You mean a gold mine, don't you?"

Her eyes were steady, unwavering. "Yes, I mean a gold mine."

"It'd be a hard trip to get there. You'd have to travel light."

"I can travel light."

"I couldn't very well guide you there, ma'am. I'm sorry, but I got some business of my own down here. People don't come here this time of year unless they've got business."

I could see her eyes wince.

"How can we get there?" she asked.

"You can't. Not with that outfit you've got."

She sighed. "Well, then," she wanted to know, "how can we get back to water?" And that question showed me just where I stood.

"You can't, ma'am, not with the outfit you've got," I replied. "I guess I've got to take charge of you. My name's Bob Zane. I'll just let my own business go for a while."

I did some internal cussing, kissed a thirty-five dollar investment good-by, and wished to thunder they'd passed a law keeping tenderfeet and fools out of Death Valley after it warms up. Seems like I've tried to prospect some during my life, but I've never done over a few hours of it. Most of the time has been spent getting to the place I wanted to prospect, running out of grub, chasing burros, getting back and ready for another start, chasing more burros, and rescuing fool tenderfeet that go busting into the desert without knowing what they're there for.

"We'll pay you," she said.

I nodded. They could pay me, but never enough to make up for what I was missing. I had a hunch that the man with the scarred forehead had been pulling a fast one, another hunch that my thirty-five dollar investment, if played right, would have netted me a big return and given me the laugh on some of the wise guys at camp. But it was gone now. I had to chaperon these two tenderfeet to water; and by the time I'd done that, it'd be too late to do anything with the other. So I figured I might as well go whole hog as nothing, and guide 'em in to where they wanted to go.

They had the car loaded with the sort of provisions that weren't much good in the desert; heavy canned stuff, fruits that were put up in a heavy, sickeningly sweet syrup. There were only two cans of tomatoes.

"You should have brought more tomatoes and not so much sweet stuff," I said.

The girl stared.

Ted Wayne shook his head. "I like sweets," he said, "and I don't like tomatoes."

I shrugged my shoulders, took my knife and opened the cans of tomatoes. The way we were traveling, we weren't going to be able to load the burros with canned stuff.

The girl tackled the tomatoes without enthusiasm. Then, as she got a couple of swallows, her eyes brightened. She lowered the can.

"Why," she said, "they're delicious—the most wonderful things I ever tasted!" She passed the can over to Wayne.

He shook his head. "I'll taste 'em," he said. Then the aroma struck his nostrils. He took a gulp, looked surprised, and drained the can. We killed the other can in record time. Then I gave them their first lesson on the desert.

"When you get out in the desert you sweat a lot. That leaves a lot of acid stuff in the body. The only thing that'll cut that is the right kind of fruit. Tomatoes are better than anything I know of. Orange juice'd be great, only you can't carry it. Load up with canned tomatoes when you head for the desert. Now we'll start."

We started. I'd had to pack my saddle burro with the extra stuff I'd taken for the pair, and we were all walking. It wasn't pleasant walking. If there'd been any shade, I'd have given them a rest; but I knew the chap was going to be pretty well all in, and I wanted to haze him along before he got to the point where he'd blow up.

Starting the way I did, they'd have the cool of the evening for the last part of the drag. They'd need it.

## IV. WHISPERS

I HADN'T GONE A MILE before I saw what was happening. The desert was getting Wayne. He was afraid of it. Fear was in his eyes, in the too rapid steps which he took, in the frightened glances he gave over his shoulder, and in the way he kept trying to talk—not saying anything—just listening to the sound of his own voice.

The desert does that to people. The first time you see it, you're either afraid of it or else you feel a strange fascination for it. And when I say "see it," I mean get out in it. Anybody who whizzes through the desert on an improved road in an automobile, or rolling along in a shaded Pullman car, has never really seen it. The only way to see the desert is to get out on foot; out where the eternal silence grips you; out where the heat makes the horizons dance and the mirages glitter; where you get that feeling of being less than a needle point in the universe, and then feel that needle point shrivel away to nothing. A man has to fight to keep from feeling that he's going to shrivel on himself until there's nothing left. It's a funny feeling. You can't tell about it. You've got to experience it to know what it is.

But the girl looked at it the other way. She was one of those who sees the desert, likes it, and fits right into it.

The desert's that way. Some she adopts and takes to her breast without a murmur. Some she fights and burns, and strips away the veneer until she's got just the naked soul to deal with. Sometimes she rebuilds on the foundation of that naked soul, and sometimes the soul just shrivels and vanishes. The desert's the kindest mother a man ever had, because she's the cruelest. Things seem sort of out of place to us when they're cruel. That's because we're soft. But it's cruelty that develops character. Man learns by fighting.

I've seen men stand on the edge of the Grand Cañon and say that it was a manifestation of the Eternal, a temple of nature and so forth. It's all of that. It's God, showing himself. But those same people turn away with a shudder when they see a cat torturing a mouse. If they only knew it, there's just as much of God manifesting himself in that as there is in the Grand Cañon. It's the law of life.

The reason men don't know the law of life is because they're afraid to look Eternity in the face. Out in the desert they have to look at Eternity. It's on all sides of them; they can't turn their eyes away. That's the spell of the desert.

We got into the drifting sand in about an hour. Those are the sand hills that drift on the wind, marching across the face of the desert, always shifting, never stopping, a ceaseless slithering march of hissing sand.

Lois Beachley was dead game. She would have gone on until she dropped; and she was almost ready to drop. She hadn't accustomed her muscles to walking, and walking in sand isn't the same as walking on pavements. Wayne was stronger physically, but it was his nerve that I was afraid of. There was a light in his eyes that I didn't like. The girl was walking because she wanted to make good. The young man was walking because fear was spurring him on.

The sun was casting shadows from the big sand dunes. I dropped the outfit down into a little gully between the sand hills, where purple shadows broke the glare of the light.

"We camp here to-night," I said. "If you'll show me the

map, I think I can take you to the place you want to go tomorrow."

"Map?" said Lois Beachley.

"Yeah," I told her. "Don't think I'm a fool."

She hesitated a minute, then took out the map. It had been drawn in pencil. I looked at it and didn't say anything.

"How about water, for washing and drinking and washing dishes and all that?" asked Ted Wayne.

"Plenty of water for drinking, if you drink desert style. You can have a cupful to moisten a rag with, if you want to scrub off. Dishes won't get washed because they won't need it. We will scour 'em out with sand, give 'em a dry cleaning. Anyway, there won't be many dishes."

Wayne looked at me, and I could see the panic in his eyes. Lois dropped down into the sand, scooped out a little hollow and relaxed. I could see that her knees were pretty weak. I unsaddled the burros and looked around for firewood.

Firewood is a problem in those sand hills, though there are some places where sagebrush grows on stilts. Sounds funny, but that's exactly what it does. It begins to grow like ordinary sage. Then the wind comes along and blows the sand away from the roots. The sage pushes the roots down deeper into the sand, and the wind blows away some more sand. It gets to be a race between the sagebrush and the wind; the old struggle between life and death that characterizes the desert life everywhere you find it; whether it's human, animal or plant.

I got a little fire going. It wasn't over eight inches in diameter, for we had to be careful of fuel there in the desert. We had a supper that was perhaps less than they expected; but I knew it would keep their strength up. Most people eat too much anyway, and their bodies can't handle the poisons that are generated from the waste. But I can tell you when they're camping with me in the desert they don't eat too much.

The sun went down and the stars came out and silence

gripped the desert. The girl dropped off to sleep. Ted Wayne tried to keep talking. It's a way they have in the desert. When they make noises with their mouths they feel they're entities. When they keep quiet and the silence grips them, they can feel their souls shrivelling.

After a while sheer fatigue had its way. I got Wayne to lie on his blanket and talk. He got his words twisted, the talk got thick, and then quit altogether. He snored.

Damn him! He couldn't keep quiet even when he slept.

About midnight, just as the moon was getting pretty well down, the desert itself began to talk. The wind hissed the sand along, and the sand gave forth whispers. The desert always talks when the wind blows and the sand starts to drift along. Sometimes it's just the sand rustling against the dry leaves of sage or the stalks of cacti. But out in the land of the drifting sand hills, it's the sound of sand slithering along on sand, a hissing whisper that almost seems to make words and sentences.

Men that have lived long in the desert absorb its personality. They get gray of eye and their voices get that whispering undertone in them. Such men will swear to you that those sand whispers mean something. They'll tell stories of hearing the sand say things they can understand, just when they're dropping off to sleep.

I lay in my blanket and listened to the sand whispers as the moon slid down. I like to hear the soft sound of slithering sand rustling along on sand; a dry, hissing whisper that's only heard in the desert.

I knew Wayne was awake because I could hear him move, and he'd quit snoring. Then I thought I heard a distant voice. It wasn't a whisper. It sounded human. And there seemed to be steps sounding through the noises made by the sand.

I sat up. I'm not overly given to imagination, and I certainly thought I'd heard steps.

I rolled out of the blankets, pulled on my boots, and started slipping along the little ravine between the two big sand hills where I'd made camp. When I got a hundred yards from camp, I climbed up on top of the ridge. The desert stretched out, silent and desolate. The sand hills were like the waves of some great white ocean, lashed mountain high, and then suddenly frozen. The moon was just angling down the edge of the Panamints.

I thought I saw specks off to the southwest, specks that moved, black things that were just moving into the black rim of the surrounding night. Then the moon dropped out of sight, and there was a hushed blackness that gripped everything. I sat and listened, and the night got darker and darker. Then I heard steps again.

This time there could be no mistake. They were running steps, and they were close. They crunched in the sand, floundered down hills, toiled up hills, swung to the left, circled, came toward me.

I crouched. I could hear the running body, the thudding crunch of the feet, even catch the panting intake of the laboring breath. Then a shape loomed up against the glow of the sky.

"Ted Wayne," I said, "come here."

He gave a mighty bound. A wild deer couldn't have been more startled, nor given a quicker reaction to fear.

Then he stopped, quivering, gasping.

"Come on over here," I repeated, keeping my voice perfectly normal, not showing that I felt there was anything at all unusual about a man running around in the desert. "I'm afraid our outfit's been stolen."

The words brought him to me, panting, shivering; but the full significance of those last words, about the outfit having been taken, did not register.

"I couldn't sleep," he said.

"Sit down," I told him.

He sat down.

"Now just why," I asked him, "should any one want to follow us and steal our outfit?"

He didn't answer that question. He sat there, panting and quivering, like a horse that's just begun to run a race and has then been pulled out of it.

He didn't answer me, and I didn't say anything more. He got his breath. The desert got blacker and blacker until only the very faintest tinge of gray marked the outlines of the sand hills, which were now illuminated only by the light of the stars. Then he burst out into speech, and his words were the words of panic.

"It's got me! I'm a coward—I'm a failure! Lois sees that I'm a coward, and she's scornful. I can't help it. It's too big. It's too God-awful empty. The silence, the big spaces, the cruelty of it! Then, when the wind comes, the sand starts to mock me. It whispers threats to me, makes me feel that it's lying in wait for me!"

He stopped his mad torrent of words, choked back a sob, and flung himself erect, poised, ready to start running again, seized by that blind panic which grips men when they find their entities slipping from their grasp, being absorbed in the Infinite.

I began to talk to him, to make soothing sounds, not caring particularly what I said, but knowing that the mere sound of my voice would hold him, just as a trainer talks to a highly strung race horse.

"Did you ever hear of the law of drifting sand?" I asked him. "The noises you heard when the wind blew were the noises of the marching sand hills. They keep moving—at the rate of half a mile a year. It's all been figured out.

"The railroads wanted to run through the desert, and the drifting sand worried them. They got a young engineer who loved the desert, a man who had something of the Arab temperament in his nature. His name was Randall, and he didn't know what failure or fear meant.—They sent him into the desert to stay until he found out how to conquer the drifting sand. He lived among the sand hills, and he developed the greatest gift the desert can give to any man, the gift of patience. He lived with the sand, and he worked out a law, the law of drifting sand.

"He found that the hills were whisked about by the wind, that they drifted half a mile a year, until they piled up to a certain height. After they reached that height they didn't drift any more. They absorbed the other drifting sand hills that were pushed up against them. And from the data he got while he lived in the desert, he found the law of the drifting sand; that the big ones don't move. It's only the little ones who drift. That law which he discovered has been the basis of road construction in the desert.

"Now you ought to sit down and take stock of yourself. You've never done it before. You've been drifting through life, making motions because everybody else around you was making the same sort of motions. When you get out in the desert and find that there aren't a lot of people all around you who are doing the same things you are, you get frightened.— But always remember that the desert is the best mother a man ever had. Remember that she's cruel, and that cruelty is the essence of kindness. It's the law of nature that only the fittest survive.

"Man gets to be the fittest by fighting. That's what the desert does to you. It makes you fight for existence. That's why she's so kind. You stay here, and quit trying to avoid the desert. Get right down on the surface of the desert and talk to it. Remember what I said to you about cruelty being kindness, and remember that it's only the little ones who drift around with every passing wind."

I got up and walked away. It was a cruel thing to do, all right, but I was practicing a little of what I preached. It is true that the desert is kind just because it's cruel, and I was handling him the same way the desert would. I knew that we were up against something, that it was going to be a hard fight if we were going to win out. Some one had been following us, keeping us spotted, and that some one had swooped down and lifted our stock. That was serious. It was certain to mean suffering, and it might mean death. I owed it to the girl and I owed it to myself not to complicate things any by having a desert-frightened tenderfoot running around in circles, screaming with fear. That's what the desert will do to a tenderfoot such as this one, if he tries to get away from it. It's only human nature for a man to react that way. When he becomes afraid of something, he wants to get away from that something. When he starts to get away, he wants to run. When he starts to run from the desert and finds that it's all around him, he goes clean batty.

### v. A Shot for Each Burro

I walked back to camp. By that time the girl was sitting up. I could see her form blotched against the slithering sand.

"What is it?" she asked in a low voice.

I sat down beside her. "I don't know," I said.

"Why don't you know?"

"Because there's so much about you that I don't know."

"Yes?" she asked.

"Yes," I said. "When I met up with you, I figured that your business was your business, and mine was mine. You could mind yours and I'd attend to mine. I didn't ask you how come you happened to be running around the desert with a young man. I didn't ask whether you were engaged, or brother and sister, or husband and wife. I didn't even ask what you were doing here.

"When you pulled that story on me about the homestead, I didn't ask any questions, although I wanted to make certain it was a mine you was looking for, because there wouldn't have been any use going on if it had been a homestead. No one could live in this country; it would be impossible to raise enough to feed a hungry grasshopper.

"But now things are different. Some one's snooped around here and nosed us out and swiped my burros. Maybe I can trail 'em in the morning when it gets light. Maybe I can't. I've got a six-gun, and that's all. Maybe I'm running up against rifles.—Furthermore, we've got precious little water here in camp, and we don't stand a very good chance of walking out to where there's water. If we make it, it'll be because we travel light and go without food. We can't carry any weight and make it.

"I've got to reach a decision. If we're going back for water, we should start right away and take advantage of the cool night. If we're going to try and get our stock, I want to swing out to a spot where they won't be looking for me, and I'll have to do it before daybreak."

I said that much and then I quit talking. The silence of the desert weighted down the darkness, made it seem like a black velvet blanket.

She sighed, "You wouldn't be helped any by what I know. It's nothing that concerns the present situation."

"No?" I said, and my tone was sarcastic.

"No," she said.

I kept still for a time, and the desert, too, was still.

That silence started things. The girl drew in her breath as though she was going to start talking, then waited a minute, then made another start. At last she got out the words.

"I'll tell you the whole truth," she said. "I think I can trust you, and I don't usually make a mistake in judging men. I'm a stenographer. I worked in a big office. I knew a man named Bloom—Harry Bloom. He was a friend of my father's."

I straightened up. "Huh?" I said.

"What?" she asked.

"Nothing. Go on."

She went on, talking in a level monotone, her knees

crossed, her hands holding them with interlocked fingers. She seemed to take to the desert, to be a part of it.

"Harry Bloom wrote to me and asked me to finance him on a trip. He called it 'grubstaking' him. He didn't need much money, and he seemed sort of hopeless, inclined to quit. I had a little money, and I sent it to him.—Then I got a letter from him, a long while later. That letter had been carried around by some man who wasn't very clean. The envelope was all grimed with dirt and smeared up with smudges from the penciled address. In it he said that he'd struck it rich, that he'd started back with a whole burroload of gold, and that his heart had commenced to go bad on him. He'd fainted twice, and he was afraid he'd die in the desert, and that some one would find his body and the gold, and that I'd never get my share.

"So he'd buried the gold, and had written me the letter to tell me about it. He was going to leave that letter near a cross-trail which he was coming to, and he knew that some teamster or prospector would come along within a day or two and pick it up.

"But in that letter he didn't dare to tell me the secret of where he'd buried the gold, for fear some person might open it. He said he'd communicate with me again and let me know where the gold was buried. He said the second letter would just be a brief line that wouldn't mean anything to anybody else if they should open it. It'd take the two letters put together to make sense.

"Of course I was all excited when I got that letter, and I could hardly wait. I figured there wasn't much chance he'd die from his heart, not if he took it easy. I waited, expecting to get a wire from him when he reached a town. Then I got another letter. This time it was in a cleaner envelope, and it looked as though it had been purchased in a store, then dropped in a post office without having been carried around any.

"That letter just had a scrawl which read: 'Here it is.' That was all the letter said; but there was map in it, and this is the map."

She took out the map that she'd shown me before, the one that had been scrawled in pencil.

I struck a match and studied the map by the light of that match, and when it burnt down lit another one.

The more I saw of the map the funnier it looked.

"I don't know any cañons that look like those," I said, "and I don't like the way they drain. They don't look natural. That right-angled turn in the cañon, where the mine's supposed to be or where the gold's supposed to be buried, doesn't mean a thing, except a double-cross . . ."

I broke off and looked over toward her. Her face was startled, the eyes wide. Then the match went out.

"Do you know a good looking fellow who's built for dancing?" I asked suddenly. "He's a man who has a deep, thrilling voice, a well-shaped mouth, and on his forehead a scar shaped like a star. Maybe he got it when he was pitched through a windshield."

She gasped. "Why that description fits Fred Trask!" she said.

"I thought it would," I told her, "and I take it that Fred Trask works in the same office you do, and that your mail came to the office. Maybe Fred had been trying to make love to you, and was jealous?"

She was leaning forward now, and I could hear the quick breathing as she stared into the darkness, trying to see my face. "Yes," she said. And then, after a moment, "Why?"

I laughed. "Because," I told her, "Fred Trask was jealous. He saw how excited you got when you received that grimed-up letter in a man's handwriting, and he decided that he'd see who the letter was from. You probably put the letter in your purse, and Fred had a chance to steal a look at the purse.

"Knowing what to expect, he watched your mail; and when the second letter came, he simply kept it from you. He got it first and kept it."

She spoke slowly. "But I received the second letter. That was how I got the map."

"No," I explained, "that second letter was pocketed by Trask. He knew you'd be expecting a second letter, and so he doped up this letter with the phony map. That lulled your suspicions. Then, I presume, you heard of Bloom's murder."

"Yes," she admitted. "I read of it in the paper.—And Ted Wayne had been a very good friend of mine. He liked me, and I liked him. He wouldn't listen to my coming out here alone. He had the car, and he said he was going to drive me and see that nothing happened to me.—Fred Trask laid off from work because he was sick. How did you know that I knew him, or that he'd mixed into this thing?"

"Because of certain information," I told her, "for which I paid thirty-five dollars. And now it looks as though the investment had been increased slightly."

I stopped talking. For a few minutes we both kept silence. Then I heard four shots, muffled by the distance—*powieee, powieee, powieee, powieee!*

She jumped to her feet. "Shots!" she said.

"Yes," I told her. "Four shots—one for each burro. My thirty-five dollar investment has been increased by the price of four burros!" I went over to my bed roll and buckled on my six-gun.

A quavering voice sounded from the darkness. A moment after there came another call, louder, stronger. I answered with a "Hulloa!"

"Who is it?—Ted?" she asked.

"Yes," I said. "Do you like him as much as you did?"

I could see the outline of her shoulders against the gray background of fine sand as she shrugged.

"I don't like cowards!" she said.

"Sometimes people get branded as cowards when they're only sensitive," I said. "I've seen people like that before. Some of them are real cowards, but some of them are just so sensitive that some sudden new experience jars them. It isn't that they're afraid. It's just that their systems are more highly strung."

She turned away and didn't answer.

Ted Wayne called again, this time closer. I answered again. I could hear his feet then, and a minute later he showed up against the blank gray of the sand.

"I heard shots," he said.

"Yes," I told him. "Somebody was celebrating the Fourth of July. Sit down and take a load off your feet. I'm going out to explore. You can't come with me, because you'd get lost."

He didn't sit down. "Why can't I come, and what's it all about?"

"You're entitled to know," I said. "You're probably going to be shot in order to keep your lips from giving damaging testimony. Or else you're going to be left out in the desert to die of thirst.—You may as well know what it's all about." Then I told them the whole story.

Neither one of them interrupted me. I told them all about meeting the man with the scarred forehead, the attempts to buy the chunk of conglomerate from Jose Diaz, the gambler; and the finding of the disk of gold concealed inside that chunk of rock.

"So you think that disk of gold held the key to the location of the buried gold?" asked Lois Beachley, when I had finished.

"Yes," I said.

"And you think that Fred Trask stole our burros?" Ted Wayne wanted to know.

"Not exactly," I said, "but Fred Trask is behind it, and he's taken the other two into his confidence. They're Sam Pitch and Dick Rose, who stole the burros. They've been sitting up here on some of these points, looking through glasses at us. They saw us make camp, knew just where to come to make their raid. Now they've left us in the desert, where we can't carry any grub or blankets. We'll have to fight for life."

"Then," said Lois, "we'd better start going for water right away, and let the mine go."

"That's the wise thing," I told her. "Only I think I'd better go and look the ground over first."

"You're the doctor," she said. "But I thought you yourself said that if we were going to have to go for water it'd be better to start while it was cool."

"I've sort of changed my mind," I said.

She sighed. "Go ahead then, and look around."

"I want to go, too," said Ted Wayne.

His voice was quiet, controlled, seemed to have something of power in it.

"Yes," I said. "I've changed my mind on that, too. I want you to come."

The girl pulled her blanket over her shoulders. "Well, I'll be here when you get back. Don't take chances."

## VI. Battle

We started out, climbing over the sand hills.

Ted Wayne tugged at my sleeve. "Thanks for what you said about the desert," he said. "I was all worked up, nervous—frightened, I guess. Then I sat down in the silence, and I thought over what you said. All of a sudden things seemed to change. It was just like being turned around, and then suddenly seeing something that puts you straight on your directions. Everything seemed to whirl for a minute, and the desert didn't seem to be anything to be afraid of any longer."

"Attaboy!" I encouraged him.

He was going to need all his nerve before we got out of there.

"Wait a minute!" he went on. "I want to tell you. I know what you're holding back."

I stopped in my tracks. "You know what?"

"What you're holding back. There was a murder done, remember. Harry Bloom didn't die from his heart. He was shot because somebody thought he had the gold with him. It was probably one of those two men who are guiding Fred Trask. They don't want us to testify afterwards. If we don't die of thirst, leaving the desert, they'll see that we die some other way. That's why you're trying to go to them instead of trying to get to water."

I saw that he knew so much that I let him have the real truth.

"You're only partly right, Ted." I told him. "If we weren't interfering with those men, they'd have let us alone. Now that map the girl has was forged before Fred Trask got the gold disk and knew where he wanted to search. It was drawn by a desert man, so Trask probably had Sam Pitch in with him all the time, after he got that first letter.

"They steered you folks out to these drifting sand hills so they could get you on a false trail, out of the way. Then they got that gold disk, and we find that they've gone into the desert, that we're crowding right on their trail. We make a camp, and they come along and run off our burros, shoot them, and try to stampede us. What's the reason?

"The reason is," I went on, not waiting for an answer, "that we're camped right near the locality they want to search. If we don't start moving, they'll try to attack. If we do, they may kill us or they may not.—Now, I figure they're coming into camp here in order to see what's happened. I'm going to sort of look around. I want you to go and get Lois and take her out some place where you can sit tight until you hear from me. There's no use alarming her.—Will you do that?"

"Can I do more good doing that than helping you?" he asked.

"Yes," I said.

He gripped my hand.

"Then that's what I'll do. Good-by, until I see you again."

"So long," I said.

I listened to him trudge back. Then I sneaked along behind him. He didn't know that I was anywhere around. I followed him in to the camp, hid behind the ridge of a sand hill while he talked with the girl, heard them move away.

After that I began to do something that was difficult and a little dangerous. I began to bury myself in the sand, just as kids do at the beach. Only this time, I was worming my way into the slope of a dry sand hill, with sand pouring down over me every time I made a move.

I not only wanted to get in out of sight, but I wanted to leave the slope of the sand hill so that it wouldn't show that it had been disturbed. The sand was dry and fine. It ran like water. I worked my way back into the side of the hill, cascading sand down on my body until only my arms were free. I had my six-gun in my right hand, and I worked with my left.

By the time I finished, I was fairly well concealed, but I couldn't make any sudden moves, except with my right hand and the six-gun.

I waited. The sky became gray in the east, and the silhouettes of the mountains stood out against the flare of color that followed the gray. The desert was whispering again, the wind whipping the sand, wiping out trails, smoothing over the tracks that I'd left when I wormed my way into the sand. It was a break for me—but the desert always gives me the breaks.

The light became stronger. Then I could feel little jarring noises that thudded along through the sand. They seemed to come as impulses along my spine before they reached my ears as sound. They were footsteps. I got ready.

I'd holed in where I could see the camp. It looked pitifully meager, the saddles and blankets, the few dishes and the little sacks of provisions.

Then a man walked down the little wind ravine between the sand hills.

"I told you I saw 'em walking away. Caught a glimpse of 'em against the sky."

It was Dick Rose who spoke.

"Well, they'll start for water—and they won't make it."

That would be Sam Pitch.

There was a laugh, and I knew who would give that scornful, sneering, reverberant laugh. It would be Fred Trask.

"What gets me," said Rose, "is that they had to make their camp right where we figured the gold had been cached. It ain't a hundred yards from here—not the way I dope it out."

"Well, it ain't luck," said Pitch. "That damned Zane has some way of getting what he wants in the desert. They say the sand whispers secrets to him, and tells him what to do. I've about come to the conclusion that that's about what happens."

Dick Rose rasped out a single word.

"Baloney!" he said. "You're gettin' superstitious. Get these burros ready to pack up that camp equipment. No use leaving it here. Somebody might stumble on it and ask embarrassing questions."

I could see the string of burros now, plodding along not far behind, on the end of a lead rope. I drew in my breath, ready to play my final card. But I wanted a little more information first, if I could get it before that fateful command of "hands up" would start the action.

However, I didn't get the information—not directly—and I never shouted the command. There was a whirling cloud of sand, then a black figure plunged down over the crest of one of the sand hills. Ted Wayne had found a stick of wood and a stone, and he'd tied the stone to the end of the wood, Indian fashion, making a very effective war club.

The sudden attack, the very unexpectedness of it, carried his first objective. Fred Trask yelled, leapt to one side, and the rock crashed a blow on his forehead.

He went down like a sack of sugar being dumped on the scales.

Ted charged, swung his club. A revolver roared. Then they were too close for shooting. It was a case of clubbed guns against stone war club, of man against man. Nor could I shoot. The three were mixed in a whirling gyration of flying arms and legs, of faces that were distorted with effort.

It was Sam Pitch who got him pinioned, but the kid had inflicted a lot of damage in the meantime. There were some casualties on the other side, too.

Dick Rose raised his revolver. "You damned whelp!" he observed.

Ted Wayne stood there smiling. I heard the girl scream. She had been watching it all over the crest of the sand hill.

Dick Rose snapped a command to his lieutenant. "Grab the girl," he said, "as soon as I kill this swine. Bob Zane's around here somewhere. Get to one side, so the bullet doesn't go through and hit you . . ."

Then I spoke, keeping my tone low, so it would be the more difficult to locate me.

"Drop that gun, or you're a dead man!"

He hesitated, pursed his lips, whirled. "Drop it!" I snapped.

But he had located me, perhaps because of some flicker of sunlight on the barrel of the gun which I held. Perhaps it was just the sound of my voice.

He fired, and the bullet *thunked* in the sand within a matter of inches from where my head was held imprisoned by the burden of the sand.

He fired again and ducked to one side for shelter. Matters had gone far enough. I squeezed the trigger of my gun—I heard the bullet strike, saw Dick Rose spin to one side, stagger, slump to his knees. For a moment his graying face, twisted with hatred, stared at me. He tried to raise the gun for a third shot, and failed. He pitched forward, on his face.

Sam Pitch flung Ted Wayne to one side, took a snap shot at me, then swung his gun toward the lad. I fired. The bullet clipped Pitch on the shoulder. I was ready to fire again, when Ted Wayne swung his club. The stone hit Pitch a glancing blow on the ribs, knocking the wind out of him.

The next moment Ted was on him like a tiger. He flung the war club to one side, using his fists.

I floundered out from the sand slope, and it was slow work, for the sand held me like silken bonds.

Ted was sitting astride of Sam Pitch when I reached him. The girl was laughing and crying all at once. I took some rope from the packsaddle and tied up Pitch. Then I went over to Fred Trask and tied him up. There wasn't any need to tie up Dick Rose.

I went back to Trask, searched his pockets, found what I wanted. Sam Pitch stared with sullen eyes while I studied what I had found. It was a map, a map made from a button of hammered gold. The surface had been carved into a relief map, and there were three bearings scratched on it, with the point of intersection marked.

That point of intersection was in the slope of a sand hill, one of the big ones that wouldn't move.

I looked down at Sam Pitch. "You'll hang for the murder of Harry Bloom," I said.

His lips twisted. "I didn't kill him. It was Dick Rose who did that. He was on the trail of the gold that Bloom was supposed to have had. Then he found he'd been tricked out of it.—Along comes this boob, to play into our hands. We were going to get the gold, and then kill the boob."

I nodded. It had happened just the way I had figured the play.

I looked at Ted Wayne. He had a cut on the side of his head. His lips were puffed out, and one eye was swelling shut. But there was something proud and self-reliant in his bearing.

"You were going to keep the girl safe," I told him.

He stared at me, unflinchingly. "We knew you were coming back to face danger. We knew they didn't intend to let any of us get away. So we decided to come back and see it through with you, shoulder to shoulder."

I sighed. "You had the breaks. You should have done what I told you to do. If those crooks had used any sense, and deployed, you'd have been shot down like a jackrabbit."

He grinned. "Anyway, we got away with it! And I guess, from the looks of your face when you inspected that gold button, we're as good as sitting on the gold right now!"

I looked at him. He was grinning, battle scarred, and I thought of the change that had come over him. The desert had adopted him, and the law of drifting sand had impressed itself upon him. The big ones stay put. Only the little ones are whisked this way and that by the changing winds of adversity.

My eyes drifted to the girl. I saw that she, too, was cognizant of the change that had taken place in her companion. Her lips made no sound. They didn't need to. The story was in her eyes.

I knew that the desert had done its work well. When you burn off the veneer of convention in the tempering fires of the desert you find what's underneath. When that engineer named Randall discovered the law of drifting sand for the railroad companies he discovered a law that relates to other things than sand hills. It's a law that applies to character as well as to sand. Little characters are whipped about by winds of adversity. The big ones stay firm.

# THE WHIP HAND

## 1. Shots That Missed

Up north of Mojave the desert goes crazy.

I was camped, up on the shoulder of the mountains where the Joshua trees start to spot the barren waste. Off to the east the mountains flung themselves up into a jagged tangle of bright reds. To the west was a plateau country. In between was everything.

Wind, sun, and an occasional cloudburst had eroded the cañons, carved miniature cities out of the varicolored strata. By day there were reds so bright they flamed in the sun; blues that were like the ocean, glittering expanses of eye-blistering white. Now it was all a golden monotone. The moon, but a little past the first quarter, was sinking down toward the western plateau region.

My camp fire was smoldering down to red embers. I yawned a couple of times and stared upward at the stars blazing down with fixed intensity. I knew that there was a wind coming up.

Then the sand would start to talk, as it slithered along on the wings of the wind, rustling against minaret, cacti, Joshua-palm; rustling, finally, when the wind got strong enough, against the sand itself. Those are the sand whispers. Desert dwellers will swear they whisper words when one is just drifting off to sleep.

It's just fancy, of course. Yet, if you've never heard those sand whispers you can't appreciate how much they sound like mysterious night voices hissing soft words.

I kicked off my shoes, rolled into the blankets.

The first faint wings of the night wind caressed my cheek.

I snapped bolt upright.

It was a rifle shot, crackling, crisp, deadly.

I reached for my boots, pulled them on. My rifle was in the saddle scabbard. My six-gun was over the horn. I grabbed the belt, heavy with cartridges.

"Crack!"

A second shot disrupted the night. This time there was the long-drawn snarl of a whining bullet, glancing from a rock down the cañon, humming over my head.

I reached the fire in two swift strides and kicked sand over it. Three seconds and there wasn't the faintest flow of light from it. But there remained the unavoidable stream of light smoke drifting off downwind.

The echoes of the second shot were still booming back from the different cliffs when a third shot rang out.

After that there was silence.

I moved off a little ways and sat with my rifle on my knees.

The desert wind whipped up into a series of hard gusts, then died down. The night was calm, warm, star-studded, mysterious.

The moon slid down the vault of the sky, bright enough to

give some faint light, but not bright enough to dull the stars.
Somewhere down the slope I heard a rock rattle.

My burros were up the slope. The rock hadn't been dislodged by the burros.

After a few minutes I heard the scrape of a boot heel over a bit of rock.

I cocked the rifle.

Steps. They were coming up the steep slope—toiling, hurrying, panic-stricken steps.

There is something uncanny about the desert night when stumbling steps sound through the oppressive silence which reaches down from the stars, a silence so intense that it makes the ears ring.

I could hear every step now.

The person was keeping to the east, would miss my camp by fifty yards.

I strained my eyes into the deceptive, golden glow of the weak moonlight. I thought I could see motion, rubbed my eyes, and the thing vanished. Ten yards farther up the slope my eyes snapped to a blur which seemed solid. They blinked and focused.

It was a figure, toiling upward.

I waited.

Twenty steps more, and I could hear the sobbing, anguished breath coming and going through laboring lungs. There was a slightness about the figure, a suggestion of small-boned physique which was puzzling.

It turned, walked a dozen steps toward where I sat motionless, hesitated, started back down the slope with staggering steps.

Then I knew.

It was a woman.

I continued to wait, trying to determine what had caused this mad rush up the slope, the zigzagging about.

She crossed down below where I was camped. The wisp of smoke blew down toward her, yet she did not pause. I spotted her then for a city dweller.

A desert woman would have checked instantly to rigid attention.

I listened to see if any one followed. I could hear no one. She started up the slope again, now on the other side of me. She was breathing a little more regularly now.

"I know it was here," I heard her say, and the words were fraught with inner anguish.

I got to my feet.

"Was there something you wanted?" I asked.

The hissing of her breath sounded sharply, clearly audible against the background of desert silence.

For a moment she was rigid, then she started toward the sound of my voice.

"Yes, yes! I saw your fire. I want protection!"

I could see that she was unarmed.

"Come over here and sit down. You're all in."

Her lungs were laboring, but she was as gracefully alert as a deer. She came to my side.

"Sit down."

She sat down, sprawled out along the slope, her bent elbows behind her, propping her back. She had on boots, whipcord breeches and a silk blouse, low in the neck.

The moonlight showed her face. It had been burnt an angry red. Evidently she was new to the desert.

"You want protection?" I asked.

"Yes."

"From what?"

"From the awful silence of the desert. I tried to camp by myself. The silence drove me crazy. I started to run. Then I saw your camp fire."

"You found the silence terrifying?"

"Yes."

"It was broken a few moments ago," I told her, "by several rifle shots."

She sat up, stared at me with a surprise that was manifest in sagging jaw, in widened eyes, a surprise that was too ludicrously assumed to be convincing.

"No!" she exclaimed incredulously.

I said nothing.

We sat in silence for several minutes. She looked about at my outfit, packsaddle, riding saddle, canteens, blankets, grub.

"You know the desert, don't you?"

I said nothing.

"It's wonderful to think of a man who can go out all alone in the desert and be so calm, so in tune with nature!"

I motioned toward the stars.

"You're not alone, ma'am, when you've got the stars."

She glanced up. Her features turned toward the stars, studying them.

"I wonder . . ." she said softly, but her voice trailed off into silence and she didn't say what it was she was wondering about. After a while she spoke again: "Men have been murdered under these stars," she said ominously.

I shrugged my shoulders.

She made no further attempt at conversation. Her breath came back, and I could see she was nearly all in. She had evidently had a hard day and was close to the limit of exhaustion.

"You can prop your head against the saddle," I told her. "That'll take the strain off your arms."

She thanked me as I dragged the saddle over to her.

That tilted her back, back so her eyes were staring upward at the stars. The moon slid down below the horizon. The wind freshened. Little wisps of sand started to scurry by. In a short time the desert would be whispering to itself. But the girl didn't hear the sand.

Her breathing was more regular now. I glanced over at her. Her eyes were closed. She was asleep.

That was what I'd been waiting for.

I took my rifle and six-gun and slipped quietly down the slope. I didn't know who had done the shooting, nor why. But I didn't propose to have daylight find me as an animated target.

The shots had come to the east of me. The girl had been over on the east side of the slope. I figured the moonlight, the shadows, and doped it out that the only place a man could have seen the girl was from a little saddle over on the eastern ridge.

I angled along the slope, made a detour and started to climb. After half an hour I came to a place where the ridges joined.

It was dark now, save for the starlight. The wind had freshened. It was a warm wind, and it blew in savage gusts, sending little wraiths of dry, whispering sand slithering along the surface of the slope.

I took advantage of the wind and kept well over to the side.

After a while I got a whiff of distant tobacco. I smelled along upwind, tracing that tobacco smell as though I'd been a hound. It was coming from the saddle in the other slope, and I wanted to be pretty sure of my ground before I did anything.

It took me fifteen minutes to cover fifty yards. Then the tobacco smell stopped. I sat down and waited. A man learns patience in the desert. I had all night before me.

The wind rose to a fierce frenzy of rushing air and then abruptly stopped. Night winds will do that in the desert.

I waited. It was calm, and still.

After a while, a match scraped. I saw the flicker of flame. Then the end of a cigarette glowed, waned, and glowed again.

I inched my way along, stalking over the sand and loose rock, through the scrub sage, as carefully as though I'd been coming up on a deer.

I could make out his outline against the lighter color of the light slope behind him. It wasn't a clear outline, just a blob of black, punctuated with a glowing red cigarette tip.

I worked closer, my rifle cocked.

I estimated the distance at twenty yards.

He took the cigarette from his mouth. I saw it sweep downward, then raise in a half circle as he stretched his arms. I was close enough to him to hear him suck in a great lungful of air as he yawned. Then he put the cigarette back in his mouth.

I kept working closer, hugging along the side of the slope, but keeping close to the ground.

I figured the distance at ten yards.

He saw me.

The cigarette end drooped, then dropped, scattering a little shower of ruddy sparks. I could hear the scratching of feet on sand as he crouched over and made fast motions.

"If you don't sit quite still, my friend, you're going to get shot!" I told him.

## II. Double Crossed

HE WAS STARTLED at my voice, so near to him. And then, perhaps, he had been waiting for a woman's voice. He must be the type of man who would shoot at a woman, otherwise he'd never have fired those shots.

He sat quite still.

I strode up.

"Get those hands 'way up."

He stretched them.

I unbuckled his belt and took the revolver and ammunition. The rifle was leaning against a sagebrush. I took that.

"You're too careless with your guns," I said.

He spoke then, for the first time. His voice was smooth and purring. He spoke with the easy glibness of one who relies much upon his tongue.

"You're making a big mistake, my friend. I wasn't shooting at you. I could see your camp fire, but I wasn't shooting at it, or at you."

"Shooting at a woman?" I asked, and he could sense my feelings in my voice.

"No," he said. "I shot up in the air, to frighten her."

"Frighten her out in the desert without blankets, food or water?"

"That," he said, his tone suddenly changing, "is none of your damned business."

In the darkness, my sweet smile was wasted on him.

"Which is exactly why you're losing your hardware."

I looked around me.

"Where's your camp?"

"Don't you wish you knew."

"Hard boiled, ain't you?"

"Yes!"

He snapped out that last answer, and I laughed at him.

"Listen, my talkative friend," I told him. "You're evidently from the city. You think you're tough. But you're out in the desert where everything is plunged into an acid bath that takes off the coating of bluff and leaves only the real stuff. Unless you assay a certain percentage of courage you won't last."

His laugh was a sneer, but it was uneasy.

"Now you started out by shooting at a woman. I'm warning you that the buzzards are going to make a meal out of you if you try it again. That plain?"

He was surly now.

"Maybe you better find out something about the woman you're stickin' up on a pedestal before you go shootin' off your face too much," he growled. "She's an adventuress!"

I laughed at him.

"Therefore you should have the right to murder her, eh?"

He fidgeted around, sucked in his breath to say something,

then thought better of it. There was a period of silence.

"That ain't the point," he said, after a while.

"What is the point?" I asked him.

"The point is that you're buttin' in on somethin' that's none of your business. The point is that woman's a dirty crook, and you'll find it out. She's got a baby face and a cooing laugh, and her eyes are wide an' innocent. But you stick around her and she'll rob you of every damned thing you've got and leave you out in the desert for the buzzards to laugh at.

"I know. I trusted her. I fell for her line. She told me a great story about being robbed, about men who had followed her and tried to take away her rights. I fell for the line. She took every cent I had. I came back just as she was robbing the cache.

"Even then I only tried to scare her, but she lit out like the devil was after her. That was because she'd seen your camp fire, and figured you'd be another sucker. Now you come along and take away my guns, and give her refuge. That's just the same thing as helping her steal the dough."

"S'pose you come along with me," I invited, "and face this woman."

He laughed harshly.

"What a sucker you are! What a poor blind sucker. You think she'll be there when you get back?"

"Of course she'll be there," I said.

For a full five seconds his mirthless laugh cackled, then he waved his hand.

"Go on, sucker. Go on back. You can talk it over with her. I don't want to see her again."

I looked up and down the slope.

"If she robbed you and you started shooting at her to frighten her, then your camp should be somewhere around here," I said.

"Think so?" he asked, sarcastically. "I s'pose you've

teamed up with the woman now, and you've come back to see if she might have left something you could grab."

I turned on my heel.

"You're as poor a liar as you are a marksman," I said. "Shots that are fired up in the air don't ricochet off of rocks and whine past my head!"

I left him with that. He snarled some retort, but I didn't listen.

I waited after a few yards, listening, to see if he was going to try and follow me; but he was sitting perfectly still. Then the wind started again, a swift blast of warm air that came rushing up out of the darkness of the star-studded night, and I went back up the ridge.

He knew where I was camped, so there was no use in taking a roundabout way back. I angled along the contour lines, making the best progress I could in the dark.

It was slow work, particularly being burdened with the double set of hardware. In the middle of the wash between the two ridges there was a rock outcropping with a windswept cave. I put the captured guns in that cave, and climbed on around the slope to my own ridge.

The wind was blowing steadily now. Sand was drifting along, whispering as it passed, singing the age-old song of the desert.

I came to the place where my camp should have been.

It wasn't there.

I was certain about the place. There was the smell of wood smoke, faint but distinctive, coming from my covered camp fire. I found the little pile of dried sage branches that I'd gathered for a quick breakfast in the morning.

Visibility was poor in the starlight, but I could make out what had happened. My camp had been packed up, the burros saddled, and the whole outfit moved. It was too dark to see tracks, and, if the wind didn't go down, the tracks would be covered by morning.

I was in the desert without grub, water or blankets.

I sat down and cursed under my breath.

The outfit had either gone up the ridge or down. I guessed up, and started feeling my way through the darkness of the desert. It was slow progress. By three o'clock, I'd reached the upper rim of the slope. I lay down, put my coat over my head and kept sand out of my hair and neck and caught a little sleep.

With daylight I sat up and scanned the desert.

It was a tumbled succession of washes, ridges, caves, wind-corroded slopes. Colors flung themselves at the eye in a vivid profusion. Off to the east, the level floor of the Mojave was glittering in the heat. To the west, there was a suggestion of cool air about the pine-clad ridges of the high and rocky mountains. A fleecy cloud even hung about one of the distant peaks.

I sat perfectly still, waiting and watching.

I knew every foot of this desert, and I could get to water. Also, I had an old mining claim up here that had about petered out. I had a few supplies cached there. But I didn't propose to be euchred out of my outfit and not do something about it.

The wind was still blowing, making tracking almost impossible, sending the scurrying sand zipping along the upper ridges. But the air was clear. The sand hugged along the ground.

At last I saw something off to the north, a flicker of motion. I strained my eyes and caught it again. It was a wisp of smoke, whipped about by the wind.

I lined up two landmarks and started.

Within ten minutes the wind had gone down. It was flat calm and the sun beat down from the brassy bowl of the sky. My shadow grew shorter and the weird ridges commenced to dance in the heat.

It's up here that the desert goes crazy.

Volcanic, sedimentary, conglomerate, ridges, washes, outcroppings, red rock, blue rock, white rock, black rock; all mingled into indescribable confusion.

I came up out of a little draw and saw a moving speck, a speck that could only be a human being, man or woman.

I sat down and watched.

It was moving backward and forward in a peculiar manner, as though searching for something.

I worked my way forward, cautiously, keeping every bit of cover between me and the speck that I could.

By nine thirty I was up to where I could see him plainly. It was a man and he had a shovel. From time to time he would select a spot and start to dig.

He didn't dig deep, just scratched around at the sand. Then he'd move along. All the time he was walking he'd look back over his shoulder at an arched rock on a big ridge. This rock formed a natural arch with a hole in the center that might have been twenty feet high by fifty broad.

I eased down behind a clump of sage and waited for him to come toward me. I figured he'd be working up the slope, and he did. It took him half an hour or so to get where he was exactly where I wanted him. Then, when his back was turned, looking toward the arched rock, I got noiselessly to my feet, carelessly dropped the rifle in the hollow of my arm, and was yawning when he turned around.

"Hello." I said. "Hot, ain't it?"

### III. Ambushed

He jumped as though he'd planted his foot down on a rattlesnake, and sprawled on the rocks. His hand started to streak toward his hip, and then paused, as he thought better of it. A slow grin spread over his face as he got up, a sickly sort of grin.

He was tall, raw-boned, and there was a look in his eye I didn't like. He started to say something, then snapped his mouth shut and nodded instead.

"Camping here?" I asked.

He shook his head.

"Looking for something, eh?"

He paused a moment, then nodded. And I started to laugh.

He stared at me, and dull rage came to his eyes. I waited for him to say something, but he wouldn't speak, simply stood there, lips clamped, eyes glittering.

I was certain of my ground then, and I called the turn on him so we could get the agony over with.

"And you're afraid to talk for fear I'll recognize your voice as that of the man who shot at the woman last night. Well, I recognize you anyway, so go ahead and say something."

That started him.

He said plenty, about men who sneaked up on other men who were going about their legitimate business in the desert, and a lot of other stuff along the same line, until I hitched the muzzle of my rifle around a little bit so that it was pointing squarely in the middle of his belt buckle, and slid my thumb gently back to the hammer.

That sapped the enthusiasm from his remarks.

When he had calmed down, not so much because of having shot off steam as because he didn't know just how far he could go, I bored my gaze into his eyes.

"Where's the girl?" I asked.

"What girl?"

"The one that you shot at last night, the one that came running up the slope to my camp."

He laughed at that, and his laugh was the same mirthless cackle it had been the night before.

"So she took a sneak on you, did she? Haw, haw, haw! That's good, that is! Mind what I told you? And I'll bet she stole you blind when she left, didn't she? Yeah, I can see it in your face, can see it in the fact that you ain't got no camp equipment. I bet she'd cleaned you out by the time you got back to your camp, brother.

"And it serves you right! You wouldn't listen to reason, an' you went around throwin' guns down on folks and takin' away their artillery, just because they objected to havin' a woman rob 'em.

"Well, sucker, I seen a pack train headin' down the pass toward Inyokern about daylight this morning, and I bet that's where your lady friend's gone to. Maybe you can overtake her if you start humping, but it's goin' to be a dry trail without no water."

I waited until the silence had furnished weight to my words, then I talked to him in low, level tones.

"All right. That's your story. Stick by it if you want to. Now listen to mine. This girl came into my camp. You were shooting at her. She was a tenderfoot. Her face was all burned red by the sun. She was all in. She was so dead tired she dropped off to sleep before she'd been with me for ten minutes.

"My camp was a four burro affair. It took some skill to get those packs on so they wouldn't slip, get the burros saddled up and on the trail. I wasted a lot of time working over toward you, but not enough for a woman tenderfoot to have got four burros in and saddled and packed.

"My best guess is that there were at least two men, both of them pretty wise old desert rats. They sneaked up the ridge, pounced on the woman, tied and gagged her, and then made off with the outfit."

I could see that my words told.

"Ain't you clever!" he sneered.

"I don't have to be," I said. "I'm right. Now where's the girl, and where's the camp equipment? You've got just ten seconds to come clean. I've got the whip hand here and . . .!"

And that was as far as I got.

It was a look in his eyes that warned me; that, and perhaps

the instinct that comes to one who has lived long in the desert. I flung myself to one side.

The man who shot at me was about fifty yards away on the crest of a ridge, and he had intended the bullet for a hit. It hissed through the air right where my stomach had been but a split second before.

I fired the rifle without taking it off my arm.

And I hoped the bullet would find its mark as I pulled the trigger. It was a high velocity shell, and if the softnosed, steel-jacketed bullet caught him it would rip him to mincemeat.

But the bullet struck in the sand, just ahead and below of where he was crouched, elbow on the ground, gun in hand. The bullet sent up a shower of sand and gravel, a stinging geyser that caught him full in the face and blinded him for the moment.

He shot twice more, but the bullets were as wild as though he'd been shooting in the dark.

But I had other things to think about. Off on the other side, some one had opened up on me with a rifle. The first bullet was a little to my right and low. I saw it shiver a rock outcropping into flying bits of rock dust as it smacked into the ledge, then went whining off into the blue air.

The man I'd been talking to had his gun out, and was firing as he ducked for cover. They were three against one, and they had me from different angles.

And it was murder they meant, too!

I flung down behind the outcropping of rock, took a chance on the man I'd blinded with the sand from my rifle bullet, and swung around on the man who had fired with the rifle.

My shot hit him.

He flung his arms in the air and the rifle swung up in a glittering arc of sunlight on blued steel. Then he howled with agony and rolled over behind his ridge.

The man who had been talking with me had vanished—down the slope, apparently. I could hear his feet, scudding "clumpety-clump, clumpety, clump," like the hoofs of a big buck deer going places in a hurry.

I turned around to where the man had been who had been shooting blind. He was gone, down over the slope.

I figured my quick shooting had disconcerted them a bit. I couldn't tell how seriously the man with the rifle had been hit, and I wanted to find out about that.

I worked back down my ridge, watching the ground like a hawk, rifle ready. The sun beat down with such terrific heat that I could almost feel the impact of the rays as a weight, pressing me down. The sand sent up little drifting clouds of dust under my feet, and the odor of gunpowder was in my nostrils.

I was mad clean through, and I was just a little bit alarmed. I was out in the desert without any water or food, and there were three men, temporarily routed, but bound to try and see that I didn't leave the desert alive.

They wouldn't have dared go so far unless they had determined to go farther.

I finally gained the ridge where the man had been located who had shot at me with the rifle. It was empty. I worked my way along on my stomach, taking care to keep out of sight of the other ridges.

A brass shell gleamed in the sun, the empty cartridge ejected from the rifle when he had flung that first shot at me. I wormed my way to it. The imprint of the place where the body had lain in the sand was plain.

There was a red spot about which a few desert flies buzzed in angry circles, and there were some big splinters of walnut.

I knew what had happened then. I'd shot him in the hand, and the bullet had ripped off a part of the rifle stock. The shot had put him out of commission as a rifle shot, but he'd been able to grab his weapon and run down the slope.

I could see where his tracks showed great running strides. He'd joined the lanky one at the bottom of the draw then, and they'd managed to signal the third.

I crawled up on the ridge.

I could see them, five hundred yards away, three specks that worked their way along, keeping close to the shadow of the ridge. One of them seemed to be supporting the second. The third had the rifle and was covering the back trail.

I could have smoked them up a bit from where I was perched, but I preferred to let them think I'd either been hit or had left the country. I figured they'd go to their camp. And I wanted to see their camp, the worst way.

But there were gusts of wind blowing, and I knew there was a big blow somewhere in the offing. Drifting sand covers tracks pretty rapidly in the desert country.

I worked down the blind side of the slope, took up the trail. I'd gone two hundred yards when a bullet zinged through the air and clipped off a few twigs of sage within a couple of feet of me.

I ducked for cover and tried to locate the man who had shot.

I didn't have any luck. He would not shoot again until I had come out and given him a fair mark. And he was probably up on a ridge somewhere, just below the skyline, barricaded behind a rock fort that would give him all the advantage.

Round one had gone for me, but I couldn't follow up the advantage.

I inched down into a coulee and followed the dry wash back. I made up my mind I'd find out what they had been searching for—if I could. Perhaps there was an advantage to be gained in doing that, particularly now that I was in sole possession of the ground they'd been searching.

I found the little holes he'd shoveled out, but couldn't make any sense out of them.

I looked back at the arched rock, and made a discovery.

Every one of the excavations was in line with the tip of a peak that showed through the hole of the arched rock.

But there were three peaks visible through the arch, from different angles, and the three men had evidently separated, to line down those peaks. That showed that they were looking for something buried at no great depth in the sandy slope of the hill opposite the arched rock at a point where the top of the arch lined up with the top of a peak in the range beyond.

I wasn't kidding myself any.

These three men were desperate.

They'd gone back to their camp to get treatment for the man who had been wounded. But they were coming back. I was alone in the desert, with neither food nor water. They'd be back after me, and before very long.

## IV. The Skeleton

THERE WAS ONE ACE IN THE HOLE that I held that they didn't know about. That was the mining claim I had a mile or so farther up the cañon, on a ridge. I'd cached an emergency ration there when I'd gone out, and there were some canned tomatoes in the cache.

Canned tomatoes!

Those are a godsend to the man in the desert. They neutralize the acids that are left in the body as the result of fatigue and perspiration. They are cooling, refreshing, and they give more quick strength and ease than any amount of water.

But I had to have something more than that one ace in the hole to get me what I wanted. I was virtually certain they held the girl a prisoner. Probably there were four in the party. One had been guarding the girl. Now they would leave the wounded man as guard, pick up rifles and start after me again, reënforced by the man who had been guarding the captive.

I looked at the arched rock.

It was peculiar, distinctive, yet not individual. I knew of another arched rock a half a mile down the cañon, on a little ridge. It wasn't so high as this one, and it wasn't so big. I figured it might be possible to line up the tip of a peak through the hole of that arch, and not have over three or four places to search.

Of course, it was only a chance, yet it wasn't such a wild guess at that. They'd been digging around here in almost every likely place, and it was only too apparent that they hadn't had any results—otherwise they wouldn't have kept on with the search. Therefore they might have picked the wrong arched rock.

I kept to the wind-swept side hills as much as possible so my tracks would not show.

The wind was whipping sand along like fog wraiths now, and tracks did not last very long without filling in.

The particles of sand stung the skin across my cheeks, and the sunlight seemed a little weaker now that the sand diluted the desert air. It was the big wind that the little gusts had presaged, and it would last for two or three hours at least.

I came to the side hill oposite the ridge, looked up, and could see the opening of the arched rock. Then I started angling around until I could get the skyline of the high ridge in view through this arched opening.

It was slow work. There wasn't a great section of ridge, in the first place, and the slope wasn't one that lent itself to the running of contour lines.

More than that, I had to watch the upper cañon, to make certain that my attackers weren't spotting me. After what had happened already, I fancied they'd try to ambush me again if they could.

Finally I struck a place where a saw-toothed peak showed through the opening in the arch. The saw-tooth just filled the arch, and I felt reasonably certain that if anybody had picked a landmark, that would be the one.

I studied the spot. It was just an ordinary slope, without even an outcropping. It was simply sand, cacti, a little sage and sunshine, and the dry sand was sifting across it on the wings of the desert wind until it seemed as though a fine curtain of white mist were being dragged over the ground.

The particular spot wasn't one that would seem to be mineralized, but, in the desert, gold's where you find it. I stood there on that slope, let my eyes range about me, and was reasonably certain that half a dozen fortunes existed within the sweep of country that was visible. It was only a question of finding those places, and . . .

I started.

The wind was shipping sand against something I had thought was a dead sage, white, sand-blasted, dry. But it wasn't sage. It was bone.

I looked again. It was a part of an arm bone, and there were finger bones scattered about on the sand.

I dropped to my knees and started to scoop out the sand with my fingers.

I found what was left of the skeleton. Originally the grave had been deeper, but the wind had whipped away the loose sand on top until the skeleton was all but exposed. There were two round holes in the forehead, small in front, but jagged cavities in the arch of the skull out behind. I knew them for what they were—bullet holes.

The man had been murdered, buried in a shallow grave.

I started poking around. There had been clothes, but they were reduced to rags of stiffened fragments that even the clean sand of the desert and years of time hadn't fully purified.

I found a little glass container that seemed to be stuffed with cloth; opened it, after some difficulty, and found what had been a handkerchief wrapped around a piece of paper.

The paper was yellowed with age, brittle, spotted. But it

had a rude diagram drawn on it with a heavy pencil, and the penciled lines had remained firm and visible.

I spread it out as well as I could, entirely engrossed in what I had found.

It was a map, and the principal peaks were marked on that map. It was a section of the desert that I knew like a book, and I could identify the place that was marked with a cross without much trouble. It was shown as being on a ridge about three miles away, and the place marked with the cross had a three way bearing; a peak, an outcropping of red rock and the North Star.

The bearings had been taken with a compass and the readings, in degrees, had been noted at the end of the lines.

I sat there and did a lot of thinking.

A man who had been murdered years before, a map that had been carefully preserved in a glass jar, a shallow grave, and three men who came and searched, evidently having some knowledge of the place where the body had been buried.

I looked again at the sheet of paper, and thought I knew the answer.

The map took up a little more than half of the sheet.

I took out my knife, folded the brittle, dehydrated paper, and hardly needed the knife to separate the map portion from the blank portion. Then I took a pencil from my pocket, a stub that I carried for notes on ore samples and locations.

I traced a map on a bit of paper that remained, and the map that I traced, making lines so faint that they were barely visible, was a map of the ridge where I had my mining location, the one that was about petered out.

If I was going to deal with murderers and camp-outfit stealers, I was going to be prepared for anything that might happen.

The exact location of my mine I marked with a cross. I

didn't have compass bearings, but I tied the thing up with certain land-marks that were easily identified.

Then I returned the jar, scooped sand over the skeleton, leaving it half exposed, smoothed everything over, and eased my way back up the ridge. The wind was whipping up a gale and the hissing sand, scurrying along the surface of the ground, was like fog wraiths.

Half an hour, and my tracks would be obliterated.

I waited for that half hour. Then I started back to the south. When I had gone a good mile, I worked my way up the ridge to the mine where I had cached a few provisions against an emergency.

I had a location notice, and a recordation on that mine. I'd called it "The Sand Ghost" because of the way the sand always whipped over the ridge when there was a wind. It came up in spirals of white; hissing, slithering, whispering. It was a place where the desert always talked when a wind blew.

The wind was blowing when I arrived, but it went down by the time I had uncovered the cache. I was satisfied that would be the last of the wind until night.

I didn't have any water handy, but I had two full cans of tomatoes against emergency, and canned tomatoes are a luxury in the desert, also a necessity. I drank one of the cans of tomatoes, had some cold canned beans, and felt a little better.

It was hot, the sun broiling down with a sizzling heat, sending dazzling rays beating against the sensitive retina of the eye.

But my eyes had become accustomed to desert glare long since, and I could stand the sun. There was shade in the little drift I'd started to bore in on the outcropping, but I wanted to keep outside where I could watch the slope.

The sun crept overhead. The shadows were almost absent. The horizon did a devil dance of heat torture, but the slope was free of motion.

# THE WHIP HAND

The shadows started to lengthen once more.

I got a little worried over my stores, but had another can of food and waited.

It was three o'clock when I saw them, three shapes that toiled up the slope, coming fast.

I didn't have any too much ammunition, and only a few provisions. If they decided to wait me out I'd have a hard time of it. But I thought I could force their hand.

I sighted along the rifle barrel, figured the range and the wind and pulled the trigger.

I'd done some pretty fair shooting that day, and this shot just about capped the climax. It hit almost exactly where I'd planned that it should, within four yards of the leader.

The bullet slapped up a cloud of hot, dry dust, skipped off on a glance, and droned away into the hot afternoon, singing a song of death.

If the bullet had been shrapnel from a field gun it couldn't have caused any more consternation. They scattered like a bunch of quail, scurrying for cover, too much upset to think about returning the fire.

My position was almost impregnable, up on the slope above them. Given food and water, I could have held them off as long as I could see. Darkness was their ally, but, even so, a man doesn't want to come marching up a ridge with sand crunching beneath his feet, and an armed man waiting at the top, ready to shoot at the first form that silhouettes itself against the stars.

I gave them that first shot as a warning. It had been close enough so that they didn't want to take any chances on coming closer.

After a while they started to creep out from cover a bit, but they didn't get out to where they'd make a real target, and didn't move around any.

The silence of the desert weighed down heavily on the slope, and I could hear the sound of their voices as they called comments back and forth, the noise coming up the slope with startling clarity. I couldn't make out the words, but I could tell they were discussing a situation that had suddenly assumed complications they didn't like.

Finally I saw one of the men pull off his shirt and undershirt. The undershirt was supposed to be white. Even in the distance, it had a drab, grayish color about it that showed it had absorbed a lot of the desert.

He tied it on the end of his rifle and waved it back and forth.

I grinned then, and heaved a sigh of relief. It had been touch and go, and I hadn't been certain that I could save the girl. Now I stood a chance.

I took out a white handkerchief and waved it in an arc.

They took in their own white flag, had some more discussion, and finally one of the figures started toiling up the slope. He had left the rifle behind him, but I had an idea there was a six-gun stuffed in the front of his waistband, underneath the blue shirt.

It was a game of bluff now, and I was prepared to play it.

I took all of my cached provisions and stacked them in a pile that was visible from behind a little rock shelf. They were carefully arranged so that they looked like one end of a large pile.

There was a two-quart canteen with a hole in it. I'd thrown it away after the burro had punched a hole in it, coming around a quartz outcropping on a narrow trail. Now I plugged the hole with a wisp of cloth and started to pour dry sand into the canteen. When I had enough in it so the canteen was heavy, I screwed the top back on and sat the canteen in the shade.

The figure was toiling up the slope, coming face on in spite of the heat. I figured they were anxious.

It happened that I had the recorded location notice with me, showing on its back the official stamp of the County Recorder of Kern County, in Bakersfield. I got that in my pocket where it could be reached easily, and waited. The cards were all set.

The man came on up.

## V. "Even Murder"

"That's far enough," I said, and stuck my rifle barrel around a bit of float. "We can talk from here."

He stopped dead in his tracks, kept his hands up, level with his shoulders.

"We want to reach an understanding," he said.

He was a man I hadn't seen before, a chunky, mahogany-skinned chap who looked tough. There was a scar down one side of his cheek, and he'd evidently spent a lot of his time in the open. Somehow or other, he looked like a mountain prospector and adventurer to me, rather than a desert men.

I kept the gun on him.

"What do you want to understand?"

"We went off at half cock," he said. "You riled Sid Grame and he started to swap lead with you when you jumped on him this morning."

"I see," I said, "and I s'pose you came all the way up here to apologize!"

"We don't want no trouble," he said.

There was a silence for a moment. I could see that he was turning about, surreptitiously lining up the landmarks that I'd put on the map, and I felt a delicious relief oozing through me. I had him taking the bait now, hook, line and sinker. They'd found the skeleton, and the map.

"We're in a position to make you a lot of trouble," he went on, "and you could make us a lot o' trouble. You might mention that we was shootin' at you, and that'd make the sheriff come out here and we wouldn't like that."

"Sure," I said cheerfully, "you got the right idea there. I

can make you a lot of trouble, but what I don't see is how you figure you can make me a lot of trouble."

He twisted his lips.

"We could keep you from talkin' to the sheriff," he said, grimly.

I laughed.

"Boloney! You've already tried that, and it didn't work. I hold all the winning cards now."

"Yeah?" he said. "Well, brother, get this straight. If we don't let you go, you ain't never goin' to get out of here, and you can't stay here. You ain't got food nor water. You can't walk out without provisions. Now we're willin' to let bygones be bygones, and you can leave, if you'll agree that you won't say anything to anybody about what's happened ... an' that means you'd get your outfit back."

He paused.

I let my eyes get wide.

"Shucks," I said, "don't you know?"

"Know what?"

"That I got enough provisions to last me for a month. That I got enough water to let me hike out clean to Bakersfield if I want to. And when it gets dark you can't stop me from leaving. I can slip past you any old time."

"You got provisions?" he sneered. "Got 'em out of thin air I s'pose!"

"No," I told him. "I had 'em cached."

"Cached."

I nodded. "Stick your hands way up, and come in and look."

He hesitated for a moment, then his curiosity got him; he put his hands up and came up the slope, around the bowlder. He took one look and his eyes were like marbles.

"You got a claim here!"

"Sure," I told him.

His eyes got hard.

"That changes things," he said; then added after a moment, "changes 'em all around."

I pretended ignorance.

"How d'yuh mean?"

He stared at me and puckered the corners of his eyes. He had resolved that I should die, but even then he didn't want to give me any information, even though he wanted to get a lot.

"How come you sneaked up here and located this claim to-day?" he asked.

That gave me my opening.

"I didn't locate it to-day, you chump. I had it located for over sixty days. I stumbled onto the ruins of an old shack here, and some old mortars and pestles. It looked as though some one had opened up a prospect and then closed it again. I poked around and found some high-grade, regular jewelry ore that had been taken out.

"So I located, came in and cached some provisions, and was coming back to work the claim when you birds grabbed my outfit."

I could have hit him on the chin without jarring him as much as did that wad of information.

He walked around, his hands high, looking at the prospect. He took occasion to kick the canteen with his foot, a pretended accident, but really to see how full it was. The sand had the canteen anchored, and made it seem chock full of water.

He sighed.

"That there changes the situation all around," he said.

"Yes?" I asked.

"Yes," he said. "We're goin' to locate this here claim."

"Oh, is that so?" I said.

"Yes," he said, "that's so."

"And a little thing like murder won't stand in your way?"

He was cold, grim.

"A little thing like murder won't bother us at all," he said. "You can either quit now and walk out with your life, or you can stick around and stop lead."

"What'd you do if I walked out?" I asked.

"Locate it, of course."

I grinned at him.

"Take a look at that," I said, and tossed over the recorded notice of location.

He read it and his hand quivered. I could see his face twist as thoughts raced through his mind. If they killed me they couldn't get title to the claim. They might take possession, but as soon as the claim proved up there'd be a stampede and questions. You can't hush those things up in the desert.

"Maybe you'd sell," he said. "I don't think she's worth much, but I want it. It's sorta in my family. My dad located this for me years ago, an' wrote me to come out an' work it. I kept puttin' it off until after the old man died. He cashed in last week, an' his dyin' wish was that I'd come back here an' work this claim. He gave me a map showin' where it was."

He looked at me, and, as I didn't seem too doubting, he rushed on with his story. His voice had a smooth, rapid purr to it, a glib ease of enunciation that showed him for a ready liar.

"I'm Bill Kelley," he said. "Sid Grame's my partner. Also Indian Pete. They all can vouch for what I'm sayin'. It was sentiment with the old man, but I promised him on his deathbed, and you know how those deathbed promises are."

I nodded.

"Well, now," I said, "since you put it that way, I'll walk down a ways with you and see if we can't talk it over. I think she might be rich, but I'll always sell a claim."

I got to my feet, motioned him on down the slope.

"Now," said Bill Kelley, in that purring voice of his, "you're commencin' to talk sense!"

We started down the slope. I couldn't see either one of the others, but as we walked, one of the men came into sight, then a bulge of clothing over the top of a rock showed where the other was crouched.

"Tell the men to lay down their guns," I told Bill Kelley. He pursed his lips.

"You lay yours down, and we'll all meet unarmed an' friendly."

I shook my head. "No. Not yet. I want to know how much you'll give me for the claim . . ."

It was the rattle of a rock that gave me warning.

I jumped, and I was too late.

The Indian, naked as the day he was born, had jumped up from behind a rock, and his rifle was leveled at my head. Its muzzle looked as big as the entrance to a drift, and there was red murder in his eyes.

He didn't say a word. He didn't need to. I dropped my rifle as though it had been red hot and hoisted my arms high over my head.

The Indian had played a smooth trick. He'd left his clothes where I could see them, and had sneaked on up the slope, moving as only an Indian can.

Bill Kelley held up his hand.

"For God's sake, Pete, don't shoot! He's located on it an' recorded his location notice!"

The words didn't mean too much to the old Indian, but evidently Bill Kelley was the boss.

"Here's the location notice, all recorded," he went on. "This man's Bob Zane, and the notice shows he's got legal title to this claim."

The other man, the one he'd called Sid Grame, the one who had shot at the woman the night before, was running up the slope. He arrived, triumphant, breathless.

Kelley broke the news to him. He didn't get the full significance at first.

"All right," he said, "kill him. What the hell do we care? We want the claim!"

I laughed at them. "Try and get it!"

The Indian moved suggestively.

"We've got it," said Sid Grame. I kept smiling.

"No, you haven't. Remember that it's registered in my name, duly located *and* recorded. Nothing you can do out here is going to help."

That was a disconcerting thought for them.

Bill Kelley shuffled his feet. "You see," he explained, "we sort of feel that we're entitled to this claim. It's a family matter. Maybe there's something here, maybe there ain't, but my father located it and willed it to me. You blundered onto it. Now we've got the whip hand here."

He paused significantly.

I could tell he was getting ready to run a bluff.

"You mean you think you have." He shook his head.

"No, Zane. It's hard luck for you, but we're going to have this claim. If we can get a legal title to it, so much the better. If we can't, we aim to have it anyway."

"And a little thing like murder won't stop you?"

He shuffled his feet.

"I told you that already," he said— "a little thing like murder won't stop us."

There was silence for a minute, then he cleared his throat.

"If you'd take five hundred dollars and get out, we might raise that much money," he said.

I laughed, but the laugh wasn't quite as care-free as it might have been.

"What," asked Kelley, "do you want?"

I let him have it straight from the shoulder.

"There was a woman. She came to me for refuge. I went out hunting Grame, and while I was doing that you two were sneaking up on the camp. By the time I got back you'd gone on in, gagged the girl, packed up my things, and dusted.

"I'll sell you this claim for five hundred dollars. But I want the girl, and I want my outfit. When I have them, you get a bill of sale."

The men looked at one another.

"Okay," said Kelley; "we'll take you up. Make out the bill of sale."

I laughed in his face.

"And get a bullet in my head as soon as it's signed."

His shifting eyes showed that that was exactly what they had planned.

"Well," he said at length, "how're you going to plan it?"

"Produce the girl and the outfit, all ready to travel. Hand me the five hundred dollars, give me my guns and a mile head start. Then I'll sign the bill of sale and leave it."

Sid Grame raised his voice.

"Haw, haw, haw!" he jeered. "And then just keep on going!"

I kept looking at Kelley.

"*I'm* a man of my word," I said. He fidgeted.

"You give me your word, Zane, that if we do as you say you'll sign the bill of sale and leave it?"

"Exactly one mile down the trail," I said.

## VI. The Whip Hand

KELLEY LOOKED AT GRAME. "That is the only way, Sid. One side has got to trust the other. He's got the whip hand. He won't give it up until he gets what he wants."

"Let him trust us, then," growled Sid Grame.

"He don't have to, and he won't."

'We've got the drop."

"He's got the claim."

"Guns talk!"

"Shut up. The damned claim is recorded; that does the trick. You can't seem to understand what that means!"

Bill Kelley looked at me.

"I'll take your word on one condition."

"What's that?"

"That no matter what the girl says, you won't back out of the deal. We'll make that deal here and now. Then neither side will back out of it."

I nodded.

He sighed, and his face showed relief.

"Pete, you stay here and watch this man. Keep the drop on him. Don't let him escape. If he tries anything, shoot to smash a leg or the left shoulder, but don't hurt his right arm. We need his signature."

The Indian didn't say anything. He hadn't said anything during the discussion.

I knew that he wouldn't say anything in the wait that was to follow. And he didn't.

He squatted there in the sunlight, the rifle aimed on my left shoulder, and he kept it there.

The shadows lengthened rapidly. The cool tang of late afternoon was in the air.

I could hear steps, voices, the clink of shod hoofs.

My outfit came up the hill, plodding along, the burros wriggling their ears sleepily, inching their way along the hot slope.

After a while they stood on the rim of the level place where we were sitting.

Kelley handed me a bill of sale, duly filled out, ready for signing.

"Stick your name on that when you're a mile down the trail," he said.

The girl was with them. By daylight she was beautiful, but her face showed the angry red of the sun's punishment and her eyes were swollen.

"Is it true you're getting five hundred dollars for this claim?" she asked.

I nodded.

"Shut up, Elizabeth," said Sid Grame.

The girl glared at him. "I won't shut up," she snapped. "I'm going to talk. I've nothing left to live for, anyway. Don't be a fool, mister, whoever you are; that claim's worth a million. My grandfather located that claim, took out a small fortune by crude hand methods. He started for town to file his location notice and get supplies. He was carrying the gold. Indians murdered him. Pete's father was one of the crowd.

"Grandpa had gone into partnership with another prospector. They agreed to separate and work different sections. Later on the prospector got a letter from grandpa saying that he'd struck a bonanza and had taken out a small fortune in high grade jewelry ore. He said in the letter he was starting out with the rock, but that if anything should happen and he'd die of thirst on the way he'd have a map of the location of the mine in a little glass jar inside his shirt.

"In those days they hadn't located any water holes in this section of the desert, and people shunned it. But it wasn't the desert that killed granddad. It was three Indian murderers who found out that the burros were loaded with highgrade.

"Pete's father was one of those murderers. They buried grandpa near where they shot him, not so the buzzards wouldn't get him, but so their circling wouldn't attract the attention of some prospector and lead to a discovery of the murder.

"They didn't search his clothes, and didn't know anything about the sealed jar. Nobody did until I happened to uncover the story in some old letters on file in the Los Angeles Museum. Granddad's letter to his old partner was in there, as showing some of the risks the prospectors took in the early days.

"I got this man, Kelley, to help me. We started a search.

Finally he located Pete. Pete had heard his father tell of killing the white man and mentioned that the murderers had buried him up on this ridge where the top of a high mountain showed through an arched rock.

"We got Pete and started up here. Last night Kelley demanded I surrender three-fourths of the half of the claim that was to be my share. I knew then they intended to get my signature and then kill me. I pretended to be willing, until I'd got them to relax their vigilance, then I ran away.

"I'd seen your camp fire, and I figured you'd help me, but I wanted to wait until morning to see your face better before I talked. Then I was so tired I drifted off to sleep, and while I was asleep you went away and Pete and Bill Kelley trailed me to your camp, pounced on me, choked me, and made off with your outfit.

"And now you're going to part with this claim for five hundred dollars!"

She stopped, panting, out of breath.

Bill Kelley grinned at me.

"You promised," he said.

"I promised," I told him, my face showing intense gloom, "but you lied to me."

"You've got the whip hand," she stormed. "I heard them say so! Don't be a fool!"

I shook my head.

"No," I said. "They lied to me, but my word's good. Come on."

Kelley handed me the five hundred dollars. It ranged through all sizes and sorts of money probably the joint wealth of the three men. I started down the trail. The girl followed along. She was too mad to ride the burro. She was walking, letting off steam at every step.

"Of all the fools! You've played this whole thing like a dumb egg. And I'm swindled out of my rights. Because you sold them the claim, they dare to let me loose. Otherwise, if the title had been in me, they'd probably have had to kill me to keep me from going to court. I'd never have signed over a thing to the murdering crew!

"And you, you desert rat! Bah! What a fool you were! Why, I heard them say you had the whip hand with your recorded notice. You may have had the whip hand but you let them take the whip away. Now I suppose you're going to sign that bill of sale. Then I'm finished. It's your mine. They've bought it. You sell it. I'm just out of luck!"

She was sobbing as she talked, the bitter sobs of defeat.

I said nothing.

The afternoon sun had slid down over the ridge when I signed the bill of sale and dropped it. They were watching me through glasses. I saw the murderous crew come boiling over the run of level space and start rushing down the trail.

I pushed the burros to speed. I wanted a good start before dark.

They reached the paper, picked it up, paused and looked at me, then back at the western sky. They'd cut the distance down in their mad, downhill rush, and they'd probably planned on coming on and murdering me. I had five hundred dollars, and they'd have murdered me for half of that. But I'd figured the light and the desert and the distance.

They were three against one; but they'd have to make an attack on ground of my own choosing, and I had my outfit. Tackling me in the desert wouldn't be an easy murder.

They paused in a huddled knot while they talked it all over. Then they slowly turned back up the slope. We kept on, and dusk turned to darkness. The darkness was illuminated by the golden moonlight.

The woman had quit her storm of words now. She was sobbing.

I worked down the ridge shown on the true map.

I managed to line up the peaks and then get a bearing on the North Star. I made a camp right where the cross was shown on the map, but the girl didn't know it.

"We won't show a fire," I said.

We had a cold snack in silence. I spread out blankets.

"Think you can sleep?"

She almost spat at me, like a cat.

"I hate you," she said, "and I hate this damned desert with its stars and its sand that hisses and slithers along the ground and makes little whispers.

"Do you know what that sand seems to me to say? Know what it seemed to say all morning when I was lying bound and gagged in a cave?

"Well, it seemed to say, 'Jus-s-stice! J-u-s-s-s-s-t-i-c-e! J-u-s-t-i-c-e!"

She paused and her silence was more eloquent than words.

After a few minutes she started to sob. Then she spoke again.

"Justice! All morning I kept thinking of you. You'd seemed so steady and calm! I made up my mind the sand was telling me the truth, that out here in the big, open spaces God would have a chance, that these men would be outwitted. It wasn't only myself that mattered but my crippled niece. This money would have been a godsend to her . . ."

Sobs choked her throat.

I got up and walked away, leaving her there sobbing.

There was a flash light in my saddlebags. I shielded it with my coat so the rays wouldn't be seen and started to walk around a little bit.

I came across some old iron, a few real old signs of human occupancy. Then I came to a rock outcropping with a little hole in it. I thrust the flash against the side of this hole. It was simply alive with gold. Gold speckled it like an exhibit in a jewelry store. The hole wasn't big enough to bury a horse in, but a man had evidently taken out all the gold he could carry from it.

I came back to the girl. She had quit sobbing now, was lying back staring hard-eyed up at the stars.

The wind began to blow, suddenly.

I waited until nature asserted itself and the girl drifted off to sleep. Then I put the saddle under her head, a blanket over her. The sand was drifting rapidly, hissing its subtle whispers.

She spoke drowsily, her mind far, far distant.

"Hear it . . . Jusssssss-s-s-stice!"

Then she slept again.

I located the claim in her name, put up the notice, took samples of rock. About the time the moon was down, I shook her awake.

The sand was talking.

"What is it?" She sat up.

She saw me standing over her. I could see a sneer on her lips.

"Damned brute," she said.

"We've got to go," I told her.

"Where to?"

"Bakersfield. We go to Kernville over the mountains. Then we get an automobile and go to Bakersfield."

"What for?"

"To register 'The Whip Hand.' "

"What's that?"

"Your claim."

"What claim?"

"The one your grandpa left you."

Her breath came in a hissing gasp, just as it had done the night before when she had first discovered I was watching her.

"What are you talking about?"

I took her hand, led her to the rock, switched on the flash light.

She looked at what was disclosed in the ancient diggings,

the crumbling quartz, rotten with gold. Her eyes bulged. She tried to talk, but no sounds came.

"Come," I told her, and then I showed her the location notice.

She read it. By that time she had her speech.

"You tricked them after all! Beat them at their own game!" she said.

I nodded.

"It's half yours!" she exclaimed impulsively. "You get the share they were to have."

I shook my head.

"No. I've got five hundred dollars for a claim I was going to abandon. That's enough for one day's work. And I'll make those desert slickers the laughing stock of every camp between here and Needles."

Her lips were firm.

"I'll sign over a half of it to you. You can't stop me."

"You can sleep on that," I told her. "In the meantime, we'd better see that we get the claim registered. Otherwise you might not have anything after all."

We traveled the ridges in a short-cut I knew of. By daylight we could look down on the Kernville road. The sand was still whispering, wiping out our tracks.

"Does the sand seem to talk to you?" she asked.

I nodded my head.

She looked to the east. The sun was getting over the rim of the desert. The sky was a vivid red, shot with gold.

"I guess there's a God after all," she said softly.